FOR PROMISED JOY

ABOUT THE AUTHOR

This is Oonagh Morrison's first published novel, though over the years she has contributed to various newspapers and journals. She holds an Honours degree in English literature and an M.Ed., both from Edinburgh University, and has taught English in her home town of Falkirk and later in Glasgow. Married now for forty-three years and living in Helensburgh, Argyll, she has two married daughters and four grandchildren. Apart from writing and reading her main interests are her family, bridge and travel: they have taken over now from sailing, which was until recently almost a way of life.

For Promised Joy

OONAGH MORRISON

But, Mousie, thou art no thy lane,
In proving foresight may be vain:
The best laid schemes o' mice and men'
    Gang aft a-gley,
And lea'e us nought but grief and pain,
    For promis'd joy.

    Robert Burns 1759–1796

For Bill,
who patiently drove me around North Carolina while I researched
this novel, helped me with my manuscript and tolerated me while
I inhabited another century.

British Cataloguing in Publication Data
A catalogue record for this book is available
from the British Library

ISBN 1 899863 75 3

Typeset in Monotype Baskerville by XL Publishing Services, Tiverton.
Printed in Great Britain by SRP Ltd, Exeter
for House of Lochar, Isle of Colonsay, Argyll PA61 7YR

AUTHOR'S FOREWORD

Much has been written about the Highland heroine Flora MacDonald, whose courage made possible Charles Edward Stuart's escape from South Uist to Skye in 1746. Her name has been romantically linked with his in song and story – so inextricably, in fact, that most have chosen to forget that the man she eventually married and had seven children by had fought on the Hanoverian side during the Jacobite rebellion. Eighteenth-century folks, it would appear, could be ambivalent in their political affiliations in a way we find puzzling today.

Nor is it universally known that in 1774, when she was in her early fifties, Flora, her husband, two sons and a married daughter emigrated to North Carolina. There they joined hundreds of friends and kinsfolk who had already been forced from the Highlands by ruthless absentee landlords, a series of killingly harsh winters, and cruel economic conditions. All might have been well there – Flora's husband Allan was an experienced cattleman and the grist mill on their plantation was a sound source of income – but the outbreak of the American Revolution found him committed to fight on the British side. Ironic, isn't it, that the heroine of the '45 should have ended up rallying volunteers to champion the English? Once again, of course, it proved a lost cause.

This book tries to explain the political anomaly by exploring Flora's personality, her relationship with her husband, and the changing fortunes of the years they spent in America. Because of its imaginative nature I must therefore classify it as a novel but as far as possible I have adhered to known facts. All the historical background is accurate; the main characters, (apart from the Boyds, the Strachans, and the slaves, who are fictional) did exist, and I have attempted to describe eighteenth-century North Carolina as authentically as my reading and travel there allowed. As a recent biographer of Flora's, Hugh Douglas, put it in a letter to me, 'I quickly discovered that very little had been written hitherto about the American side of her life ... The reason I believe is simply that very little is available on life in Carolina at that time. The Scots were very unpopular, especially at the time of the Revolution, so no-one wrote much about them.'

Much of history is speculation. We all interpret facts differently. This is only one very personal view of what an obscure episode in Flora MacDonald's fascinating life might have been like.

ACKNOWLEDGEMENTS

I am most indebted to the following for their help:

My agent, David Fletcher, whose encouragement kept me writing and who has worked unstintingly on my behalf; Hugh Douglas, whose biography of Flora MacDonald was an inspiration, and who put me in touch with vital American contacts; Julie McDonald of Davenport, Iowa, who generously sent me her account of Prince Charles Edward's escape in *The Heather and the Rose*, and suggested valuable texts; Dr Margaret Mackay of the School of Scottish Studies, University of Edinburgh, who let me have the text of John MacRae's poems; Mr Ian MacDonald of Clachan, who has made a study of the Largie MacDonalds; Bill Caudill and Professor Margaret Houston, both of St. Andrew's College, Laurinburg, who gave generously of their time when I went there to discuss the site of the MacDonald plantation; and the many good friends, both here and in America, who kept insisting that I could do it.

PART ONE

I

September 1773

'Quick, Allan, they're coming! Oh, I do hope to God that mutton stew still tastes fresh. And will there be enough salmon? They say he has a prodigious appetite, that Doctor Johnson...'

'Don't fret, woman. We have a whole turkey there, don't we, not to mention mince collops, and haggis, and the muirfowl old Neil brought in yesterday? Anyway, the man's coming to meet and talk with us, not to criticise our fare.'

Flora MacDonald smiled to herself at that 'us'. Well she knew that the great Dr Samuel Johnson's interest was in her alone, but not for the world would she disabuse her husband of his self-conceit. Hadn't she spent the last twenty-three years consciously subordinating her own fame to Allan's ambition, underplaying for all she was worth the star-studded, adventurous life she had led before she married him? She felt fluttery and nervous about the forthcoming meeting, yes, but the frisson of apprehension was due more to her fear of the limelight than to humility in the presence of a literary celebrity from London. Better then to let Allan go and welcome him. She would stay meek and wife-like in the background.

So she watched from the window as Allan ran to help his famous guest dismount, and felt her mood change without warning to one of sheer frivolity. She did not usually see her husband as a figure of fun, but he looked so large and stocky as he trundled along, noticeably incommoded nowadays by a developing paunch, and with his coal-black pigtail jumping comically up and down. Seeing Allan stop beside the great man's horse and brace himself she almost laughed out loud. Oh, what a pantomime! So this was the celebrated Dr Johnson, this gargantuan, blubbery figure! How he must have weighted that poor horse down, all the way from Corriechatachain! It would take all Allan's considerable strength to dislodge him, let alone lift him down. To her relief, however, she noticed that the Doctor's travelling companion – James Boswell, no doubt: she observed with a start that he looked remarkably like a smaller version of her husband – had dismounted and was hastening to Dr Johnson's aid from the other side, so that a kind of tug-o'-war ensued, whereupon the Doctor spoke sharply to his friend and summoned him round to share Allan's burden. Then at last, with extra persuasion from the two indolent Highlanders who had been leading the horses, the mound of shapeless flesh that literary London had lionised for years was deposited at the front door of Kingsburgh House. By now the wide, bushy, iron-grey wig had toppled to a precarious angle, while the brown suit and black worsted stockings were travel-stained and rumpled. After all he was but human, this luminary, and well into his sixties now.

The thought sobered Flora, had her mastering her mirth and composing her features into the staid mould expected of a fifty-one-year-old matron. As mistress of Kingsburgh she was dispenser of hospitality to all who came here. It was her duty to make these visitors welcome.

She soon realised, too, that in the case of Dr Johnson physical attributes counted for nothing. Ugly to the point of repulsiveness, his face scarred with the pox and his dropsical body bordering on the grotesque, he yet commanded instant respect. She felt her amusement give way first to admiration and then to the emotion she had least expected – a warm sense of kinship. To think this paragon had come all that way, daring bog and mountain, moorland and rushing torrent, simply to see her! For he made it clear, as he deposited a brotherly kiss on her cheek, that she had been his sole reason for making the journey.

Suddenly she felt twenty-five again as she remembered how she had once met the leading lights of the London social scene on equal terms. Her old, carefully submerged vivacity came bubbling up, and with it a flirtatiousness the dour island folk scarcely ever saw.

'I heard that Mister Boswell was coming to Skye, and one Mister Johnson, a young English buck, with him!'

The temerity of it, speaking like that to the master! But clearly he was lapping it up, and the tone was set for the visit.

With quiet satisfaction she noticed her visitors' surprised appreciation of her home. Kingsburgh House looked west across the loch, to a view of heather-clad mountains. It was large and spacious, two storeys high and built of stone. It had five bedrooms, a hall, and ample kitchen accommodation. The parlour the family used for entertaining was high-ceilinged, with hangings on the walls and curtains at the windows. Flora's spinning-wheel stood in one corner and a huge fire burned in the grate. There were books scattered around too, and among them, prominently displayed, was Dr Johnson's own Dictionary. They might be on the Isle of Skye and far from centres of learning but these Highlanders were no strangers to culture.

'You'll be having a glass of good Holland gin, Doctor? And you too, Master Boswell?' Allan was bustling proprietorially about, obviously eager to impress as the hospitable host, and Flora withdrew tactfully into the background. She felt very proud of her husband then, acutely aware of his handsome, sensible presence. He had put on his blue tartan philabeg and matching hose, and his waistcoat was new, with gold buttons. His features were as clearly defined as when they had married twenty-three years before, and his sleek hair was still jet black, as if in defiance of life's vicissitudes. Watching him dispense the usquebaugh Mr Boswell had requested (the Doctor had asked only for lemonade) she consciously fixed the scene in her memory. Yes, her Allan was the epitome of the educated Highland gentleman. Every movement reflected his military training. He was always meticulously polite and distinguished in any company.

Such a pity that for all his social qualities he was no businessman, and not much of a farmer either. Poor, self-opinionated, lovable Allan, with his fanciful plans for improving the land that never came to anything, and his determination to live at a level that Skye simply could not support. His total lack of business sense exasperated Flora at times, yet he was not entirely to blame for their poverty now. From the moment of their move to Kingsburgh they seemed to have been beset by financial worries, many of them occasioned by the stagnant economy at the end of the Seven Years' War. She remembered one disastrous year in particular. 1764 it had been. Allan had travelled to Crieff with 2,800 head of cattle, only to find that they were worth £1,400 less than he had paid for

them originally. Perhaps, had the new young chief Sir James
MacDonald and his mother Lady Margaret been more amenable,
he would have got by, but all he had encountered in that direction
was greed and antagonism. Allan had worked on tirelessly,
building on the estate, sowing rye grass and clover, introducing
new varieties of potato and involving his tenants in breeding sheep
and pigs, until Sir James himself had died and been succeeded by
young Sandy, who had found kelp more productive of revenue
than the land. Then, disastrously, a succession of bad winters had
depressed livestock prices even further all over the country. She
pursed her lips, remembering the cattle plague of '69 and the Black
Spring of '71, when snow had lain on the ground for all of eight
weeks and the land had been devastated again.

Nor had the islanders' attitude helped. They insisted on
bleeding the cattle for food, as they had done since time
immemorial: she shuddered, recalling how she had actually
watched some cottars lifting the ailing beasts to their feet one
freezing dawn, and carrying them bodily to pasture. Thrawn,
ignorant peasants! They refused to accept Allan's innovations as
desirable because the hated English had inspired them and her
own Jacobite money had financed them. For though such as Dr
Johnson might honour her, Flora had no illusions about how her
own Skye men regarded her. She had succoured the Pretender,
the source, it had turned out, of all their present subjugation and
misery, and had profited from it.

But Flora knew she was powerless to change things. 'I shall see
to supper, dear,' she ventured from her stance at Allan's elbow,
and he nodded absentmindedly, his whole attention riveted on his
illustrious guests.

The Doctor was hugely appreciative of his meal.

'That pheasant was an epicurean's delight, dear lady, as were
the syllabubs and puddings. Four days we spent with your
chieftain, Sir Alexander MacDonald of Sleat, and never a collation
like this! The food at Armadale was fit only for dogs. No wheat
bread. No claret. Not even sugar tongs! I had to take up my sugar
in my fingers! And of course my good friend Boswell here did not
help matters by tactfully declaring that we had crossed the water
expressly to see you alone...'

Flora blushed modestly at this while Boswell simply shrugged and accepted another glass of porter.

'Aye,' he agreed. 'I must say I had expected better, considering that Sir Alexander's wife Elizabeth is my cousin. The drink they regaled us with was but a punch without souring and with little spirits in it, and our host served it with the same pewter spoon he had used for the broth. My Scottish pride was black affronted!'

Flora noticed that while Johnson was remarkably abstemious regarding alcohol Boswell applied himself with serious concentration to its consumption, and the more he drank the more tactless he became.

'This is indeed super-excellent claret,' he declared contentedly now, delicately lifting a pinch of snuff to his nostrils and proceeding rashly to open yet another can of worms. 'We talked much of emigration while at Armadale. I myself went aboard the *Nestor* at Portree and we saw the *Margaret* pass, full of folk desperate to escape these shores.'

'Yes indeed,' the Doctor put in. '"Twould seem the island's life is draining away westwards. Why, when we wanted to cash a bill for £30 the only place we could do it was on an emigrant ship moored in Loch Bracadale! I fear I could not keep silent. 'Tis those lairds, as I believe you call them, to blame. They are never at home to care for their own people. No Highland chief, I told Sir Alexander straight, should be allowed to go further south than Aberdeen!'

Allan smiled grimly at this sage analysis and Flora's sympathy went out to him. The Doctor's rapier-sharp mind had certainly probed straight to the heart of things. For seven years now, ever since the young laird had dismissed him from his post as factor, her husband's life had become progressively bitter and precarious. She remembered him sitting at the table, head bent, that terrible day when a proclamation had appeared on the church door warning clansmen not to sell their cattle to Allan MacDonald, because the bills would not be honoured. Oh, the humiliation of it!

For a brief moment something of the helpless anger she had felt returned. She herself had always been a shrewd manager of money and Allan's improvidence was the one aspect of him she found hard to forgive. But she had to be fair. Given different circumstances his enterprise and energy might well have triumphed.

Meanwhile Boswell's voice rumbled relentlessly on. 'You would consider leaving too, sir?' The question was respectful enough but there was no mistaking the undertone of sheer nosiness.

The reply was tense. 'Aye, we would that, and of necessity. Flora's stepfather Hugh has gone already. He went two years ago, after the Black Spring, with her half-sister Annabella and her husband and children. Their letters speak of a good life in North Carolina. Land can be got there for the few shillings it costs to have a holding surveyed and registered.' He sighed and added, 'We would have left ere now, but could not while my father lived. But he has been dead this eighteen months past – he was eighty-three – and there is naught to keep us now but our fear of the unknown and concern for our bairns. The youngest, Fanny, is not yet eight.'

Listening, Flora felt the onset of tears. Furious with herself she bit her lip hard and got up to busy herself at the side table.

Then came Boswell's answer. It had a ring of calm certainty and authority. 'So spirited a man as you, sir, would do well anywhere.'

They might ridicule him for an obsequious Lowland ass, this Boswell, but from that moment on he had Flora MacDonald's complete affection.

II

September 1773

The visitors spent the night in the very room Charles Edward Stuart had occupied twenty-seven years before, while fleeing from the Hanoverians. Dr Johnson had the Prince's bed which Flora had draped with tartan. There were maps and pictures on the walls, among them Hogarth's famous print of John Wilkes with the cap of Liberty beside him. All very civilised, and totally unlike some of the hovels where the travellers had been obliged to lay their heads.

It was only at breakfast next morning, over the porridge,

oatcakes and ale, that Dr Johnson raised the subject of the Young Pretender's escape and Flora's part in it.

Over the years Flora had been deliberately reticent about the episode despite determined efforts to prise the details from her. There had been many reasons for this: her own innate reluctance to promote herself, especially at her husband's expense; the widespread anti-Jacobite feeling on Skye, that blamed the Stuarts for the island's woes; and particularly her conviction that her own part in the drama had been exaggerated by popular rumour. Why had other protagonists, like her clever unassuming cousin Neil MacEichain, or Captain Felix O'Neil, or even Lady Clanranald, not been similarly recognised? She suspected it was simply because she had been young then, female, and comely enough, that she had become the focus of so much attention.

But somehow it no longer mattered, even though James Boswell was sitting over there diligently noting down every word she said, for soon she and Allan would quit these shores for ever. Besides, she liked these people, felt relaxed and secure in their company. They were intellectual and urbane, and brought a salutary breath of a sane outside world to this remote, inward-looking island. So she opened up to them gladly, recalling that moonlit Friday night on South Uist so long ago, when she had first set eyes on the Prince at the sheiling on Sheaval Hill.

'I swear I had never dreamt of such a thing. I had simply gone from our home on Skye to the family farm at Milton, to visit my brother and his new wife. It had never even occurred to me that the Prince might be on the island. He had been skulking in the heather for three months, ever since the devastating defeat at Culloden, with a price of £30,000 on his head. I marvel still that through all his journeyings not one of his Highlanders was venal enough to betray him.'

She felt herself flush with pride when she said this, even after twenty-eight years: her people's devotion to their outlawed Prince had been extraordinary, though it had brought them nothing but grief in the end.

'Come June 20th he was indeed on South Uist, however,' she went on. 'He had been hounded there relentlessly, and was holed up like a stag at bay in a gamekeeper's hut in Glen Corradale. Two warships, the *Trident* and the *Raven*, lay at anchor in Loch

Boisdale, and the Minch was patrolled constantly by ships of the Royal Navy, so that no French vessel dared venture near to rescue him. The two notoriously murderous Hanoverian commanders, Captain John Ferguson at sea and Captain Caroline Scott on land, planned to land troops at both ends of the Long Island and have them march in a kind of pincer movement to intercept him. It certainly looked, that night, as if the hunt was over.'

Flora paused for breath, remembering how she had climbed the hill late that afternoon, thinking of the young man and the merciless fate that would befall him now. Doubtless he would be transported to London and if Butcher Cumberland had his way would be despatched to meet his Maker in the cruellest way that could be devised, a lesson to all who dared question His Majesty's right to reign. She remembered how she had cleared the little turf-roofed cottage of cobwebs, fetched fresh heather for a bed, called to the cattle to come and be milked, and wondered, as the moon rose, if it would ever get properly dark on this mid-summer night: for only in darkness could the Prince and his protectors move with impunity.

'I had just washed in the stream, had my supper of bread and cheese, said my prayers and settled down to sleep when who should come and seek me out but my cousin Neil MacEichain and the soldier-adventurer Felix O'Neil, whom my brother had introduced to me just the previous evening. All their talk was of the Prince. I was amazed to learn that many of the island chiefs whom I had assumed to be opposed to the Jacobite rising were in fact sympathisers – MacDonald of Boisdale, my kinsman Clanranald, Hugh MacDonald of Baleshare and even my stepfather Hugh of Armadale, 'One-eyed Hugh', who was with the King's militia on Benbecula. Lady Clan and Lady Boisdale had been sending him secret gifts of food and clothing, and even Lady Margaret of Sleat, prevaricator though she was, had sent money, clothes and broadsheets.

'Even so I was appalled and terrified when Felix told me of their plan to disguise the Young Chevalier as my maid and row him back to Skye, where nobody would dream he was hiding. I refused at first to consider such folly and Felix, thinking I feared for my reputation, offered to marry me if it would help allay my doubts.'

Flora felt herself suddenly blush, for there in her mind's eye was

Felix, tall and dashingly handsome, with his mother's passionate Spanish eyes and his Irish father's instinct for well-chosen blandishments. She heard his voice, its soft Irish inflexions intermixed with subtly foreign vowel sounds and occasional awkward idioms that betrayed his continental roots. What had possessed her to deny him? Most young women would have jumped at such a magnanimous proposal, and held him to it!

'But it was not Felix who changed my mind. It was the Prince. After all those weeks of existing in caves he was in a wretched state when they called him in to meet me, covered with midge bites and terrible sores. His diet had been meagre to say the least – wild berries and whatever food his henchmen could borrow or steal, with the occasional fish from the burns or small animals and birds – so that his stomach was racked with diarrhoea. Add to that the number of times he must have been soaked to the skin: it is surprising he had not succumbed to the ague long ago. Yet there he was before me, still with such majesty in his bearing! They talk still, you doubtless know, about the Stuarts' irresistible charm, and I must admit that I fell victim to it that night. Nor was I the first or the last, male or female. 'Twas when he accepted the bowl of cream I offered him, not without gratitude yet as if 'twere but his due, that I decided, and from then on nothing would have turned me.

'You see, looking back, I think that in our secret, romantic Highland hearts we were indeed Jacobites, all of us. Even Allan here – yes, Allan, don't you be denying it! – for all he was a lieutenant in the King's militia. And my stepfather Hugh might have been captain of a company but Felix told me 'twas he who had thought up the disguise, none the less.'

She told them then of the five days spent with Lady Clanranald, 'Lady Clan', at Nunton, how the womenfolk sewed frantically into the wee small hours, thankful for the long lingering light of these northern latitudes, and gradually the Prince's disguise took shape. As the Irish maid Betty Burke he would sport a quilted petticoat, a calico gown patterned with lilac, a white apron, a hooded cloak, blue velvet garters and a huge, floppy, face-concealing bonnet.

In his military capacity Flora's stepfather Hugh had greatly assisted the Prince's getaway by always ensuring that the militia were never in the right place to catch him. Hugh was a very strong character, much thought of by the islanders, and his judgement was never questioned. He it was who gave Flora the letter that ensured her safe passage, declaring that she was returning to Skye lest she be 'frightened with the troops'. Betty Burke, 'a good spinster', was her maid and Neil MacEichain was going as escort.

Flora remembered with a fresh pang how chagrined Felix had been when she adamantly refused to include him in the party. Her stated reason, that Felix was too patently a stranger and could not speak the Gaelic, had been valid enough but there had been more to it than that. She had felt she could not trust herself with Felix close at hand, feared his very presence might disrupt the whole venture: for the young man had aroused feelings in her that she was reluctant to acknowledge and examine even now.

Avoiding further direct mention of him she said simply, 'There were eight of us, crossing the Minch. The shallop we used was only eighteen feet long but it needed five boatmen, four to row and one at the helm. I knew them all. The helmsman John MacDonald of Dremisdale and his brother Roderick were my cousins. The other oarsmen were Lauchlan MacMhuirich, a cheery soul if ever there was one, another Roddy MacDonald of Glengarry, and Alexander MacDonald

'But for all I knew and trusted them I was still scared out of my wits. Ever since my half-brother came to grief in the Kilbrannon Sound I had hated to be on the water, and panic always seized me whenever I lost sight of the shore. That night thick mist blotted out everything and for most of the way and I thought I would die of fear. But the Prince was unperturbed and his lack of concern gave me courage. There he sat, quite light-hearted, drinking Jack-fellow-like out of the bottle of milk Lady Clan had given us, and never turning a hair.

'I still don't know how the boatmen found their way, for the night was pitch black and we had no compass. We used a sail in the open Minch but had to take it down in the grey dawn when the mist temporarily cleared and we spotted an English man-o'-war in the distance. I dozed off at one stage – I must have been dog weary to do that – and was conscious of the Prince's hands spread above me, to keep the boatmen from stumbling over me. He was even easy enough in his mind to sing, the gommeril!'

She took a deep breath, and for a moment felt the sickening, lolloping motion of the boat as it surrendered itself to the waves and the calm, reassuring presence of the grotesquely-dressed figure watching over her. Still marvelling at the Prince's nonchalance she heard again in her head the haunting Jacobite air he had sung:

'For who better may our high sceptre sway
Than he whose right it is to reign?
Then look for no peace for the wars will never cease
Till the King shall enjoy his own again!'

When at last she opened her eyes he was quick to offer her a draught of reviving wine. Then he pointed eastwards towards a lightening in the sky, and a dark distant shadow looming up out of the mist. 'There! Can you see it, mademoiselle? Land!'

Waternish Point was a forbidding headland, a towering bastion of black basalt fretted with waterfalls and crowned with sparse vegetation, home only to gannets and puffins. But it was solid and enduring and on that bleak Sunday morning Flora felt it was the most desirable place on earth.

The ordeal was far from over however. Flora found herself clutching the boat's gunwale, petrified with fright, when a sudden gust from the west overwhelmed them and a curtain of torrential rain came down. John MacDonald frantically baled out the rainwater, the oarsmen pulled mightily on the oars, and Flora was convinced that her life was over. Even when the sun came up and land was clearly visible there was still an hour and a half of hard rowing ahead, for the wind had veered to the north and was blowing hard against them.

'The Hanoverians intercepted you, did they not?' Boswell's voice was impatient, craving more details.

'Yes indeed. We were fired at by militia on the beach at Ardmore, but it was low water and before they could launch their boats we vanished behind a cliff and they lost us. We rested then in a sea cave. Never in my life have I tasted bread and butter more satisfying than that Lady Clan had given us, and the water from the burn was sweeter than any wine.

'There was still a long row after that, of course – it was twelve miles across Loch Snizort yonder to Kilbride and Monkstadt, home of the Chief of Sleat – but things were quiet. 'Twas a Sunday, you see. Everyone was at church.

'But as luck would have it by the time we got to Monkstadt Lady Margaret was at dinner and she had company – Allan's father, who was her factor, and the head of the local militia, Lieutenant Alex MacLeod of Balmeanach. It did not help that Lady Margaret panicked on realising who her strangely-dressed guest was. Her whole concern was to get him out of her house and save her own skin.'

At this point Flora could not keep the bitterness out of her voice. She still found it hard to forgive Lady Margaret for the disdainful way she had treated her all through her life. But she continued gamely. 'I think, looking back, that that was when I was most on my own, and most vulnerable. I had to keep the lieutenant occupied with small talk while the others considered the safest place for the Prince to hide. Eventually they decided to bring him here, to Kingsburgh House.'

At this point she smiled over to her husband, inviting him to have his say, and he eagerly took up the tale. 'My mother never stopped talking about it afterwards, how my sister Anne came running to her crying, 'Oh, Mother! My father has brought in a very odd, muckle, ill-shapen wife as ever I saw!' Even when the peculiar female with the long stride kissed her hand she still did not suspect that it might be the Prince. She was quite won over, my mother: she begged Anne to get a lock of the fugitive's hair, and forbade anyone to wash the sheets he had slept in, for one was to be her shroud and Flora here would have the other.'

His voice shook. He had been devoted to his parents and rarely trusted himself to talk about them. So Flora said simply, 'Ah yes. The dear lady has lain buried in it in the kirkyard yonder these past seventeen year. God rest her soul. And I have mine still. Wherever I go it will go with me.'

Then her fears for the future suddenly surfaced again. She struggled to keep her voice steady and serene, and to betray nothing of the despair that might signal disloyalty to Allan.

For he too was fighting to hide his bitterness and maintain the image of the trouble-free, self-reliant host. Flora suspected, too, that his old jealousy had returned as she warmed to her theme. Sensing his fretfulness she therefore condensed the rest of her account, consciously playing down her own part in helping the Prince reach Portree in safety.

Perhaps something of Allan's restiveness had transferred itself to Dr Johnson also, for he suddenly growled, 'Help me out of this armchair, James, else I shall be tempted to sit here all day, entranced by this dear lady's reminiscences. Would we could stay, but we yet have calls to make and London beckons at journey's end. 'Twill be winter ere we get home if we keep overstaying our welcome as we have so happily done here at Kingsburgh.'

Flora demurred at this, and meant it. 'Please, please stay!' – but again she felt Allan bristle with impatience. He did not add his own plea to hers but did manage to stay magnanimous. 'You must not ride back the long way, by those narrow rutted paths. See, I shall row you across Loch Snizort. We can have the horses sent on ahead to Grehornish.'

For this Dr Johnson was both relieved and grateful. He had complained repeatedly that conversation and thought were quite impossible while negotiating Skye's rough terrain on horseback. So with much grunting and groaning he was raised from the chair and then he turned to take his leave of Flora.

'It has indeed been a most memorable visit, my dear,' he said warmly, and bent to kiss her cheek. 'Please know that if ever you find yourself in London you will be welcome in my house at any hour of the day or night, and I know that Mr Boswell here echoes my sentiments.'

'I do indeed, kind lady,' said the Doctor's faithful amanuensis as he gallantly kissed her hand. He was clearly embarking upon a fulsome speech of thanks when the Doctor mercifully cut in. 'Come, James, we must not keep our host waiting' – whereupon Allan, accommodating to the last, bundled his illustrious visitors down to the lochside.

Watching them go, Johnson so fat he could scarcely waddle along, Boswell all bustle and perkiness, Flora marvelled at their resilience. Boswell, Allan, Donald MacQueen the minister and Allan's brother James had drunk three bowls of punch the night before, not to mention gallons of claret and porter. But oh, how sorry she was to see them go! She could have talked for weeks to these clever, sophisticated people and never felt tongue-tied or at a loss for something to say. All at once her sense of desolation was almost insupportable and she felt her eyes fill with tears.

Then the memories the visit had evoked came crowding in and

she could not hold them back. Thoughts she rarely allowed herself to entertain, of all the eligible, gallant men she had met and turned down in her brilliant youth, clamoured for attention. Might she have found rapture of a totally different order with Felix O'Neil? She had met him only once after the Prince's escape, when they had both been imprisoned on the warship *Furnace*, and she vividly remembered the impression his physical presence had made on her. She had pretended light-hearted coquetry to cover up her fear and confusion, and he had advised her to stick by her story when questioned and never publicly repent of what she had done. Then he had been taken forcibly ashore.

It had taken four months to transport her to London and she knew now that the kindness she had experienced at the hands of various naval officers had been largely due to her sex, her youth and her social status. Young Nigel Gresley had befriended her on the *Eltham*, which had taken her round the north of Scotland and down to Leith, and again on the *Bridgewater*, on the passage to London. She would never regret having given him the portrait Richard Wilson painted of her. Commodore Smith had been like a father to her, giving her a gown and a new suit of riding clothes, as well as linen to make shifts for her maid, while the captain of the *Bridgewater*, Charles Knowles, had also gone out of his way to indulge her. She knew all too well that had those gentlemen willed it otherwise her two-month enforced stay on board ship in Leith harbour that miserable, wind-swept autumn would have been intolerable. She could see Charles Knowles now, a likeable, melancholy-looking man with a long nose. She had thought him ancient at forty-five but blushed now, realising that her conscious efforts to retain his good opinion might have aroused other feelings than mere sympathy. How innocent and totally unawakened she had been! She had been visited on board by the Jacobite gentry of Edinburgh: the redoubtable old Lady Bruce of Kinross had come, as had the countess of Dundonald's daughter, Lady Mary Cochrane, and Rachel Houston, who was destined to marry Bishop Forbes and become a firm friend. And she had taken all that flattery quite calmly, as a matter of course! She recalled now that her main emotion had not been gratitude or relief but irritation, for she had heard that Felix O'Neil was in Edinburgh and they would not allow her ashore to see him.

The adulation had continued in London, where she had been lodged with other Jacobite prisoners at Messenger Dick's house. Lady Primrose, the young widow who entertained supporters of the Stuarts at her house in Essex Street, had not only befriended her but had set up a fund to pay her lodging fees, and had raised £1500. Flora had met a string of notable people, among them the distinguished banker Aeneas MacDonald and John Burton, the young doctor from York whose friendship she would always cherish. Ah, John. She had been half in love with him, and had been so disappointed to discover he was pledged to another.

It had been strange to be held prisoner and yet be treated as a celebrity. Impassioned pamphlets had appeared, extolling her exploits. The eminent Scottish artist Allan Ramsay had painted her portrait. Then, the ultimate accolade, she had been honoured with a royal visit by Frederick Prince of Wales, and an invitation to Vauxhall Gardens which she had graciously declined! Asked how she had dared assist a rebel against his father's throne she had replied quite simply that she would have done the same for him, had she found him in like distress. The cheek of it! But she had sensed his admiration none the less.

Later, back in Edinburgh after her pardon and release, Bishop Forbes had made a great fuss of her. Then in his late thirties and still a bachelor, he had been rector of the Episcopalian Church in Leith, and had been assiduously collecting those anecdotes and details about the rebellion which would later be collated in 'The Lyon in Mourning'. He was another whose regard she had been careless about. She knew now that she ought to have let him know when she and Allan got married, instead of having him hear the news at second-hand, from John Burton.

To think that she had had London at her feet, the elegant world of Hogarth and Handel, Smollett and Fielding, and had taken it all so calmly. But she did recall that any gratification she felt had been mixed with fear. Why should she have been spared, when Aeneas was sentenced to death and only pardoned much later, Lord Derwentwater was executed, and a whole row of victims' heads grinned ghoulishly at Temple Bar? Mercifully her youthful resilience had refused to acknowledge the full extent of the danger. She had emerged after three years away from Skye more self-sufficient and with a new determination to improve herself – hence those handwriting lessons from David Beatt, in Edinburgh. Strange, though, that she had had to come home to Skye to find the man who would claim her life and heart.

Now, in her bitterness, she seriously questioned whether those years had benefited her at all. Others who had helped Prince Charles had been left sick and impoverished: their resentment of her fame and fortune was understandable. Better perhaps if she had stayed obscure and comparatively penniless on Skye. Allan might well have fancied her just the same and she would have worshipped him blindly, never comparing him with others she had known and never questioning his grandiose schemes, his reckless buying of livestock he could not afford and his bids to improve land that could never be other than rock and bog.

But she had been free to make her own choices. Allan had been most insistent that she marry him – he was stubborn and invariably got his own way – but she had not been bound to accept his suit. He had appeared in her life, however, at the critical moment when she was ready to turn her back on fame. And the match had seemed most appropriate at the time. Her husband had already been hailed as the great drover of the Isles, able, with his dog, to handle fifty beasts and cover twenty miles in a day. Not only did he belong to Skye's most powerful family but he had been groomed for the eventual factorship of the MacDonald estates, having distinguished himself in the army after being educated in Edinburgh at his chief's expense. Yes, she might occasionally hanker after might-have-beens but she had not done badly for herself.

The early years had been hard, though, fraught with adjustments and compromises. Their first son had been born in October 1751, just eleven months after their marriage. What maverick impulse had possessed her to call him Charles, she wondered, despite the family tradition that decreed the continuance of patronyms? And after that she seemed to be constantly in the family way. By 1757 she had four sons and a daughter to care for, as well as Allan's old and ailing parents. Yet they had been blissfully happy in their farm at Trotternish, any differences of opinion soon gentled away by the felicities of their marital bed. She had sedulously avoided any mention of the old days, her Jacobite associations and friendships. All of that was in the past, for only fanatics ever dreamt, now, of a Stuart returning to claim the throne. So why disrupt the even tenor of her days by recalling something that could only drive a wedge between them? Politics and love were undesirable bedfellows.

Allan's voice called from the doorway and her heart leapt. 'Are you still there, woman, dreaming at the window? I thought you'd have cleared away the breakfast things long ago, or at least have got Morag to do it!'

Then his voice softened. He came over and fondled her hair. She felt his rough skin on her cheek and smelt the familiar odour of horses and tobacco, and wondered if he guessed the line her thoughts had taken. That was the problem, when you had been married all those years: you became so finely attuned to each other's moods and memories.

She sighed. 'They've gone, then? Would they could have stayed!'

His fingers were busying themselves with the silver brooch at her throat, the one she had had made from the rhinestone buckle Prince Charles had given her at Portree, all these years ago. He laid it on a side table and then set to work on the minuscule buttons of her gown. 'Where's Fanny?' he asked thickly. 'Could we sneak back to bed awhile?'

'I sent her up to fetch the tea Aggie MacLeod promised me. She'll be away a good hour.'

The remark meant consent, of course, and Allan smiled. 'We'll lock the door, just to be on the safe side.'

She rested her head on his shoulder – he was a good foot taller than she – and murmured languidly, 'You'd think we'd be past this houghmagandie nonsense, at our time of life.'

'We'll never be past it, Florrie. Without your loving, lass, I honestly don't think I could carry on.'

He was rarely so frankly dependent. She felt a great surge of protectiveness and with it the familiar, creeping warmth of desire. Yes, her recent life had been beset by poverty, by the envy and malice of their island neighbours and the rigours of survival in a wild, remote place, but she could still hold her head up high. Above all, despite her occasional disloyal thoughts about the past, she loved this man. She knew the greatest challenge lay ahead in that untried world across the waste of ocean, but she was ready. With Allan she would gladly journey to the earth's end.

III

Winter 1773–74

The winter months served only to confirm Flora's determination
to emigrate. Harsh, salt-laden gales came hammering in from the
Atlantic, bringing driving rain and freezing hail-storms.
Kingsburgh was a large house, built in and for more prosperous
times, and it was impossible to keep it warm. They would spend
their evenings huddled in blankets round a single peat fire, gazing
desolately into the flames.

Allan reached the nadir of his despondency in mid-January,
when five cows died of cold, hunger and blood-letting in so many
days.

'I can take no more, Florrie! That's three hundred and twenty-
seven head of cattle and horses gone in the last three years! If things
go on at this rate there won't be enough money left to pay our
creditors, far less start a new life in America!'

Flora's heart went out to him. Normally ruddy and ebullient,
he had lost weight recently. His face was lined with worry and his
voice had a new bitter edge to it. He had worked so hard. Some
might see his destitution as just punishment for pride and folly,
but not she.

'I know, my love, I know,' she soothed. 'But we must hold on
a while longer. There will be no ships leaving until the spring.
What captain would brave the ocean in this weather? Better to
work towards leaving, packing our possessions and arranging
places for Sandy, and Jamie, and Fanny.'

She swallowed hard. This was the rub, the possibility of having
to leave their family behind. She loved them all, all seven, with a
fierce, uncompromising love, and daily thanked God that he had
spared every one of them from disease and early death. Four of
them were no longer at home, of course. Charles had a commission
with the East India Company. Ranald was a lieutenant in the
Marines through the good offices of Captain Charles Douglas of
the *Ardent* ship-of-war, whom Flora had known on the *Eltham* in
'46. And Johnny, the bright one, was living with their lawyer friend
John MacKenzie of Delvine, while a pupil at the High School of
Edinburgh.

Then there was Anne, nineteen and married for three years

now to the redoubtable Alex MacLeod. Alex, an ex-officer in the Marines, was wealthy, distinguished and far-travelled. He had been with Wolfe at the Siege of Quebec, had fought in India and in the Philippines. He was so masterful and experienced it was no wonder he had swept Anne off her feet. Flora felt a glow of satisfaction. How happily that marriage had turned out. She had had understandable doubts at first, seeing her beloved Anne married so young to a man twenty-four years her senior, and a widower at that, but the match had proved singularly harmonious. Anne was cheerful and adaptable, and seemed able to accept every decision of Alex's without question – a characteristic which Flora found alternately enviable and irritating, depending on her mood.

But perhaps this accommodating nature of Anne's was particularly fortunate now, when the MacLeods had also come to a crossroads in their lives. Alex, though illegitimate, had been the acknowledged MacLeod heir, but on his father's death a family row had erupted, obliging him to resign his factorship of the Dunvegan estates and sell his tack of Waternish. He talked now of joining the MacDonalds in their foreign venture and Flora, while knowing that she did not dare actively interfere, prayed daily that he would not change his mind. Amazing, how emotionally dependent on Anne she had become recently. The girl had matured so rapidly. She now had two children of her own and was more like a sister than a daughter.

But what of the ones who were left, eighteen-year-old Sandy, sixteen-year-old Jamie and little Fanny? Their fate had caused Allan and Flora much anguished soul-searching those past few months. Not only did they worry about having three extra passages to pay, but the children's welfare was a constant preoccupation. Sandy had already shown a fondness for the opposite sex which, though natural, had to be channelled in appropriate directions, while Jamie was at the malleable stage and needed role models, his father being the most obvious and desirable. As for Fanny, she was still a child, but a sweet and loving one, and the thought of leaving her behind broke Flora's heart. Yet might not all three be safer morally and physically if they grew up in familiar surroundings, rather than being uprooted and transferred at a tender age to an alien land full of uncertainties and danger?

Flora was all for finding work for the boys at home and taking

Fanny with them. 'You will write to the Duke of Atholl and ask whether he can find a place for Sandy, and maybe Jamie too? You knew him once, after all, and as Lord George Murray's son he may well have a soft spot for me.'

But months passed and despite Flora's nagging Allan made no move. He had a most frustrating habit of evading the issue whenever there were letters to be written. He had a pain in his side, he would say, or the light was bad, or there was other more pressing business to attend to.

Eventually, one day when she had attempted a particularly desperate plea, he turned on her angrily and burst out, 'Can't you see I'm sick and tired of begging, Flora?' She knew then that it was no use. He had no intention of writing. He had lost faith in himself.

So young Sandy sat down himself and penned a letter to the Duke. No reply came. Not even a kind word. In the end it was Fanny who was offered a home with the MacLeods of Raasay, while Sandy and James were obliged to accompany their parents.

It was the outcome Flora had most feared. Fanny was so thin and waif-like and her almost preternatural sensitivity – had it something to do with her being a seventh child, Flora wondered – made her doubly vulnerable.

'Can't she come with us, Allan? I know the voyage will be a test of strength and courage but would it not be better that we be all together? Fanny is but eight. She needs her mother.'

Allan's reaction was patient but firm. 'The child's constitution wouldn't survive the voyage. And even if she did win through she would be one more mouth to feed when we got there. Who knows what hardships we are going to find?'

Flora knew that further remonstrance was useless. After all, Allan was largely right. Fanny would thrive at Brea. The sixty-two-year-old Laird of Raasay, Malcolm MacLeod, was a bluff, accommodating man: he would readily welcome Fanny into his rumbustious family of ten daughters and three sons. Again, Flora realised that his kindness could well be a tribute to her, for he had been imprisoned on the *Furnace* with her for his part in the Jacobite drama, and they had returned to Scotland together after the general pardon. She and Allan had much to be grateful to him for: she still winced, recalling how he had lent them £500 in a particularly worrying financial crisis.

But despite the ultimate advantage Flora still felt guilty and unhappy and flung herself into a desperate indulgence of the child. She spent hours sewing new nightgowns and petticoats for her, and stitching aprons she adorned with embroidery and lace. In the evenings she would laboriously bind the girl's raven-dark hair with strips of cotton and come morning the shining ringlets would be lovingly brushed into place, more for Flora's gratification than for Fanny's own

'You'd think she was a duchess's daughter, Florrie! You'll have her totally spoilt. She mustn't go to Raasay with fancy ideas about her own importance. Nobody there has any time for that kind of nonsense.'

'Nothing can spoil our Fanny, Allan. You know that. And she must not think we are casting her off. She goes to Raasay as a Kingsburgh MacDonald, not as a pauper lass!'

Allan's face darkened at this – what were they now, if not paupers? – and repenting she went to him and laid her head on his chest. 'I am truly sorry, husband. It is hard for you too, I know. But whatever happens we must hold on to our dignity.'

She expected solace from him then, for they had consistently turned to one another through all their misfortunes, but his eyes were hard as granite as he roughly pushed her from him. The rejection brought a bleakness she had never felt before.

'The sooner we leave this Gehenna of wretchedness the better,' she managed to gulp through her tears. 'Another winter here would surely kill us. This misery is poisoning all our lives.'

IV

April 1774

Somehow they struggled through what remained of that dark and dreary winter, until the pale northern sun brightened towards spring. Something of Flora's old spirit revived then and she found herself thinking more constructively of the future.

'Come with me to Flodigarry tomorrow, Fanny,' she burst out impulsively one evening in late April. 'It will be at its best just now, with the daffodils out. Neil's taking the cart round the coast road to Kilmaluig. We'll walk round from there under the Quiraing, then he'll bring the horses round later.'

The words brought a vivid mental picture of green and gold, and she vowed to take a trowel with her. Six bulbs. Only six. Yes, that would do as a memento. She would take them with her and plant them in the new land.

'The weather promises fair,' she continued, 'for all there's mist on the Cuillins, and if we're up at sunrise we can have the whole day. Who knows, it may be our last chance to see the old place.'

Fanny's face beamed at the prospect of a holiday, then clouded as she remembered the changes her mother was hinting at. She had spent the winter dreading the threatened departure of her parents and brothers, hoping against hope that some miracle would bring reprieve. Maybe, if she did not think of it, the threat would go away: so she asked simply, 'Who will milk the cows and gather the eggs?'

'Oh, Morag will do that.'

So they set out together before dawn on the long trek to the other side of the island. Allan and the two boys were already out working in the fields. Flodigarry, where Allan and Flora had lived for the first eight years of their married life, was fifteen miles away by the twisty coastal track but once Neil had left them to continue on foot Flora knew of secret paths under the mountains.

Mother and daughter were both tuggingly aware, as they scrambled up the myrtle-scented slopes, of the unspoken but indissoluble bond between them. Each knew that this expedition was both significant and symbolic. For Flora it would be a sad farewell to the place on earth where she had been most happy, while Fanny, young and exuberant though she was, sensed her mother's melancholy. Where normally she would have frisked on ahead and made nothing of the rocky climb she realised that Flora was finding the going heavy and hung back.

'Here I am, peching up this hill like an eighty-year-old,' Flora complained. 'That winter must have taken more out of me than I thought. I'll pay for it with aches and pains tomorrow, I'll wager!'

'Never mind, Ma. We'll be at the top in an hour or two. Let's rest awhile by the waterfall there. We're making good time. See, the sun's just up!'

It was certainly an idyllic morning. The thin clouds had lost their opalescent pallor and were blazing into brilliant hues of rose and lavender. The birds were awake, their first sleepy chirpings giving way to a crescendo of sound. Within yards of them a lark rose suddenly from its nest in the undergrowth, the loud whirr of its wings making them start. Rich and golden and unbearably beautiful its song flooded the sky, a torrent of mindless notes that tumbled over and into one another as if the singer could not contain its rapture. For some minutes the poignant music hung in the air, detached and solitary; then the bird plummeted to earth, its outpourings ceasing as abruptly as they had begun.

For a while they sat in silence. Flora heard the lush melody echoing in her mind and sighed to herself. Would there be larks in North Carolina? Were there mountains like the Cuillins, and wild flowers like the primroses at their feet? Did the lochans lie dark and mysterious in the hollows, home to herons and wild swans? It wasn't natural, this uprooting! How could she bear it?

In an access of tenderness she smoothed Fanny's hair and kissed her cheek. 'Come, wee one. I'm rested now. Not far to go. The worst's behind us.'

This was not altogether true, for the final part of the climb proved steeper, rockier and more exhausting than it had seemed from below, but at last they crested the hill and looked down on the whole north-east corner of the island, the Trotternish. Behind and above them towered the sheer, serrated crags of the Quiraing; to the south rose the dramatic, improbably-shaped pinnacles of the Stoor; and away below, beyond a downward-sloping series of hummocky hills, the blue sea glittered.

Flora felt her breath catch at the beauty of it. 'Oh, Fanny! We could not have chosen a clearer morning. See the hills of Torridon and Gairloch on the mainland yonder, and the point of Ruibh Reigh away in the distance! I can't remember many days as sharp as this!'

They sat under a rock and ate their bread and cheese. The spring sun had some warmth in it now and a pleasant languor crept up on them. The scattering of houses in the bay below looked deceptively near. Flora lit her clay pipe and smoked contentedly: nothing like a pipe of good Virginian tobacco to soothe the soul.

That was one item she craved that would probably be abundant, and cheap, in America!

It was only as they started down that she began to feel apprehensive. The winter rains had soaked the peat bogs of the lower slopes, rendering them treacherously muddy to the depth of a good foot.

'Take off your pattens and hose, Fanny. We'll have to wade through this glaur.'

In a moment of blind panic she imagined them being sucked helplessly down into the ooze of that dun, unpeopled landscape, and despairingly reproached herself for having contemplated this expedition.

Fanny, however, was fleet of foot and buoyant of spirit. 'Keep to the tussocky bits, Ma, and we'll be all right. See, I'll show you!' And she leapt lightly on ahead, full of confidence, until they reached solid ground again.

The terrain was now achingly familiar to Flora. All she had to do was clamber down a few yards more and there the cottage would be, huddling secretively under the tall lava cliffs. Would it still be as she remembered it?

Speaking almost to herself, she murmured, 'Strange to think you weren't even born when we lived here, lass. Oh, it was that bonnie in the summer! We grew kale and potatoes and deep red roses, and your father and I would sit there in the evenings watching the otters playing in the bay. Aye, we were happy then right enough. I wouldn't have changed Flodigarry for a royal palace.'

She tried to stave off the memories but they would not be dismissed. Annabella and Alexander's wedding day, when people had come not just from Skye but from the mainland and the Outer Isles, to feast on roasted sheep and oxen and consume gallons of whisky. The times when Allan had come back from Crieff or Falkirk or Edinburgh, always bringing some welcome trinkets for her, or a piece of lace or some special tea, even if the cattle sales had not come up to expectations. The days spent cutting and stacking the peats, hard work but companionable: they had always sung as they laboured, in these days. The pedlars who trudged over the moors, bringing bolts of cloth and needles and thread and always the latest gossip from near and far. Then Allan reading morning and evening from the big family Bible, and heading the ritual Sunday pilgrimage of family and servants, rain and shine, summer and winter, to hear Donald MacQueen preach in the church at Kilmuir, on the west side of Trotternish.

It was all too much to bear. Ashamed, she hastily brushed away the tear that rolled unbidden down her cheek.

The green, wholesomely fertile land around the shore had attracted crofters, and in the old days the few cottages had constituted what on Skye amounted to a rudimentary township where Allan's tenants helped him work his land and grew some oats and kale for their own use. But now the life of the place had gone. Abandoned and forlorn, the crumbling walls and gaping thatch of the houses bore witness to some dire disaster. Flora remembered a conversation of just a few days before and Allan's despondent shake of the head as he said, 'One more summer of emigration, and the only folks left in Sleat and Trotternish by the name of MacDonald will be old Aird and three other ancient bodies.'

She had thought he was exaggerating but the tumbledown state of these buildings here at the end of the island brought home the gravity of their plight. Everyone was leaving, harried by the new breed of mercenary lairds and their heartless stewards. If Allan and she stayed it would be rather like growing old and realising that there was no-one of one's own generation left.

With a determined effort she hauled her mind back to the present. No point in being either sentimental or bitter. The world had changed and she must adjust to it or perish. It was just that every so often she was reminded that she herself had played a not inconsiderable part in the events that had led, with cruel inevitability, to her own people's humiliation, and while she would not change what she had done she deeply regretted the consequences.

They were down on the shore now, and just over there was the rocky islet their farm had been named for. Under the bluff the air had turned balmy. Wood anemones and violets peeped shyly from grassy clefts and the daffodils she herself had planted in the copse by the cottage were coming into bloom: their faint woody scent drifted towards them. For a moment she was reminded of rural England, then realised that those slender young birches were essentially Scottish, as were the tender fronds of bracken just starting to unfurl. The rowan by the garden gate would have a haze of green on it too, she reckoned, and if ever a tree spoke to her of home it was the rowan.

Approaching the house from the side they only gradually became aware of the property's dilapidated state. A thicket of massed holly, ash and elder crowded in upon it. The garden that had been Flora's pride and joy was knee-high in docks and nettles, and the path to the door was so overgrown with weeds and moss that it was scarcely visible.

The house itself was a shambles. Great swathes of thatch had fallen away, leaving cavities open to the sky. The door hung precariously on its hinges. The windows no longer served any purpose: their frames were warped and the glass so encrusted with grime and obscured by encroaching greenery that no one could hope to see in or out.

'Oh, Fanny! We were so proud of that house! So few of the island cottages had windows, far less glass, and your father was planning, had we stayed, to put on a slate roof. Poor Flodigarry!'

So saying she stooped to busy herself by a clump of daffodils. She carefully chose an area where the bulbs had spread abundantly, and carefully deposited each uprooted bulb in the small sack she had brought. Only six. She must not be tempted to take more.

Meanwhile Fanny was prattling on. 'It's all that Mistress Martin's fault, isn't it? They say she's a witch and that she hates all us MacDonalds. And we never see her in church. Will she spend her Sundays working spells against us, do you think?'

Flora shuddered at the innocent words. Here was the old family enmity perpetuating itself, though she had never consciously fostered it in her children.

'Don't talk nonsense, Fanny. Mistress Martin's just a poor widow body who's not quite right in the head. She's too crippled now to leave the house and doesn't have the wit to do anyone ill.'

'Then why don't we call on her?'

To Flora's horror Fanny had taken her mother's reassurances at their face value and was making to push the rickety gate open.

'No! No, Fanny! Please come back! We would not be welcome, lass!'

She knew only too well how true that was. Martin Martin had

died eaten up with hatred for Allan. The hostility had begun away back, when both men were mere youths. There had been what Allan still insisted on referring to as a friendly wrestling match in the courtyard at Kingsburgh, and just when Allan was getting the upper hand he had caught his spur in some sacking on the ground and had thrashed out frantically, grabbing his opponent in a crushing bear hug. This trouncing of the dour Martin had been acclaimed by Allan's supporters who subsequently embroidered it until it achieved almost Homeric status in the island's folklore. There was even a song about it.

More recent events had fuelled the rankling animosity. In '51, at the end of his lease, Martin had been evicted in Allan's favour from the 960-acre farm, and his resentment had been so open and vocal that old Kingsburgh had branded him a turbulent, unsafe tenant. Since his father's death Allan had tried to make amends and had offered Martin the tenancy again, but the man had continued feckless and troublesome. His death ought to have ended the feud but the widow and her fusionless sons had put it about that their paterfamilias had been virtually murdered by Allan, for according to them he had never recovered from that youthful trial of strength.

All this was going through Flora's head as she tried desperately to restrain her impetuous daughter. 'No, Fanny! Better if we just sit here by the shore a while and then start back along the road to meet Neil.'

But the words were scarcely out when an eldritch screech rent the air. Marion Martin had burst out of the cottage door and was rampaging down the path towards them. Though probably little older than Flora she looked to be in her seventies. Her jaundiced complexion had been ravaged by the pox and was deeply wrinkled, long white hair straggled over her shoulders, and her ragged, unwashed clothes gave off a fetid, diseased odour that was quite discernible even at fifty yards.

She was brandishing an axe and howling imprecations in Gaelic. 'Begone from my house, ye poisonous MacDonald bitches ye! As if 'twas not enough to kill my man ye think ye can come snooping about my place and steal my daffodils! We all have but ye to thank for the state o' Skye, ye and a' yer fancy gentry kind!'

There followed a string of foul oaths in which she condemned

the whole MacDonald clan to the fires of hell. May they never find
peace wherever they wandered on this earth. May their children
and their children's children be cursed to the end of time. May
they ... And the tirade rose to a crescendo of garbled rhymes and
weird maledictions that smacked of ritual necromancy, as she
hurled herself upon them.

Appalled, Flora saw the axe blade suddenly poised within inches
of her daughter's head, and realised that Fanny was too petrified
to move. She had turned ash-pale and her eyes were blank and
staring, as if she had been hypnotised. Quick as a flash Flora
grabbed her by the shoulders and pushed her aside. 'Run!' she
hissed, and leaping aside saw the deadly weapon descend and fix
itself harmlessly in the ground on the very spot where Fanny had
been standing.

Her own first instinct then was to flee, but her stubborn self-
possession held her back. Determinedly she pulled herself up and
faced the frenzied crone, looking unflinchingly into the mean,
simian little tinker eyes. Then she replied, using the same homely
Gaelic that sprang as naturally to her lips as to those of her
adversary.

'Good day to you, Marion. Please forgive me. We did not mean
to disturb you. I had come but to gaze awhile on Flodigarry, since
it was once my home. I would remind you, however, that these
daffodils are as much mine as yours, since you hold the land from
my husband. They are not even in your garden, and what's more
I planted them myself years since, with my own hands. But let us
not quarrel. There is no need, considering we shall be here only
a little while longer. May the good Lord be with you and yours.'

A puzzled frown appeared on Marion Martin's face then, and
she stopped in her tracks. She was still muttering incomprehensibly
but the diatribe had fallen away to a low, confused grumble that
lacked both venom and conviction. Only then did Flora turn on
her heel, and only when she had seen the crazed harridan close
the cottage door did she quicken her pace and run to comfort the
shaken, weeping Fanny.

'It's all right, lass. All right, I tell you. People often go that way
when they feel old and poor and abandoned. See, we are whole
and unscathed. She did not mean to harm us.' And she made a
dogged effort to smile, even laugh.

Fanny looked decidedly doubtful at this but the terror had gone from her eyes. Flora knew that the incident would soon be, if not forgotten, at least pushed to the back of the child's mind. Marion Martin's curses continued to sound in her own ears, however, as they took to the coast road to meet Neil and the horses. Here they were, trudging along as if the day had been uneventful, but how close to tragedy they had come! The lustre had gone from the day. What had started as a pilgrimage in search of old remembered delights had rendered up nothing but insanity and malice. She told herself to be charitable, to discount the ravings of the poor ignorant addle-wit, but the horror of being so hated, even by a lunatic, kept torturing her.

And though largely reassured Fanny was too conscious of her mother's thoughts to let the subject drop. 'That Mistress Martin is a horrid, hateful old woman, isn't she? I hope she dies soon, so that Skye will be rid of her. Satan take her! There, Ma, I can curse too!'

Suddenly overwhelmed with love and relief Flora took the fragile little body in her arms. 'Oh my darling, you're as dear to me as life itself! No matter what happens you'll always remember me, won't you?'

'Aye, Ma. I promise.'

The deep hazel eyes that turned on Flora then were full of warmth and trust. Young though the child was she was showing a determined intelligence and the ability to survive deprivation and disappointment. Flora, too doubt-ridden right then to realise that her own character was reflected in these eyes, was proud of her.

V

August 1774

That summer Allan sold the livestock he had conscientiously nurtured, and the buildings he had laboured so hard to improve. The whole lot fetched £800, a paltry sum after twenty-three years of struggle.

Flora was appalled. Her first instinct was to protest. The words were on the tip of her tongue – 'But that's surely impossible, Allan! Why, £800 is scarcely more than I brought to you as a dowry in 1750!' – and then she saw the haunted look of desperation and hurt pride in his eyes and bit back the impulse. It was no wonder Allan was bitter. The sad state of their finances was only partly due to his lack of business sense. Involved in this wholesale exodus from the islands were people of all shades of temperament, from the frugal to the most prodigal. She herself might always have been shrewd and careful with money but she could not be sure that their fate would have been any different if she had been running Kingsburgh instead of Allan: Lady Margaret and her grasping absentee-landlord son would have seen to that.

But there was so little left! Even Flora's own savings had gone. Allan had undertaken to pay the passages not only of his own family but of eight of their servants too. Cabin accommodations for Flora, himself and their two sons amounted to £20, while below-decks fares were £3 .10s each. Half of this sum would be paid to the ship's owner in advance and the rest on embarkation. She hoped that once they had bought food supplies – they had to provide their own on the voyage – they would have no more steep claims upon their capital.

But now that preparations were so far advanced she had to look to the future. It was good that Morag, her personal maid, had agreed to come. Large, bovine and somewhat deaf, the lass was yet loyal to the point of idolatry and would be a constant solace. The others too, including the old retainer Neil and his indispensably capable wife Deirdre, seemed happy enough with their indentured servant status. Neil, the seventh son of a seventh son, was known far and wide for his psychic powers. They said he had the taisch, the second sight, and he had made gloomy predictions about the outcome of the emigration scheme, but Allan pooh-poohed them as superstitious rubbish. 'The man grows senile,' was his uncompromising verdict.

What a mercy, too, that Anne and Alex were joining them. It had been difficult enough to say goodbye to Fanny, who would spend the winter at school in Edinburgh with Malcolm's girls, but to abandon Anne as well would have been heart-breaking.

At last, in early August, when they were beginning to despair of having word, a courier arrived to tell them that passages had been booked aboard the 115-ton brig *Ulysses*. Flora's Argyllshire cousins knew the owner, Walter Ritchie, and had arranged for the MacDonald party to be picked up at Campbeltown in the middle of the month. Suddenly the emigration was all too terrifyingly real. Flora squared her shoulders, made a supreme effort to smile, and addressed herself to the task of packing their belongings.

Allan had had wooden crates made by the local joiner, and into these she stacked their fine collection of books, glass and silver which she was sure would be the envy of many in the land they were going to. There were rugs, prints and family portraits, clocks and a mirror. Their household linen was lovingly folded away – tablecloths and napkins, and the bedding that included blankets, counterpanes and bolsters. She paid particular attention to the sheet the Prince had slept in, and to the red damask curtains that had been a gift from Lady Primrose, and down the side of it all she tucked a little bag containing her six daffodil bulbs from Flodigarry. Their furniture would go too: the hand-carved desk; the long stretcher table; the fireside bench with its tufted Turkey carpet upholstery; leather-seated chairs; tapestry footstools; and of course her indispensible spinning-wheel. What a load it would be, especially when you added clothes, sacks of meal, crates of poultry (Flora had a pet hen called Beanie), and all the paraphernalia a family acquires over the years!

Yet even on the very last morning, when the floorboards and walls were bare and Kingsburgh an empty shell, she could scarcely believe it was happening. Only when she heard the cartwheels trundling on the gravel did she realise that the wagons had indeed come to carry their possessions to Portree. Hastily she wiped away a tear. On no account must anyone see her give way to despair.

A cheery sound outside the parlour door interrupted her thoughts as she bundled up the very last of their possessions. Sandy, whistling that song Iain MacRae of Kintail had composed. He could whistle like a blackbird, could Sandy. How did the words go again? 'Dod a ah'iarrudh an fhortain do North Carolina.' Going to seek a fortune in North Carolina. Oh, how she hoped MacRae was right. All the evidence pointed to golden opportunities over there. Both her stepfather Hugh and her half-sister

Annabella sent glowing if infrequent reports. But Annabella's last
missive had hinted at some unrest among the colonists. Something
to do with objections to British taxes. Impatiently she brushed the
moment of fear away. Every society had its hotheads.

Sandy was overjoyed that Iain MacRae, with his wife and
family, would also be sailing on the *Ulysses*. Flora frowned, seeing
in her mind's eye the flaming red hair of the young maverick poet.
She hoped Sandy wouldn't be too much influenced by him, for
he was a mass of contradictions, one minute a languid dreamer
and the next a reckless mischief-maker. And people said that he
was a bit of a womaniser, for all he was a married man.

'Mother! Is everything ready? Father and the ghillies have
brought the wagons round. They want to get away!'

Sandy's voice thrilled with excitement. He couldn't wait to
board that ship, he who had made few sea passages and those
always in sight of land. Flora remembered her own voyages in
1746 and shuddered. It was only in nightmares that she fully
confronted those memories and she still had not come to terms
with them. Little did the youth guess what might lie ahead, of
sickness and danger.

But the lad was young and she knew he needed the stimulus of
new surroundings. He had been getting into trouble lately, what
with that Peggy McKinnon adventure and his subsequent brush
with Donald MacQueen the minister. She herself didn't think
Sandy had done anything wrong. Why not tryst with a girl under
the hazels by Loch Snizort, if she had asked for it? Sandy was
certainly not the kind to say no, and all the local girls adored him,
a circumstance which Flora totally understood. What lass could
resist that frank and radiant smile, the clear grey eyes and curly
brown hair that flashed red when the sunlight struck it? And he
had his father's tall, muscular physique: Peggy must have been
positively jubilant when she won his sole attention.

So serve Donald right if he had caught them with no clothes
on, happily fornicating, but he hadn't: the only crime he could
accuse them of was walking out on a Sunday. She smiled grimly
to herself. Donald was over-zealous at times, a typical, sour-faced
product of Skye's uniformly dour landscape, without intimacy or
humour. A pity that he had appointed himself custodian of her
boys' moral welfare, for since Charles and Ranald had gone –

'escaped' was the expression Sandy used – the lad had found himself under constant surveillance.

But she mustn't admit her real thoughts to the eighteen-year-old, and spoke now with deliberate briskness. 'Almost finished, tell your father. But first help me lug some of these bundles.'

They met Allan and the servants in the hall and Allan relieved her of her load. 'No need for you to carry things, Florrie. That's what the ghillies are here for. Now I don't think we should linger. The *Jessie* is waiting for us at Portree. See, Neil has brought the carriage round. We'll get those last bundles in there: the wagons have gone already, with the heavy stuff. I'll fetch Jamie and Morag and the other women and you can get started. We'll follow on horseback.'

Flora knew that Allan's peremptory tone masked his own distress at leaving. She wanted them to stand entwined at the door and say goodbye to the place together but knew neither of them could bear it. So she cast one last loving look over Kingsburgh's plain, solid facade and let Neil help her into the coach.

As if to make the leaving even more difficult it was a perfect August morning, promising heat. Beyond the loch on the MacLeod shore the fields lay laughing with grain, and even the harsh moorland and grim rock of the Trotternish were softened by a purple veil of heather. So often eerie and menacing in their dismal shroud of mist, the mountains looked positively benign. On the approach to Portree the cottage gardens smiled, full of hollyhocks and roses. Skye seemed determined to disown all the hardship it had caused by presenting its most amiable face; but Flora knew this seduction for the meretricious veneer it was, and hardened her heart.

As they entered the town she had to fight to maintain her detachment, for memories kept crowding in. There, high on the hill overlooking the harbour, was the whitewashed inn where she had last seen Bonnie Prince Charlie. Gallant and regal till the end, he had kissed her hand and murmured, 'I hope, Madam, we shall meet in St James's yet.' Then Donald Roy had bade him make urgent haste and had hustled him off towards the harbour and a possible haven on Raasay.

She let herself savour the recollection for a moment and then shoved it aside. Far from being summoned to St James's she had

had not a word from the Prince, over all the years. By all accounts he was living a life of debauchery on the Continent – the latest rumour had him in Florence – and shunned many who had been prepared to sacrifice their all for him. Even Clementina Walkinshaw, who had borne him a daughter in 1753, was abandoned.

Portree harbour was milling with emigrating islanders and the friends and relatives who had come to bid them farewell. Heaps of possessions lay all around. The squawking of seagulls vied with the droning of bagpipes and the shouts of the jostling mob, the whole cacophony seeming to throb as bursts of sound were followed by sudden, solemn oases of silent awareness. The MacDonalds' carriage came down the steep hill and debouched its human cargo in the midst of the throng, with the men clattering down on horseback immediately behind.

Their arrival caused quite a stir. One man, a cottar of around Allan's own age, came up and almost prostrated himself before them. 'My two brothers are going with you, master, and they are all I have in the world. Would you be minding taking me as well? I promise I would be loyal and trustworthy, and give you no cause for regrets.'

Flora watched Allan's face working and knew the dilemma he faced. 'No, Donald, I fear I cannot, man. The places are all spoken for. But I promise that if things go well out there I'll send for you, and pay your passage gladly, for I know your worth.'

'God bless you, sir. You are a true Highland gentleman and should you agree to have me one day I shall gladly serve you for the full seven years.'

Flora knew Allan's instinctive dislike of the indentured servant system which was somehow more demeaning than the natural hereditary pattern of hierarchy within a clan, and understood Allan's brusque rejoinder.

'So be it, Donald, if that is the only way. But I assure you, friend, that it is no slave you would be but a trusted servant.' And he turned away with tears in his eyes.

Soon they were rowed out to the *Jessie*, which was lying at anchor just off the pier. They found the decks of the little brig that would take them to Campbeltown even more congested than the town jetty had been. The passengers were jockeying for comfortable positions, settling themselves against their crates and bundles and spreading pallets to serve as beds. Allan and Sandy began to organise the stowage of the family's gear, helped by Alex, who with Anne and their two children had been on board for the last two hours.

Everything happened very quickly after that. Flora was aware of another lull on shore. The men were taking off their bonnets and the women stood reverently while the old Portree minister, Hugh MacDonald, offered up a prayer. Flora could not make out the exact words from the distance, but she knew it had to be the ancient, incantatory Gaelic blessing she had learnt in her childhood, and found herself murmuring, 'Preserve them from danger, Let the Holy Ghost be around them, Who knows every harbour under the sun.'

There was a lump in her throat, for the minister's son John was one of their number. Chances were the two would never see one another again.

A loud shout of 'Amen!' echoed over the water and as if at a signal the sails were hoisted, the windlass creaked, and the little ship sped from the tight haven with its encircling hills out into the Sound of Raasay.

VI

August 1774

The wind was north-westerly and the weather fine, encouraging a reminiscent, elegiac mood. The gentle hills of Raasay reminded Flora that she was leaving Fanny. The parting with her daughter two weeks before had been heart-rending and she found herself avoiding Allan for much of that first day, afraid that he would see her tears.

They spent the night at anchor in the Kyle of Lochalsh, where a tender brought aboard some emigrants from the mainland, among them Iain MacRae of Kintail, his heavily pregnant wife Siobhan and their children. Their arrival made Sandy's day.

Next morning the *Jessie* ventured into the usually terrifying tidal race at Kyle Rhea, but the skipper had planned his departure so that he would enter the race at slack water and they found the channel mercifully calm. Flora's spirits sank, however, when they encountered a herd of cattle swimming across. She had hoped Allan would not see anything like this but there they were, perhaps fifty of them, predominantly black in colour but some of them brown, dun or brindled. In the water they presented an impression of rolling, heaving shoulders and rhythmically plunging horns. Her concern for Allan then made her seek him out, where he stood by the ship's rail.

'That's Callum McEwan and his lads,' he said dully, 'on their way to Falkirk Tryst. A lot of my bullocks there, I'll warrant. Pray God they fetch him a good price. They're certainly bellowing loud enough!'

His eyes had gone dreamy and she went with him in spirit on one of his annual droving expeditions. He had told her about the damp and dirty inns he had been forced into for shelter, less healthy always than sleeping in the open air, which he relished in good weather. The cold itself did not faze him: he would just dip his plaid in the burn before wrapping it round him, and the wetness would thicken the tweed and keep the wind out. She saw him negotiating the loose scree and barren rock of fearsome remote passes where only deer and ptarmigan dwelt, heard his voice ringing out as he and his dog worked with boot and stout stick to keep the beasts together, plodded with him through the oily black ooze of peat hags and the boggy rushes that grew by the lochans.

'Never mind, love,' she said chokingly. 'There are cattle in America too.'

She gently covered his hand with her own to signal her sympathy, and was rewarded by his smile.

The last of the herd had just clambered ashore on the mainland side as the *Jessie* was carried through on the first of the flood, her sails lifting in the following breeze. Flora had the impression of being sluiced helplessly along, totally at the mercy of the tide. Then they emerged from the narrow strait into open water and the ship began to sail sedately again.

But still the memories flooded relentlessly in. Over there to port was Glenelg, where the old chieftain Sir Alexander MacDonald of Sleat had died in November 1746. Allan had been with him.

They had been bound for London to plead for the release of Allan's father, imprisoned for his part in succouring Prince Charles. An equivocal character the old chief had been, a Hanoverian sympathiser one minute and a Jacobite the next, but who knew what pressures he had been subject to? Lady Margaret's attitude had been equally ambiguous: she had unreasonably blamed Allan for her husband's death and had been obstructive ever since.

Though nothing was said Flora knew that Allan's thoughts were running on the same lines as her own. She felt him remonstrating with himself, reiterating the litany of regret she knew he felt but rarely voiced because it touched on the forbidden area of politics. We all strove so hard to save my father yet did nothing for Flora, he might well be thinking, though she was a prisoner in London too by that time. How could we have brushed her fate aside, as of no account? Lady Margaret was positively dismissive, damning her as a foolish girl, a mere gypsy. And here she is beside me now, my dear helpmeet. But how was I to know that, then?

The words lay between them, as sharply sensed as if they had been spoken aloud. To break the uncomfortable silence Flora pointed ahead and to starboard, towards Isle Oronsay, and said chattily, 'That's where the *Furnace* lay stormbound for two nights, in '46. I was so sea-sick, I remember, that they were glad to shed responsibility for me, and allowed me ashore under guard to see my mother. That was when our maid, Kate, came back on board with me, and a great comfort she was to me all through my travail. I remember how fearful she was, though, and her having no English did not help matters.'

Allan said nothing. Perhaps he was thinking that she had never told him this before? But to her relief the moment of unease passed and the ship flew on down the Sound of Sleat towards the wedge-shaped island of Eigg, where they planned to lie for the night and pick up another party of emigrating crofters. Coll and Islay yielded yet more. Each new contingent crowded the decks further and contributed an extra clamjamfry of objects, an additional dimension of smells and noises, so that Flora was infinitely relieved when the *Jessie* eventually rounded the Mull of Kintyre, having spent the third night off Port Askaig. Campbeltown was still fifteen miles away but she knew that the journey was as good as over.

If only some great magic bird would swoop down now, lift them up on its swift wings, and deposit them directly in America! Suddenly the stuff of her nightmares came savagely to the surface. Entering Campbeltown Loch, she visualised her brother Ranald overwhelmed as he rowed against wind and tide. His death had devastated them all. Thoughts of her own five months at sea in 1746 came rushing back too. Though she had been kindly treated and had scarcely been out of sight of land she had still hated her cramped quarters and the constant violent motion of the ship. When she was well enough to go above decks for air she had gazed longingly towards the shore, envying the beasts in the fields and the birds in the trees their tranquillity and freedom: but mostly she had lain helpless below, her stomach heaving. Uncertainty about the fate that awaited her had compounded her terror. She remembered hearing, in the August, about the execution of the two Scottish rebels, Kilmarnock and Balmerino. That ought to have made her want to stay, comparatively safe, at sea; but no, reaching London and walking on dry land again had been an enormous relief whatever was in store. She had vowed never willingly to board a ship again. The prospect she faced now, of six weeks on the open ocean, could scarcely be contemplated.

The little town of Campbeltown was quite visible now and there, tied up at the quay, was the ship that would take them on their journey.

'Well, she's substantial looking enough,' Allan said at her elbow. 'This little *Jessie* will look tiny alongside her. Don't worry, Florrie. I have every faith in the *Ulysses*, now that I see her. She will get us there, never fear.'

But Flora was unconvinced. She had seen ships of that size before, and knew how insignificant and helpless they could be when battling against the might of the ocean.

Greatly to Flora's delight her cousin Elizabeth, who had taken over Largie House on the death of her father in 1760, had ridden over to Campbeltown with her husband Charles Lockhart as soon as she heard of the *Jessie*'s imminent arrival. They were waiting on the quay to greet the Kingsburgh contingent, and so for a few hours Flora was able to put the forthcoming ordeal to the back of her mind and give herself over to the nostalgic pleasure of their company. It was years since she had seen Elizabeth and there was so much to talk about. Flora remembered how Largie had seemed the essence of sophistication when she had first met her cousins, back in her early twenties. She had spent all of nine months at Largie then, and at that time the great stone mansion had echoed with the fun and laughter of seven sisters – Elizabeth, Jessie and Kate, Julia and Marjorie, Lilias and Molly. Flora had felt overwhelmed by the grandeur of everything, the vast panelled hall hung with shields and claymores, the rich tapestries, marble fireplaces and family portraits in golden frames. Its luxury had even outdone Monkstadt, seat of the laird at home.

Then she sighed. No doubt the house would have lost the patina which her youthful enthusiasm and the gilding of memory had bestowed upon it. Nothing ever stayed the same. She could be sure, though, that it would still be a happy house, for Elizabeth and Charles seemed well suited to one another. They had four little girls ranging in age from nine to two, and were rejoicing in having produced a son and heir at last: baby James, just a year old, was their pride and joy.

It both amused and exasperated Flora that Elizabeth and Charles were clearly embarrassed by what they saw as the MacDonalds' poverty. Anxious to help their kinsfolk save face they refused openly to acknowledge the reason for their very presence in Campbeltown. But they were kindness itself and fussed over Flora, Anne and the children while the men saw to the purchase of last-minute provisions and the transfer of their belongings from the *Jessie* to the *Ulysses*. Understanding that it would not be practical for their cousins to make the journey to Largie in the time available they had left the children with their nurse, arranged to spend the night with friends in the town, and had been instrumental in organising a ceilidh in the local inn that evening. The punch flowed, the pipes played, and the carefully vetted local company danced their way through a succession of reels and strathspeys, culminating in the reel called 'America' that had so intrigued Dr Johnson at Armadale. Its involuted, whirling movements came to a frenzied climax in which everyone was spinning round at once, and Flora emerged from it flushed and breathless.

'Oh, Allan, haven't Elizabeth and Charles been kind! I shall never forget this evening!'

Then she broke off, unable at first to interpret the opaque look in her husband's wide-set eyes. Then realisation came and her heart sank. He thought the gathering had been held in her honour, for these people were her kin, not his! He felt upstaged, his vanity bruised, for he saw himself suddenly as a mere adjunct to a Jacobite legend. Quick to make amends, she raised her eyebrows questioningly and reached out to touch his arm. But he turned from her abruptly and escorted her to her seat without a word.

The evening ended with singing, which Flora loved. As a young girl she had been well known for her pleasant voice and knew all the Gaelic melodies by heart. The tunes, so varied in mood and tempo, took her back across the years to the time when she had been uncomplicatedly innocent and happy. Then, in a sudden lull, young Fergus McFarlane from Carradale embarked upon the mouth music so dear to the Gaelic soul, and Flora found she could not listen to the poignant tribal ululations without weeping. She was thankful then that someone had put out the candles to enhance the melancholy atmosphere, so that only the fire gave light.

When the performance ended in a tremulous hush she turned to Elizabeth.

'Do please forgive my tears, cousin. The music, and all this hospitality, have touched my heart. I had quite forgotten how dear you all were to me, and still are. Close ties like ours outlast time, do they not? But now I must return to the ship. It has been such a long day and tomorrow will be hard for us all.'

She turned to look for Allan, expecting him to join her without question, but he had ensconced himself by the ingle with the menfolk. He had a stoup of ale in his hand and was obviously settling down to another hour's drinking.

Trying to keep the querulous note out of her voice she said, 'Come, dear. We have had a full day and tomorrow will be even more demanding. Besides 'twill soon be dark, this town is strange to us and the roads uneven and unlit. Go fetch a lanthorn and bear me company.'

At that he got up but with an ill grace, making a great show of being put upon. Flora wished he were not so morose in his cups but knew in her heart that his truculence was fed by old, barely-acknowledged resentments.

She sighed. So much for their last night in their homeland.

VII

August 1774

She awoke panic-stricken on the *Jessie*, full of premonitions of disaster: then the truth gradually dawned. This was the day she had been dreading for months. They must embark today on their great, irrevocable adventure, and it did not help to remember that she and Allan had been decidedly out of tune the night before. She wondered where he was. Had he gone to bed at all?

But Morag was all reassurance as she regaled her with a dish of tea.

'The master has gone aboard the big boat to see to things but he says there is no hurry for you. The ship will not be sailing until the tide turns, in the early afternoon. Didn't you sleep well, ma'am? You're looking a wee bit pale.'

Flora tried to smile and act normally. 'Oh, I'm fine. Perhaps too much porter and tobacco last night. I should know better at my age, but what is a ceilidh without a good jug of ale and a pipe? It's nothing some good fresh air won't remedy. And we'll be having plenty of that soon, no doubt. Too much, maybe.'

She could not keep her voice from trembling. It did not help that Anne was also distinctly out of sorts and was finding it hard to keep food down. Only the children wolfed down their bacon and eggs, seemingly oblivious to their grandmother's fears and their mother's sickness.

So it was late morning before Flora had pulled herself together, gathered the last of her possessions and clambered off the *Jessie*. The cousins were already patiently waiting on the pier, full of last-minute advice and concern. Flora tried to relax but could not, especially as Elizabeth seemed as edgy as she was.

'You'll write regularly, won't you?' she twittered. 'See, we have addresses for you here, of people you can get in touch with. Hugh Campbell's family is at a place called Cross Creek – his son Farquhard's a big merchant there – and Alex McAlister of Islay's flourishing: they say he has had three wives and any number of bairns – fifteen at the last count! Then there's Colin Shaw of Jura, who's a merchant in Cumberland County. But of course, I'm forgetting so many of your own family are there already! Oh, you won't weary for your own kind, Flora!'

Not to be outdone, Charles put in with, 'They say there'll soon
be more Highlanders in North Carolina than there are at home!
And the Gaelic's flourishing. It's used in all the church services
and even the African slaves speak it.'

But Flora found little solace in their well-meaning, nervous
chatter. She tried to breathe deeply and compose herself but felt
a wave of stomach-churning weakness come over her. She saw
Allan approach and managed a tentative wave but her hand fell
helplessly to her side when she realised that the tatterdemalion
mob that had suddenly assembled on the quayside seemed to have
only one objective: to catch a glimpse of her. Most of them had
come ashore from the *Ulysses*, having embarked the day before at
Greenock, and were rougher, more intimidatingly alien, than the
wistful clansmen who had seen the MacDonald party off at
Portree. Flora's natural fastidiousness recoiled at their raggedness,
their uncouth Lowland accents and their rancid, unwashed smell.

'That's her! That's the wife that succoured yon Pretender!'

The voice was a triumphant shriek. It issued from a barefoot
woman in a holey grey shawl, with a company of urchins in tow.
She hurled herself at Flora, who was aware of two wild red-rimmed
eyes, the stink of rotten fish, the clutch of a claw-like hand. The
menacing figure seemed to sway and swim before her eyes and
she felt herself crumble. It was like the Marion Martin incident all
over again, just when she had thought herself free at last. After all
those years of avoiding publicity were there still people in the world
at large who resented her, and was she to be exposed to their rude
attention in the narrow confines of an emigrant ship?

A voice rang in her head. 'Allan, I can't! Take the boys and the
servants. I'll stay here at Largie and you can send for me once
you're settled.'

She opened her mouth to speak the words but they would not
come. Instead a homely voice with a pronounced Glasgow accent
intervened. It belonged to a tall, commanding gentleman in a frock
coat and a tricorn hat, clearly a man of substance.

'Off with you, you ramscallion lot you! Can't you see the lady's
like to faint away? Welcome, Mistress MacDonald. I am Captain
Chalmers. 'Tis honoured we are to have you sail with us. So this
is your family here. I have already met your husband' – he nodded
acknowledgement to Allan – 'and Sandy's on board already so

this must be young Jamie …'

Then, as if he sensed her misgivings, he added, 'Be not afraid for them, lady. The *Ulysses* there is a well-found ship with a sturdy crew and we'll get you to the Carolinas safe and sound, never fear.'

Flora felt herself respond to the captain's reassuring, fatherly demeanour. Resolutely she told herself that this was no time for weakness. She dared not let herself – or Allan – down

'I thank you, sir. Forgive my gaucheness. Alas, as you have doubtless guessed I am no lover of the sea. But come, let me introduce my daughter Anne, my son-in-law Alex MacLeod of Glendale, and their little ones, Norman and Allan.'

She was so busy trying to sound self-possessed and gracious that she scarcely took in what happened next, hardly realised that Captain Chalmers had dispersed the mob as if by magic and was ushering her family group across the wharf. Before she knew it she had been helped down a rope ladder on to the ship's deck. A stench of tar and fish with an underlay of rum and oakum assailed her nostrils. Now there was no going back.

Sandy came running over to them, all bustle and enthusiasm. He had foregone the ceilidh the night before but that had vexed him not at all. The evening had been spent exploring the many taverns of Campbeltown with Iain MacRae, and then he had elected to stay aboard the *Ulysses*. He looked now as if he had been at sea for weeks.

Allan received him jovially, as man to man. 'All well, son? Everything stowed?'

'Aye.'

'You managed to get that barrel of hard apples I mentioned, and an extra sack or two of potatoes? We can't exist for weeks on nothing but salt meat and dry biscuit.'

'Aye, I got them.' He did not say, 'Don't fuss, Father' – that would have been impertinent, and would justifiably have aroused Allan's wrath – but his tone implied it.

Flora cut in. 'And Beanie? You found a safe place for Beanie?'

'Aye.'

Flora made a little choking sound, halfway between a sob and a laugh. 'Tell me, then. Where is she?'

'Up there by the mast, beside the other hens. She'll be quite safe there, Ma. The mate said so.'

'Did you get any sleep last night? Where did they put you?'

Sandy grimaced. Usually taciturn, he let the words tumble out. 'Och, it was the worst place I've ever slept in, that cabin! It's like those pictures you see in the history books of the catacombs in Rome, with narrow shelves for bunks and scarcely a ray of light getting in. At night they lash a row of hammocks down the middle for extra sleeping space – I had one of them – and the stink's worse than the byre at Monkstadt.'

Flora felt her face pale, and then realised that Sandy was actually revelling in all this discomfort. To him it was no last-resort, gut-wrenching test of stamina but a wonderful, euphoric experience. He was being given the opportunity, at eighteen, to leave this god-forsaken country and start life afresh in Arcadia. If she could summon up even half his enthusiasm she would be content, but the knot of fear had come back and was tightening with every passing minute.

Sandy was elaborating on the ordeal to come. 'And to think that was just the Greenock folks, last night. 'Twill be more cramped yet, when our men from the *Jessie* come on board.'

As if this mention of the island emigrants had sparked off a signal Flora saw then that the mate had started to bundle the new intake of passengers aboard. Allan's face darkened as he watched the ghillies and crofters, many of them friends and relatives, being hoisted unceremoniously from the *Jessie* by two burly sailors.

'A real ruffian, that mate fellow,' he muttered. under his breath, 'and with a palm that's easily greased, so Sandy tells me. Name of Roger Anderson.'

Sandy grinned broadly. 'Oh aye, We have his measure. We managed, Pa and I, to persuade him to give up his quarters in the stern cabin to you, Ma. You'll have to share it with Anne and Morag and the children and 'twill be very crowded, I fear, but a great sight better than the common sort have.'

Flora marvelled at this resourceful son of hers. Perhaps this move to America would be the making of him after all. And was this the Allan who had been so diffident before, even to the point of evading writing a letter on his sons' behalf? She was pleased and yet fearful: she could not afford confrontations, especially unspoken ones.

They watched as the men, women and children, old people, babies and young folk from the islands were deposited on deck like a herd of sheep. Uprooted from all that was familiar, many of them barely literate and yelled at now in a foreign language, they stood around looking bewildered. Flora sensed Allan's rage at the way they were being treated.

Anderson was a louche-eyed, loose-limbed Lowlander wearing knee-breeches, a red-and-white spotted neckerchief and one ear-ring. Swaggering up, he proceeded to lecture the new arrivals as if all they merited was blanket contempt.

'You lot'll bunk down in steerage and it's your responsibility to keep it clean, whatever the weather. Ye'll supply your ain victuals or go hungry, so mak siccer that ye hae ample supplies o' biscuit and oatmeal. Ye can cook forward in the cab-house when it's calm but nae fires are allowed if it's blowing hard, so I'd advise ye tae cook in advance if there's a storm threatening. Oh aye, and if ony o' ye's maybe fleein' the law ye'd better get doon below and stay there until we sail. We dinna want tae be discovered harbouring criminals.'

Most of the Highlanders barely understood him, and stood stunned, their heads bowed. But Iain MacRae, Sandy's new-found crony, was not so easily intimidated. His face flushed with anger, he retaliated fiercely.

'Ye'll be minding, sir, that we island folk have paid our way and will be expecting courtesy from this ship's company. We are none of your dastardly Lowland slubberdegullions!'

The words came out calm and controlled, the lilting Highland accent lending them an edge of sweetness and light, but Flora sensed their menace. She saw the look of enraged astonishment on Anderson's face and wondered if the battle of wills would end in fisticuffs, or worse.

Sandy was standing beside her at the ship's rail and she felt him stiffen. Quickly she put a restraining hand on his sleeve. 'Let it be,' she said. 'We don't want any trouble before we're even away.'

And fortunately the mate chose to ignore the interruption, though Flora knew he had marked Iain as a troublemaker and would make life difficult for him, given the chance.

'Ye'll be sleeping doon there,' he was saying now, opening the hatch to the great cabin and releasing a wave of warm, stale air, 'and the women and weans'll be in the foc's'le. See and keep the place clean, mind'

Then to Flora's consternation he turned disgustedly from his charges, strode over the deck, and came over to introduce himself.

'Roger Anderson, at your service, ma'am. I've met young Sandy here a'ready and a great credit he is tae ye, gin I may say so.'

He leered sycophantically and Flora saw Allan master his distaste with an effort: better to stay in this fellow's good books.

'How many passengers does that make, now?'

Flora heaved a sigh of relief. Allan was managing to keep the conversation polite and impersonal.

'Upwards o' a hunner and twenty, I'd say, maist o' them the scum o' the earth as far as I can mak oot. But that's no' the maist we've ever had. Last voyage we had a hunner and fifty o' the puir sods. It was hell, man. Sheer hell.'

'You have cargo as well, of course?'

'Oh, aye. We hae that. The Carolina gentry are great ones for their luxuries. There's linen and woollens and shoes and port wine' – he licked his lips – 'no' to mention linseed oil, and iron goods frae Carron, and paint, and glass. There's even some gunpowder … It's a' in that hold doon yonder, the one that's a' locked up.'

As he spoke his eyes were roving over the decks, taking in every move by the crew. He might be a rascal but Flora suspected that he was an expert seaman. Suddenly he broke off.

'But if you'll excuse me now, sir, I see the Captain beckoning. Time for sea. The tide's on the turn.'

The scene was one of frenzied but coordinated activity now. Sailors swarmed in the rigging. Hawsers were being flung aboard by hands on the quay.

'Break out the mizzen!'

Flora felt the surge as a brisk wind caught the sails and the *Ulysses* drew away on the ebb tide amidst a squawking flurry of seagulls and a whoosh of spray. Then the ship gathered speed and ran smartly out of Campbeltown Loch before the prevailing westerly. The cheering died away. The skirl of the bagpipes lost its swagger and faded to a reedy, melancholy wail. Even the most substantial figures had receded and were scarcely distinguishable, save for the tear-blurred white blobs of their fluttering handkerchiefs and the bright pink blotch of Elizabeth's bonnet.

It had all happened so quickly! A silence fell on deck as realisation sank in. People who had hitherto pretended cheerfulness gave way to tears. Some grown men were crying and their distress naturally affected their dependants.

Flora heard a father comfort his son while manfully stifling his own sobs.

'Aye, lad, it's no' exactly a palace, this brig, but it willnae last for ever. An' it was this or starve. Weel ye ken that.'

The answer was a low moan, followed by a series of sniffs as the boy tried for his father's sake to control his weeping.

By common consent most people were staying on deck in the fresh air. As the *Ulysses* rounded Davaar Island Flora looked back at the receding hills. The landscape was gloriously vivid in the sun, the brilliant purple of the heather conspicuous against the yellow of birches and the russet of bracken. A stag stood proudly silhouetted against the skyline, symbol of steadfastness in the wild: above it the pale fragile wisp of a daytime moon. Would she ever see such beauty again? She felt her eyes mist over.

'You're not feeling queasy, Florrie? And you, Anne, are you all right? Shall I fetch you some ale?' Allan's voice was full of concern.

'No, Pa. Just leave us be. 'Tis quite pleasant here.'

Anne's usually rosy face had turned an unhealthy grey colour, like a dirty mushroom. The suspicion that she might be with child again flashed through Flora's mind. It was just like Anne to keep such a thing to herself as long as possible, for Alex's sake.

'If we can find somewhere comfortable and sheltered to sit I'll spread my plaid and we can stay till nightfall,' Allan said. 'See, there's our crate with the hens in. We'll lean against that.'

They had rounded Davaar and were out in the Firth. Flora looked up Kilbrannan Sound and over to the mountains of Arran. There were gannets fishing just offshore, whole flocks of them swooping and plunging, spearing their prey with deadly, instinctive accuracy. Their screeching was audible above the muted murmurs of the assembled emigrants. How she admired their ruthless efficiency, their economy of movement and unerring eye.

'For days, nay weeks, we shall see no birds.' She sighed. 'They cannot live on the vast ocean. 'Twill be all whales and giant leviathans, there.'

'Better get your meat cooked afore we round the Mull,' the mate broke in, and there was a movement of maids and ghillies in the

direction of the galley. Greatly to her surprise Flora thoroughly
enjoyed the supper Deirdre brought them – herring fried in
oatmeal followed by cheese and apples, with some strong Falkirk
ale to wash it down. She had not expected food and drink to taste
so good at sea.

'A pipe of tobacco, Florrie, before we turn in?'

For Flora tobacco was a real treat rarely indulged in and here
she was, enjoying it two nights running! Allan produced their clay
pipes and they sat companionably tamping and savouring the
sweet, comforting weed.

The evening continued calm, and the *Ulysses* made steady
progress under full canvas. Anne and the children had gone below
now and Sandy had joined the mate at the helm. Allan had made
to hold him back at first but then had second thoughts.

'Might as well let him go. 'Twill do him no harm to learn some
sea craft. But I still can't take to the man.'

Indeed the mate, far from objecting to the youth's presence,
seemed actively to be encouraging it.

'We should make Rathlin by dawn at this rate,' he told Sandy,
who stood by as Anderson made the evening's entry in the ship's
log. Then, 'Alter course to starboard!' he yelled suddenly. 'Steady
on! Easy as she goes!' as with a grating creak of cordage and a brief
pitching sensation the ship came about and settled gradually into
a new rolling motion.

'That's us round the Mull now,' he explained. 'From now on
the course is westerly, to clear the coast of Ireland. See here, on
the compass…'

This sea-lore was totally new to Sandy and Flora sensed his
fascination with it. She listened drowsily for a while and then felt
her head fall on to Allan's broad, tolerant shoulder as exhaustion
engulfed her. The summer dusk was giving way to darkness now
and stars were beginning to prick through the vast velvety vault
of the sky. She felt Allan's hand reach out to fondle her breast and
let out a sigh of sheer contentment.

'Oh my dear, 'tis sorry I am to sleep apart from you this night.
It pains me not to have you near.'

He kissed her then in a bid to allay her fears, and probably came
as near to succeeding as any mortal could.

VIII

August 1774

Worn out though she was sleep kept evading Flora that first night. The cabin Sandy and Allan had inveigled the mate into giving them was only six feet long by five feet wide, and she had to share it with Anne, Morag, and her two grandchildren. She and Anne each had a berth in the curve of the hull while the others slept on the cabin sole, all huddled up together. The only light was from a smoky lanthorn that swung from the deckhead and cast green flickering shadows, as the ship lurched, upon the lurid faces of her sleeping companions.

Anne had fallen asleep almost immediately and lay purring gently, like the cat Purn they had had to leave behind. The thought brought many other memories of Fanny and home crowding in, and then Morag started to cough, a dry, hacking wheeze that became more irritating the more Flora tried to ignore it. Behind those human sounds were the continuous creaks and groans of the ship's timbers as she ground her way westwards. At intervals these were punctuated by scuffles and shouts as sail-changes were made or watches called and then, just before dawn when she was on the verge of sleep, a cock in the long-boat above Flora's head began to crow and set all the chickens cackling. Beanie, don't cluck so, your chirring's getting on my nerves, she was murmuring to herself as she gradually fell into a fitful doze, only to be wrenched awake what seemed only moments later by sunlight filtering through the half-hatch, Norman and Allan's chiming voices, and the bustling sounds of morning on the deck overhead.

Red-eyed and weary though she was she soon realised how salubrious her sleeping quarters had been compared to what the others had endured. The hatch to the main cabin had just been opened and she gagged, her nostrils assailed by the stench of sweaty unwashed bodies, the concentrated reek of whale-oil and tar, and mingled with it all a whiff of something more elusive and disturbing, the hum of fear. Heaven help us all, she found herself praying, if we meet bad weather.

Allan and the boys were up already and old Neil had fetched them some porridge.

'How did you fare, Florrie?'

Allan's question was fearful and tentative, making Flora doubly conscious of her lack-lustre eyes and how wan her ageing skin must look in the unforgiving morning sun. But she was damned if she would sound complaining.

"'Twas not so commodious as the cabin we had on the *Jessie* but then one does not expect comfort. We shall just have to get used to it I suppose. 'Tis early days yet.'

'Commodious, Florrie! Did you say commodious? 'Twas sheer hell! All those poor folks crammed in together, spreading lice and disease! And the stink! No human being should be expected to live in those conditions! I intend to challenge Captain Chalmers about it!'

Small chance of that, Flora thought wryly. If I know Allan he'll bluster away in private but do precisely nothing. But to her amazement the new, masterful Allan did not hesitate when the captain appeared on deck.

Captain Chalmers was all ready with a polite greeting but his brows darkened when Allan registered his complaint.

'I am afraid I can do nothing, sir. The hold was clean enough when your people went in. 'Tis up to them to keep it that way. As for overcrowding, many a master would cram in double that number. I fear you have no case, sir. Good day to you.'

Allan came back to her seething with rage: he was unused to such high-handedness. 'Boorish Lowlander!' he growled. 'Such truculence makes my blood boil! And we thought he was a gentleman! I fear there is little more we can do, though, Florrie. We must just help those poor creatures come to terms with it.'

Flora shared his anger but also felt a glow of satisfaction. She had noticed the 'your people' and realised that Allan had been acknowledged by the ship's company as the emigrants' leader and spokesman. It was as if, by leaving home, he had come into a deserved inheritance.

And he did work hard for the rest of the day, helping the passengers find their sea legs and persuading them to keep their gear safely stowed and the steerage quarters aired out. The second night passed, and the next, and yet another, while the *Ulysses* ploughed steadily on, rolling easily into a slow westerly swell.

Meanwhile Flora was observing her fellow passengers, aware of friendships and antipathies developing among them as inevitably happens when people are flung together at close quarters. She talked to a twenty-year-old, Aeneas Mackay, who was going out to teach, having heard that tutors could make between £16 and £20 per annum. She observed him striking up a friendship with George Grant, who was going to North Carolina as factor to a Glasgow tobacco business, and noticed that the two were frequently in the company of the ship's surgeon, young Dr Talbot. It really was astonishing, how quickly people of like spirit and education were drawn to one another regardless of their provenance, whereas the normal run of Highlander was restricted by language and culture to the company of his own kind.

Rather to her consternation she also realised, however, that she was not immune to prejudice herself, for while she could not help regarding some of her fellow passengers with sympathy others aroused only irritation and even contempt. The woman who had accosted her on the pier at Campbeltown was a very vocal presence and Flora conscientiously avoided her, sure that she would not improve on acquaintance. She was accompanied by two snotty-nosed children, a boy and a girl, who were obviously her offspring, and a girl of about sixteen who resembled her in everything but looks, having the same vulgar forwardness but striking marmalade-coloured hair and a voluptuously sinuous figure. Flora could not help being intrigued and her curiosity turned to alarm when she accidentally intercepted a meeting between the girl and Sandy. It all looked entirely innocent, their encounter – just a locking of eyes, a lightening of glances, a quick passage of a missive from one hand to the other – but the girl's mother was ever on the watch and quick to reprimand anyone in the family group who lagged behind. Flora saw her whip round, snakelike, and grab her daughter by the shoulder.

'Come here, ye brazen hussy ye! Dae ye think I canna see ye, oglin' the lads a'ready? Is it no' enough that ye've shamed us a' wi' yer wantonness but ye hae tae mak up tae a Highlander, and him likely a Catholic intae the bargain? Get ye doon intae yon hold there and bide till I tell ye ye can come up!'

The girl went in silence, but not before she had cast a glance at Sandy that would have had the least susceptible of men ready to die for her. Flora hesitated a moment – was it any of her business, this philandering? – but her instinctive distrust of the older woman eventually prompted her to seek Sandy out.

'What do you think you're about, encouraging a wench like that? Can't you see that she isn't our kind?'

At first the youth pretended puzzlement but then blurted out, 'Oh, you mean Rachel? Well, you see, Ma, Iain and I met her ashore, in the tavern. 'Twas really Iain that fancied her. and wanted a tryst with her, and I undertook to give her his message because Iain's that conspicuous, like, with his height and his red hair...'

'Aye,' Flora parried, 'and his wife and bairns! I'm amazed at you, Sandy MacDonald! Well you know that a lass like that means nothing but trouble!'

A moment's discomfiture, and then Sandy came out with his shocking revelation.

'Don't blame her, Ma! Her mother's taking her to America to get her away from her employer in Falkirk that's been making her life a misery trying to get her into his bed! Her father died when she was but a babe and they needed the money she brought in but this old apothecary that's sixty if he's a day and a greasy old goat into the bargain wouldn't let her be. He kept pressing her to marry him – imagine it! – and give the mother her due even she baulked at that. So they're going out to stay with an auntie that's married to a doctor in North Carolina, in Cross Creek. Oh, Ma, have some pity! Rachel's maybe a bit flighty but she's not all bad. It wasn't her fault that the apothecary wouldn't leave her alone, though she says her mother blamed her for it and has treated her like dirt ever since.'

The tale made Flora's gorge rise. Disturbed though she was at the thought of her son being involved with such a person, she still felt reproached by the earnestness of Sandy's plea. But, 'I think you should be more circumspect about whom you befriend,' she said, more gently now. 'You're too ready to give everyone you meet the benefit of the doubt. Those people are not like us. And try to see less of Iain MacRae. His influence is not good.'

She brought up the incident with Allan later and was surprised at how calmly he responded. 'Aye, Florrie, 'tis a mite unfortunate, the lad's choice of company, but there's little we can do. He has to make his own mistakes. And when we reach America he'll listen to us even less, believe me. We'll just have to trust him to use his common sense. And to tell you the truth I'm relieved that his bent is towards females, of whatever kind. I was beginning to wonder if we had done wrong, encouraging him to take lessons in navigation from that blackguard Anderson. I was afraid he had designs on him, the bugger. I saw a lot of his kind in the army and wouldn't trust him an inch.'

So that was it. Suddenly Allan's contempt for the mate was explained and Flora marvelled. Clearly, among males things happened that she knew little of, and she preferred it to stay that way.

IX

August 1774

On the fifth morning they awoke to a red and angry sky, the sun obscured by a high veil of mist. Ahead of them black clouds were piling up and the sea around had grown gurly, with foaming white caps to the waves. The light had taken on an eerie, apocalyptic quality and the air was strangely menacing, as if storm demons inhabited it.

The mate and crew were hurrying hither and yon, their movements and voices charged with ill-restrained excitement.

'Take in the jib and bend on the storm jib! Double-reef the main! You there, be quick about it or you'll end up in the crow's nest, storm or no storm!'

Other lads were ordered to double-lash the boats on the deck-house (where Beanie was, Flora remembered fearfully) while the passengers were advised to cook porridge for sustenance during the storm and then take refuge below.

Sandy was most reluctant to leave the deck. He was stimulated by the drama of it, seemed not to mind the pitching and heaving or being drenched with flying spray.

'Get below, boy. This is no place for you,' the mate said gruffly. 'This is likely to be a bad blow. We often get hurricanes at this time of year and I tell you, lad, you don't realise the power of the sea until you've weathered one. But we'll call you if you're needed, never fear.'

The captain had temporarily allocated his cabin for the MacDonalds' use. It had a stove and lashed-down armchairs, and though claustrophobic offered comfort that none of the ordinary emigrants would be enjoying. Nevertheless Sandy was restless, peeved that his bid for seamanship was being thwarted. He kept prowling around like a caged animal, with a scowl on his face.

'Wheesht, lad,' Flora said at last. 'Come, read to us.'

She knew that Sandy would be flattered by the request. Though a good reader he had always been overshadowed at school by Johnny, the clever one. But Johnny wasn't here. Determinedly she pushed aside her sadness.

They had three books to hand – the Bible, Lord Kames's 'Elements of Criticism', which Alex had been reading (he was something of an intellectual and had brought a huge library of 324 books with him), and a well-thumbed pamphlet entitled 'Informations Concerning the Province of North Carolina' which had been published just the previous year. Sandy chose the last although most of them already knew it by heart, knew where it described the colony as 'the most temperate part of the earth on the north side of the equator', with winter skies that were 'commonly clear and serene'. Spring there brought 'gay and glowing colours promising rich fruits in their appointed seasons', and though summer might indeed be called hot you could stay cool indoors, and in autumn there could not be a better climate, the weather being fine for the space of forty or fifty days together.

Sandy's voice thrilled with anticipation as he read about the new land of opportunity with its pleasant farmhouses, rich fields and forests. Nobody said a word: the only sounds were the creaking of the rigging, the groaning of timbers and a strange, distant screech, as of a thousand banshees, that they concluded could only be the scream of the approaching storm.

The boat began to toss uncomfortably as Sandy finished reading and laid the tract down, but his eyes were shining.

'The paper won't stay still, but oh, it makes all this seem worth while, doesn't it? 'Tis to freedom we go, freedom to wear the kilt again, to play the pipes and speak the Gaelic without fear of reprisals!'

Flora almost added, 'Aye, and freedom to kiss the lassies without

Donald MacQueen's interference,' but Sandy had launched into one of Iain MacRae's poems, and was too wrapped up in it to hear.

'We shall all go together,' he intoned, 'to where we shall find game of every kind, the most beautiful game to be seen. We shall get deer, buck and doe, and the right to take as many as we wish. We shall get woodcock and woodhen, teals, duck and wild geese. We shall get salmon, and white fish if it pleases us better. Imagine how prosperous they are yonder: even every herdsman has his horse!'

But the sounds of frenzied activity above them were drowning out his words. Rushing feet were stamping on the deck and a desperate voice was yelling, 'Get the deadlights fixed!' They were aware then of wooden shutters being nailed over their only sources of daylight and simultaneously a solid wall of water overwhelmed the ship. The impact yanked Flora's chair from its station and flung people and fittings helplessly together. Boxes and crates they had trusted to be securely wedged came sliding down the inclined sole and tipped over. Then the cabin door burst open, the sea flooded in, and they found themselves swimming in a confusion of chests, joint-stools and tables, bottles and papers and navigational equipment.

'May the good Lord in his mercy preserve us!' Morag had turned ghastly pale and was reaching in vain for a basin. 'Dear Jesus, if ye but spare me now I'll never set foot on the sea again!'

As she whimpered the ship suddenly gave a lurch to starboard. The cabin door slammed shut again but the water on the floor continued to slurp and swish back and forth. The noise was deafening: waves kept crashing on deck, there was a jarring, squelching sound as water poured out through the scuppers; the shrouds rattled; and there was a concerted keening from the steerage quarters, where the other emigrants were confined.

Through it all Anne had been ominously silent. She lay clutching her belly and holding on to her two boys, while Alex tried in vain to soothe her. Oh, let her keep the babe, Flora prayed.

Somehow, sick though he was like the rest of them and with an ugly gash on his head where he had been flung against a bulkhead, Allan managed to prepare mulled wine on the stove. He offered it first to Anne, and the combination of claret and spices seemed to bring some comfort. Flora gamely sipped at it too but a sudden whiff of tar and oil had her retching and grabbing her smelling bottle. Then her discomfort was compounded by a recurrence of the heavy bleedings she had been suffering for some months. The lack of privacy grieved and embarrassed her: afterwards she would maintain that only Allan's constant attention kept her sane: even in her discomfort she marvelled at this new, competent Allan who had taken all their troubles on himself.

The gale lasted for six hours, with torrential rain and deadly, battering winds. Then suddenly there was silence. Limp and bruised and empty Flora wrenched her aching body out of the bunk.

'Thank God we have been spared. Come, Morag, we must see Anne comfortable and then set this place to rights. We don't know how long the calm will last.'

And Morag, bless her, braced herself to help.

Fresh air was a priority too, and the only place to find it was on deck. They scrambled up to confront a scene that was even more chaotic than the one below. The deck was awash with sea-water and debris. Each emigrant family travelling steerage had been allowed to bring one timber chest and these, carried in a long-boat, had been dislodged and broken up by the storm. The contents – sodden clothes, bed linen, smashed china, shattered glass and precious mirrors – floated pathetically, and their owners were trying desperately to salvage the undamaged stuff before the crew callously swept it overboard. Flora realised to her horror that the hogsheads of precious fresh water which had been lashed on deck had gone, and of the hen-coops there was no sign. She mourned Beanie then, her pet hen of the knowing eye and soft, gentle plumage.

The captain and Anderson stood in the midst of it all, insisting that the passengers stayed clear of the deck and left the crew space to work.

'We're still not out of danger. Far from it,' Anderson was saying. 'This is just the eye of the storm and there's no knowing what's still to come. All we can do is keep the deadlights up and see that everything's well lashed. Make sure you have food ready and if anyone needs medical help now's the time to seek it. And see that you ration the water. There's hardly a drop left.'

Queasy though she still felt, Flora was anxious to find out how her servants in steerage had fared and was just about to descend to the stinking hold when she came on Iain MacRae huddled weeping by the mast beside a shaking heap of blankets drenched in vomit and blood. All his customary swagger was gone and his freckled face was shiny with tears and sweat.

A nauseating, sour-sweet smell emanated from the bundle and for a moment Flora wondered if she could stomach being near the girl. Then the compassion that had prompted her to help the Young Pretender came to the fore and she found herself taking charge.

'You've done the right thing, Iain, bringing her up into the air. She'd never have survived in that hell-hole. Now go and find Sandy's father. Tell him to give you a bottle of wine and the hartshorn drops I have in my medicine chest. There now, Siobhan, be still. You've lost the babe, yes, but you're still here for Iain and the rest of your bairns.'

When Iain came back Siobhan was quiet and some colour had returned to her cheeks. Together they helped her swallow a few drops of the medicine and saw her lapse into sleep.

'She'll get over it now, I promise. Don't take her down below until you have to. I'll see if I can find some dry clothes for her.'

She was rewarded by the kind of smile that should have been reserved for a saint. 'God bless you, Mistress MacDonald. Me and Siobhan there, we'll never forget this. We'll be your friends till the end of our days.'

'Just look after her now and be a good husband to her,' Flora said shakily, and turned away so that he would not see how moved she was.

Allan came to join her then and as his hand went round her waist she almost blurted out a stricken protest – 'What has happened to Scotland, that good people like these are uprooted and subjected to this torment?' – but prudence stopped her. She knew, anyway, that every single one of them had come because he had no choice.

The storm had taken its toll of the steerage passengers. Already two children and one woman had died. It was rumoured that fever was raging, and this was confirmed when Flora suddenly felt a proprietorial hand on her sleeve and turned to find the girl Rachel standing at her elbow. She was bonnetless and the wind caught her hair, making it dance and adding to her distraught appearance.

'My Mammy's ill o' a flux, and a fever wi' it. She's lyin' there shakin' and cursin' and we need your help. The surgeon's too busy to come: he's cutting off somebody's leg that got hurt in the storm. Mind ye, it's no' her I'm bothered about, if I'm honest – she can end up feedin' the fishes for a' I care – but there's the rest o' us tae think about.'

The words shocked Flora profoundly. That a daughter should talk so of a dying mother! She stood hesitating. She certainly owed nothing to the family who had shown her only hatred since the very moment of her arrival at Campbeltown. They were not even of her own nation, far less her own clan. Then sympathy stirred in her. 'Tell her I'll come,' she said grimly, and the girl ran off without a word of thanks.

The whole incident had unnerved her and she paused a while to regain her composure before facing the shambles of the hold with its smells and sickness.

But Captain Chalmers had spotted her and was bent on conversation.

'Ah, Mistress MacDonald, I trust I find you well? 'Twas unfortunate, that squall, but the wind has gone abaft now and we're making a good ten knots. Perfect sailing weather, until the next blow comes along.'

Flora felt her heart quail. She had been hoping against hope that the mate's earlier prediction might have been wrong. 'We must endure another storm?'

'I fear so, dear lady. This is but a brief respite. But we shall weather it as we did before, no doubt of that. Everything is well battened down.'

Then his practised eye scanned the western horizon, where angry black clouds were piling up. 'See, here it comes. I'd give it five minutes at the most and then we're for it. Better to go below at once and lie down, Mistress MacDonald. But tell your menfolk we'll be needing them. 'Twill be a case of all hands this time, I fear.'

Despite his urgency Flora found herself protesting. 'But – but I promised to help them down there, to take some food and ale for a woman that's dying of fever…'

The words elicited a frown that expressed not just simple displeasure but fury that anyone should dare gainsay him.

'Mistress MacDonald, you may see yourself as some kind of benevolent chatelaine on land but I am master of this ship and responsible for all who sail with me. Please do as I say. Return to your cabin.'

She might have ignored the order but for an undercurrent of pleading desperation in it. Besides, no sooner had the captain spoken than he had turned away and made a bee-line for the bridge, and she realised to her horror that the sky had gone black and the ship was pitching violently. She had to accept then that her place was with her own family, and scurried down to join them.

She found Anne in a state of hysteria and Morag prostrate with fear. Norman and young Allan were clearly unsure what response was the more appropriate, manly excitement and curiosity or frank, realistic terror. Jamie had already decided how he felt: it was not fair that he should be prevented from joining Sandy and the men-folk on deck.

Afterwards Flora was to look back on the three days that followed as among the most miserable and helpless in her life. Somehow Allan managed to scramble down in the occasional lull and bring them a few slices of cold boiled ham, some raw potatoes or a dish of what the emigrants called 'lobscourse', neck beef or salted pork which had been hung in the water to soften it, then cut up and stewed with vegetables and pepper.

'This is all I could find,' he apologised. 'Most of our food has gone. I managed to salvage a keg of butter, though, with a barrel of flour, half a cheese and some eggs. Oh, and we've some onions. But the ship's biscuit is mouldy, has been all along. I wouldn't risk eating it. Last lot of it I saw was crawling with maggots.'

Flora felt her stomach rebel but forced herself to eat some ham and swallow a mouthful of porter. Then she saw Allan flung across the cabin as the *Ulysses* pirouetted on the crest of a freak wave, briefly balanced herself, and then tumbled with deadly violence into the trough. The whole ship shuddered with the shock and there was a rending noise as the fore-mast splintered and came crashing down.

Despite his cuts and bruises Allan insisted on going back on deck. 'They need every able-bodied man,' he gasped, 'but I'll be back as soon as things calm down, I promise. Be brave, my love.'

Flora was lying bracing herself for each lurch, determined not to give in to hysteria, when with a sudden roar of wind and waves the *Ulysses* broached to and lay on her beam ends for a few agonising seconds that felt like eternity. Water poured in while in the airless darkness, cold and sick and hungry, Flora prayed as she had never done before. She felt her guts lurch as the ship righted itself, only to roll sickeningly back to the other side again.

The agony continued for what felt like a hellish eternity while she lay there, sick and petrified with fear, expecting each harrowing oscillation to be her last. Every bone in her body was braced and bruised. She scarcely cared whether it was night or day.

Then gradually – only later was she to realise that the storm had raged for two catastrophic days – the sea began to subside and it was borne in upon her that survival was possible after all. Tentatively she lifted her head from her pillow and at last, with a supreme effort of will, she rose from the berth and found that she could put a shaky foot on the floor. Ravenously hungry and almost euphoric with relief she rallied Morag and together they tended Anne and the children.

Shaken and weak though they were, however, their plight was as nothing compared to that of the other emigrants, many of whom had spent days without light, meat, or fresh air. Those who were able had congregated on deck amidst the tangled rigging and ragged ribbons of sail. A barrel of molasses had burst and its contents were sticking to everything. From the newly-opened hatch came a sickening stench of vomit, urine and faeces, with an overlay of something more sinister – the smell of death.

'Ye didnae came and help my mammy like ye promised, and noo she's deid and my wee brither and sister wi' her!'

The stunning accusation came rattling at Flora the moment she ventured out of her cabin. Rachel stood there in a lather of tears and rage, her face and clothes drenched in sweat and ordure.

Flora's immediate reaction was to reach out to the girl in sympathy – she even stepped forward and made to embrace her – but to her horror the gesture was met with a frenzied snarl.

'I spit on ye, Flora MacDonald, ye and a' yer murderous Jacobite kin. But for ye and yer like my Auntie Kate would never have gone to America. We'd never have got on this foul ship and my mammy and Bobby and Lizzie would still be here!'

Flora felt the spittle on her cheek as the wench flounced off, leaving her in an agony of remorse and indecision; for much as she deplored the girl's vulgarity she could still find it in her heart to feel for her loneliness and desperation.

Later that day the pity was doubly felt when the mother's body, together with those of five old people and seven children, were committed to the deep. Two women had gone into premature labour and had also died, as had their babies, but greatly to Flora's relief all their own group had survived, including Siobhan MacRae. That they had not succumbed was due largely to Flora's own efforts, for she had seen to it that all of their people got a good helping of chicken broth as an antidote to their sea sickness.

The funeral service presented the only emigrating minister, a man called MacKeogh, with a chance to air his snivelling sanctimonious zeal.

'Ooh, Lord, that has in thy great wisdom ta'en untae thysel' the spirits o' these oor brethren and sisters, look on us noo in pity and bring us safe tae oor journey's end. And we promise, gin ye keep this fragile cockle shell on an even keel, we'll never doubt thee mair, nor take thy name in vain.'

Whether the Lord did indeed hearken and have mercy, or whether it was simply in the nature of things that storms should subside as the ship entered more temperate zones they would never know, but certainly the worst was over. After a few days of an uncomfortable residual swell the sea began to smile and a blessed calm set in. Sick emigrants who had spent nine days without light, meat or air ventured out of the hold now, to savour the clean air and look around them.

Not that better sailing conditions meant less work for the crew. Although their hands were torn and bleeding from hauling on wet ropes and many of them had sustained injuries in the storm they still laboured to bend on new sails and rig up a stubby jury-mast to attach to the stump of the old one. Allan, Alex and Sandy helped with this last operation and marvelled at the mate's dexterity.

'He might be a rogue, that Anderson,' Allan conceded, 'but he's a great man with a tackle. What you can do with a length of rope, a few pulleys and some able seamen at the crosstrees to manhandle the spar! Aye, it takes a special kind of person to manage a ship.'

Just as it takes a special kind of person to keep his head in an
Atlantic tempest, Flora thought, and Allan has proved himself
special. So too have all our menfolk, inspired by his example –
Sandy, and Alex, and old Neil, and Iain MacRae.

Gradually as the days passed the wind died completely and the
weather turned balmy. Hours passed when the ship sat becalmed,
her sails languishing in the breathless air. There were worries over
supplies of food and water but nevertheless Flora began actively
to believe now that they had done the right thing, braving the
ocean. Porpoises plunged and played around the keel; flying fish
darted about the bow and frequently landed on deck; and to her
infinite delight they were visited by new exotic birds. Then one
morning she thought she caught a scent of flowers on the soft air
and – hallelujah! – there appeared mirage-like on the horizon the
outline of mountain peaks floating above a narrow band of mist.
Their closer approach revealed a landscape of vineyards and rich
pastures. They caught tantalising glimpses of clean whitewashed
houses with red-tiled roofs, then a building that looked like a
monastery and another that could only be a fort. At the same time
the sea miraculously changed colour, from deep ocean blue to a
luminous shore-sea green.

The Azores. Paradise.

X

September 1774

'I'm going ashore with the captain,' Allan announced when they
were safely anchored in Horta harbour, on the island of Faial. 'We
have to arrange for fresh supplies of food and water. That stinking,
brackish stuff we've been forced to drink has been affecting
everyone's health. We'll get really pure water here and we'll all
know the benefit of it, I'm sure.

'Alex's coming too but I don't think all of you can go ashore. It
seems we can't linger in these waters. Something about pirates.
We have to go to the consul and collect what they call a
Mediterranean pass, to give us protection.'

Flora swallowed hard. So there were serpents in Paradise. Of course, there had to be. 'You mean those Barbary corsairs we hear about?'

Allan frowned. 'Now don't be dramatic, Florrie. I'm not denying the danger but no, they're not the Algerian rascals exactly but rather a band of international renegades and bandits who harry legitimate vessels, steal them and their cargoes and sell everyone on board into slavery. But it's to foil them and ensure our safety that we've stopped here, so don't worry.'

Flora sighed. She would dearly have loved to go ashore and acquaint herself with this colourful Eden, but she knew better than to protest. She would not be at a loss for something to do while the men were away, however. Anne, Morag and young Jamie still needed her, she had not abandoned the servants and Siobhan MacRae, and in snatched moments of leisure she could marvel at the kaleidoscopic scene before her. It was all so exciting. Another world. Everything was as new to her as if she had been but a day old.

The harbour was milling with all manner of people. Many had arrived in carriages drawn by small grey mules, while beneath the shouts and clamour there throbbed a strange disturbing music: Roger Anderson told Sandy it was called the flamenco. Already bum-boats were plying between the ship and the quay, bringing piles of fresh fruit and vegetables. The hawkers spoke Portuguese, a language Flora had never heard, and their attempts at English were causing much hilarity. Naked boys were diving for pennies and dusky, scantily-clad girls with bougainvillea in their hair were exercising their powers of seduction, eager to be invited aboard.

Watching their erotic antics Flora felt a pang of unease. Hitherto, throughout all their marriage, she had never once doubted her ability to hold Allan faithful to her. If some wanton wench had inveigled him into her bed on one of his journeys to the mainland, or when she had been great with child and he had felt randy, then he had never told her and she had had no wish to know. But if he should deceive her now, when they were already well into middle age and starting afresh in totally different surroundings, she did not know how she could cope.

A cold hand gripped her heart. He was still handsome and virile, her Allan, a man to be proud of. Those last rigorous weeks, far from daunting and enfeebling him, had hardened his physique and restored his faith in himself. She, on the other hand, had lacked the stamina to confront the elements without its showing. Seeing those vibrant young island women she felt old and haggard, her body flaccid and her features blurred with age.

Then her innate resilience reasserted itself. Had she not had the admiration of princes? She drew herself up to her full height, so that she felt all five feet two of her towering above those playful island children. Of course she could trust Allan!

But it was evening before her husband returned, flushed with brandy and his new-found sense of self-consequence. 'Zounds, it's the strangest feeling, going ashore after weeks at sea. Everything seems still to be moving as it did on board! Takes a lot of getting used to!'

'Aye indeed,' Flora almost retorted, 'especially when you've had a skinful,' but bit back the words. She must not nag.

Then, to her consternation, he told her that Captain Chalmers wanted to weigh anchor that very night – so much for her lingering hopes of getting ashore – but added temptingly, 'Let's sleep on deck. Who wants to be in a stinking hot cabin on a night like this?'

The captain had an awning stretched over part of the poop for them and she was amazed at how comfortable and soothing it was, lying there with just one sheet to cover them. Phosphorescence glittered in the water, as if reflecting the myriads of wheeling stars. Right then, with her man beside her and the ship gently rolling, she almost understood why sailors longed to return to sea. Her sleep was calm and dreamless, the storms but a vaguely remembered nightmare.

Everyone sensed the contentment. The days scintillated with sun and promise now, their pleasant monotony broken only by the excitement of spotting some strange sea creature – a wallowing whale, a fifteen-foot-long manta ray with huge winged fins, a lolloping turtle or some new species of seabird.

Easier too now to look halfway appealing, when the hand-mirror stayed steady and the slop-bucket could be emptied regularly. Flora saw her face take on some colour again and rejoiced that Anne was no longer pale and ill-looking. Thin clothes helped too: somehow the women had unearthed bright muslins and cool calicoes to wear, and it was obvious why chip hats had been so assiduously touted by the hawkers in Horta harbour.

The optimism affected everyone. When the Highland girls sang their essentially plaintive songs – 'Lochaber no more' or 'Heaven preserve my bonnie Scotch laddie' – it was not broken-heartedly but with a remote nostalgia, as if they had accepted their uprooting and were even beginning to rejoice in it. At last there was a sense of leisure hard-earned and unashamedly indulged in: the men lolled on deck playing cards or backgammon, the sailors danced jigs, there was a lot of flirting among the young. And it was hot. Even the ship's cat sought the shade.

Flora kept an eagle eye on Sandy, anxious that the acquaintanceship with Rachel did not go any further, but she spotted them together only once and that seemed innocent enough for Iain MacRae was there too. She was still sure, however, that Rachel had her cap set at Sandy, and knowing how susceptible her son was to female charms she determined to stay vigilant. The girl was blooming now that the weather had changed; her eyes had regained their come-hither sparkle and her skin glowed. Of course, she herself was trying hard to avoid Rachel and if ever their paths crossed she made a point of turning her gaze away. Even so she never encountered her without feeling the hatred that sizzled in the air, spoiling the idyllic languor of those tropical days.

Only one other doubt gnawed at her peace of mind, and that was occasioned by a comment of Allan's. 'That consul fellow in Horta was a Scot, and not exactly encouraging. Wanted us to stay and settle in the Azores, I reckon, else he wouldn't have been so scathing about the colonies.'

Flora felt herself stiffen. 'What do you mean? What did he say? Tell me!'

'Oh, nothing you need to bother your bonnie head about, Florrie. Just more about those rebels in Boston. Remember that trouble last year, when they objected to being taxed on imports – declared it wasn't right to have taxes imposed on them by the British Government, when they had no representatives there – and ended up throwing a whole cargo of tea into Boston harbour? Then just in May we closed the port of Boston completely and caused all kinds of hardship?'

'Aye, 'twas in the broadsheets, and Hugh mentioned it in one of his letters.'

'Well, according to that consul in Horta General Gage, the new Governor-General, is expecting more protests and has asked for extra troops to be sent. It seems the New Englanders have been trying to stir up sedition in the other states, through bodies they call Committees of Correspondence.'

His account of the problem was flat and matter-of-fact. There was no reason for Flora to feel any apprehension. Then why was it as if his words had been emblazoned unforgettably across the copper-hot sky?

'He ... he didn't talk of any trouble where we're going?'

Allan sensed her alarm and was quick to set her mind at rest, bringing forward every possible argument to reassure. 'Of course not, Florrie love! You must realise that Wilmington, the main town in the area we're going to, is seven hundred miles from Boston and we're likely to be well up country even from there, and far away from any bickering that might be going on. Besides, the North Carolina Governor, Josiah Martin, is a colonial himself, brought up on his father's plantation in Antigua. He understands his own people, knows how to smooth ruffled feathers. No, those Boston folks can't be speaking for the colonies in general. It would be madness for them to fight the British, who are their own kin! It's through trade with the home country that they make a living after all. Why kill the goose that lays the golden eggs?'

He sounded totally convincing and carefully avoided mentioning the negative side of what he had heard. He purposely did not add that various people in Horta had advised him to stay aloof from politics when he eventually got settled, because the American colonies were a powder keg ready to explode at the touch of the tiniest spark. As for Governor Martin, he might be cultured and well-intentioned but he was also impulsive, over-confident and no judge of men. North Carolina might seem remote from the centres of sedition but distance didn't really prevent people from communicating with one another – especially when there were pockets of discontent there as well.

If Flora had been less perspicacious she would have accepted his reassurances without a qualm, but instinct told her he was keeping something back. She rejoiced at having the Allan of the old days back again, with his overflowing self-confidence and optimism, but remembered how it had been that same Allan's refusal to face facts that had led to their ultimate ruin on Skye.

'Hold me,' she whispered. 'I'm cold all of a sudden, as if it were daytime and the sun had gone in, instead of just a cloud covering the moon.'

Under the thin sheet he laid his hand on her crotch and gently stroked the bush of springy black hair. She felt desire stir and waited joyfully for his kisses. But even after her need had been assuaged she lay for hours gazing into the darkness, feeling the sea slurping beneath them and the great creaking sails carrying them ever westwards towards an unknown destiny.

PART TWO

I

October 1774

Their landfall on the American continent was not as memorable as the approach to the Azores had been, for the coastline was shrouded in a thick mist. Flora sensed the unease among the officers and crew, sensed too that she must not betray any distrust of their competence. But she found herself hovering around them, listening to their exchanges in the hope that she'd pick up clues.

'We mustn't find ourselves too close inshore in this fog. Better heave to until it clears, and start sounding.'

'You think we're that far in?'

'Aye, I feel it in my bones. I smell the tar. And the rum. And the darkie women.'

The mate squirted out a quid of tobacco as he spoke and Flora intercepted a look of disgust on the Captain's face. But Anderson's instinct was unerring, as always, and ten minutes later the fog lifted like a curtain on a lighted stage, revealing a low promontory ahead with sea-birds flying around it.

'Must be the Cape Fear. Make sure we keep it to starboard and that island there to port. And see that the lads keep the lead line working. It's spring tides, mind, and we've got to avoid the Frying Pan Shoals at all costs. Don't want to find ourselves aground at this stage in the game.'

I should think not, sighed Flora. Two months we've been at sea and while the last weeks have been pleasant enough I long to feel solid land under my feet again. Land and trees and houses and mountains.

But her dreams of mountains were to remain insubstantial memories, for sea and river simply blended imperceptibly into one another. She for whom a coastline meant a dramatic configuration of hills laced with waterfalls, of waves crashing against craggy rocks, and all in an open, sparkling airiness, found herself entering an ambiguous fenland of white sandy wastes and water-logged swamps covered in impenetrable brushwood.

Even more forbidding was the first man-made structure they saw, a small defence-work on the west bank of the river.

'Yonder's Fort Johnson,' Anderson informed them. 'We'll pick up a pilot there.'

'So that's the Americans' idea of a fort,' Allan remarked at her elbow. 'It looks as if it would crumble away if you flung a stone at it.'

Roger Anderson laughed wryly and spat. 'Aye, some fight they'll put up there, if it ever comes to war. The walls are built of tapia – the negroes call it 'batter' – and it's nothing but a mixture of lime, sand, oyster-shells and water. As for yon Captain Collet that's in charge, he's no' worth a doaken. He's the last man they should have in authority there – a rash, greedy devil that like as not'll squander the fee we pay him on some trollop in Brunswick. And see yon hulk yonder, lying just offshore? That's His Majesty's Warship the *Cruizer*, and a fair disgrace she is too. She's lain there for years, being eaten away by the barnacles. I doubt if she could sail a mile if she had to dodge an enemy. Pshaw! Some protection these poor colonial fellows get from us, the mother country! No wonder they're crying out about having to pay taxes! If I stayed here I'd be bellowing too!'

Captain Chalmers looked thoughtful and shook his head; then he turned to Flora and Allan. 'Don't pay any attention to Anderson there. Things aren't as bad as he's making out. He's got a bee in his bonnet because he has a brother a farmer in Massachussetts. Just a lot of rebels, those New Englanders are.'

So saying he shouted to one of the crew to get a tender launched and said over his shoulder, 'No matter what we think of Fort Johnson's Captain Collet I still have to pay my respects to him, present my papers and hand over a fee. To attempt going up that river without a pilot is to invite shipwreck.'

The tide was just beginning to make as they entered the river channel, which began just after Fort Johnson. 'That's us over the bar now,' Captain Chalmers said, clearly relieved. 'There's only twelve feet at the most there at low water springs, and we draw ten and a half. But with the tide under us, and a following breeze if we're lucky, we should make Brunswick in four hours or so.'

They crept on, every hour taking them deeper into what Anderson called the 'pocosins', evergreen shrub bogs covered with pond pines and bayberry. Sometimes beyond the sand bars there were clearings where trees had been deliberately burned off to make the ground suitable for human habitation. Coarse grass had grown in the peaty soil and here log houses had been built, usually a storey and a half high, with end chimneys and gable roofs pierced with narrow obtruding dormer windows. But for their timber construction, columned porches and shuttered windows these homes were reassuringly Scottish-looking, but their isolated situation was daunting.

'Why do people build such houses in this wilderness? Don't they go mad with loneliness?' Allan sounded perplexed and incredulous. 'Surely nobody can graze cattle in country like this?'

The captain shrugged. 'That's just the way it is here, I'm afraid. These are wealthy planters' houses, and very special.'

He pointed over to one particularly attractive house as it hove into view. 'That's Snow's plantation yonder, on the north side of Sturgeon's Point – the road north starts there – and we're just coming to Harnett's. He and Howe and Lillington and Hooper, they've all bought land down on the Sound. They bring their wives and children down from New Bern and Wilmington for the summer, to get the sea breezes and escape the heat, the mosquitoes and the snakes.'

'Is it that bad inland?' Flora shuddered. She was already aware of the mosquitoes, had heard their whine and felt their sting.

The answer was terse. 'Aye, it's that bad. No point in pretending otherwise. But you've come at the best time of year. 'Tis bearable, just, in the fall. You'll notice the houses are all shut up for the winter now because the worst of the heat is past. The wives will be glad of that, I'll warrant, knowing what the likes of Howe and Harnett get up to when their womenfolk aren't there. A census of the mulatto children's dates of birth would reveal a lot. But enough. You'll soon find out for yourselves that moral values in the colonies aren't what they are at home.'

What a maze of waterways! Flora was sure that without the pilot the *Ulysses* could never have negotiated that bewildering estuary. The whole outer coastal plain, which Captain Chalmers referred to as the Tidewater, was less than a hundred feet above sea level, and covered almost exclusively with pine forest. They gazed in awe at those trees, which were fantastically festooned with mistletoe and with a greyish-green, hair-like moss that looked menacing and spectral.

Flora tried to sound matter-of-fact. 'Can you do anything with that strange stuff? I've never seen anything quite like it.'

'Oh yes,' Captain Chalmers replied. 'There are few things the negroes don't find a use for. They use it in upholstery, to stuff chairs and the like.'

'I don't like it here, Ma,' Norman, the baby, suddenly piped up. 'Can we go home to Skye now?'

That gave his elder brother his cue. 'I don't like it either. This America place is too dark and hot and stuffy and I thought we'd get away from the midges but they're worse here than they were at home! Do you like it, Uncle Jamie?'

Flora saw sixteen-year-old Jamie's lip quiver, but he was too busy pretending to be a man like Sandy these days to betray his fears to his nephews. Instead he said gently, 'We'll be coming to a town soon. Won't we, Captain Chalmers?'

'Aye lad, that's right. The tide's running fast. We'll be at Brunswick by mid-day at this rate.'

Then he broke off suddenly, a smile of sheer wondering delight on his face.

'See there! The snow geese! That must be the first of them this year! They must have been flying all night! They come all the way from the Arctic Ocean, seeking their winter feeding grounds. Know by instinct where the juiciest seeds and grasses are.'

The *Ulysses* had just emerged from a thickly forested area and had entered a wide savannah where the sky above seemed solid with birds. The air throbbed with their honking cries and the sound of battering wings as they glided in perfect vee-shaped formations and swooped down clamouring to feed.

Anderson immediately raised his musket and fired. 'Goose tonight, boys, roasted with onions and peppers!'

But shooting a single goose was like knocking down a snowflake in a blizzard, so closely huddled together were the birds, and the Cape Fear tide refused to be tethered. Flora was not sorry. She remembered the skeins of geese at home, dark against the red sunsets of the islands, and her heart lifted.

They continued through solid walls of pine forest, every creek that branched from the river looking very much like another. As the trees crowded in mosquitoes droned around them and sent them scuttling below for relief from their stings. Then they'd drift into a clearing and expect respite, only to find clouds of flies dancing in the sunbeams. At one point there was a swirl in the water and a sinuous form flicked past them. 'Water moccasin,' Anderson said dismissively. 'They're all over the place.' Flora felt her face pale and was conscious of little Allan's trembling hand in hers. He had no idea what a water moccasin was but sensed his grandmother's fear.

Every so often they'd glimpse another fine house nestling in a clearing.

'Yonder's Howe's Point,' Anderson explained when they remarked on a large three-storey mansion with a brick foundation. 'He's a great one for the horses, Bob Howe. They say he'll starve his household if it means he can make a showing at the Virginia races. Something of a ladies' man, too. Aye, he's quite a character, is Bob.' And he leered suggestively, putting Flora off the idea of this Bob Howe before she even met him.

Then they came on a cultivated area of rice and indigo fields, with an elegant brick house fronting the river, sloping lawns, and away to the right a group of dilapidated log cabins with sloping thatched roofs.

'That's Nathaniel Moore's plantation. York, it's called. The Moores are an old wealthy family and highly respected: must be fifty-odd years since they set up their estates here... More or less own Brunswick. Must have at least a hundred slaves.'

Flora was about to ask about the slaves – she found the whole idea of them both repellent and fascinating – when Captain Chalmers pointed to a huddle of buildings on the edge of the woods, poised above a low bluff on the left bank of the river.

'That's Brunswick yonder. Our official port of entry. We can anchor within half a musket shot of the town. Don't expect too much of the place, though. It's a mean apology for a town, and though it has its share of sea captains and merchants, lawyers and doctors and the like, the folks can be unruly at times. But don't let on I said that, especially to Master Dry or Master Quince, whom you're sure to meet. They fought long and hard to keep Brunswick going when Wilmington began to take over. 'Twas doomed, though: too near the coast to be secure from pirate raids, and ridden with disease in hot weather. So Dry and Quince were forced to give in and their wee town has gone down the hill a bit.

'A pity. Back in '48, during the Spanish War, Spanish pirates captured the town and it was Dry, who was Port Collector then, that rallied the townsfolk and routed the invader. They seized a Spanish ship and the treasure in it helped finance the building of St. Philip's Kirk .

'Then ten years ago they were up in arms against the Stamp Act. Surrounded Russellborough, where Governor Tryon was living. Unloaded unstamped goods from ships in the harbour and forced the port officials to resign: meant you could go up the river without stamps. Aye, quite a colourful, turbulent history, has Brunswick. Of course Dry and his cronies have found another, more sinister cause to fight for since the trouble over taxes. See themselves as great American patriots. Call themselves the Sons of Liberty and talk treason by the hour.'

He went on to explain that whereas most of the gentlemen of Wilmington had firm ties with England or Scotland the Brunswick families had come from South Carolina and regarded people of British birth as foreigners.

'Not that they'll impose their views on you, of course,' he said finally. 'They're too gentlemanly for that. I'd keep off politics when you're with them, though. Don't want to ruffle any feathers.'

Again Flora felt that creeping sensation of premonitory unease but shoved it aside, caught up in the general excitement that always attends the arrival of a ship in any harbour the world over.

As the captain hastened away to oversee their safe arrival he flung at them, 'I'll see you ashore, of course. Messrs Dry and Quince will already know that you're on your way. News travels fast in these parts and I've no doubt they'll be waiting on the quay there, vying to give you hospitality.'

The harbour was thronging with people, horse-drawn carriages, heavy wagons and chaises. Longshoremen and labourers bustled about in their hundreds. Flora found herself hanging back when she was handed ashore. Not only was it physically disconcerting to feel dry land under her feet after weeks afloat but her senses were assailed by the sights, sounds and smells of a new continent.

Colours pulsated and clashed in the brilliant sun and she realised with a shock of recognition that it was not only clothes and wigs and personal adornments that provided contrasts in hue but faces too, for while about half of them were predominantly pink, rubicund and vinaceous or pale and creamy, depending on age and sex, a large number were coal-black, bronze or coffee-coloured.

The noise was deafening. A ship from the Indies had just docked and was unloading its cargo of rum and sugar. Cart-wheels clattered. Off-duty sailors swaggered and roistered, and shouted to one another in incomprehensible tongues. It took Flora some time to realise that much of the language she was hearing was in fact English, but a nasal, distorted kind of English, while the blacks had a patois all their own with only the occasional recognisable English word in it.

But it was the overpowering pungency of the smells that affected her most. Exaggerated by the intense heat, they were predominantly of tar, turpentine and timber, with an underlay of human and animal sweat, dung, spices, tobacco and molasses – a potent mix for nostrils unused to that particular chemical combination. She staggered, suddenly overcome by the intense foreignness of it all, and Allan had to steady her with a well-timed hand under her elbow.

At that two figures, obviously gentlemen of some substance, detached themselves from the mob, came confidently towards them, and bowed low. Both looked to be in their fifties and were dressed much as gentlemen of their age and status would have been in Glasgow or Edinburgh, in blue broadcloth, nankeen breeches and clean frilled shirts. They even wore their hair as Allan did, drawn back in a club. But while one was tall, thin, and serious-looking, with a pale, ascetic face, the other had the plump, well-fed air of a bon viveur, and on closer inspection they saw that the buckles on his knees were of silver and the cuffs that fringed his sleeves were of the most delicate Brussels lace.

'Richard Quince, merchant, of Rose Hill, at your service,' said the tall thin one.

'And I am William Dry of Belleville, Collector of Customs. We sure are delighted to make your acquaintance and shall be most honoured if you and your family will be our guests while you are in Brunswick.'

Richard Quince gestured towards a carriage some yards away. 'I have my phaeton and four there. Let me show you around our little town, such as it is, and then we can partake of some refreshment at my town house.'

It felt surprisingly airy and comfortable inside the carriage but as they trundled away from the quayside dust rose in clouds from the horses' hooves and the black coachman had to dodge past piles of barrels that lay everywhere.

'Tar,' Mr Dry explained. 'Brunswick ships out half the colony's naval stores. You'll know, of course, that we North Carolinians go by the name of 'Tarheels'? There's good money in those forests of loblolly pines!' And he laughed with huge flesh-quivering self-satisfaction.

Flora reckoned that Brunswick contained no more than fifty houses, built on two unpaved streets running parallel to the river. In fact, there seemed to be more rice mills, indigo works and timber mills than houses.

'That's our church yonder. St Philip's,' Mr Quince pointed out, – Flora recalled the captain's description of how it had been founded – 'and of course there's the Customs House, domain of Willie here, and we have a courthouse where the colonial assembly used to meet, and a jail and one or two stores. And there's a tavern – Roger's – that's most proud of its Delft-tiled fireplaces but is better known locally, alas, for the disorder of its clients.'

Flora was more interested in the people than in buildings, however. The negroes she found particularly fascinating. There were two black servants riding beside their carriage, constituting a kind of bodyguard, and she was intrigued by their air of self-importance: then every so often their natural high spirits would spill over and they would wave like children to groups of darkie women wearing vibrantly colourful turbans.

The Quinces' house, though one of the town's largest, was very like others they had seen on the Tidewater, two-storeyed, built of wood, and with a verandah along the front. Mistress Quince had clearly been expecting them. A compact, bustling little person, she was doucely dressed in black and white, and though her face was largely obscured by the muslin cheek-wrappers of her crisp dormeuse cap Flora got the impression of an open, no-nonsense personality. She received her guests in a wide, wood-panelled hall with a large Carron stove in one corner and an assortment of comfortable chairs and tables. Flora's eye was attracted by an array of fine glasses and delicate porcelain tea-bowls.

'A refreshment, Mistress MacDonald? We can offer port or claret wine, persimmon beer, a cold flip, or punch, or sangarie, or perhaps a dish of tea?'

'Oh, please, the tea!'

Allan, determined to be adventurous, asked what the sangarie was, and on being told it was a mixture of Madeira wine, water, sugar and lime juice, very popular in the West Indies, he decided to sample it.

Sipping the tea, Flora wished she had done likewise. The brew was harsh and bitter and bore no resemblance to the Indian beverage she was used to: this despite its having been stored in a handsome tea chest of mahogany and kingwood, with elaborate silver fittings.

Richard Quince noticed her reluctance to drink it. 'You don't care for our yaupon tea? At first we did not fancy it either but it's surprising how one acquires a taste when one is forced to it.' And he turned to his wife. 'Find some of that Dutch tea, my dear. I'm sure our guest will enjoy that.'

Then he went on to explain. 'You've probably heard that we've had big problems with your government recently over taxes, and somehow tea has become a symbol of the goods they would impose restrictions on – the poisoned leaf, in fact. Boston ain't the only place that had a tea party, you know. We had one of our own up at Edenton not so very long ago, and it was the women who were the hot-heads then. Ain't that so, my dear?'

Mistress Quince blushed but did not gainsay him. 'Indeed, and quite right too. Most of us consider the holly-tree tea a vile substitute for our Indian tea and we do cheat a little sometimes and accept the smuggled Dutch stuff. But we're ready to make sacrifices if 'twill promote our cause and free the American people from foreign oppression.'

Then she bit her lip and looked fearfully over towards her husband, who was frowning in displeasure. Clearly they had agreed not to embarrass their guests by talking about politics and she had gone too far. The Dutch tea was duly served. Flora found it very palatable and said so, then carefully steered the conversation into less controversial channels – the weather, the vegetation, the animals, those impenetrable pine forests. Flora asked if they were likely to encounter wild Indians in the woods on their journey north, and was told that the Tuscarora Indians had been decimated in a bitter war sixty years before. As for the Cherokees, their lands were away to the west beyond the mountains and they gave North Carolina little trouble. No, there was nothing to fear from the native peoples. Bears, wolves and snakes were much more dangerous. Flora blanched at this but pretended nonchalance. After all, had she not heard of the wild beasts before, and vowed to take their presence in her stride?

Their hosts insisted, as Captain Chalmers had done, that they had come at the best time of year. The harvest was in, they would have the winter months to find land, and the worst of the hot, mosquito-ridden weather was past.

'Hurricanes ain't so usual in winter, either,' William Dry volunteered, 'though we did have a devastating one in January not so long ago. Two years past was it, Dick? Oh, the havoc that caused! Nearly unheard of at that time of year, too.'

'The negroes have a rhyme that puts it well,' Sophie contributed,

> 'June, too soon; July, stand by;
> August, come it must;
> September, remember;
> October, all over.'

Clever of you then, to arrive in October!'

Flora sighed. 'Aye, so it may be. But 'twas not so well-advised to set sail in August, as we did, and find ourselves facing the tempests in mid-ocean!' And she proceeded to tell them about the tribulations of the voyage, the sea-sickness, terror and death that had attended them for so much of the way.

The storm seemed like a safe enough topic but mention of it prompted an unexpected reaction from Sophie Quince.

'Oh, Dick, how remiss of us! We should have remembered that Roddy and Kate Boyd asked us to look out for their sister-in-law and her children, whenever ships came in with immigrants from Scotland! We've been so anxious to fête the Scottish heroine that we totally forget! You did not happen to meet a Mistress Strachan on board? From a town called Falkirk, where I believe that Carron stove yonder was made? Like you they would be going to Cross Creek, where they would stay with our good friend Dr Boyd at his Mumrills plantation, until they found a place of their own.'

Why was this conversation so doomed to follow difficult paths, no matter how hard Flora tried to avoid them? Evidently the Strachan woman, for all her vulgarity, had had decent family connections here. So it fell to Allan and Flora to describe how Mistress Strachan and her two children had perished, leaving Rachel as the only surviving member of the family.

'Indeed 'twas most sad,' Flora said finally, 'We tried to show sympathy but the lass is dour and would have none of it. Of course, nothing rendered a personal acquaintance necessary between us, and 'twas not surprising she should be stubborn and withdrawn in her grief.'

'Aye,' Allan put in, and Flora's heart quailed, suddenly sensing what he was about to say, 'Her grief, and the mistaken idea that we are hardened Jacobites still, secretly yearning for the return of the Stuarts. As if that dream had not faded into legend long ago! People seem not to realise that I fought on the side of King George in the '45, and am still his loyal subject!'

At that an awkward silence fell while Flora's emotions alternated between admiration for her husband's new self-confidence and regret that he could not have been more tactful. Fortunately their hosts were too well-mannered to rise to Allan's bait, if he had indeed intended to provoke them, and Sophie was too upset about Rachel to pursue any other subject.

'It's all so tragic! You will go straight to the *Ulysses*, Dick, and bring that poor girl back here. We can't leave her alone to fend for herself in a strange country, at the mercy of thieves and rogues. We'll get a message to Roddy and Kate, telling them we're looking after her, and Roddy can come and fetch her next time he's down-country. Shoot, it's our Christian duty, and the least we can do for a friend!'

Flora sensed a hint of dismissal in this ultimatum and made to take leave of their hosts, feeling that the pleasure and interest of the occasion had outweighed the embarrassment of any inopportune remarks. Surely the Quinces, and Mr Dry, would realise that they were new to the intricacies of American politics, and forgive them? Sophie Quince certainly seemed to have done so for she urged them to stay longer.

William Dry, refusing to be outdone, came up with his own invitation. 'And you'll come and visit me at Belleville, when you come on to Wilmington? It's just north of here, south of Eagle Island...'

Whereupon Dick Quince interrupted with, 'Yeah. Willie here owns the boats that ply back and forth between the island and the town, and a leaky lot they are!' Then he softened the dig by adding good-humouredly, 'But you cain't get a better dinner anywhere in the colony than you'll get at Belleville. 'Tis known far and wide as the house of universal hospitality.'

To all of which banter the expansive Willie Dry simply beamed and chuckled, basking in his friend's approval.

Rachel presented a further challenge, of course. Flora reproached herself for feeling at all responsible for her since she had received nothing but defiance at her hands, but when they arrived back at the *Ulysses* and Dick Quince went to track Rachel down she and Allan stayed on deck, anxious to show no ill will.

The girl soon emerged under Dick Quince's wing. The harrowing month in steerage and the loss of her family seemed to have made little outward impression, apart from leaving her thinner and harder. As she passed she left a sickening whiff of urine, sweat and grime in her wake. Flora was sure, too, that her tattered clothes harboured fleas and that her hair swarmed with lice – was anyone on the *Ulysses* free of them, after all? – yet Rachel was clearly determined to make the most of this unexpected visitation by one of Brunswick's dignitaries. She had combed her hair, washed her face and tidied her clothes, and as she swept off the ship clutching her pitifully few possessions she tossed her head with an air of triumph, as disdainful as any high-born lady of fashion.

'See you all in Wilmington!' she crowed, gloating at her change of fortune, and the peals of her exultant laughter echoed back to them as she was received by the Quinces' waiting equipage.

Sandy and Iain MacRae had also seen Rachel's performance and had the grace to be amused by it, as Flora was too but rather more grudgingly: she could not but feel that the orphaned girl was not so ingenuously transparent as she pretended. Everyone was obviously relieved to see what they thought might be the last of her, however, and Sandy had other things on his mind.

'The broadsheets are full of your arrival, Ma! We've seen two, the Cape Fear Mercury and the North Carolina Gazette, and they describe you as 'the idolised saviour of the last Stuart claimant to the throne'! Everybody in Roger's was talking about you. One old man, not knowing who we were, said that a whole crowd of people from Cross Creek have gone down to Wilmington to meet you. There's to be a reception in your honour, Ma, and even Governor Martin will be there! The old man wasn't very flattering about the Governor, I'm afraid – said he'll make the most of you because he thinks government's a matter of bowing at balls and paying compliments. The old codger wasn't very well disposed to us Scots either, come to think of it. Now how did he put it? I must get it right. Yes. He said we newcomers don't understand the issues here. "They're raw and ignorant," was what he said, "and at the mercy of the first man who will speak them fair; and nobody will speak them fairer, and mean less, than our Governor Martin."'

But Flora had heard only the words about the planned reception at Wilmington. The last thing she wanted was to be fêted and fussed over. She felt the blood drain from her face.

Jamie looked at her in amazement, his eyes wide. 'You never told me you were famous, Ma! Why? What did you do? It must have been something very brave or important if people thousands of miles away know all about it. Tell us! What did she do, Pa?'

Allan, however, had turned and walked away. Not, though, before Flora had seen the shattered, hunted expression in his eyes.

II

October 1774

Wilmington, the county seat of New Hanover County, was on the eastern shore of the Cape Fear River only fifteen miles from Brunswick. Its sheltered harbour had developed at the point where the river split into two tributaries, one going north and east towards New Bern and Virginia, the other west towards Cross Creek and the border with South Carolina. Captain Chalmers explained that the town had been promoted by Governor Johnson, a previous governor, in the face of opposition from Messrs Dry, Quince and Moore, and had now gone far towards eclipsing Brunswick altogether, being closer to the producers of naval stores and grain, less swampy, and strategically situated on a main road.

'We'll be up there in an hour or two,' he assured his passengers as the *Ulysses* weighed anchor and drew away from Brunswick. 'We've lightened our load, and we have a spring tide under us, so there's no worry about clearing the Flats, as they call the shoals seven miles upriver. And you're bound to like Wilmington. It's altogether more genteel and has fewer of those American liberty-mongers.'

Allan looked thoughtful at this. 'Maybe so, Captain, but our experience back there taught us that those colonial protesters aren't all riff-raff. Many of them, like our friends Quince and Dry, are deep-thinking people and highly respected in their communities. I'm beginning to realise that the social system here is entirely different from the one that prevails at home. It would be crassly presumptuous of us raw newcomers to make judgements, far less take sides.'

Flora felt a surge of admiration for her husband then, for what he had said so exactly summed up her own reaction. While they had to know what was going on and show themselves to be interested, they had not come here to get involved in politics. Just as long as Allan was prepared to forget that he had once been a military man and get on with his career as a farmer they could avoid awkward confrontations.

She certainly felt in no mood for argument herself. Her whole body itched abominably and her flesh stung and tingled as if it were on fire. She had been trying not to touch the small pink weals of mosquito bites on her neck and wrists but found herself scratching instinctively. Her lips felt parched and sore. Everything – the shifting spectacle of barges stacked with tar-barrels and timber, the fleeting, tantalising glimpses of cool plantations, the ooze of the swamps and the evanescent dazzle of brilliant, nameless birds and wild flowers – flashed and swam and danced before her eyes, the stuff of feverish dreams.

Her age again, no doubt. She absolutely had to steady herself and take in all the Captain was telling them, concentrate hard while he described the foremost families in the colony and linked them to their various plantations. Her head rang with the litany of names – Joseph Eagles of The Forks; John Rutherford of Point Pleasant; Cornelius Harnett of Hilton; Robert Schaw of Schawfield. Oh, she'd never remember them all!

'That's Russellborough Plantation over there,' the Captain was saying now, pointing to an elegant two-storeyed house with wide, double verandahs all round. 'There's fifty acres in cultivation there. It belonged first to Governor Dobbs, then Governor Tryon lived in it until they built his magnificent palace at New Bern. Everyone agrees that there's nothing in the colony to touch Tryon's Palace, of course, but you'll see that for yourselves one day, no doubt.'

His voice went on, interminably it seemed to Flora. Was there no respite from its tedious monotony, nor from this enervating heat, the relentless assault of insects and the subaqueous gloom of these brackish, primeval swamps? The drone of flies and voices blended into a leitmotif that underscored the nightmarish unreality of the scene. The river seemed full of half-submerged tree-trunks and she shuddered, seeing in them the man-eating alligators which some of them, indeed, might well have been. At places the river narrowed and they sailed so close to the bank that they could pick wild grapes from the trees – clusters of luscious fruit that normally would have cooled and refreshed but seemed to stick in Flora's parched throat. She felt as if an implacable bottle-green wall was closing in on them, ready to swallow them in its all-consuming maw. The ripe-smelling tunnel suggested some distant, dark primordial age and having entered it she was certain they would never again emerge into the blessed sunshine of the here and now.

Panicking, she made one heroic effort to speak and sound normal. 'Och, those creatures you call chiggers are worse than midges, Captain Chalmers! They're burrowing away under my skin something awful!'

But the last words trailed away into a mere whisper and she felt herself stagger and grab the ship's rail in a desperate effort to stay upright.

'You're all right, Florrie?'

Allan's voice sounded distantly in her ears. He caught her as she fell and she submitted to merciful oblivion in his arms.

When she came to she was back in her cabin and young Dr Talbot, the ship's surgeon, was bending over her and pressing a spoon with some kind of infusion in it to her lips. The stuff tasted gritty, metallic and bitter and she gagged violently.

'What is that vile concoction? I will have none of it!'

The surgeon smiled, infuriatingly condescending. 'There there, Mistress MacDonald! Try to sip a little of it. 'Twill do you good, I promise.'

''Tis poison! Take it away!'

In vain the doctor protested that the purgative was a well-tried mixture made of ten grains of calomel to fifteen grains of jalop, which if ingested three times a day was guaranteed to rid the body of fiery humours. If she would also submit to blood-letting he was sure he could have her back in fine fettle for the jollifications at Wilmington.

But all she wanted to do was sleep.

Morag eventually roused her and with some extra help from the men folk Flora clambered back on deck just as the *Ulysses* was approaching Wilmington. Still hot, fevered and drained of energy though she was she yet felt a sharp sense of déjà vu when the town hove into sight. There, just where she had expected to see it, was Eagle Island, with William Dry's leaky little craft plying back and forth, and off the town various vessels lay moored beside rafts of timber and lighters of naval stores. Furthermore the town itself had a reassuringly planned, permanent look. The buildings did not sneak away into the woods as the Brunswick ones had done: instead, behind Market Street, where the wharves and official town houses were, residential areas rose to the east and south and formed a backdrop of impressive brick-built homes. Many of these were two-storeyed, with wide double piazzas and windows of costly imported glass. A metropolis indeed!

Captain Chalmers was most solicitous. 'You have introductions to some of the Wilmington gentlemen, I trust? Mistress MacDonald must not stay in a dirty, vermin-infested inn in her state of health.'

Allan was quick to reassure him. 'Ah yes, we have letters to various people from our good friend John MacKenzie of Delvine, our lawyer in Edinburgh. The main one is to a Robert Hogg, a native of East Lothian who runs a mercantile business here called Hogg and Campbell. Perhaps you know him?' Then there is a John Rutherford, who I understand began his career as a protégé of Murray of Philiphaugh and is now a Crown official of some kind.'

The Captain nodded, satisfied. 'Good. Couldn't be better. Good, solid Scottish stock, and staunchly loyal to the King even if their forebears did arrive in Covenanting times. And look, see yonder where yon carriage is standing? That'll be the Hoggs I'll warrant, come to take you under their wing.'

Allan was more animated than Flora had seen him for years. He grabbed her hand and hustled her impatiently to the gangplank, clearly forgetting how ill she had been.

'Come, Florrie girl. Oh, how good to be among our own kind again!'

And true enough, though the crowds that flocked on the quay were every bit as tatterdemalion, multi-coloured and smelly as their Brunswick counterparts Flora was quick to notice that the shouts, cries and snatches of conversation were mainly in Lowland Scots. It was only because she recognised the words behind the American drawl that she realised with the old, familiar stab of despair that the crowd was waiting specifically to catch a glimpse of her. They were surging forward now and it took Captain Chalmers and Roger Anderson all their time to hold them back.

'Off with you, you thoughtless dolts! Make way!'

'Come Florrie. See, they've cleared a way for us.' And Allan half-carried her down to the quay-side where a pair of strong outstretched arms lifted her bodily into the waiting carriage.

A slow, lavender-scented voice took command then. 'There now, Miz MacDonald hon. What y'all are a-needin' is a long sound sleep in a good feather bed and that's what you're gonna get jes as soon as we get you home. Pammy! My smelling salts!'

Flora was aware of other, more elusive odours as a huge amorphous shape with a red turban round its head loomed not unkindly over her. She felt the draught wafted under her nostrils and relaxed, knowing she could trust the large, soft brown eyes that gazed into hers from a round moon-face that was shiny black as midnight.

'Now you jes lie back and rest, ma'am. Pammy and the good

Lord above, we gonna look after y'all. Yeah, ma'am.'

So assured, Flora slipped into a merciful oblivion, unaware that she was dangerously ill.

The next few days would always be hazy in her memory. She spent them in a turmoil of delirium, now haunted by fiery nightmares and now plunged into semi-consciousness. Certain isolated vignettes were to stand out, however, vividly sketched against the flickering background of dim candlelight or curtained daylight. When she first came back to full awareness after hours of fever she thought herself in heaven, for she lay in a downy bed furnished with sheets and pillows of fine lawn, and above her rose a tented pavilion of pure white gauze. Exhausted but clear-headed, she realised that someone must have washed her hair and given her a bed-bath, for the sweatiness had gone and her skin had the sweet, slightly astringent scent of lavender.

'Open the shutters and let in the light, Laura. I'm sure some fresh air will do Mistress MacDonald no harm.'

The voice was firm and the accent reasssuringly Scottish, and it was as if God Himself had spoken, for sunlight flooded the room and with it came a breath of air smelling of roses, river traffic and pine resin. And there came sounds – a tinny church bell, a cock crowing, the rustle of leaves, the wonderfully varied song of some divinely archetypal bird.

Strange what she said then. She felt that she had known the man for ever – his identity could wait – but the bird was new.

'Tell me. That bird. What does it look like?'

Nor did he seem to think the question irrelevant. 'That is the mocking-bird, Mistress MacDonald. You do not have them in Scotland. It is small, about the size of a thrush perhaps, blue-black in colour and with a white breast and head.'

She sighed. So much to learn… 'This is Wilmington, isn't it? And you… you are…'

'Doctor Boyd. Roddy Boyd. I have a plantation called the Mumrills near Cross Creek, and know your half-sister and step-father well. Oh, they've been so excited at the prospect of your coming! They just can't wait to see you!'

With that he turned away, though not before Flora had noticed the startling blue of his eyes, and she realised that there was someone else in the room besides the maid Laura.

'But I am forgetting my manners. This is our host, my dear friend Dr Tom Cobham. It was agreed to bring you here, to his house on Front Street where we could watch over you while you were ill, rather than to the Hoggs' place which is rather busy and noisy at the moment.'

'I have been that ill?'

'Yes, ma'am. Gravely so, I'm afraid.'

As he spoke he reached out to grasp her wrist, routinely checking her pulse. Confidence and strength seemed to flow from him then, and she was also suddenly, poignantly aware of something else, something she had not felt so sharply for years and acknowledged now only with slow, almost shameful reluctance: a powerful, undeniable sexual magnetism.

He was continuing to explain. 'You've had some kind of fever, probably contracted in the Tidewater swamps. The climate is most unhealthy down there, causing all manner of agues, pleurisies and bilious complaints. But you are a tough old bird' – he seemed to know that she would not take offence at this expression – 'and will survive this setback, never fear. The Peruvian bark I've been treating you with contains quinine, the perfect specific against the exhalations of the marshes. Now we are going to leave you to rest for a while. Don't attempt to get up yet. Laura will bring you a posset of rum, and Tom here will get a message to your husband and family, telling them that you are recovered. They have been quite beside themselves with worry.'

Alone, she lay back to reflect. How kind everybody was. She ought to have made an effort to thank her host, this Dr Cobham, but the Scotsman with the blue-eyed charm had quite overshadowed him. Where had she heard of this Dr Boyd before?

And suddenly it struck her with the force of a thunderbolt. He was the Strachan girl's relative! How could such a thing be possible? For of all the people she had met so far she liked this Roddy Boyd most of all. Steady, reliable and clever, he embodied everything she admired in a man. What was more, he was handsome with it, so handsome that if she could have turned the clock back thirty years she would have found herself hopelessly in love with him.

But was she losing her mind, thinking this way? That fever must have gone to her head! Concentrate, instead, on the insistent birdsong – so aptly named, the mocking-bird, taunting her pathetic, middle-aged fancies and singing silly old woman, silly-silly-silly – and on the incredible russets and golds of the autumn trees outside her window.

Above all, don't fall to speculating about what Roddy Boyd's wife is like, she told herself firmly. But of course, the more she determined not to let her thoughts travel along that road the more she gave them full rein. And to her horror, every time her imagination wandered in that direction she retreated in confusion, convinced that there was danger there.

III

October 1774

The next day almost tired Flora out because the family were so anxious to see her. All of them came in turn, bringing ripe melons, large juicy apples, fresh hazelnuts and walnuts, armfuls of brilliantly-coloured flowers. Her bedroom was like a queen's bower.

Sandy's eyes were shining. 'Those wild grapes in the forest were as nothing to the fruit that grows in the orchards here! The peaches are past but those apples are luscious, and as for the berries and nuts – you have to taste them to believe how sweet they are! Oh, Iain MacRae was right. There will be no shortage of good things to eat. The woods abound with deer and rabbits and quail, and the rivers are teeming with fish. I just can't wait to go hunting and fishing!'

Jamie had other concerns. 'Is it true what Morag said, that if I stay too long in the sun I'll turn black, like those darkie folks? And will my hair go all pitch black and curly?'

'Of course not, silly,' his brother scoffed. 'You mustn't listen to the servants' tales.'

Flora would have said the same, but realised that Morag might well have been speaking in all earnestness. If so, she must disabuse her of this peculiar but understandable notion. Poor Morag: she must be hopelessly out of her intellectual depth here.

Allan was all praise for the kind people of Wilmington. 'Bob Hogg has been so good to us, you just can't imagine! I think his heart's still in Scotland – he keeps pumping me for news of home, and is touchingly full of childhood reminiscences – yet they tell me he's one of North Carolina's richest men. His firm, Hogg and Campbell's, is the main supplier to the Highlanders up in Anson and Cumberland counties. His brother James has just recently arrived from Caithness to work with him. And I get the impression this James hasn't just brought his wife and five children, all under eight, with him, but a whole village! Oh, what a country this is, Florrie! Full of promise!'

Allan had not been idle. Although he had decided to store the bulk of their furniture in Wilmington until they found a place of their own he still had to arrange for some of it to be carried by wagon to Cross Creek. And he hated uncertainty, wanted desperately to have their plans cut and dried.

'Thank God you're well again, Florrie. Anne and Alex have been chafing to get away but wouldn't go while you were ill. Now they can enquire about river transport. They say it takes about seven days to cover the ninety miles upstream to Campbellton, rowing against the current at a rate of fourteen miles a day. They'll have to depend very much on the plantation people for shelter at night, for that north-west branch of the river is the lesser one and there are no towns until you reach Cross Creek.'

He paused then and looked doubtful. Flora knew he had something more, and that probably controversial, to say. 'What is it, Allan? Tell me!'

She watched him take a breath and frame his words carefully. 'Jamie wants to go with them, and I'm inclined to let him. I've never seen him so excited. And he's good with the little ones, would be a help to Anne in her condition.'

'Then let him. Just as long as they all come and see me again before they go.'

She saw the relief on Allan's face but then the troubled look came back again. 'I want Morag to go too, with Neil and Deirdre and the ghillies.'

'Morag! But I need her! She's my maid!'

Even as she spoke Flora realised that since she had come to the day before in the Cobhams' guest bedroom there had been no sign of Morag. Her every need had been met instead by the indefatigable negro servant Laura. At Dr Cobham's direction the black girl had pampered her with possets, turtle soup and goat's milk, had helped her out of bed whenever she wanted to use the commode and had taken the chance, while Flora was up, to plump out her pillows and smooth the sheets. No Morag.

A terrible suspicion came into her mind. She remembered Morag as she had been during the storm, petrified with fright. 'Morag is all right? She hasn't been ill of a fever, like me?'

Allan shook his head. 'Nothing like that. But she's a strange one, is Morag. Her devotion to us has its darker side, for she furiously resents anyone else who seeks to do things for us. And that's the trouble here, Florrie, as you will soon discover. No white person, unless he is utter trash, is expected to do menial work. It's all done by the slaves. And the slaves themselves, especially the faithful household ones, see it as a point of pride to do everything for their masters and mistresses. It's a whole new concept of service which will take a lot of getting used to, and I'm afraid Morag never will accept it. She has been downright troublesome about the Cobhams' servants nursing you. Someone has been feeding her stories about African black arts and I verily believe she suspects them of poisoning you! We're going to have to be very tactful with her. So meantime I think the answer is to have her go with Anne and Alex. We can say Anne needs her. I understand, anyway, that there aren't so many negroes up in the back country, where people aren't quite so well off. Morag may settle in more happily up there.'

Flora marvelled for the umpteenth time at how quickly Allan was adjusting to the peculiar mores of the new land; marvelled too at his perspicacity, for though he had always cared for his servants' physical welfare he had not been one to probe into their private feelings. There had always been concern for the members of his clan but this was new: this was as if they were all his family and he the undisputed head. She wondered, with a wild, half-fearful leap of surmise, whether he could already be seeing himself as some kind of chief among the people they were going to. A warning framed itself in her mind but she said nothing. She had watched him cowed and thwarted for too long to grudge him prominence now.

'Do what you think fit, my love. If anyone can placate Morag and persuade her to go, you can.'

Allan smiled and patted her hand, glad to have his opinion so readily trusted. 'Have some rest now,' he soothed. 'You'll be having so many folks coming to see you, now that you're well enough for visitors. Apart from the fame that has gone before you that Roddy Boyd fellow has been singing your praises and has the whole of the town agog to meet you. I tell you, if we were thirty or even twenty years younger Morag's jealousy would pale to insignificance beside mine! I'd be challenging the bounder to a duel at dawn!'

There was absolutely no rancour in the comment, even about her erstwhile fame, and Flora felt relief and thankfulness surge through her. Yes, America was indeed proving to be Allan's remaking.

So she laughed, she hoped not too wryly. 'Och, Allan, well you know we're all too old for such folly. 'Tis all just friendship now.'

She hoped her sigh had not been audible, that her expression and the catch in her voice had not betrayed her longing and regret. After all, Allan could still arouse passion in her. Even now he could, as his hand came under the coverlet to caress first her breast and then the moist yielding centre of her.

'I can't wait to get you back,' he said thickly. 'Promise it won't be long.'

'Nor I to be with you again, my dear. They say I mend quick. 'Twill not be long, and all the sweeter for the wait.'

* * *

Tom Cobham's wife Mabel came in shortly afterwards, to sit by Flora's bedside and talk. And further talk, for it soon became obvious that talking was Mabel Cobham's favourite occupation.

'Lawd-a-mercy, Miz MacDonald,' she simpered, ''tis sure a pleasure to see y'all restored to health. Tom was quite despairing, and that's the truth, but 'twould seem y'all have a cast-iron constitution.'

Weakly Flora tried to interpose profuse thanks for all the Cobhams had done for her but the protestations were flung aside as irrelevant to the young woman's chatter.

Mabel was determined to impress, though in the most charming, ingenuous way.

'Ah'm Tom's second wife an' jes eighteen – a doggone sight younger than he, as y'all will have reckoned. Never did have any practice at running a big household. All those ornery slaves to see to an' order about! Then there's pickles to put up, an' the sewin' and mendin' an' jam-makin' an' all with a baby comin'...'

Far from complaining, she was clearly revelling in her new-found responsibility as the bride of a prominent professional figure. Her husband featured constantly in her conversation. Tom this. Tom that.

'Tom says we gotta move house when the babe comes. We have our eye on the ol' Neilson home, the Lodge, that's gonna fall vacant when ol' Granny Neilson's gathered to the Lord – which Tom says is bound to happen this comin' winter, if not before. It's near the river, between Princess and Chestnut, and has a beautiful portal.'

Flora tried to take in the substance of what Mabel was saying but was so fascinated by the girl's voice that she found herself lulled and almost mesmerised by it. It was slow, deep and languid and reminded Flora of a rich syllabub laced with rum. The sentences merged into one another, the only perceivable punctuation being what could only be interpreted as a question mark, and that in the most unlikely places. Why sound doubtful, for example, about that beautiful portal? Was Flora supposed to doubt its beauty? She tried to accustom herself to this strange drawling accent with its diffident rising inflexions.

'This ain't our only home, of course. We have a half-share in a plantation over and above, with Roddy and Kate Boyd. Thirteen hundred acres and two sawmills up country, near Cross Creek. Tom and Roddy may be among the colony's best doctors, but they still need commercial interests, Ah guess, to keep themselves in some style. Not that the life up country appeals to me. Ah'm Wilmington born and bred . Yeah ma'am. Ah'm a city gal. Likes ma comfort.'

She preened herself, fingering the immaculate brown ringlets that framed her face and then drawing her hand down towards the large red rose that lay, modest and dewy but unmistakably provocative, at the cleft of her snowy white bosom. It was not a Scottish gesture, at least among the ladies Flora consorted with, though she found herself reflecting that the likes of Rachel

Strachan might resort to it on occasion.

The old unease stirred again. Could it be that colonial people in general were more blatantly sexual in their social congress than the general run of the British? Or had it something to do with the hot climate, and the further south you went the more sexually charged life became? Undoubtedly there was a heightened carnality, a voluptuousness of dress and attitude here that proclaimed a confident disregard for hypocrisy and puritanical scruples. Yes, these folks might speak the same basic language but there was much that was strange and new about them. They were indeed a fledgling nation, separate and different from the mother country, and Britain would have to come to terms with that one day. And so, she thought ruefully, would she.

The languorous voice droned on. 'But I do declare I must be tiring y'all out with ma thoughtless talk. This town won't ever forgive us if we don't have you up and fit as a fiddle come Saturday. They're calling it the Flora MacDonald Ball and not a soul but's rarin' to get an invitation – all exceptin' the doggone spoil-sport Sons of Liberty, of course.'

'Ball? What ball?'

'Ain't nobody told you? There's to be a reception first, just for the town gentry, at the new Burgwin House, then a ball in the Town House after, for all comers. Ah'm gonna wear ma new gown. It's green, with white roses embroidered on the bodice – in your honour, of course, as the Jacobite heroine.'

Flora felt her face blanch. How would she ever persuade those kind, well-meaning people that the last thing she wanted was to be fêted? If she protested they would interpret it as false modesty and press their attentions on her all the more. It was all so ironic, too, since these very people made so much of their loyalty to the British king: very few of them would have been of the Jacobite persuasion, had they been living in Britain thirty years before. At last, with reluctant resignation, she realised that her only course was to accept their blandishments graciously and try to keep a low profile. This adulation was none of her doing. Surely Allan would see that.

Alone at last, she lay for a long time drifting towards sleep. Sometimes, in her reveries, she imagined Anne and the children journeying north on the river. Sometimes she reflected on Morag,

so faithful and yet so touchy. Nor could she banish her longing for
Fanny, who flitted in and out of her dreams like a pale, insistent
ghost. But her thoughts were dominated by all the new, larger-
than-life people she had met, and Roddy Boyd was always there.
At one point panic seized her. If she could let her mind wander
unchastely, remembering those quizzical, startlingly blue eyes,
what kind of temptations were Allan and young Sandy facing right
now?

It was then that she resolved to get better in record time. Flora
MacDonald's menfolk would not fall prey to the predatory females
of North Carolina if she could help it.

IV

October 1774

The morning of the MacLeods' departure dawned calm and cool,
with a woody autumn fragrance in the air, and Flora awoke
determined to see her family off. She had been staying with Allan
at the Hoggs' house for two days now, and felt restored by the
more normal routine and particularly by her husband's loving.

Their hosts pressed the use of their carriage upon them but
Flora had decided to walk and nothing would change her mind.
She felt she had to make up for lost days.

'I'm not an invalid any more, Allan, so don't treat me as one!
For five days I've missed seeing the sights of this town, and the
trees are so magnificent in all their autumn colours! Besides, this
cooler morning air will do me good, I'll warrant!'

'Then at least see that you wear a pair of solid pattens over those
flimsy velvet slippers,' Allan insisted. 'Wilmington's streets are no
better than our cart-tracks at home, unpaved, full of pot-holes and
covered in dung. And it isn't just the horses. People let their hogs
and poultry run around loose and the mess is deplorable. Bob here
has been telling me all about it. Haven't you, Bob?'

'Aye, I have that. It's a darned disgrace. We've had to appoint
a scavenger to clean the streets once a week. As for maintenance,
all adult men are responsible for keeping the colony's roads in

order but it's a duty folks are quick to ignore. One of our biggest headaches, it is. Why should gentlemen feel obliged to labour in the streets? 'Sblood! I'm darned if I'm going to sweat and toil to suit a law that goes back to the colony's earliest days! They can fine me to their hearts' content, I'd rather pay the niggers to do it!'

Clearly the conversation had hit one of Bob's sore spots. Flora noticed the veins standing out on his forehead. Realising that there was more at issue than the road maintenance question – Bob was objecting, really, to what he saw as the levelling tendency of American society – she decided to say nothing, and was glad when he had the grace to look sheepish.

'But none of that concerns you,' he said finally. 'We're lucky this morning that the day is young and everything was cleaned up only yesterday, so I don't think we need worry too much about the muck. Not too many prying eyes about either, this early in the day. Come, Mistress MacDonald, do me the honour of letting me accompany you to the harbour. 'Tis not very far, and I can point out some of Wilmington's landmarks.'

So saying he took Flora's free arm and tucked it under his elbow. The three of them set off lightheartedly, Flora feeling safe and protected by her escorts' masculine presence. She could see already that the town invited exploration. Not only did it boast shipping docks lined with warehouses but also a farmers' market and several shops selling imported luxuries as well as locally-grown produce.

'We're on Market Street now,' Bob was saying. 'That's the Town House yonder, and the jail. There's the public whipping post. Pity it's necessary but we're not soft on crime in these parts. You'll see we have a new ducking stool, too, for the correction of prostitutes, gossips, scolds and brawlers. Too many of them around. And there's the building that houses our fire-fighting machine. Fire's a terrible scourge here. Aye, terrible it is right enough. You see, they insist on burning pitch and tar on the wharves and rubbish in the streets, so it isn't surprising that we get sparks flying. Then householders refuse to have their chimneys swept. The law insists that chimneys be at least three feet above the ridgepole but you can imagine, with those frame houses and shingle roofs, that fire spreads – poof! – all too easily.'

Flora supposed that Allan was taking all this in but her own attention was straying too readily to the blazing colours of the trees and to the gaudy flowers – zinnias, petunias and canna lilies – that lingered in neat cottage gardens. Convolvulus cascaded over fences, a riot of large white and purple flowers with huge bees and citrus-yellow butterflies hovering over them, and Flora exclaimed at the profusion of it.

'Aye, we can't control it, that morning glory weed,' Bob grunted. 'They say the roots protect against rattle-snake bites, though, so I guess it has its uses.'

Whereas Flora could see little to complain about in this settled, orderly community the town environment was obviously not perfect enough for Bob Hogg, who seemed obsessed by its shortcomings.

'The fire hazard isn't lessened, either, by wooden buildings encroaching on the street,' he was going on. 'Structures like George Moore's stable yonder, and John Burgwin's tar shed, and John Lyon's tannery. Some folk think that because they're gentry the law doesn't apply to them!'

Flora smiled to herself, amused at the blatant inconsistencies in their friend's arguments, but fortunately he changed tack then.

'That's Mistress Heron's house yonder. The cemetery's in behind it, on Third Street. A Scot called Duncan who hails from Edinburgh lives down there below the jail, where William Dry also has a house – he has a foot in both camps, Brunswick and Wilmington, has Willie – and George Parker's below that. But here we are at the river. I guess that's your little party yonder.'

The quayside was milling with people and piled high with crates and barrels. The *Ulysses* had gone back to Brunswick with a cargo of grain, timber and passengers, but a variety of craft were plying back and forth, mainly scows, yawls and piraguas. There were also huge rafts piled so high with timber that Flora reckoned that the individual planks could be counted in their thousands. To make use of every inch of space the sides had been hung around with barrels of tar, and turpentine, and a thick black sludge oozed from the seams. Clearly the port was prospering.

Bob pointed to one particularly impressive barge which sported an awning and was crewed by negroes in colourful uniforms.

'That's John Rutherford's barge yonder. Must be here for the shindig. You'll likely meet him. He has a big plantation and sawmills at Hunthill, up New Bern way.'

Anne and Alex's group were clustered around two long, blunt-nosed dug-out barges tethered to a piling at one of the wharves, and the menfolk were handing bundles aboard. The children were first to spot Flora and came running up to cling to her skirts and demand attention.

'You coming too, Granma? We're going to see Papa Hugh!'

'Not today, darling, but yes, I'll be joining you in a day or two.'

Anne held out her arms to her mother. 'Oh, Ma, I'm so glad you came! We've been feeling so guilty about leaving you! You are quite recovered I trust?'

'Of course, lass. No need to worry about me now. Think only of yourself. 'Tis pity you cannot stay for the junketing tomorrow, but we can understand that you want to get away and settled, with the little ones. But you'll remember to give our love to Annabella and Alexander, and to Papa Hugh?'

'We will! We will! Oh, Ma, isn't it exciting? I feel already that going up river is like going home. You'll join us before too long, won't you?'

With that she turned away, as if hoping that Flora would not catch the tremor in her voice. Hearing it however Flora took her hand.

'Bear up, little one. We women all remember what 'twas like, to be in the family way. Feelings are heightened. We become fiercely protective of our young and passionately possessive of our men. But you need have no fear on either score. The children are sturdy and Alex as faithful and steadfast as a rock.'

She wondered what had spurred her to say that: but if she had had to reassure herself about Allan's straying what might Anne be dreading, in her delicate and vulnerable state? Not that Anne had lost her comely looks. Far from it. She had recovered quickly from the ordeal of the voyage and was blooming now. Today she had draped a kerchief of fine blue muslin round her neck and shoulders and had cunningly tucked the ends into the voluminous breast knots on the bodice of her dress. The wide bows carried the eye away from her thickening figure and up towards the porcelain-white purity of her skin. Even in her pregnancy she would have graced any ball and it would have taken a particularly skilled seductress, Flora knew, to deflect Alex from her side. Even so, Flora understood her daughter's reservations. Anne just wanted to have her husband to herself, no matter where.

'Make sure you keep your head covered. They say the forests are less dense, north of here, and that sun can burn you up.'

'Aye, Ma. I will. See, I have my parasol ready. And they tell me they can rig up an awning of sorts, if it gets too hot.'

Flora's gaze took in the tiny cabin, little more than six feet square, saw how the vessel was rapidly filling with people and baggage, and feared for her pregnant daughter's comfort, but restrained herself from further comment. They kissed. Flora embraced the children and then returned to the menfolk.

Jamie had been chattering non-stop. 'They said I could take an oar! Don't you wish you were coming too, Sandy?'

His brother reached down and ruffled his hair. 'Aye, lad. Maybe so. I've been drawn both ways. But you see, Father can use my help and besides, Iain MacRae's still here. And I like Wilmington whereas there's no guarantee that I'll like Cross Creek!'

Jamie grinned cheekily. 'Ye canna fool me, Sandy MacDonald. It's yon Strachan lass, isn't it, that's holding ye here?'

Flora saw Sandy blush and her heart sank. What had been going on there, during her illness? Had the Quinces brought Rachel up from Brunswick to be claimed by the Boyds and had the two young folk somehow engineered a tryst? It would be easy enough, while Sandy stayed at the inn with the MacLeods and the servants.

The servants! She suddenly remembered Morag, and turned at that very moment to confront two black, adamantine eyes.

'Morag. Goodbye lass. We shall be with you ere long. Take good care of yourself. Cuidreach and Annabella will rejoice to see you, as will Father Hugh.'

But all the girl offered in return was a brief, peremptory nod. Then she pointedly turned her back on her mistress and handed a carpet bag to a waiting negro who deposited it in the waiting vessel.

'Morag! Come here! How dare you ignore me like that!'

The words were on the tip of her tongue but she bit them back. She had seen Mabel Cobham berate a little negro maid, slapping her hard across the face and yelling, 'You dare sass me, you nigger slut!' and the sight had been far from uplifting. No, she would not stoop to such indignity. Let the girl go. All that ailed her, after all, was a surfeit of sensitivity. Loyalty was Morag's middle name. Give her time. She would come round.

Suddenly Flora realised that all the passengers had clambered aboard. The deep-laden barge was pulling away from the wharf, its oars, all save the one Jamie was plying, rhythmically dipping and lifting, and everyone was waving energetically. Everyone but Morag, who sat impassively sulking in the bow, her sphinx-like gaze fixed firmly in the direction of Eagle's Island.

At last the barge rounded the bend in the river and vanished from sight. Flora tried to stifle a sigh and failed.

'That Morag will need careful handling. I hope we have done the right thing, sending her with Anne and Alex. She may never forgive us.'

Allan simply shrugged and took her arm. 'Too late now, I'm afraid. We must just do our best to gentle her out of it when we see her again. Come. Bob says there's a slave auction at Ancrum's. They're selling the latest cargo to come in. It should be quite a spectacle, he tells me.'

'You mean they're actually selling people?'

'Yes. that's how they get labour around here.'

Flora was holding back, repelled by the idea of human beings so demeaned, but her curiosity was whetted and she was particularly intrigued by a notice she saw prominently displayed on a tree. It read:

JUST IMPORTED IN THE SCHOONER CHARITY
THOMAS MOON, MASTER,
FROM AFRICA, A PARCEL OF LIKELY HEALTHY SLAVES
Consisting of Men, Women and Children, which are to be
sold for Cash or Country produce,
By Ancrum and Schaw
On October 10th,
beginning 9 a.m.

Even when they were a street or two away it was obvious from the racket that something was going on. Contemptuous male voices rent the air, interspersed with a shrill hysterical keening.

'Obviously a lot of interest in this lot,' Bob said calmly. 'I heard there might be some bargains. Some of the local owners are also trying to resell some rejects, runaways and the like. Could be I'll get me a new drayman, and someone to sweep the warehouse.'

And he pushed forward towards the raucous noise. From behind Flora watched him merge with the would-be customers who had assembled outside Ancrum's store. They were an unsavoury-looking lot, the kind, Flora felt, who would delight in persecuting anyone weaker than themselves. Almost to a man they were tall and rangy, with lean faces and hard eyes, and they walked with that peculiar roll of men accustomed to living in the saddle. Flora saw that when Bob Hogg approached they made no move to stand aside for him. There was no place in their vocabulary for words like respect, humility or deference. These people would kow-tow to no-one, not even to a king. Least of all, perhaps, to a king. Gradually it was being borne in upon her that the typical North Carolinian was a different breed from his counterpart at home.

The gaggle of human merchandise had been stood up for display on a wooden platform outside the store. All were barefoot. Most were still in chains and many were in a pitiful physical condition, with weals from the overseer's whip visible on their backs and their bodies covered in sores and scabs. Even at ten paces they smelt abominably and what few clothes they wore were vermin-infested rags.

The white bidders were having a field day, revelling in what they saw as their God-given position of power and privilege. Flora knew at once that she ought to leave this arena of degradation but found herself unaccountably drawn to witness the scene, prey to a strange, voyeuristic fascination.

A man just in front of Flora turned to his companion, spat out a gobbet of tobacco and said, 'Yeah, man. Ain't much wrong with that there specimen. 'Bout eighteen, would you think? Real sturdy. Muscles all firm and knotted like he was used to hard outdoor work. What say we take a look at him?'

The other man nodded and together they mounted the platform. Clowning was clearly their speciality and there was a ripple of anticipation as they made much of their disgust, approaching the young man with hands holding their noses. Then they proceeded to scrutinise the youth's body as if he were a cow or a horse, prodding his biceps and prising his mouth open the better to inspect his teeth.

The final humiliation came when they removed his loin cloth. 'Eeh, man! What have we here? Look, ladies! Bet you often wondered what colour a nigger's prick was! Now you know!'

This evoked shrieks of laughter, both male and female. Evidently the crowd relished such scenes: Flora suspected that was why many of them had come. The young negro stood passive through all the hilarity, his head bowed. Only when bidding began and his two taunters were successful in purchasing him did he lift his gaze, as if something of what had been going on had got through to him, and Flora had never before seen such hatred blaze in anyone's eyes.

But his triumphant captors pulled him down off the platform and drove him forward like a recalcitrant ox.

'Giddee-up, Caesar! You's a-workin' for me an' Joe here now! We find you slackin' an' your life's sure gonna be hell. Yeah, man!'

At last Flora's sense of decency asserted itself then. 'I've seen enough, Alan. Take me back to the Hoggs'.'

But to her consternation she realised that there was no way back through the press of people: in fact, they were almost at the front of the crowd now – a circumstance that the claustophobic Flora would have welcomed had it not also meant that she had to witness those distressing scenes at close quarters.

And worse was yet to come because another group of negroes had been man-handled on to the platform and Flora saw to her horror that they were all women and children. A roar of prurient appreciation went up from the watching men. No matter if the females were just budding towards puberty, great with child or wrinkled with age, they became the objects of jeering, insolent comment.

'Ah'll be doggoned, Abe! If that ain't Farquhard Campbell's half-breed wench! The one wid the star on her brow! Must have been playing up some, for him to be selling her!'

The man who spoke, a dark, hairy countryman in moleskin breeches and a wide-brimmed hat, was gigantic. He was standing just a few paces from Flora and seemed double her height: she was suddenly visited by the memory of herself as a child, lifting her gaze from her father's deerskin broghans up to his face away above her. Looking upwards now she felt herself recoil as the man removed a straw from his mouth, revealing a row of black, misshapen teeth. Then he let out a randy whoop.

'Oh boy, Abe! We can have ourselves some fun wid this one! She's proud, that Stella! They say she was spawned by Harnett, or maybe Howe – one of the quality, anyway – on one of his Ashanti slaves. And she sure is a honey, ain't she now?'

'Sure is, Leroy. Ain't saw a whore in a long time wid such a fine upstandin' pair o' bubbies! An' the colour! Like a ripe walnut! Feel maself risin', jes lookin' at her!'

The last words echoed above the murmur of voices, occasioning a chorus of guffaws that encouraged the two men to push forward, mount the platform, and approach the girl slave.

Flora could well see what it was in the girl that excited them. She looked to be at least fifteen but was probably younger, for her body had not quite lost its pubertal plumpness. Yet she was tall already, at least six inches taller than Flora, and the impression of height was enhanced by the long, silky dark hair which fell loose about her coffee-coloured shoulders. Her facial features too were remarkable – flaring nose, heavy lips, startlingly white teeth – but even these were overshadowed by the two aspects that set her apart: her flashing tawny eyes and the star-shaped birth-mark on her forehead.

The slave flinched as the men approached but did not alter her defiant stance. She continued to hold her head high and to stare steadfastly ahead, seemingly ignoring the jibes of the onlookers and the vile intentions of of her two tormentors. But Flora saw her stiffen, noticed the marked whitening of the star-shaped scar and the determined clenching of her fists.

An expectant hush fell on the crowd as the man they called Leroy stationed himself in front of the girl, put out his hand, and with exaggerated casualness tore away her meagre homespun bodice to reveal a shapely brown bosom. For a moment his calloused hand cupped her right breast, and his index finger pointedly traced the outline of the aureole around the nipple: then he stepped back, feigning repentance.

'My humblest apologies Ah'm sure, Ma'am! No offence meant! But maybe you would care to feel this member here, and put it out of its misery, eh? For ever since Ah set eyes on you it jes won't stay down!'

This lascivious horseplay aroused a roar of laughter from the mob. Ancrum's auctioneer was standing by with a lax, stupid grin on his face, and even substantial-looking citizens like Bob Hogg were doing nothing to intervene. It was as if being present at a slave market conferred on every white man a licence to commit rape. Incensed, Flora turned to Allan and was appalled to see no trace of disgust or pity on his face.

'How can you stand here and tolerate this?' she demanded. 'Can't we stop it?'

His answer stunned her. 'Why? They do no harm. Besides, 'tis the custom here. 'Tis not our place to change it, we who arrived but days ago.'

In the event protest was indeed forthcoming, and from an unexpected quarter. Stella's persecutors were making to unbutton their breeches when a frenzied female figure darted forward from the line of slaves and planted itself, arms flailing, between the men and their victim. The woman was old and shrunken, with wiry grey hair that looked strangely incongruous against the shiny ebony of her skin, but age had not put out her fire. A jungle savagery still seethed and clawed and scratched in her as she turned to face her adversaries, a wild cat defending her cubs. And Flora was amazed, as the vituperations came spitting out, to realise that spattered among the alien curses were words she knew. Gaelic words. Nor were they all imprecations; many of them, words of comfort and assurances of love, were directed at the girl.

'Grab that old shotten herring, you doggone yellow-livered bastards!' The auctioneer had at last been spurred into action and Leroy, his courage questioned, delivered a violent cuff on the old woman's head which by all the rules of physics ought to have sent her reeling. But somehow she stood her ground, her head went down, and charging her assailant she butted him sharply in the vitals.

He staggered back, clutching his genitals and bawling with pain. Delighted taunts from the crowd exacerbated his fury and humiliation. Flora was sure, from the evil look in his eyes, that murder was going to be done.

But instead he showed remarkable constraint. Few heard the chilling words that came hissing from his lips, but Flora did and her heart quailed.

'Yew gonna regret this, granma! Yew gonna wish yew had never been born. Ah's gonna buy yew an' make yer life a livin' hell. Ain't nobody else gonna have yew!'

Having snarled his ultimatum he then turned to the auctioneer, putting on his most affable, unconcerned persona and feigning admiration for the old woman's spirit. 'Real sassy old cow, ain't she Tim? And strong! Still years o' field work in her. What say Ah give yew ten joes for her? Ain't nobody here gonna make yew a better offer!'

He pulled a handful of gold coins from his pocket. The auctioneer's eyes registered greed.

'If yew's so wealthy all of a sudden, Leroy, what say yew take the girl too, the mulatto wid the star? She's a real honey. Ain't she, Abe? Yew'd have some fine sport wid her. Better'n her old turkey buzzard of a mother.'

Leroy stood for a moment, considering. 'Naw. Not now. 'Twould make for trouble, havin' two vixens on ma farm that's in cahoots. They'd conspire to steal ma chickens an' hogs, and like as not turn ma other hands against me. Guess Ah'll leave the young biddy to yew, Abe.'

With that he grabbed his most recent purchase by the hair and dragged her screaming off the platform. She wriggled ineffectively in his grip and even tried biting his wrist but her owner had the upper hand now.

'Struggle, woman, an Ah swear Ah'll kill yew!' He had a pistol in his hand and was belabouring his victim round the head. Flora knew that he could just as easily pull the trigger and not a white soul there would question the action. She stood helpless, tears of rage and pity in her eyes. She had seen people demeaned and reviled before, would never forget the punishments she had witnessed being meted out to captured Jacobites by the notorious Captain Caroline Scott and his like, but there was an arrogant sadism about those American yahoos that filled her with horror.

Recent events seemed to have fazed Tim Farrell, the auctioneer. He knew he had lost control of the proceedings and departed from the preferred order of sale. Besides, the newly-arrived slaves had seen the treatment meted out to the old woman and had become fearful and restive. The girl Stella, standing there tall and silent but with tears streaming down her face, seemed to be the focus of disquiet. Get rid of her and the auction might continue smoothly.

'Quit that shoutin', folks, an' let's get on wid the sellin'! What say we start wid Stella here, the half-breed? Guess she'll be a much-coveted item. Through her feather, into her twat, and you're in a real blissful Garden of Eden, I'll warrant! Yew there, Leroy's buddy Abe Crawley ain't it – yew want her?'

'Yeah, but Ah cain't afford her, Ah guess. Ah don' have a pocket full of joes like ma friend Leroy. Reckon he must 'a sold some cattle, he's that flush wid gold all of a sudden.'

'Aw, you're jes kiddin'. Come on. Get the biddin' started.'

'A'rightie. Ah'm sayin' ten joes.'

The low bid occasioned much merriment. There followed a fast-escalating run of offers, and as the prices rose the comments sank to unplumbed depths of indecency. Finally it looked as if Abe Crawley had acquired the girl after all, for the bidding came to an abrupt stop at fifteen joes, an unprecedentedly high amount for a female slave, no matter how nubile.

Flora would never know what came over her then. She watched the auctioneer lift his gavel to clinch the deal, saw the successful customer dash forward to possess his prize, and a mad impulse seized her.

'Wait! The bidding is not yet closed! I want that girl!' And turning to Tim Farrell she said, adopting a haughty tone but inwardly quaking, 'Make out a bill of sale on my bank, at a sensible price.'

She heard Abe Crawley growl. Allan glared and muttered something about their not being made of money. But she did not care. She stepped forward, took Stella by the hand and said in Gaelic, 'Come. Work for me. Let me give you a home. We may not be wealthy but we are kind. It is not right, that you should see you mother degraded by those hooligans, and have to suffer such obscenities in your turn.'

Her intervention caused quite an uproar. People all round were speculating as to who this audacious woman was, and the name 'Flora MacDonald' was bandied about like a talisman. It had a markedly quietening effect. Even Abe Crawley stood back, dumbfounded, and as Flora led the girl slave away the crush of people meekly opened to let them pass.

V

October 1774

Allan was furious. Though he had parted with a letter of credit to Ancrum's agent and had asked Bob for temporary lodgings for the girl in the Hoggs' slave quarters he had done both with an ill grace.

'What were you thinking of, Florrie? As if we did not have enough problems, both domestic and financial, without you having to complicate things further!'

The very sense in his protest put Flora all the more firmly on the defensive.

'But can't you see, Allan? I simply had to rescue her! Common humanity demanded it! We could not have her sold like some chattel into the hands of that lecherous brute!'

Allan's expression said, 'Why not?' but his spoken words were an attempt to reason with her.

'You don't seem to understand, Florrie. Those slaves are like animals. They don't feel pain beyond the moment. Only the present touches them. That girl may feel gratitude to you now, but she could make big trouble in the future. I've discussed it with Bob and he is quite anxious for us. Please consider, Florrie. 'Tis not too late to sell the girl back again. Bob has offered to trade her in for us. Not that we could expect anything like the money we've pledged, of course.'

He scowled, recalling what he saw as a waste of money they could ill afford, but Flora was adamant.

'Your heartlessness appals me, husband! I may have been over-impulsive, yes, but I have no regrets. 'Twas not merely compassion that prompted me, but a feeling that the lass will be of ultimate value to us. She served in Farquhard Campbell's household in Cross Creek, remember, knows the area and its people. You will recall Bob's mention of this Farquhard Campbell, who is one of the region's wealthiest and most distinguished Highlanders?'

At that Allan simply shook his head in exasperation and went off glowering. He did not leave the matter there, however – that was not this new Allan's way – and Flora was not surprised when Bob Hogg added his plea, approaching the subject from a different angle.

'Please, good friend, consider my advice on this question of the Campbell half-breed. I have been in this country for eighteen years now, and know these people and their ways. The pure-bred black slaves are difficult enough to handle, being lazy and irresponsible, but the mulattoes are a spurious and degenerate breed, insolent and licentious. Because they were begotten of white men, frequently their masters, they think themselves above the others. You will have seen already, how this Stella wench you have bought gives herself airs!

'Matters are made no easier by this particular girl's undeniable beauty. Farquhard Campbell himself has told me that she and her mother threatened the safety and cohesion of his whole household. The mother brought knowledge of the black arts from her home-land, and did not hesitate to use them whenever her daughter's virtue was threatened. No one doubts, either, that the girl herself has inherited this African lore. Obeah. Voodoo. Understanding of poisons and potions, evil spells and deadly sorcery. I feel I really must warn you, madam, even should it mean giving you offence. If Farquhard Campbell could not cope no one can, and an inexperienced newcomer least of all. She could tempt your menfolk with her wiles and cause resentment among the white servants you brought with you. Please. I beg you. Think twice about this disastrous decision.'

For a moment Flora's resolution wavered. Bob Hogg's warning had summoned up a blood-curdling mental picture of obnoxious brews being prepared in black cauldrons over jungle fires, of a primitive necromancy no white man could begin to combat or comprehend. And that comment about Stella's power over men brought to mind those dusky maidens on Faial. She shuddered, a prey to dark imaginings.

Bob Hogg must have guessed at her fear then and sought to make capital out of it for he proceeded to enlarge on this theme, and Flora sensed his relish in it.

'You must have noticed that my house slaves refuse to consort with the piebald girl. They see her as a threat, interpret that star on her brow as a proof of her witchery. Of course, we more enlightened ones are not so gullible. We believe there must be a more rational explanation for the unfortunate stigmatism. Her mother might simply have loved to lie under the stars, or had milk spilt upon her, while she was a-carrying Stella. But be that as it may she is not as the others are, and to have her among us stirring up trouble is most unwise. You see, we slave-owners walk a tight-rope much of the time. We have to keep the upper hand, as masters, yet avoid confrontation. They can cause untold trouble, can slaves, if they but bear you a grudge. 'Tis not all benefit having them in your house, and that is what I fear for you, dear lady.'

His argument was irrefutable and Flora was quick to recognise the notes of reproach, appeal and admonition in it. Yet she could not dismiss the persistent suspicion that Allan had put Bob up to it. A stubborn perversity born of pity – that very aspect of her character that had led her to befriend a fugitive prince – came defiantly to the fore then. She was damned if she would give Stella up!

She did see the need to choose her words carefully, however. She dared not repudiate her host's wise advice too roughly.

'Bob, you are indeed a dear friend to us and I greatly value your advice, for we are so raw in our experience and new to the ways of this new land. Nor would I wish to cause trouble in your household through any deeds of mine. You will appreciate, however, that I have committed myself to this mulatto girl. She depends on me now for sustenance and employment and I feel I cannot betray her trust.'

'Trust! Pshaw! She knows not the meaning of the word! But if you will not take my advice then there is nothing more to say.'

Flora felt his annoyance and hastened to make amends. 'Please, Bob. Do understand. All I can say is that I'm sorry to have given you trouble. One thing I can promise, though. I shall do my best to keep the girl by me, make sure she does not have too much occasion to mix with your house servants. She can sleep in the little closet off our bedroom, and 'tis only for two more days, after all. Then we shall be gone.'

Bob appeared slightly mollified by this but there was a new formality in the bow with which he took his leave of her.

'Very well. So be it. Would I could change your mind, but you are a lady of great determination, as reports of you have always claimed. I shall pray sincerely that on this occasion your judgement may be less fallible than before.'

Chastened though she felt Flora was all the more conscious now of the need to keep Stella by her, and busy. Not that the girl had been shirking any light duties that fell to her. Ostracised by the other slaves she had clung to her new mistress and had been quick to tidy up discarded garments, swat annoying flies, throw out withered flowers.

She had also been full of promises. 'You jes wait till we's home, Miz MacDonald. Ah show you den how clebber Ah be. Ah kin weave, an' quilt, an' make soap an' candles, an' all de ol' African medicines. Anybody in your house hab an illness, Ah kin make 'im lik new agin.'

It was also clear that she regarded herself as infinitely superior to the rest of the slaves, not just because she was half white but also by reason of her phenomenal star. According to her, even some of the slave-owners held her in superstitious awe.

'Massah Campbell, he allus kind to me, an' dose gentlemen dat came a-visitin' at de big house mostly polite, specially Doctor Boyd: he de best ob all. But udders, like Massah Howe and Massah Harnett, dat ma mammy says be ma daddy, dey gibs me scared looks.'

'And the ladies, what of them?'

The girl's wide nostrils flared in contempt. ''Part from Miz Campbell, de mistress, an' Miz Harnett, who be too busy udder ways to care, dey all hate me. Tink Ah gonna steal deir men. Specially Miz Boyd, dat's allus suspectin' the doctor ob doin' tings he ain't.'

Her young features registered unmitigated scorn then. 'Guess Ah could get any man Ah liked into ma bed, wid de arts ma mammy has taught me, but Ah swear ba de good Lord above, Miz MacDonald ma'am, dat Ah be pure as de dribben snow. Doctor Boyd lik a fadder to me. Nebber did de tings Miz Boyd say.'

'What things? What happened?'

'Oh, 'twas dat Miz Boyd made me and ma mammy run away. Us'd nebber hab done it but de Massah believed de tings Miz Boyd said 'bout me an' de doctor, an' declared he'd whip me an' make me do field-work. Me!'

With this Stella flung back her fine leonine head and her yellow eyes flashed. Flora could see why people feared her. In her were combined the warlike qualities of an ancient Amazon with the erotic seductiveness of a Jezebel or a Delilah.

The slave was embarking now upon an extraordinary tale of hardship and survival against fearsome odds. She told how her mother, years before, had been marched by slave-dealers through the Congolese jungle to Luanda, where she was imprisoned in a crowded barracoon before being shipped to Cuba. She had almost died on the voyage, locked in a pitch-dark hold, beset by sea-sickness, disease and filth. Here in the New World she had been sold with callous disregard for her health and dignity, but had been content enough on the Campbell plantation until the previous May, when Kate Boyd's jealous accusations had forced her to flee.

So Stella had existed with her mother in the forests all through the summer past, knowing they were being hunted unmercifully by Farquhard Campbell's overseers and their dogs. Mainly they had eaten rabbits, small animals, and berries, with rats and occasional chickens stolen from isolated farmsteads as special delicacies. They had been befriended by a group of runaways in similar case who together had constituted a small community but one day they had witnessed the leader of the gang being cornered by dogs while he took refuge in a tree. The animals had torn the clothes off him and savaged him so sorely that there was no fight left in him; then covered in blood, with the bones showing white through his wounds, he had been manhandled onto a cart and trundled away for punishment.

'Seeing dat ma mammy tink better ob stayin' in de woods. De winter come. De bears an' wolves hungry. We not safe. So we goes back to Massah Campbell an' gib ourself up. An he kind. He even weep when he see de state ma mammy in, thin an' pawley. He say he jes pretend to believe Miz Boyd but wid hab to sell us jes de same. An dat how Ah be here wid you.'

Flora felt a rush of anger and pity. Every country had its outlaws and America, with its sub-society of imported slaves, was compounding an already existing problem. She would see to it that Stella did not undergo such privations again. She would be the girl's stay and protectress.

'Come,' she said at last on impulse, taking a dress from the closet and examining it critically. 'Let's visit the store and do some marketing. You shall help me choose some ribbon to brighten up this old green gown of mine. So dull and worn it looks in this harsh sunlight, and with this grand ball only hours away 'tis time I gave it thought.'

The gown was of light green satin, with a billowing hooped skirt and full slashed sleeves lined with white. Fashionable enough perhaps to wear to a ceilidh in distant Portree, but could it stand the scrutiny of the ladies of Wilmington, especially if one were the focus of attention? Flora had decided not to take the risk. The gown was crying out for repair. Who better to do the job than Stella, who claimed to be such an accomplished needlewoman?

It was Flora's first venture out of doors without male company and she felt self-conscious and conspicuous as she closed the gate in the Hoggs' picket fence and stepped out into the street. It was late afternoon but the sun was still hot and its slanting rays dazzled her eyes, rendering her parasol necessary: she welcomed the shade it provided but found it doubly useful as a screen for her features.

It soon became obvious, however, that had she craved anonymity she would have been better advised to walk out un-accompanied. People seemed to materialise at every corner and she soon realised that their glances were directed not so much at herself as at Stella. Folk would look at the slave with a ghoulish curiosity and then their gaze would slide away, discomfited and tremulous.

Far from evading their stares Stella actually seemed to court them. A good foot taller than Flora, she walked with a sinuous grace that made other, daintier women feel and look clumsy and insignificant. Flora suddenly understood why the Kate Boyds of this world distrusted her.

And no sooner had she let the thought cross her mind than she felt Stella stiffen and heard a particularly venomous Gaelic curse come snarling from the girl's lips. She looked up and saw the beautiful features – the slightly hooked nose with its full nostrils, the wide, sensuous mouth, the tawny, big-cat eyes – transformed by hatred into a feral mask. Fearfully she followed the direction of that malevolent gaze and realised that four perfectly innocuous-looking people had rounded the corner and were coming towards them. They walked in two couples, a man and woman in front and two young women bringing up the rear. The man was all smiles, and was approaching them with hands outstretched, determined to outface whatever dark forces Stella might be

summoning to her aid. But Flora knew that it was not Roddy
Boyd that was the object of Stella's wrath, but the woman on his
arm.

She was small, dark and bustling, and probably around forty-
five. Flora found her attention held, surprised: 'tis not often, she
reflected, scarcely registering the impression as a conscious
thought, that one sees oneself as one used to be so precisely
reflected in another! Then she looked more closely and saw the
pell-mell succession of emotions in the woman's face: astonishment, fear, and stubborn black resentment. So this was Kate Boyd.
The woman Roddy Boyd had chosen for his wife. How on earth
had such a mésalliance ever come to pass? For Flora had no doubt
that it had been a disastrous marriage.

Her eyes went from Roddy and Kate to two girls walking
behind. The first she did not know, but the other made her want
to turn right round and make her escape homewards, for there,
large as life, was Rachel Strachan in all her brash, red-headed
carnality. She had decked herself out, at the Boyds' expense no
doubt, in sprigged muslin and an elaborately be-ribboned bonnet,
and for a moment Flora felt unjustifiably ashamed of Stella's simple
osnabung shift, checked kerchief and childish necklace of painted
lilac seeds. Dear God in heaven, she found herself muttering
inwardly, what kind of hornets' nest of bitterness have I stepped
into now?

But if Roddy Boyd was aware of the sizzling cross-currents
around him he was determined to ignore them.

'My dear Mistress MacDonald! How good to see you walking
abroad, and looking so well! I trust you are fully recovered, and
that we shall see you at the ball tomorrow evening?'

His gaze turned then to Stella. 'And I see you have acquired a
new maid. I had heard about that. This is a chance to redeem
yourself, Stella. See that you make the most of it and give your
new mistress no trouble.'

Having delivered this school-masterish admonition he then
made to introduce his three companions to Flora.

'First you must meet my wife Kate. I am sure you will be firm
friends when you come up to the back country to live. And this' –
his voice registered pride – 'is our daughter Jenny. You have
encountered us on a very auspicious occasion, Mistress Mac-

Donald, for we have just had the Quinces deliver Rachel here safely into our hands, and have had a happy hour buying clothes for her at Ancrum's. She is our niece, and now our ward. But how silly of me. You have met already, of course, having braved the ocean together.'

He hesitated then, non-plussed and wondering what to say next. Flora felt his discomfiture, knew that his openness had to be met with similar good humour.

'I am glad to make your acquaintance at last, Mistress Boyd. And Jenny,' And she held out her hand.

Jenny was first to respond, with a respectful but amiable curtsy. Flora was aware of a ready dimpling smile, creamy skin and large grey eyes. Here, she knew instinctively, was Roddy's reason for living. Kate, on the other hand, seemed taken aback and disconcerted, and for a split second Flora wondered whether her gesture of friendship was going to be ignored altogether. The pause was certainly long enough for the rest of the company to notice it, but Kate appeared at last to think better of her rudeness and with obvious reluctance extended a lace-mittened hand. There was no friendliness or warmth in the gesture, however. The eyes that looked into Flora's were as hard as the rock of the Quiraing, and she was left marvelling at the difference in temperament between Roddy Boyd and his enigmatic wife.

Roddy must have realised that the stalemate could not be relieved by small talk for he made haste to wind up the conversation and salvage what good feeling he could from it.

'Well then, Mistress MacDonald, we shall certainly meet again within the next few hours. Keep well.' And he bowed low over her hand.

At that very moment some genetic affinity must have prompted Flora to lift her eyes from Roddy Boyd's discreetly-powdered head: for there, within yards of them, was Sandy. He had just come round the corner, seen them, and decided not to infiltrate the group, for when his eyes met his mother's he raised a finger to his lips and turned back. Flora saw, however, that it was not only she herself he had been aware of. He had certainly seen Rachel. And Stella. And she knew that being Sandy he must have noticed the Boyds' daughter, even if only from behind.

Three girls. All different. And every one exuding her own

particular brand of sexual attractiveness. Flora's heart turned over. She wondered what Sandy's had done.

VI

October 1774

'Beautiful,' Allan breathed, fingering the side ringlets she had been at pains to curl. 'And that old green dress! Why, it looks like new! You think I do not notice feminine things, Florrie, but it has worried me those past years, not to able to buy new gowns and gewgaws for you. You who deserve them so.'

Flora gave a light laugh. 'Fiddlesticks, Allan. You know I care not for fripperies. A few fresh ribbons, some ingenuity and a moderate skill with the needle and any woman worth her salt can transform a worn garment into a perfectly presentable one.'

Then she frowned and added unthinkingly, 'Stella yonder assured me she was a needlewoman but her efforts at stitchery were deplorable. I had to take the work out of her hands or the whole effect would have been ruined.'

Allan's hand stopped in mid caress and dropped to his side. She felt the reproach in his eyes, heard the unspoken what-did-I-tell-you. She ought to have had the sense not to voice her growing doubts about Stella. The girl had become one more forbidden topic between them.

'Are you almost ready? The carriage is waiting. Bob says that the Governor is a stickler for punctuality. And we have a strict timetable to keep, with this supper at the Burgwin House before the actual ball.'

There was indeed a crunch of wheels on the gravel outside, a creak of harness and the small, expectant sounds of horses pawing the ground.

'Just a second to adjust my brooch, and I shall be as ready as I can be.'

As she fastened the rhinestone talisman she took a last, appraising look in the glass and was not displeased with what she saw. Perhaps her cheeks were a trifle red from the sun and she had always known that a few extra inches in height would have enhanced her general appearance, but her comely brown hair retained its hint of auburn and the gaze of her blue-grey eyes was still clear and direct, registering interest in everything around her. She had been careful to include the odd Jacobite touch in her dress, too, knowing that the Americans, loyal though they might be to the English king, would expect it: hence the brooch that the Prince had given her, the three cockades of white ribbon at her bosom, and the symbolic white rose, culled from the Hoggs' still-prolific garden, that bloomed modestly in her hair.

The night was balmy and flower-scented, scattered with stars and noisy with crickets. Bursts of laughter and anticipatory human voices followed their progress as drunken revellers debouched from Wilmington's many taverns, but seated next to Allan in the carriage Flora felt herself inhabiting a landscape of dreams, cocooned in the luxury of assured love and protectiveness. Would that this could last for ever, she murmured to herself, knowing however with the accumulated wisdom of five decades that it is when one feels most secure that fate can deal its cruellest blows. But why question the future, when there was so much to savour in the here and now? She lay back upon the cushions with a sigh of sheer sybaritic contentment.

As they approached the grand Palladian facade of the Burgwin House uniformed negro grooms and footmen rushed to help them descend. They were escorted to the columned portal like the central figures in a Roman bridal procession, illumined by torchlight and surrounded by deference. Then directly into a huge open hall whose main feature was a vast stairway with turned balusters and carved consoles. Flora's quick eye took in the marble facings on the mantels, the scrolled pediments above the mirrors, the magnificent crystal chandeliers swinging from elaborately corniced ceilings. Her eyes blinked, dazzled by the sparkling splendour of it all.

The guests were being formally received by Governor Martin and his wife Elizabeth, and by their Wilmington hosts, the Burgwins, all four of whom, though reassuringly middle-aged, had clearly taken great pains with their dress and appearance. The men wore coats of exquisitely embroidered brocade while the women struck Flora as having carried their sartorial efforts to comic extremes. Both sported towering, liberally powdered wigs and prominent face-patches; their fans were enormous and their cork heels precariously high; while their dresses, widely hooped and of expensive damask, featured low necklines and elaborate Callamanco sleeves.

All four were inordinately gushing in their appreciation of Flora.

'How honoured we feel, to be meeting you at last! You are completely well now, we trust?'

One by one the women curtsied and the men bowed. Flora, who had come prepared to do the curstying, felt quite disconcerted until Elizabeth Martin took her elbow and steered her away from the little reception line and into the centre of the hall, where twenty or so pairs of curious eyes turned to gaze on her. Liveried flunkies appeared from all quarters bearing trays of generously-charged glasses and it was clear from the crescendo of conversation that most of the guests had already sampled the refreshments.

'What an overwhelmingly beautiful house!' Flora could not restrain her admiration.

The Governor's lady gave her a sideways look and Flora could have sworn she neighed. 'Oh yes, indeed, though a little ostentatious don't you think? One wonders where those tradespeople find the funds for such extravagance. We are much indebted to them for this little reception, however, though 'tis a pity the house is not large enough to accommodate the ball.'

Flora was just wondering how to respond tactfully to this damning with faint praise when the call came for the guests to assemble for dinner.

She had not expected to be seated in the place of honour at the Governor's right hand and to be regaled with course after delicious course served on finest porcelain: duck and goose, pheasant and turkey; hard- and soft-shell crab; scallops and salmon; an array of fruit pies, comfits and sorbets. Above all, the colonials' capacity for alcohol astonished her. She toyed with her glass, afraid she would be ill if she joined in the endless succession of toasts she was expected to drink.

The Governor noted her reluctance and laughed indulgently. 'Come, dear lady! You must be prepared to hob and nob with the rest of us! Surely some Madeira will do you no harm! I assure you the Burgwins serve only the very best of wines!'

Then he relented and called to a footman to bring a jug of lime juice and water. Flora gratefully sipped the cool, scented liquid and marvelled at the stout constitutions of the women around her, who seemed quite unaffected by their enormous consumption of wine and spirits.

She found Josiah Martin more congenial company than his wife, though like Elizabeth he affected an air of social superiority. She soon gathered that they both regarded North Carolina as an inferior, backwoodsy sort of posting when compared with their beloved home territory of Antigua.

'Tis such a pity that you and your husband will be making for the wilds, when you bring such tone to this poor, godforsaken colony. My Elizabeth has no friends at all of similar education and standing. Most people of wealth are self-made men, and even the professional gentlemen appear to have been singularly undiscriminating in their choice of wives. A silly, simpering lot they are, with no manners, no sense of fashion, and only the most boring conversation. You'll find, too, that most of them are full of the most unbecoming so-called patriotic sentiments. We can but hold them in contempt.'

This diatribe had been spoken in a low, confidential voice and Flora felt embarrassed rather than flattered by its content. She felt on safer ground when he switched to telling her about his family.

'The children take up most of Elizabeth's time of course. We have four, and would have had seven had we not lost three of them to the atrocious climate here. Little Samuel was only two, and our little girls ... But I must not distress you. I keep telling Elizabeth that we must not despair. There is still time for her to conceive again. If only she would agree to rest. I tried to persuade her to forego this trip to Wilmington but she said she needed dress fabrics and gloves which only Hogg's, or Schaw's and Ancrum's, can supply. And she so misses properly elegant society, poor girl. 'Twas a chance to visit with the colony's few respectable people, here. Besides, of course, we had heard that you and your husband, despite being Scottish, are people of breeding and culture. You must come and visit us in New Bern when you get settled.'

Flora was sorely tempted to respond to that 'despite being Scottish' with a spirited defence of her homeland. How dare this arrogant jackanapes imply that the land of her birth was somehow inferior to England? But the Governor was in full flow now and she simply smiled graciously, encouraging him to carry on.

'I am so sorry that we could not hold this function at New Bern, where my official residence, Tryon's Palace, is without doubt better suited for such a function, but then 'twas admittedly too far out of your way, when you plan to go west.'

'You really do live in a palace?' Flora was duly impressed.

'Well, that was the name given to it by the back-country folk when my predecessor, Governor Tryon, had it built seven years ago, and it seems to have stuck.'

The comment drew a loud exclamation, somewhere between a guffaw and a snort of derision, from the person seated on Flora's other side.

'Bloody Tryon's Palace,' a voice said. 'Caused more trouble than it was worth. Just added fuel to the fire. As if ordinary folks hadn't enough to complain about, with their religion being questioned and corrupt, pettifogging lawyers denying them justice, without extra taxes being levied to build a white elephant of a palace!'

The outburst was so startlingly unexpected that Flora almost choked on the piece of duck she was eating. Who could possibly be so presumptuous as to utter what almost amounted to treason in the presence of the Governor? She turned her eyes upwards and met the shrewd, penetrating gaze of her neighbour, Farquhard Campbell. So far their only contact had been a brief nod when they were introduced on entering, but she had recognised his name as that of one of the colony's leading Highlanders, and the slave-owner who had sold Stella.

Then she had to smile, realising why there had been no retort or recrimination from her other side. For she had just been addressed in the Gaelic, and the Governor, perhaps realising that he had been over-possessive of her, had turned away to address his wife.

So this was the wealthy Cross Creek merchant who owned lands all over, had been married three times, and whose present wife was half his age. He had forty slaves and they all understood and frequently spoke Gaelic. Remembering Stella's comments she recalled that although he had decided to sell Stella and her mother the girl had not been bitter about him, nor about his wife: it was rather the overseers and senior servants she had fulminated about.

Flora had been bred to distrust all Campbells as the traditional enemy. They were the perpetrators of massacres, the betrayers of ancient trust, their name synonymous with treachery and cunning. But she and Allan had vowed to bury all those old animosities. Contemplating this Campbell now, Flora decided she was inclined to like him, and it was amazing how rarely her first instinctive assessment was proved wrong. In his fifties like herself, he was tall and lean, with craggy irregular features and a leathery, lumpy complexion. A mass of greying red hair crowned his head: he must be inordinately proud of it, she reflected, for everyone else is wearing a wig. But it was his eyebrows that most commanded attention: thick and bristling and of a grizzled ginger colour, they protruded a good inch from his forehead and gave the impression of a perpetual supercilious scowl.

The eyes beneath were not scowling now, however, but positively twinkling as he continued to enlighten her, still in Gaelic, on his opinion of Governor Martin. He was the first North Carolinian to address her in her native tongue and she warmed to him, immediately at ease. No matter if she felt Governor Martin bristle with displeasure on her other side. She smiled to herself, recognising that Farquhard Campbell would probably delight in his host's frustration at not being able to follow what they were saying.

'Aye, 'tis a palace right enough. No wonder there was wellnigh a revolution over it. It fair got folks' backs up, right enough. Tryon couldn't be content with a modest mansion. Oh no, it had to be an elegant edifice of pink stone, with a great cupola over the central atrium, and sweeping double wings and covered colonnades. And it had to be furnished to rival the finest stately homes in Europe, with Aubusson carpets and grand portals and china from Sèvres.

'Not that anyone can blame Josiah there for all that, of course. We have to be fair. He inherited the house and has worked long and hard to quell the rebellious feelings it aroused. It's just that he fails to understand the patriot mentality, wants the backwoodsmen here to submit to the very restrictions they came to the colonies to escape. He really ought to listen to advice from the people's representatives. I've been here nearly forty years. I know what folks are thinking. With my brother-in-law Alex McAlister I've been a Cumberland County delegate to the Association for a good decade, and I'm not giving up my work there to please any Governor, no matter how anxious he is to placate.'

He spoke not so much in anger or bitterness as in exasperation. Flora sensed that for all his criticism he really rather liked Josiah Martin. Seeing some comment was required of her she put in tentatively, 'But you're speaking about troubles some years back, aren't you? Everything has been sorted out now?'

He looked at her with appalled disbelief.

'But where have you been since you came here, woman? Has nobody told you about the War of the Regulators? The Battle of Alamance, just three years since? Aye, May 16th, 1771, it was. Ordinary folks, mostly from the back country, had had their fill of high taxes, dishonest sheriffs, extortionate fees and the capricious behaviour of the Crown's officials. So they took matters into their own hands, and I don't blame them. There had been a whole series of riots. At Hillsborough an attorney called Williams was set upon and nearly killed. Judge Richard Henderson of Granville County had his barn and stables burnt. JPs were hauled from their houses and forced to resign.'

His face darkened. 'Of course the Regulators were poorly armed and lacked leadership. The insurrection was crushed right away. Maybe that's why the British broadsheets said little about it. But there were a lot of good men lost in the fighting and six hanged for treason after. They made them swear an oath o' allegiance, you see, six hundred of them. There was one Jamie Few, that I kent fine, taken prisoner on suspicion of burning the Fanning house, and they hanged him when he wouldnae take the oath. Aye, I liked Jamie fine. Wasn't capable of such barbarity. I'm damned if he did what they charged him with. All these hangings... It was a terrible time.

'The government should have seen then what way the wind was blowing, and worked to put things right. But instead the King's cause lost a lot of good men, for some that had been loyal to the Governor changed sides after Alamance. Richard Caswell. John Ashe. Cornelius Harnett. They're all patriots now. Things have just gone from bad to worse, until we're on the point now of halting all commercial dealings with Britain. Aye, it's that bad, Flora. My advice to you and your husband is to get away from the Tidewater as soon as you can and whatever you do keep out of politics.'

Perhaps he sensed her panic then, because his eyes softened. 'But you'll hear about all this soon enough. Let's speak no more of it.'

He sighed. Flora was tempted to remind him that he alone had chosen the topic of conversation and she had uttered scarcely a word. She felt the old familiar stirrings of apprehension. Where did Farquhard Campbell stand in all this controversy? She just had to know, and was about to ask him outright when he switched abruptly to English and boomed out in a loud hectoring voice, inviting everyone to hear.

'And I'm hearing you bought the half-breed, Stella, the one my overseer couldn't tame? Just like the thing somebody like you would do, someone that's new to the country and is notorious for letting her heart rule her head! Did your impulsiveness not bring you enough trouble before? Will you never learn, eh?'

There was an audible gasp from the assembled diners. The audacity of it! Some of them, though by no means all, doubtless appreciated the old enmity between the MacDonalds and the Campbells. They also knew Farquhard Campbell for his fearless candour, and here he was, exercising it against their guest of honour. It was a tricky moment. You could have heard a pin drop.

Flora felt herself stiffen. She could scarcely believe that a man with whom she had exchanged hardly a word should dare to address her in so provocative and personal a fashion. It did not help, either, that he had been so unerringly right in his reading of her character, pinpointing that tendency to instinctive behaviour that had shaped her destiny.

She was just framing a suitably withering retort when she saw the teasing challenge in those hooded eyes and realised how crucial this moment was, not just for tonight but for her family's whole future here. Friend or foe, his look seemed to say, which am I to be? See! All these people are agog to know.

She knew it would be futile to explain why she had bought Stella. She could not even explain that to herself. This man Campbell indeed had her in a tight spot, and was obviously baiting her. All she could do was keep her sense of humour and retreat gracefully. So she did, and the chuckling laugh she kept only for family and close friends bubbled up. She had never quite appreciated the

effect that laugh could have on other people. Never coarse or
raucous, it rippled infectiously around the table and its sheer
spontaneous joy was picked up, savoured, and gratefully recipro-
cated. Sensing the loosening of tension Flora attributed it,
typically, to the guests' intake of alcohol. She did not realise that
she alone had transformed the mood of the evening.

Life had been so hard for Flora in recent years that she had
almost forgotten how to be frivolous. The last time, she recalled
with a wistful pang of regret, had been on the day Dr Johnson
visited Skye. Allan, for all his physical strength and leadership
qualities, lacked that cosmic humour that could transform
adversity into adventure, and she could barely remember when
they had last laughed together. Perhaps it took a man of really
powerful personality to draw out her lighter side, and she sensed
that Farquhard Campbell belonged to that category for here she
was suddenly feeling ridiculously, inexplicably happy.

Conversation scintillated, and when at last the illustrious guests
piled into the carriages that waited outside the Burgwin House
they were not only well lubricated with spirits but alive to the
felicity of Flora MacDonald's social gifts.

Only one incident marred her happiness. Throughout all her
exchanges with her neighbour she had been aware only
peripherally of Allan, deep she was sure in dull conversation with
the Martins. But his antennae had been attuned to her every word
and he could not resist puncturing what he saw as her levity as he
handed her into the phaeton she was to share with Elizabeth
Martin for the short drive to the Town House.

'Restrain yourself, woman. You shame us with this frivolity.'

The laughter died on her lips then and for a bitter moment she
felt the quick sting of tears. But the new milieu had heartened her,
as had the modicum of rum she had imbibed, and for once she
had the nerve to hold her ground. She was determined that her
husband's jealousy would not mar her pleasure.

'Och, Allan, don't be spoiling things with your soor-dook looks!
Let's show these good people how much we appreciate their
kindness!'

It was gratifying to see him look sheepish then, but her little
spurt of triumph was tinged with misgivings and she grimly
cautioned herself to curb her high spirits, for admittedly it was a

side of her that Allan rarely saw and clearly mistrusted.

Fortunately, perhaps, Elizabeth Martin was not one to encourage flightiness either, and Flora had some minutes to compose herself as her lanky companion was hoisted up into the carriage and comfortably settled opposite her. She sat regarding the poker-backed, vinegary-faced matron who had married a cousin five years her junior and marvelled that she had given him so many children. There could well be hidden depths of passion here, and possibly even some sweetness and warmth, but Flora was yet to catch a glimpse of them. She tried to picture this gangling woman and the neat, dapper little Josiah in bed but her imagination failed her. And she mustn't think that way. It was the kind of prying into other people's private lives that she found so tempting but Allan would not countenance. Determinedly she focussed her attention on being amenable. What to talk about? They certainly couldn't sit all the way to the Town House in this frosty silence.

'What a wonderful evening it has been, Mistress Martin! Altogether perfect!'

The Governor's lady's features relaxed slightly and she favoured Flora with a condescending nod, but the eyes in the bony face stayed gimlet hard.

'Yes, indeed. It has served the occasion very well. Nothing more elaborate was called for, after all.'

Duly chastened on this score, Flora tried yet again. 'You find life congenial in North Carolina?'

And to her surprise the face of the woman opposite her suddenly looked old and crumpled. The steel-blue eyes filled with tears. For a moment Flora thought that the colony's first lady was about to collapse in an embarrassing frenzy of weeping. But Elizabeth Martin was made of sterner stuff. She visibly pulled herself together, straightening her back and setting her features into a dignified, queenly mode before replying.

'I hate and despise the whole territory! It could fall into the sea tomorrow for all I care, and take every one of its goddamned ill-educated oafs with it! You have come at a time of year when the climate's bearable, but just wait until the summer, when the fevers start to take their toll. No doubt you have heard of our tribulations since we came here?'

Flora stuttered her sympathy, cursing herself for not recalling all Josiah had told her, but by this time her companion was wound up and could not contain her grief and venom.

'There is little culture here, as you will soon discover, and no command of the niceties of fashion. The men think only of hunting, whoring and cock-fighting and are totally lacking in refinement, while the women are either empty featherbrains or coarse farm-women without elegance or style. The food is greasy and monotonous. There is no theatre, no music, no literature. As for the back country, it is a heathenish wilderness where women of every degree suckle their young and men are given to violence and degradation. Oh, how I long for London or Paris or Rome! Even Charleston is better than this hell-hole! 'Twill be the death of me, this isolation!'

Then she seemed to regret her outburst and added politely, 'But I forget you are not one of us yet, dear lady. Please let me say how pleased we are that you and your husband have come. You bring a breath of the outside world to this benighted place.'

Flora murmured her thanks. She could not decide whether Elizabeth's uprush of magnanimity was a mere matter of form, sincerely meant, or perhaps a veiled apology for an uncharacteristically frank confidence: for she was sure that this woman would rarely voice her reservations about North Carolina in public: she would just hold herself aloof and wonder why nobody liked her.

Altogether she was thankful when the little carriage came to a halt outside the Town House, where a noisy crowd had gathered. Time now to confront whatever revelations the rest of the evening had in store.

VII

The civic ball was well underway when the official party arrived, but the moment Flora entered the hall on Governor Martin's arm the music stopped and the dancers drew back to let them pass.

Then a voice, unmistakably Scottish, called out, 'Three cheers

for Flora MacDonald! May she and her husband prosper in North
Carolina!'

The orchestra – three fiddles, a fife and a flute – then withdrew
to let a piper play and Flora felt an upsurge of nostalgia as
she was swept into the breathtaking figures of a series of reels
and strathspeys. It was like being home again. The good
people of Wilmington had decorated the walls of their town
hall with MacDonald tartan. Draped in swathes, its greens
and blues were the perfect foil for the cockades of white ribbon
that hung everywhere, on bannisters, sconces and mantelshelves.
She was glad her dress complimented the colour theme of the
occasion. Even the buckles on her shoes were perfect: the
diamonds and emeralds might be paste, but it would take a trained
eye to know.

She had not expected to be so lionised, and while the flattery
pleased her she feared that Allan would resent her seeming to steal
the limelight. She longed to tell him that he was attracting attention
too. She had seen more than one pair of female eyes rest on him,
appreciatively assessing his Highland dress, his sturdy physique
and ruddy, weather-beaten complexion. But he seemed not to
notice, and she could detect the old jealousy colouring his
cynicism when he handed her into a minuet. Why did he always
have to puncture her rare moments of triumph with snide
comments?

'Trust colonials to make a fuss over something that happened
more than thirty years ago! And to think most of these folks are
Lowlanders: their kin, likely as not, would have been Hanoverians
and would have rejoiced if you had been sent to the scaffold with
Kilmarnock and Balmerino. So much for the strength of the
romantic spirit! Let the years pass, change the scene to a distant
continent, and the mad action of an obscure girl is elevated to the
stuff of legend!'

Very true, she thought. There is an element of extravagant
humbug in all this. But I'm touched all the same. And she told
him so. 'Oh Allan, my dear, don't be such a curmudgeon! Look
at the trouble they've gone to! What a welcome!'

And there was no doubting the sincerity of many of her well-
wishers. One old Highland woman grabbed her by the hand,
looked long and searchingly into her eyes, and said in the Gaelic,

'Flora MacDonald! Our heroine! I'm that glad ye're here. We thought ye would never come!'

There were tears in her eyes as she said it, and Flora's confidence was restored.

She danced with Tom Cobham, who introduced her to his friend and colleague Dr Tucker. Bob Hogg was anxious for her to meet his brother James, recently arrived from Caithness. Messrs Dry and Quince were there too, of course, and she was much impressed by the handsome James Moore, who seemed to command universal respect and admiration.

All the while her eyes were scanning the room for Roddy Boyd, and at last, when she was dancing with Farquhard Campbell, they happened to finish a strathspey just at the point where Roddy and Kate were stationed. The two were obviously friends.

'I see you commandeered our guest of honour first, Farquhard. My turn next.'

'And I may dance with you, Kate?'

Kate nodded and they drifted off, but not before Flora had felt the chill of Roddy's wife's demeanour. She had scarcely acknowledged Flora's presence, confirming afresh the tacit antipathy Flora had sensed on the occasion of their first meeting on Front Street.

Roddy had noticed the coldness too – so much so that he felt the need to apologise for Kate.

'I had better explain my wife's acerbity, Flora. I had assured her that she need not come if she harboured such resentment, but she hates to miss those occasions. Fears that I may stray from her, maybe.'

He gave a humourless little laugh then, and added quickly, 'But I assure you 'tis a political, rather than a personal, grudge she bears you. See, there are two empty chairs. You don't mind if we sit out and talk?'

He then told her a tale that took her back in memory to the dark days of the '45, when nobody knew who was friend or foe, families were riven apart, and the streets of many a Scottish town ran with blood.

'I was a newly-qualified doctor living in Falkirk. You'll know it maybe, 'tis famous now for its foundry but in those days 'twas the Tryst that took folks there, that and the excellent ale. Kate was just a lass then, a servant in a lodging house on the High Street, and when the Jacobites came she fell in love with one of their lads, an Alastair MacDonald from Lochaber way. You'll remember the battle that January in '46, how the Jacobites won but things went sour on them afterwards? Well, this Alastair had much to do with it. Quite by accident he shot the young chief of the Glengarry MacDonalds, and though as he lay dying the young man begged forgiveness for his killer the clansmen insisted that the lad be punished. They dragged him through the town to the walls of Callendar House and shot him. His own father finished him off.'

Flora vaguely remembered hearing about the incident. She had twice passed through Falkirk in the old days, on the way to Edinburgh. She visualised its Tolbooth and douce cobbled streets, smelt the reek of peat-fires and horse-dung, the pungent odour from the brewery and the sharp tang of leather from the tannery.

'And Kate? What happened to Kate?'

His face darkened. 'They would have harried her too, but I persuaded her to escape with me and find a new life in America. You see, I loved her already. She was real bonnie then, with her raven-black hair and violet eyes. Steadfast and loyal, too. I'd have done anything for her.'

He paused reminiscently for a moment, then added, 'I all but lost her on the voyage. She had fallen pregnant by the young MacDonald, and had never seen the ocean, far less sailed on it. I think that but for the babe coming – his babe – she would not have survived. That was what kept her going.'

'But you won her in the end?'

'Aye, but 'twas not all that easy. For the first two years she insisted that she represent herself as my housekeeper and the babe as the product of a previous marriage. She had gone through some kind of pagan ceremony with her Alastair, you see, linking hands across a burn and vowing eternal love, and she could not see me as a husband at all. Then one day, without warning, she came to me and announced herself ready. Said people were talking and it would be better for my reputation if we wed. That was when we decided to move south, first to Pennsylvania and then down here. Tracts were cheap then. You could take up six hundred and forty acres with a mansion house for £160, and the quit rents were risibly low compared with those in Pennsylvania or Virginia. Besides, the flora and fauna of these new-found lands fascinated me.'

'And you've been happy?'

A little frown of puzzlement creased his forehead, as if the question was one he had scarcely confronted before and had to consider carefully.

'True happiness is fleeting and given to few. At first, around the time our Jenny was born, we enjoyed being together. But other passions than love of me soon began to consume my Kate. She adored her son. She became passionately interested in the cause of American patriotism. And that last interest is where you come in, Flora. She hates the very idea of kings because had Charles Edward Stuart refused to sanction the execution her Alastair might not have died.'

'She has nursed this animosity all these years? Even in a distant land, with a good kind husband and a host of blessings to thank God for?'

'Aye. She has learnt to read, and devours every tiny item she can find that concerns the Young Chevalier. She can tell you every detail of his amours, follows the sad peregrinations of Clementina Walkinshaw and her daughter Charlotte, could probably tell you the exact whereabouts of the poor dissipated adventurer right now, whether he be in London or Paris, Florence or Rome. She will not rest until he is in his grave, and even then she will find others to castigate, who have once embraced his cause.'

Flora needed no prompting. 'Like me,' she said simply. 'But surely she knows that all that is behind us now, that times have changed? Why, look at this gala reception! Would they deck this hall out in tartan if Jacobitism were still a valid political alternative? And as for me, I cannot afford to indulge in sentimental memories. My husband has aye been for the King.'

Roddy gave her a quizzical look then and for the first time since they had sat down she fancied his attention wandered. Had she said the wrong thing? She certainly felt that the mood of intimacy had been broken and it was as if Roddy feared that he had confided too much. Oh well, she thought, be that as it may. This is a strange place to choose for the telling of secrets anyway but he must have wanted me to know them, and they certainly explain much.

Right at that juncture a little group of men came over to be introduced. They were all middle-aged, all impeccably dressed in lace-trimmed brocade and powdered wigs, but they might just conceivably have spent overlong around the punchbowl, for their movements seemed exaggeratedly careful and their voices a shade overloud.

'Ah, the magnificent Mistress MacDonald! Charmed I'm sure! You are every bit as delectable as I was led to believe!'

She was aware then of a tall dandified figure towering above her and wet lips slobbering over her hand. A pair of lascivious green eyes probed the cleavage at her breasts and for a moment she half expected two groping fingers to follow the gaze and divest her of her bodice. Quick as a flash she realised who this must be. Bob Howe. The man who ate women for breakfast.

And she was right. 'Bob Howe, at your service,' an oily, suggestive voice was saying, 'And this is John Rutherford. He's our collector of quit-rents. Has his finger in other pies too, of course. We're all agog to see the improvements he makes when he takes over his new estate at Hunthill.'

The fellow he referred to looked uncertainly at Flora and smilingly extended a hand. For some reason she could not quite define she felt sorry for him.

'John's a bit deaf,' Howe explained, and then turned to the last man. 'And this here's Bob Schaw of Schawfield, my brother-in-law. Married now to my brother Job's widow.'

The man he indicated struck Flora as the most sympathetic of the three. He was self-possessed without being flashy and did not obviously put himself out to impress. He was laughing as he greeted her and said, pointedly though seemingly without rancour, 'What Bob omits to say is that I'm John's brother-in-law too. My first wife was a Rutherford.'

This gave Flora her cue. Pretending confusion she clapped a hand to her forehead and protested, 'Please, gentlemen, remember I'm new here. It will take time to work out all those complicated family relationships. Why, 'tis almost as bad as threading the maze of clan kinship at home!'

All the time she was telling herself that doubtless there would be undercurrents of animosity among those three, given connections by marriage and, most probably, political differences:

for had she not heard somewhere that Howe was a prominent rebel, while Rutherford was sure to be a loyalist? She would have to tread warily, and was wondering what to say next when much to her relief Allan joined them and after exchanging a few pleasantries with the trio claimed her for a contre-dance.

They managed a certain amount of disjointed conversation, interrupted though it inevitably was by the separations the patterns of the dance demanded, and Flora was glad to see that Allan's mood had mellowed since they had last danced together.

'See. Over there. The Rachel wench. Still setting her cap at Sandy, I'll warrant.'

They had spun round until Flora was facing in the direction Allan had indicated and for a brief moment she had a good view of Rachel, standing flushed and triumphant in the midst of a circle of admiring young local men. Her mane of long reddish hair outshone even the garish scarlet and silver of her dress, and as her gaze fleetingly met Flora's she let out a whoop of raucous laughter that was audible even above the music of the fiddles and the buzz of conversation. No doubt but she was relishing being the centre of male attention.

But Flora very much doubted that her performance was having any effect on Sandy, if indeed it was calculated to attract his interest, for Sandy's whole attention was focussed on the girl at his side. A very different kind of girl, tall, with well-formed but delicate features and a high forehead, and wearing a low-cut gown that emphasised the length of her neck and the graceful slope of her shoulders. Flora just had time to identify Jenny before she was whirled off again into another figure of the reel that necessitated her turning her back on the young folk.

But at the first opportunity she glanced over again and this time there was no mistaking the pair's rapturous absorption in one another. Sandy was gazing at Jenny as if she had just descended from heaven trailing clouds of glory, and Flora could only endorse his awe. For a moment she found herself wondering if Jenny was purposely presenting herself as a foil to Rachel – why, otherwise, the virginally white dress with its discreet touches of yellow, the long dangling amber ear-rings, the simply-coiffed swirling loops of hair and the pale powdered skin? – but whether intentional or not the effect on Sandy was obvious. He was irrevocably smitten.

And Flora knew her son well enough to realise that this would be no mere meaningless flirtation like the Peggy McKinnon episode on Skye. She felt a smug maternal smile come on. She could think of no more suitable match for Sandy, than that he should marry Roddy Boyd's daughter.

'Better join our hosts again. We've been neglectful of them,' Allan announced as the reel ended, and they betook themselves breathlessly to the alcove where the Martins were sitting with Farquhard Campbell.

'Ah, Kingsburgh, we were just talking about you,' Josiah Martin said jovially. 'Your contribution to this conversation will be more than welcome.'

Flora noticed the Governor's use of Allan's home title, noticed too that Farquhard was frowning, and wondered what they had been talking about. Politics, she supposed, and felt herself shiver involuntarily.

Elizabeth Martin's small talk was almost insultingly polite and undemanding, so that Flora was able to respond without missing much of what the men were saying. Yes, she had been right about the burden of their discussion, and from the heatedness with which they were resuming their argument it would appear to be already well advanced.

'I'm warning you, Josiah,' Farquhard was saying. 'Those trade restrictions will undoubtedly go through. Every port will be closed. It's going to mean a lot of hardship, both here and among the merchants back in England, and may even lead to violence, but some of us see it as the only way. Harnett and Hooper particularly. You'll notice none of the rebel leaders are here tonight? Surprising that Howe's here. I'd have expected him to stay away too.'

His voice was calm and certain, with an edge of threat to it. Again Flora felt that Farquhard did not dislike Martin, only found his smugness exasperating and longed to puncture it. And from the reaction his speech elicited he was little short of achieving his goal, for while Farquhard sat back unperturbed and appreciatively drained another glass of usquebaugh Martin's face turned a deeper shade of purple. Flora wondered if he were about to succumb to a bout of apoplexy.

'Fools!' The words came spluttering out. 'They'll stop trade altogether! They're cutting off their nose to spite their face! Given the trade they'd make enough money to pay the taxes and never feel it!'

To which response Farquhard smiled condescendingly and said levelly, seeming to relish his self-appointed post as devil's advocate, 'But you still don't understand our point, Josiah. There's a principle at stake here. Why should all our exports and imports be directed through Britain, even if it's a European country we're dealing with? Why should we have to pay high duty and handling charges on goods coming into America, when our counterparts in England are free of them? It just isn't fair, man, and you must know it!'

But Martin remained testy. For the first time he included Allan in the argument. Turning to him he said pedantically, 'What our friend Master Campbell really means, of course, is that Caswell and Hooper and Harnett and their like are not simply agitating for local authority and representation. They would go the whole way and demand complete independence from Britain. Believe me, sir, I have worked my fingers to the bone in an effort to meet their demands, as far as English law and and royal prerogative will allow, but those hotheads refuse to compromise and now there's scarcely a court functioning properly! As for you, Farquhard, I had counted you a friend, but 'twould seem from your words that you are one of those firebrand self-styled patriots!'

'No indeed, sir!' Campbell expostulated, furious at last. 'But I am not so blinkered by prejudice that I don't see their point of view! If judges and clerks are not enforcing the law justly then 'tis better to do away with them. And every new tax brings outright war the closer. Right now the colonies are loyal, just as I swear I am, but that can change overnight. Is it anarchy you want, friend?'

The veins were protruding in Martin's forehead now. ''Tis treason you speak, Farquhard! I had always thought that we understood one another, worked towards the same goals, but your words proclaim you a rebel! Believe me, you'll suffer for this!'

The answer came back, sorrowful rather than defiant. 'Do not be threatening me, my friend, nor telling me what to think. You know what I stand to lose if I cut myself off from my home country. But if folks like me see justice in the colonists' cause then 'tis time to take heed and put matters right before it is too late.'

Listening with more than half an ear, Flora fully expected the debate to end in fisticuffs. She was glad that Allan had declined to get involved; he had just sat quietly listening, a look of intense concern on his face. But greatly to her surprise Farquhard got up, snatched up his cloak and stretched out a conciliatory hand to the Governor.

'But I must away. I have an early start in the morning. I did not come to harangue you, Josiah, but only to warn. The committees are still willing to negotiate but their patience is beginning to run out. Thank you however for a most enjoyable evening. No hard feelings, I assure you.'

For a moment Flora wondered whether Martin was going to repudiate the overture, for she suspected he was the kind who would easily take offence and lapse into a sulk, but amazingly his anger had melted.

'Damn you Farquhard,' he spluttered, 'You're going to get into big trouble one of these days, speaking as you do to those that represent the King. Already they're bidding me watch out for you, man. But yes, we're friends regardless and for that I'm grateful.'

Exuding bonhomie Farquhard came over to the ladies then and bowed gallantly.

'Elizabeth. Flora. My compliments to both of you. Your graceful company has cheered us all.'

He bent to deposit a social kiss on Flora's cheek and she was almost sure she detected a wink. But at the same time she knew that Campbell's observations were not frivolously meant. Nor was he a deliberate mischief-maker. Her respect for him soared, yet even as she admired his restraint she could not help wondering what side he would favour should it ever come to war.

Clearly Allan was wondering too. 'Things are that bad among the colonists?' she heard him ask. 'There are some that would countenance open war with Britain?'

But Martin dismissed the query almost lightheartedly. 'To hear Farquhard speak, you'd think the country was bristling with hotheads, but he exaggerates. I assure you, sir, that if I were to raise the standard tomorrow ninety per cent of the Carolinians would rally to fight for the King. That assumes you and your Highlanders, of course…'

'Of course. There would be no question of us holding back, should we be needed.'

The pledge was firm. Hearing it, Flora's first reaction was pride in her husband's unqualified loyalty, but this gave way to the old familiar stab of fear, and that was the emotion that stayed with her for the remaining hours of that memorable evening. Most of all the suspicion niggled that the reception, while ostensibly in her honour, might also have served to get the region's most prominent citizens together and gauge their allegiance. Perhaps that 'Of course' of Allan's had been more important to Josiah Martin than all the lip-service obeisance to an ageing Highland heroine. Was the Governor far more subtle then than she had given him credit for? Perhaps so. But there, she was being cynical. She must take people as she found them, and all she had experienced at those folks' hands was kindness and respect. As for their quarrels, they were not her business, nor Allan's. Farquhard Campbell had counselled her to stay aloof from them and her whole instinct prompted her to take his advice.

VIII

November 1774

'You're sure you feel up to the journey, Florrie? We could stay a few days longer if you want to. Bob Hogg would have us here for ever but I really think we ought to go. They say there will be a sudden change in the weather now that it's November, and the further west we travel, towards higher ground, the more chance there is of frost. Besides, Annabella and Alexander and Hugh will be impatient, not to mention Anne and Jamie.'

Flora was quick to agree. Kind and hospitable though these Wilmington folks were they were not her own people. 'When do you want to leave? And do we go overland, or by river?'

'Tomorrow. There's no point in delay. And I've decided to go overland. I've seen two fine horses for sale, a big bay stallion and a chestnut mare, that will be perfect for me and Sandy. I know we'll have to think about a horse for you too but better you should be driven meantime. You're still not quite over that fever and I'm told the roads are far from easy. Bob Hogg has offered us the use of his carriage and pair. Says his brother James who runs their store at Cross Creek will arrange for them to be brought back: there are constant comings and goings, it seems, for all the two towns are a hundred miles apart.'

'A hundred miles! It's that far!'

'Aye, but 'tis a road much used. And we've travelled that far before. 'Tis the same distance from Falkirk to Oban you know. Remember 'twas nothing for you to journey from London to Edinburgh, in the old days.'

Flora's heart quailed. England and the Scottish border country were not covered in impenetrable forest. How many miles could they cover in a day? Ten? Fifteen? Certainly no more. But she sensed that Allan's mind was made up and his arrangements finalised. He was not consulting her but simply informing her of a fait accompli. So she bit back her reservations. After all, she thought, I should be glad that Allan is organising things again after years of indecision.

'The Boyds will be going home by boat but Roddy has offered us two of his best slaves as guides. Evidently they're called Hannibal and Scipio. Did you ever hear such ridiculous names? And Bob Schaw says he'll arrange protection for us beyond Schawfield. He may even come on to Cross Creek with us.'

'Protection? Are there highwaymen here then?' Flora felt a twinge of apprehension.

'No, Florrie. I don't think we have to worry about that. The odd outlaw or runaway slave, maybe, but it seems there are too few travellers to make highway robbery pay. No, it isn't human beings we have to fear. It's animals, more like. Bears and wolves and snakes. That's why we have to try to find some place to lay our heads at night, even if it's just an isolated log cabin. The area's settled enough, you see, but there are no towns at all and the country's deeply forested. And it's amazingly easy to get lost, I'm told, even if you think you're familiar with the road.'

'Are you trying to scare me, Allan? Maybe we should go by the river after all!'

'No, Florrie. I've made up my mind. The land journey won't take so long and we can trust Bob Schaw to see us right.'

* * *

They set out at dawn next morning, Bob Schaw and his man-servant Fergus McCallum riding ahead with their little equipage of slaves and the MacDonald party following. It was almost dark under the pines. A white wispy mist hung phantom-like over the swampy ground and curled around the tree-trunks. The air felt dank and smelt mouldy, and Flora drew her cloak more closely around her, conscious as much of the eeriness as of the chilly temperature.

Stella was shivering. 'Dat cold gwine freeze ma bones, ma'am. Us niggers cain't abide de cold. Ah wish Ah dinn have to go back to dat Cross Creek. De winters dere no use for niggers.'

The girl's complaints nagged on, a persistent monotone, until Flora could stand it no longer. 'Then you'll just have to work harder and get a good heat up,' she snapped.

Stella's lip trembled. 'Ah wants ma mammy!' she whimpered. 'You done be as cruel as Massah Campbell's overseer to us poor nigger folks!' And she lapsed into a sulking silence which Flora made no effort to break. She preferred her own thoughts to the girl's carping and anyway the rumble of the carriage wheels made conversation difficult even if she had wanted to talk.

For the first few miles beyond Wilmington the track was wide and well worn. Every so often Bob Schaw would stop by the carriage and refer to some plantation or sawmill nearby. 'Tom McKnight has land over yonder, by the river,' he would say. Or 'We're not far from the McLean place.' Flora found this assurance of human habitation very comforting because as the hours passed the road became more marshy and the canopy of pines more thickly interwoven, so that sometimes they could scarcely glimpse the sky.

They crossed innumerable creeks and were always aware of their proximity to the river.

'Now you can see why we want to do this journey in dry weather,' Bob commented. 'After rain some of these creeks are impassable and the morasses that seem bottomless at the best of times are truly treacherous. It wasn't easy getting the road through here, I can tell you.'

Flora looked out at that point and saw only a wide expanse of bog with ghostly cypress trees growing out of it. She realised then that the carriage was lumbering across a most precarious surface. The road, which Bob referred to as 'the causey' seemed to consist only of a series of logs laid lengthwise and covered with brushwood, the whole bound together with earth. It was a scene of utter desolation, every bit as alien to her as the river journey from the coast had been.

Perhaps Bob Schaw sensed her dismay, for no sooner had they negotiated that section than he pointed over to the right and called in to them. 'There's a good clearing over there, down where the river widens. We can stop there for a rest and a bite to eat. I'll tell McCallum to go on ahead and get the food ready.'

The sudden, searingly hot sun dazzled their eyes when they emerged from the forest and found themselves overlooking a little beach of sparkling white pebbles. The river bickered shallowly towards the stream's centre in a confusion of wavelets and then lay still and deep on the other side beneath a solid wall of pines, and Flora's heart lifted at the sight of it. There were grassy verges here where they could rest, and rocky outcrops to break the monotony of evergreens, black moss and vines. All Flora wanted right then was to get out of the carriage, take off her pattens and stockings, and feel the cool water trickle around her toes.

But no sooner had she alighted than she heard screams coming from the river bank and Allan rode up, panic-stricken. 'Better get back in. They disturbed an alligator down there. A fiendish brute. It has already attacked one of the slaves who deliberately provoked it.'

Fear and curiosity fought within her but only for a moment. With her, curiosity always won. 'Do you think I'd miss seeing an alligator? What kind of coward do you take me for?'

At this Allan only shrugged and she followed him, her heart pounding. Just to think that she had planned to paddle in that very spot!

Bob Schaw had armed himself with a stout pine branch and was standing by, ready to react if the beast came his way. 'Stand back!' he cautioned. 'We have quite a fight on our hands here. This one's an adult and really strong! See what it has done to that nigger lad!'

Flora saw the boy being carried from the scene. He couldn't have been much more than sixteen and she thought she recognised him as one of Roddy's slaves. Her immediate instinct was to run and offer help.

'Fetch some whisky, Stella! Quick! And a darning needle and some thread, or better still some thin twine. And we'll need some fresh linen if you can find it. Hurry, girl! Don't just stand there!'

The boy slave was clearly in shock. He was shaking violently and his eyes were rolling in his head, their whites round and prominent in the blue-black face. Blood was pouring from his injured thigh, from a ragged gash some six inches long. The whole limb looked to have been ferociously mauled. Flora looked over at the offending alligator and shuddered. The beast was at least fifteen feet long from the tip of its snout to the flexible, flailing tail, and its powerful arms must have been six feet in length. She had heard tales about such primeval monsters – legend had it that something of the kind inhabited Loch Ness – but here was the grim reality. She gazed in horrified fascination at the great blood-stained claws, the wild protruding eyes and wide, voracious jaws. There was a strong, sickening smell of musk and blood.

Then she realised that Sandy was in the thick of the fray. Far from being terror-stricken he seemed to relish the challenge. He had joined Bob's slaves and two older white men who had been rafting a cargo of grain down the river and seemed to know exactly what to do. They waited until the creature's jaws opened wide and then thrust an oar down its throat, choking it and rendering its teeth powerless. Then skilfully avoiding its frantically waving arms they thrust a knife into its throat. The beast twitched violently for a few tortured seconds and then was still.

Bob Schaw was jubilant. 'Good work, that. 'Gators are hard to kill. Many's the time we've been scared to tackle them, when we've found them taking our geese. It's that coat of mail, you see. They've got complete protection save for their eyes, and those soft bits under the throat and belly. You have to get at 'em there or they'll get you. God's most vicious creatures, the 'gators, and no mistake. My, that's a strong lad you've got there, that Sandy. He was fearless. Like Saint George and the dragon, eh?'

Flora laughed shakily. She was glad of Bob's nervous chatter: it kept her mind off what she had seen and the grizzly task presently to hand, of binding up the boy's wound. He was still decidedly groggy and lay writhing on the ground in a pool of blood, the gash on his leg more bruised and ugly by the minute. She frantically went through her mental list of herbal treatments, trying to remember what was appropriate to apply to wounds of this nature. Pennyroyal. St John's wort. Garlic. Angelica and thyme and wood sorrel. But even if she could recall which herb to use it was most unlikely that any of them grew in the Carolinas at this time of year, far less in this forest wilderness. Leeches would help if she could apply them to the bruises while they were still fresh, but though the creeks were doubtless teeming with the creatures it would take time to gather them and the boy needed attention now.

Then a breeze blew a pungent whiff of mint in her direction and she turned urgently to Stella who had just come back with a needle, some twine, and a bag of rags that Flora kept for menstrual emergencies.

'Go into the woods and fetch some stone root, the plant they call heal-all. Mistress Hogg told me of its properties. Just enough to put over the wound before I bind it. Why do you hesitate, girl? Go!'

But Stella was standing petrified. 'Ah's not venturin' alone into no forest. No ma'am. Dere be bears an' snakes dere, an' abter what Ah jes seen Ah too scared to move.'

'Do what I say!' Flora was sorely tempted to lash out at the girl in a fury of exasperation when Sandy appeared, his face flushed and jubilant.

'Can I help, Ma?'

'Aye. I think some heal-all would benefit this wound. See what you can find, son. 'Tis like mint at home, but taller, and has large greenish-yellow flowers. A handful will do. They say it grows in moist woodlands, and while 'tis late in the year I've no doubt there will yet be some growing.'

He turned to go then but not before Stella had attempted to work her most blatant wiles upon him. Her hand curved gracefully upwards to smooth her hair. Her gaze scanned him appreciatively, pointedly dwelling, as it journeyed from head to foot, on the neat bulge at his crotch. Then she smiled a slow, suggestive smile.

'You be a real gentleman, Massah Sandy. Maybe Ah go in de woods wid you, help find de plant. Ah knows it well, an' Ah not be afeared ib you be dere wid me. No sah.'

The lazy, insinuating drawl infuriated Flora, all the more so because her anger was tinged with an indefinable dread. She knew how personable Sandy was. It was natural that every girl would respond to his gallantry, his openness and bluff, outdoor looks, but here in America temptation stalked him at every turn, and not just among his own kind. She had already heard of the flagrant liaisons involving white masters and their slaves. People here even seemed to condone them, seeing the inevitable pregnancies they occasioned as a way of increasing slave ownership. Oh what had possessed her, to acquire this incorrigibly wanton creature?

So she found herself reaching out, grabbing Stella by the shoulder of her shift and forcibly restraining her on the spot.

'You'll stay right here, you shameless little hussy you, and help me stitch up this leg!'

She bent to her task then. She carefully lifted the flap of flesh that the alligator's claws had severed, cleaned off the blood with fresh water from the river and then bathed the fiery wound with brandy-wine. Then she began the grisly business of stitching – a procedure she had never undertaken in her life but which was clearly crying out to be done.

The boy's huge brown eyes were suffused with terror. 'Ah gwine gonna die! Dat 'gator be de debbil come to git me!' And he gazed horrified as Flora worked.

'Nonsense! The beast's dead. See, over yonder. They've killed it. There's nothing to fear. Now turn your head away and grit your teeth. Be brave. Tell me, what's your name?'

'Hannibal. Ah be Doctor Boyd's stable boy. An' Ah sure scared he'll punish me for teasin' dat 'gator, when he hears. Me an' Scipio, we jes playin' wid it, an' it lashed out…'

'Yes, that was foolish but I don't think Doctor Boyd will punish you. You've been punished enough.'

Sandy had come back with a little bundle of greenery. She stripped away the tenderest leaves and applied them to the newly-stitched wound before firmly wrapping the linen round it. 'There, that's the bandage on. Let Scipio and my son here carry you over to the carriage. You can travel with me and Stella here.'

The boy's eyes widened even further. 'Wid you, ma'am? In dat carriage dere? But Ah be jes a poo nigger boy. Ah not eben a house slave. Ah cain't ride wid you in no carriage!'

'Don't quibble!' And she bade Stella sit and watch over the boy – a task which the girl seemed all too ready to undertake. Flora smiled wryly to herself. So obviously Stella's tastes in men were catholic and undiscriminating. Perhaps she had not set her cap specifically at Sandy after all. Maybe anything in breeches would do. And she had noticed as she bound Hannibal's leg that he was clean-limbed and muscular: if she sensed this strong animal attraction how much more must Stella, who was partly of his own race and doubtless responded not just to his looks but to his smell and all the other subtle sexual signals that flash back and forth between young people?

She shook her head in wonderment at the ways of love and fervently hoped that Stella would content herself with her own kind and leave Sandy alone.

Relaxation was the last thing in everyone's mind now, shaken as they all were by their recent ordeal. A quick bread-and-cheese lunch, some ale and the little procession was off again, trundling along the twilit path through the pines.

'No distance to Schawfield now, Flora,' Bob said at length, poking his head through the carriage window. 'And I hope you've thanked Mistress MacDonald for mending you, Hannibal. Most fortunate we had her here. Next best thing to a surgeon, a woman who's a healer.'

He added that they would keep Hannibal at Schawfield until Roddy arranged for his transfer to the Mumrills. He had asked those fellows on the grain barge to look out for the Boyds on the river and ask them to make a point of breaking their journey with the Schaws – which he had already invited them to do anyway. They might well be here as early as the morrow. That way the boy would get proper medical attention and could also be with his master again.

It was growing dark when they reached Bob's plantation and the oil lamps and candles were already lit, their glow welcoming them as they approached. Flora was aware of a large plain facade surrounded by different species of deciduous trees. The leaves were beginning to fall, making a bright red carpet on the ground. Mulberry? Liveoak? Dogwood? Maple? They were all new names to her, but she had seen them growing in the Wilmington gardens and had marvelled at their vivid autumn colours.

Anne Schaw, Bob's second wife, struck Flora as a strong-willed person who was accustomed to getting all her own way. Of course, Flora remembered charitably, she had been married previously

to a Howe, and in view of that one must be prepared to forgive
her much, poor thing. Then she also had a new baby, little
Alexander, who, she maintained, demanded total attention at all
hours of the day and night.

When Flora observed, by way of making polite conversation,
that the garden's evening scents were a tonic in themselves after
the dank fungoid forest, Anne gave her a sceptical look.

'That's as may be, now, Miz MacDonald, hon, but you oughta
smell it when the rice is ripe. Bob has much of our land in rice,
and you never did smell such a putrid stench. No sirree. I jes
couldn't wait to get away, this year. The babe was a'movin' in me,
and what with the heat and the flies and the stink I was sick to my
stomick every goddamn morning. Just as well Bob bought a passel
of land down on the sand. All our friends go down there then: the
Howes and the Hoopers and the Lillingtons. You get breezes from
the sea but no big winds cos it's well protected inside the islands.
I was all set to stay but I guess it ain't so desirable in the winter.
All the quality folks are back at their plantations come the fall an'
it gits powerful lonely.'

A farmer himself, Allan was naturally curious about land
clearance and drainage, methods of cultivation and the availability
of farm workers. Bob promised that he would take him on a tour
of inspection of the slave quarters and outhouses in the morning.
He explained that he had come late to farming – he was forty-four
– after years spent developing the mercantile business of Schaw
and Ancrum's. But he had craved the outdoor life, and many of
his friends, people like William Dry and Roddy Boyd, had also
bought plantations after becoming established in their respective
callings. They saw themselves now as gentlemen farmers rather
than as shopkeepers, lawyers or doctors.

The tour around the Schawfield policies next morning was
necessarily short because Bob had an acquaintance in mind, some
ten miles north, who would house them that night: so it was decided
that Allan would be shown the sawmill, smithy and barns while
Flora saw the domestic arrangements.

'Come first to the kitchen,' Anne volunteered, and led Flora
along a covered walk-way to a separate building. 'My cook Lavinia
won't like it – she maintains that for a mistress to enter the kitchen
is low taste – but we'll butter her up with compliments.'

'You never cook yourself?'

Anne looked at her in horror. 'Fegs, no! Supervising takes time enough. I oversee the food and sometimes enjoy putting up pickles or making special pies. Then there's the dairy, the poultry yard and the vegetable garden, not to mention the seamstresses. All on top of a husband and family! No, there's no time to cook. The kitchen is Lavinia's sphere.'

And it proved to be quite a domain, a vast pine-lined room with an open timbered ceiling and a window in the gable end. A great brick fireplace spanned by an oak lintel took up the whole of one wall, and the chimney-piece accommodated two large hooks on which the hind quarters of calves and pigs had been hung to smoke. There were sinks, a large Carron stove, a pine table in the centre and various side counters, racks for pots and pans, and all kinds of pestles and mortars, mixing bowls and utensils. Sacks of potatoes lay around, there were bunches of pungently-smelling herbs and some brightly-coloured gourds that Anne described as 'squash'.

Lavinia herself seemed imperturbable. A huge, indigo-coloured negress in a turban, she was somehow managing to rule her domain while feeding two babies, her own at one overflowing breast and her mistress's at the other. Anne just nodded perfunctorily in her direction and the woman's acknowledgement was a mere murmured 'Mornin', ma'am'.

Although Flora thought that she and Allan had been up early the life of the kitchen had been going on for hours and female slaves of all shapes and sizes and degrees of duskiness were engaged in various tasks – chopping herbs and vegetables, plucking geese and duck, cutting venison into cubes for stew. Flora thought she detected a speeding-up of activity when the mistress entered. That fitted, if they were all as lazy as Stella.

'You done your duties, Matilda?' This from Anne to a scared-looking child who stood open-mouthed in the corner.

'Yesm... Ah be up at three. Ah done water de hosses an' slop de hogs. De slop buckets wus heavy an' Ah had a heap of wuck dat wus hard ter do, but Ah milk de cows, an' den Ah git back to de house an' git de breakfast.'

This occasioned a disbelieving snort from Lavinia, the presiding genius of the place.

'Dat be rubbish yo talkin', Matilda MacKenzie! Ah's a good

mind to wash out yo mouth wid salt an' water, for de lies you tell!'
And she turned to Anne. 'De gal done do no such thing, Ma'am.
She jes peeved at bein' got up early. We gonna be busy today,
renderin' de lard from de hogs dat Samuel killt. Den we have dat
lye dere to drain an' boil.'

She pointed to a barrel in the corner and Anne said proudly,
'We make our own soap here. I insist upon it, even if Bob could
bring ready-made Irish stuff from the shop.'

They then went to the laundry, where washerwomen were
busily at work in an enervating steamy atmosphere. Flora stared
aghast when a slave tossed a pile of assorted clothes into the huge
copper without first sorting them for colour or fabric. Bed and
table linen, muslins and cambrics, whites and checks and florals
were all bundled in together and a wench was bidden stir the load
with a hickory battling stick until the water boiled up. Another
copper was being emptied: the clothes were simply taken out,
squeezed, and carried off to be thrown on the pales to dry.

'You don't use blue, or bleach?' Flora was a meticulous
laundress and could not understand why the colonials grew indigo
and did not use it in their wash.

Anne Schaw tossed her head. 'That's an English idea. We here,
we leave it to the slaves to decide.'

Clearly Anne saw herself as a kind of chatelaine or Mother
Superior, a gracious protectress of her little enclave of slaves, yet
she was determined to eschew many of the agricultural routines
that Flora took for granted. When they inspected the vegetable
garden Flora asked innocently whether they used chicken dung
for fertiliser.

Anne threw up her hands in horror. 'And eat squash that has
grown through dirt?'

Gradually it was borne in on Flora that Anne Schaw, and
perhaps her husband also, though in his case it was not so blatantly
obvious, belonged to the Dry-and-Quince school. Her mind was
closed to anything she saw, absurdly, as even remotely English and
royalist. She was a bundle of prejudice. So Flora remained
diplomatically silent as they toured the slave quarters, a collection
of mean huts with sharply pointed thatched roofs where naked
black children played among the rootling hogs and scrabbling
chickens.

She was acutely, intuitively conscious of being fundamentally different in outlook from these people. She sensed a conspiracy to stay hospitable and polite but to keep one's counsel on political matters. It had been the same with the Drys and the Quinces, Kate Boyd and perhaps even Farquhard Campbell. All of them, she was convinced, were aligned against Governor Martin and the British King George. But when she tentatively voiced these fears to Allan he pooh-poohed them, determined she knew to ignore the whole controversy as irrelevant.

"'Tis all in your imagination, Florrie. And anyway, I'm assured that folks are less interested in politics the further we go from the Tidewater area. We're going to our own folks, Florrie! They're nearly all Highlanders in Cross Creek, and they say there must be ten thousand of us in Cumberland and Anson Counties alone! Come, forget it! We have far more important things on our minds, like finding land and building a house, and being prosperous again! Then we can arrange for Fanny and maybe Johnny to come over and join us...'

Flora could not hold back the sigh that escaped her then. All through these past weeks, preoccupied though she had been by the dangers of the voyage and this fascinating new land and its people, the children they had abandoned had never been far from her mind.

'Oh, Allan, how fervently I pray that you are right, for only the Almighty can guide us now.'

PART THREE

I

November 1774

Eight days it had been. Eight days of fording stagnant creeks and sloshing through swamps, always under that monotonous canopy of long-leaf pine. The treacherous mud had not only made the surface slippery: it had also hidden holes and fallen tree branches, making the going doubly difficult for the horses, whose hocks, bellies and heads were so spattered with muck that it was hard to tell the chestnuts from the bays. Twice the carriage had got bogged down, its wheels caught as in a vice, and it had taken all the men's strength to dislodge it. On those occasions Flora had almost succumbed to despair, and had found herself doubting Allan's judgement in deciding against river transport. But then surely Bob knew what he was doing, and there were always the alligators... She shuddered, remembering.

Most nights they had found shelter in some remote forest shack where the woodsman had been glad of the company and a silver Spanish dollar in payment. But one night they had not been so fortunate and had had to sleep outside. Flora and Stella had huddled in the carriage while the men had lit fires, cooked a possum stew (a new taste experience) and taken turns at keeping watch through the hours of darkness. Flora had slept very little. Owls had hooted and wolves had howled. She had imagined – was it really just imagination? – that feral yellow eyes had surrounded their camp, curious and malevolent. She had greeted the first tentative rays of dawn with huge relief, and had been glad to be on the road again, if road it could be called.

But gradually, around the sixth day, the going had become easier and Bob had confirmed that the worst of the forest was behind them. They were nearing the gentle hilly uplands of the Piedmont now, and could expect more varied, less austere scenery. And sure enough the whole colour palette of the landscape was

changing. Flora gazed entranced at the new trees they encountered, not uniformly dismal like the pines but vividly clothed in
blazing polychromatic reds.

'What is that tree there, the deep crimson one?'

'Ah, that's sourwood. And the one beside it, the yellow one, is
the sweet gum. You don't have them in Scotland. Nor the swamp
maple yonder, that's maybe the brightest of them all. Of course,
we do have oaks and elms and chestnuts. Not every tree will be
new to you.'

Bob left them for a few minutes and returned with a bag of nuts:
hickories and black walnuts and hazels. 'No one need go hungry
in the fall, in this country. It's a very Canaan at this time of year.'

Nor did they feel so isolated now. Indeed the road felt almost
busy. They met drovers with herds of cattle – fat, healthy animals
with the long, sharp-pointed horns, short legs and thick curly hair
of the home breeds. As the MacDonald convoy drew up under
the trees to let them pass, the drovers leaping around and shouting
to the beasts in Gaelic, Allan rode alongside the carriage and Flora
felt a pang of sympathy, seeing the look of longing on his face.

'Look at them, Florrie! They must be twice the size of our Kylies!
To think I might one day have a herd like that!'

Bob Schaw smiled proprietorially. 'No reason why you
shouldn't. A man with your experience will soon build up a herd,
once you've found your piece of land and cleared it. We have ideal
cattle country here. No wonder the animals thrive, with our open
grazing and wholesome Indian corn. Why, 'tis even said that old
Dan Paterson the piper once drove a cow to Charleston that
weighed all of a thousand pounds! Hard to believe but I guess it's
possible.'

He went on to explain that in these parts the Highlanders
almost had the monopoly in cattle-rearing, whereas the longer-
established colonials inclined to hog farming. It all depended on
what you knew more about.

Allan's eyes still held that wistful, covetous gleam. Alexander
and Annabella's letters had mentioned the rich soil and the fine
herds but it was different, seeing it with one's own eyes.

'Which do they favour, beef or dairy cattle?'

'Beef, I'd say. They salt it and send it in barrels downriver. The
hides are much in demand too, of course, as are dairy products.

We don't make our own butter and cheese down on the Tidewater, you see – think the salt marshes give the milk a tainted taste. It's all in the feeding.'

Flora sensed Allan's enthusiasm now, knew that he could not wait to be working with cattle again, and his impatience seemed to infect the whole company. She imagined then that even the pack-horses had a new spring in their step.

Wagons stacked high with grain also became a familiar sight, and they frequently had difficulty staying on the road as vehicles manoeuvred alongside one another. Bob explained that Cross Creek, which was just over the hill, was fast growing into the most important trading and distribution centre in the area. In fact, it had now overtaken Charleston as the principal grain-collecting town for the Moravians.

'Moravians?'

'Aye. You'll meet hundreds of them in Cross Creek. They estimate they're getting forty or fifty Moravian wagons a day down there just now. They're Europeans like us, but from Germany, or maybe further east. Farm up Salem way and bring their wheat down here for shipment. Came originally from Pennsylvania, down the Yadkin Road. A methodical lot. Careful farmers. Protestant and very sober. Don't cause any trouble.'

The horses had settled into a steady trot and Flora relaxed, confident that the worst of the journey was over. She closed her eyes and was absorbed in a gentle daydream of Fanny when she heard Sandy's voice call out excitedly.

'Come quick, Ma! We can see Cross Creek!'

The carriage came to a halt and Flora alighted. She expected Stella to join her but the girl sat sulking, her face an emotionless mask.

'Come, Stella. Get out and stretch you legs! What ails you?'

The answer was a truculent humph. 'Ah done see enough ob dis Cross Creek place in ma time, Miz MacDonald. 'Taint ma favourite place. Ah don lik de country. Lik Wilmington better. Ah lub ter see de folks on de streets, an' ter walk 'long an' see de fine close dey wear.'

They had emerged on a gentle incline overlooking the valley of the Upper Cape Fear. Away to the north and west lay the dark folds of pine-clad hills, their uniform olive green throwing into relief the vivid red tints of the trees on the lower slopes, while below them, shouting their sunshine, stretched the golden-brown stubble fields of autumn, bordered now with piles of brilliant orange pumpkins and yellow squash. Through it all, like criss-crossing streaks of silver, ran innumerable creeks, and on a little bluff at the point where two of them met there stood a huddle of houses and mills.

'They say the creeks cross there without the currents mingling,' Bob laughed, and even from this distance they could hear a hum of activity in the air and sense the purposefulness and industry of the valley.

Flora felt a sigh of sheer delight escape her, and imagined it echoed by everyone there.

'Oh, Allan, isn't it beautiful! A land flowing with milk and honey, indeed!'

'And yonder will be Campbellton?' Allan was pointing to another, smaller conglomeration of buildings some mile and a half away, where the stream debouched into the main river.

'Aye. You'll notice that the two places seem to merge into one another, from this distance. That's mainly grist mills you see on the flat land between. It's ideal ground for them. That's where they convert the grain into flour and meal, before sending it downriver to Wilmington. But some six years ago the Colonial Association decreed that the site of Cross Creek was a mistake. They wanted to eliminate the haulage of goods over the swampy ground to the river, and so they declared Campbellton would be the seat of the Cumberland County Court, the capital of the area as it were. But of course it wasn't as simple as that. Cross Creek was established already and is still growing while Campbellton stands still. I guess the two places will become one eventually and then they won't be able to agree on a name. Something entirely new, if they have any sense. Maybe a name that none of us would ever dream of.'

Bob then sent one of his men on ahead to let the Cross Creek folks know they were coming and in what seemed like no time at all the scattered houses huddled together more closely, the track widened, and they were entering the little town. Flora got a fleeting impression of dirt, dust and the smell of whisky and horse. Unlike Wilmington Cross Creek had no illusions of grandeur. It was a bustling, frankly commercial town, conscious of its pioneering situation and proud of it. The houses and shops were all of wood and unashamedly utilitarian, with their long outside porches, swinging half-doors and plain shutters. Any paintwork they boasted was peeling and shabby. The roads were unpaved, and crowded with creaking drays and barrows laden with all kinds of merchandise – wood and glass and grain. Dogs and pigs and hens wandered around unchecked. There was scarcely a tree in sight. Her heart sank. Was this the town that had for so long beckoned like a distant Mecca, and had indeed looked so inviting from the hill up there? How could they have abandoned the douce cobbled streets of Portree for this squalid, Godforsaken hell-hole of a place?

But she had little time for such reflections. She was just thinking how incongruous it was to see the words 'Murdock MacLeod, Surgeon and Apothecary' on a shingle here when she was aware of people running towards them, and saw that their little party had become the focus of wild attention. The pipes skirled. Blue bonnets were tossed in the air. A hundred well-wishers shouted homely words of welcome in Gaelic. The press of people would have been intimidating had it not been so overwhelmingly friendly.

'Better get out and walk, Florrie,' Allan advised, and she found herself surrounded by a sea of familiar faces – familiar because she knew so many of them by sight, from her other life in Skye. She recognised the lineaments of their features, the colour of their hair and the shape of their heads, the timbre of their voices and the texture of their skins, as if they were bone of her bone and flesh of her flesh. That burly character there, the one with the red hair and ruddy face, just had to be a MacGregor or a MacNeil. The dark solid one there was a Morrison for sure, and yes, that curly-headed young fellow with the piercing blue eyes was so like her half-sister Flora's husband that he could not be other than a MacQueen!

But even as they crowded round Flora's eyes were searching their ranks for the faces of her very own, and when Annabella flung herself into her arms she completely forgot what a disappointment Cross Creek was as a town. Those two and a half years in America had clearly been kind to Annabella, turning her from an ill-nourished woman with the makings of a shrew into the healthy, rosy epitome of a happy Highland matron. Behind her, grinning broadly, stood her husband, Alexander of Cuidreach. It gladdened Flora beyond telling, the way he and Allan greeted one another. The cousins had always been close and here they were, together again at last.

Annabella and Alexander's fourteen-year-old son Donald was there too, standing apart a little with a shy smile on his freckled face. He had left Skye to join his parents only months before, yet in that time his shoulders had broadened and Flora sensed that his voice would have deepened too. He had been Fanny's favourite cousin, and Flora felt that familiar pang of guilt and regret. Why had Fanny had to suffer all those partings? They had behaved so cavalierly towards her, almost as if her feelings had counted for nothing, while there she was, sensitive and vulnerable and yes, probably as much in love with Donald as any nine-year-old could be. Oh what she would give to have Charles and Ranald and Fanny and Johnny here with them now!

As swiftly as those sobering thoughts ran through her mind she caught sight of Jamie standing a few feet away. So Anne had to be here as well! Sure enough, a moment later she was embracing her and the children. Holding her daughter away from her and searching her face she realised that this was a much happier, healthier Anne than the one who had left Wilmington less than two weeks before. And she could have sworn she was bigger too. How long did she have to go? Until March? Why, that was only four months!

'And Hugh?' She looked around, scanning the crowd for her stepfather's tall, commanding presence.

'You'll see him up at Mount Pleasant. Alexander went up to Cheek's Creek to fetch him and he's waiting for you. But his farm's a long way off – fifty miles from Mount Pleasant, and that's twenty miles from here – and 'twas just too far for him to travel. He's not so agile now, though hale enough. I fear you'll see a difference in him, Flora. His hair has gone white and he isn't as straight-backed as he used to be.'

Flora swallowed her disappointment, just as she realised that yet another familiar face was missing. 'You would bring Morag, though?'

Annabella's face clouded over. 'We left her at the inn yonder. She said she didn't really care whether she came or not.'

She paused a moment, as if wondering whether to say more, and then added, 'What's wrong between you and Morag, Flora? She used to be so cheerful and helpful. Now she is downright sullen and I don't care for her as I used to. Perhaps she should not have left Skye.'

So Morag was still in a huff. Flora groaned inwardly, knowing that Stella's appearance on the scene could only make matters worse.

'Morag was jealous of the African slaves who tended me when I was ill,' she explained, 'and I fear she will be more vexed than ever when she hears about this new maid I acquired in Wilmington. But I dare say I shall be able to put everything right in time. Say hello to Mistress MacDonald, Stella.'

She was totally unprepared for Annabella's reaction then. She took one look at Stella and all the colour drained from her face. A hand came up to her mouth to stifle a cry that was somewhere between a squeal and a groan. Then, 'The good Lord in His mercy save us,' she muttered. 'That creature is evil, Flora, as was her mother! Everyone in the neighbourhood fears her! Did you not see the mark of Auld Nick upon her?'

In spite of herself Flora could not control the atavistic shiver of fear that ran through her then, but she managed a conciliatory laugh.

'Nonsense, Annabella! Why, America must have made you superstitious! Stella is but a poor slave lass! She could not help the colour of her skin, nor yet the strange configuration of a star upon it. And what a fate had befallen her! Not only had they wrenched her from her mother but would have sold her into the hands of lecherous ruffians. I couldn't let that happen!'

Throughout this exchange Stella had stood by with an enigmatic expression on her dusky features. Flora was unsure whether she had followed what Annabella was saying, though chances were she had, but clearly she had chosen to ignore it.

'Why, Miz MacDonald,' she drawled, 'Ah bin wonderin' if us wis gonna meet. You dinn tink Ah'd come back to Cross Creek ever again, did you, an' here Ah be, as if Ah'd nebber bin away.'

At that Annabella's florid face turned whiter still with rage. 'Take the wench away, Flora,' she spluttered, 'and make sure that I don't have to lay eyes on her as long as you're with us. And watch out for your men folk. Besides being a sorceress the trollop is a shameless whore, as was her mother before her. I warn you, you don't have your troubles to seek! Harbouring her is like holding a viper to your bosom!'

She was about to flounce off then but Flora put a restraining hand on her arm, having glimpsed the gleam of triumph in Stella's eye. 'Please, Annabella. We have just arrived. You must forgive us if we make mistakes.'

This rather mollified her half-sister. 'Right enough,' she conceded, "twould be wrong to let a wretched slave come between us. 'Twould be playing right into her barrow, for nothing would please her more. But keep her away from me, remember! Now, who else here will want to meet you? There's Patrick MacEachan the blacksmith over there. And yonder's Allan Cameron, who's a millwright now as well as owning a farm. Oh, and that's Angus MacDougall, standing there like a knotless thread, as always: he's doing well at the weaving, though, for all he's a gormless numpty…'

The more they saw of Cross Creek and its people the more Allan and Flora were impressed by the confident prosperity of the place. The Highlanders obviously looked up to Allan as their laird, much as they had done at home, but there was a new spirit of equality among them.

One friend of Cuidreach's, Neil MacArthur, put it in a nutshell when he said, 'It's different here. You don't have great lords possessing everything and a whole host of people with nothing. There's room and work for everybody. Nobody need fear failure.'

Whereupon Alexander snorted with laughter and cupping his hand over his mouth remarked in a low voice, 'Aye. Well may he say it. The man came here just ten years ago without a penny and now I'd wager he's worth a good five thousand pounds, with his saw-milling plant and all. That's America for you.'

Such comments from their own people gave the MacDonalds much to think about. Nobody was at the mercy of landlords here. Even kingship was a remote, irrelevant notion. And while the Highlanders still kept their reverence for clan names and the traditions, culture and language of home they were no longer dogged by poverty and haunted by the fear of eviction. They were their own people, and proud of it.

It was clear, too, that the longer people had been living here the more likely they were to have adopted typically American attitudes. Alexander had everyone taped.

'Watch the minister, James Campbell. He has served the area well for wellnigh fifteen years. Three charges he has – Rogers Meeting House, where Alex McAlister and Farquhard Campbell are elders; Barbecue Church, which we attend; and Longstreet Church, on the Yadkin Road – and he has taken on the job of teaching some of the youngsters as well. But for all we admire the work he does we can't but notice that he's a bit of a firebrand and I wouldn't be surprised if he's inflaming folk with patriotic ideas. Patriotic, indeed! It's treason, as I see it, this talk against the King! Just as well we got young John MacLeod here to help him, three years ago. It balances things out.'

Flora had just talked to this James Campbell and had not exactly taken to him. John MacLeod she would doubtless meet later. She sensed he was special, for he had emigrated from Balmore, in Skye, and was brother to Alex MacLeod of Pabbay: but it worried her that people she was meeting for the first time were being damned or upheld for their political views. Surely there were other standards to judge folks by?

Allan did not seem to take her line, however. What of Farquhard Campbell, he was asking, and Roddy Boyd, whom they had met at Wilmington? Flora's ears could not but prick up then.

'They're both rather a puzzle,' Alexander was saying. 'Both have been here a long time. Campbell came when he was but nineteen and he's in his fifties now. Quite a character, is Farquhard. His wife, his third, is little more than a girl. In fact, she was born on the very ship Farquhard was on when he was returning from a visit to Scotland. So I don't think there is pressure on the distaff side to support the rebels. But I honestly wouldn't be sure what side he'd be on, if it came to the crunch. As one of the wealthiest men in the colony he has business interests to protect, but he also sees himself as spokeman for the back country folk, and clearly thinks they have legitimate grievances.'

'And the Boyds?'

Flora could feel Alexander's hesitation and wanted to yell out, 'Quick, Alexander, tell us!' but curbed the impulse.

'He's one of the earlier arrivals too, though later than Farquhard of course. Around 1750, I'd say. Hard to say how he would tend. It would probably depend on how much hold Kate has. A very strong-minded woman, is Kate. She rules the roost at the Mumrills. Her and that son of hers, Alastair. An unsavoury piece of work, him, though I guess I shouldn't say so. Mind you, Alastair stands no nonsense from the slaves and Kate keeps Roddy's feet on the ground. Looks after the books and sees to it that he doesn't overstep their budget. For Roddy the plantation is a means to wealth, rather than a way of life. Given his head, he would go gallivanting around the country looking for Venus's flytrap orchids and exotic birds. And he's still in touch with doctors both here and in Europe, keeping abreast of all the latest medical theories. A scholar rather than a farmer, that's Roddy. And one of the finest fellows you could ever meet. If he turns patriot I guess it won't be because of outside influence, but because he has studied Francis Hutcheson and Lord Kames, and has come to his own conclusions.'

They went on dissecting the political inclinations of this one and that one. Alexander was particularly concerned that James Hogg, Bob's brother, was openly taking the patriots' side despite having arrived only recently.

'Most peculiar,' he fretted. 'Most of the newer settlers are for the King, but he makes no secret of his leanings. And that despite his having been a tacksman who brought two hundred and eighty tenants with him when he came! His land's over Hillsborough way, though, and he has dreams of buying more in Cherokee country, which the Crown would disapprove of. That's probably at the root of it all. Money. Let's hope you don't go that way, Allan!'

Flora heard Allan say, 'No fear of that,' but the snippets of information about Roddy were really all that had interested her. She reproached herself for finding him so fascinating. Why, it was almost like a girlish infatuation, this clutching at every little detail that would flesh out her picture of him.

Then, as so often happens at such junctures, the unexpected happened.

'How odd, Roddy! We were just talking about you!'

And there he was, suddenly beside them.

II

November 1774

So they were all together again – the MacDonalds, Bob Schaw, the Boyd contingent, and Farquhard Campbell, who had come upriver with the Boyds.

Roddy was delighted. 'We so hoped you would still be here! We knew there was a good chance, of course, because we had such a good, clear journey upriver. The current didn't seem as strong as usual and for once the slaves really put their backs into it. By the way, Hannibal's leg is healing nicely. You made a good job of it, Flora.'

The Mount Pleasant folks were already installed with friends for that night but Farquhard insisted that the others should all go back and spend the night with him at Rockfish Creek.

'It's not all that far out of town.We have more rooms than we know what to do with and the kitchen is bursting with fish and game, not to mention all the fruit and pickles the women have been putting up these past weeks. One thing I must ask of you, though. Keep that Stella woman out of my way. She is not welcome at Rockfish Creek, as you've no doubt guessed.'

Everyone else, however, was more than welcome. Everything about Farquhard Campbell's plantation shouted prosperity: the dock by the river, the gardens and stables, the sawmill and countless acres of pine trees.

And as it happened Stella was very subdued all that evening. Indeed Flora was quite reassured by her behaviour. She virtually hid herself away, and accepted with alacrity the decision that she should sleep in the little dressing-room off the guest-room that had been allocated to Flora and Allan. That way she would remain segregated from the slaves of the Campbell household, who appeared legion.

The girl was disarmingly helpful when her travel-weary mistress was bathing and dressing.

'You be glad to see all you family, Miz MacDonald, an' Ah be happy for you. Dey be fine people, de Mount Pleasant folks. Ah cain't tink why dey don' like me. Dey got no reason. Must have bin dat Miz Boyd dat put dem agin me. Her an' young Massah Alastair. All de niggers scared ob Massah Alastair.'

She spoke the last name with a kind of shuddering awe, like a newly-enlisted acolyte of the Devil acknowledging his superior powers, and Flora realised that she had at last discovered someone who actually put the fear of death into Stella.

Perhaps the girl's dread stuck in her mind, or maybe she was remembering Roddy's remarks at the Wilmington reception, but a shiver went up her back when she heard a hollow laugh as she entered the parlour that night, and came face to face for the first time with Roddy's stepson. She knew it had to be he from the pale, lightly freckled complexion, the glass-green eyes and the soft sand-coloured hair that was wasted on a man. Tall and loose-limbed, he came towards her with an easy, mocking arrogance and bowed.

'Ah. Mistress MacDonald, I do believe. The one who saved the Young Chevalier from the scaffold! My father speaks well of you, despite your chequered career. And what brought you here, to this benighted land where we have no time for kings?'

The words glittered with scorn. Even the reference to his father's good opinion managed to imply other than the words themselves. Their menace was unmistakable

Flora's impulse was to retort immediately with 'You young jackanapes! How dare you make such insinuations!' but bit her tongue. She had no wish to make an enemy of this fellow who was Kate's son. She wondered briefly whether his mother had injudiciously told him the whole tragic story of his father's death, and decided that it was highly likely. How else to explain this bitterness in a young man with such prospects, who had met nothing but kindness at his stepfather's hands?

So she ignored his jibe and pointedly turned her attention to the young woman beside him, who was obviously pregnant. About the same time to go as Anne, Flora reflected.

'Oh, this here's Hannah. My wife,' Alastair explained offhand-edly, as if he had been forced into the introduction against his will. 'She doesn't speak much English, I'm afraid. A racial mix, my Hannah is. German with a bit of Red Indian thrown in.'

He spoke with such unmitigated contempt in his voice that Flora could have struck him. She was glad when Farquhard came in and defused the situation with a bluff 'Ah. I see you've met. Good. Some punch now, everyone?'

His question set the tone for the evening, for here was the same overwhelming hospitality that they had encountered downriver. The meal was a sumptuous banquet of seasonal delights – turtle cooked in its shell, turkey and partridge, duck and venison, all kinds of pies and syllabubs, flummeries and trifles washed down with an unending succession of wines and spirits. Even Kate Boyd thawed a little after a few glasses of sack: Flora frequently intercepted looks between her and her son, and found herself pitying Roddy. No wonder he so doted on Jenny, for it was clear that Alastair was the apple of his wife's eye. She sighed, guessing at the many crises there must have been in that family.

Clearly Roddy had accepted the situation, however, and the conversation flowed. As if by tacit agreement the subject of politics was avoided and Scottish matters took over – so much so that Flora found it hard to believe that a vast ocean lay between her and her homeland. It was for all the world like a cultured gathering in Edinburgh.

'I get regular letters from my sister Janet in Edinburgh,' Bob Schaw explained. 'She's an inveterate letter-writer. Has an adventurous spirit, too, and desperately wants to come and see America. I've warned her that this is not the time...' – he frowned, and bit his lip – 'but she is not easily put off. Last time she wrote she was saying she might act nursemaid to the Rutherford children when they come over in a month or two's time. Trust her to find some absolutely watertight excuse to indulge her wanderlust.'

His voice was affectionate and indulgent and Flora warmed to the idea of this young woman who thought nothing of braving the rigours of that terrifying voyage. Janet Schaw, she was sure, would make the most of her visit here, would not let herself be deflected by fears of wolves and alligators, wild frontiersmen and fanatical 'patriots'. But then, Janet would be going back home again. She was not coming to stay for ever.

Meanwhile the young folk were in their element. Young Jamie had elected to join Annabella and Alexander rather than come with his parents, so that Sandy and Donald, Rachel and Jenny became a quartette of near-contemporaries. Flora watched the four of them with trepidation. Rachel was so blatantly setting her cap at Sandy, casting come-hither looks in his direction and giggling at his every word. But by some miracle all seemed smooth and friendly, a circumstance that Flora could attribute only to Jenny's good nature. Most girls would have resented the intrusion of a third party, but not Jenny. Perhaps, of course, she was sure enough of Sandy's attachment to her not to be perturbed by Rachel's antics? As for Sandy, he just lapped up the flattery and managed to share his gallantry and flirtatiousness equally between the two of them. But Flora saw the light in his eyes when he looked at Jenny, and knew Rachel didn't stand a chance.

Then suddenly it came to Flora that she had been preposterously naive in taking Rachel's conduct at its face value, for her performance had not been put on for Sandy's benefit at all. The girl had an entirely different audience in view. Someone she had met just that day, and should not even be contemplating as a possible paramour, though that was clearly what she had in mind. Alastair. Rachel's unscrupulous married cousin. For a terrible moment Flora could scarcely breathe, so strong was her premonition of disaster. At the same time, too, she realised that she was totally helpless. Interfere, and she would simply be exacerbating a situation that already existed.

From then on the evening lost its gloss, and she went to bed with a heavy heart. After all the excitement of the day she ought to have fallen asleep at once – Allan was certainly dead to the world in no time – but her hyper-active mind would not stop churning. What was ahead of them in this strange new place? It had been so comforting to feel that she was back in the bosom of her family and yet she was so conscious of those dangerous forces lurking under the surface of things. Maybe the sense of insecurity would vanish when they got even further up country, where, according to Annabella, there was a concentrated population of Highland farmers: but right now she could not throw off her feeling of foreboding, and it persisted despite all the outward show of kindness.

She was just drifting off, having willed herself to dismiss her futile worries and get some sleep for they had to journey to Mount Pleasant in the morning, when she heard a rustling sound in the room. A large moth, maybe? Or, infinitely more spine-chilling, some large, slithering, venomous snake?

Wide awake she sat up, her eyes staring into the pitch darkness. 'Allan! Stella! There's something in the room!'

She thought she heard a click then, as of a door closing, but was too petrified to get up and investigate. And Allan, rudely awakened from his slumber, was far from sympathetic.

'Get back to sleep, woman! Remember we have a long ride tomorrow!'

Determinedly she snuggled into his back then, pulled the sheet up over her head, and lay still. Everything was quiet again. She told herself firmly that in this unfamiliar tropical clime new night noises were only to be expected. She must not give in to nervous fancies. Gradually her breathing became deeper and more regular and she felt herself approach the frontiers of sleep.

Oblivion had almost overtaken her when a scream penetrated the darkness, a bloodcurdling scream full of pain and primeval terror. And at the same time she smelt the acrid stench of smoke and opened her eyes to the glare of flames. Other voices were echoing out now, supplementing the original cries. Uppermost were the hysterical ululations of negroes, high-pitched, keening lamentations in weird African dialects; and those were underlaid by the calm, measured tones of white men issuing orders in Gaelic and Lowland Scots.

'He says the cook sleeps in there! Get her out, somebody!'

'Water! We'll have to put this blaze out or it will destroy the house!'

Allan and Flora were up in a flash. Pulling on some clothes they ran to join the panic-stricken mob outside. The fire was in the kitchen which stood, like the one at Schawfield, some distance from the main house. It was however joined to the house by a wooden covered walkway, and it was this that compounded the danger of the fire's spreading.

Everything seemed to go into slow motion then. The first person Flora was conscious of was Jenny. The girl was standing desolately just outside the fire zone, and she was shivering violently despite the intense heat.

'Oh, Mistress MacDonald, thank God you're here! Sandy's in there! I begged him not to go in but you know what he's like! He had to play the hero!'

Flora wanted to scream then, to rend the air with the kind of cries the slaves were emitting, but the quiet dignity of the girl's grief shamed her into a bleak, adult resignation.

'Hold on to me, lass. Don't despair. See, we can pray. Our Father…'

The age-old words steadied them both and they clung together for comfort, scarcely daring to look at the raging flames and yet inexorably mesmerised. Flora was just saying, 'We must help! See, they've formed a chain, passing buckets!' when Jenny let out a whoop of joy.

'There he is! He's alive! Oh, thank God!'

Sandy had stumbled out of the building by way of the connecting passageway, with a bundle in his arms. His clothes were on fire and as soon as he was out in the open he collapsed with his burden on the ground. Roddy was the first to reach him, and immediately threw what looked like rugs over him to dowse the flames.

Flora and Jenny ran over and were relieved to hear Sandy speak. 'See to the woman. I'll be all right.'

Roddy knelt. They saw him take off his jacket and place it over the face of the victim Sandy had risked his life to rescue. His voice was tearful. 'I'm sorry, lad. She's dead. The smoke likely got her before she even felt the flames.'

Flora sensed his despair and knew the effort he was putting into cheering Sandy.

'It's you we have to watch now,' he was saying. 'Let me have a look at those burns. I'm amazed you're alive, man! You must have a hide like an alligator's!'

It was at that moment, like a signal from heaven, that the rain came on. Flora had rarely seen rain like it. It came with a whoosh of wind and battered down, flooding the courtyard and everyone in it in a matter of seconds. Flora heard a voice yelling, 'Hallelujah! The weather's broke! Praise the Lord!' And they all stood giving thanks for the blessing of it as the fire that had threatened to engulf the house gradually subsided.

'No point in standing here,' Farquhard was saying. 'A wee dram, and then it's back to bed. We'll face the damage in daylight.' Then he looked around him, a haunted look on his face. 'Where's that maid of yours, Flora? The Stella one? If she has had a hand in this I'll kill her with my own hands!'

His voice was infinitely desperate and weary. It was only next morning that Flora fully understood why. The dead woman had been the Campbells' long-serving and trusted negro cook, Chloe. Nor was that all. Searching in the ruins at first light the yard slaves had found the charred body of Chloe's eight-year-old son Cato, who had been a great favourite with everyone, black and white.

A pall of sadness fell over the Rockfish plantation then and the MacDonalds mourned too, marvelling at how quickly they were identifying with this new community.

But Farquhard's words, spoken no doubt when he was under stress but all the more significant for that, aggravated the suspicion that had been festering in Flora's mind ever since the outbreak of the fire. She struggled to ignore it but having entered her consciousness it kept nagging away, demanding attention.

Someone had disturbed her that night: of that she was certain. She had not imagined the presence in the room. Had Stella sneaked out, thinking her master and mistress were asleep? Allan determinedly ignored the girl's existence: it would not enter his head to wonder where she was, especially at a time of crisis. But Flora knew that her maid had been absent for at least four hours in the middle of the night. Where had she been and what had she been up to?

Speculation led her into jungles thorny with guilt and apprehension and she drew back, appalled. She was mystified by the almost hysterical hatred Stella seemed to arouse in the people around here. As far as she could see it was entirely irrational, for nobody had put forward any concrete evidence against the girl. But what was she to do? They were going to be living at Mount Pleasant as guests of Annabella and Alexander until Allan could find a farm, and here she was, inflicting Stella's unwanted presence on them all.

She decided to ask Roddy. Surely he wouldn't think Stella evil enough to set fire to the Campbells' kitchen premises? Above all, as a level-headed doctor he had to be essentially humane: Stella's strange pigmentation he might see as a scientific curiosity but certainly not as proof of some diabolical provenance.

By great good fortune she encountered him just after breakfast when little knots of people were congregating to examine and exclaim at the fire damage of the night before. Naturally he spoke first about Sandy.

'He's a brave lad, that son of yours. I sought him out an hour or so ago and put more salve on his burns. They're bad enough, but restricted mainly to his face and shoulders, and of course his hair was badly singed. He'll be able to ride today, I should think, but I'm afraid his looks have suffered. Not that that will put the girls off. You'll have noticed that Rachel has an eye for him, I guess?'

Flora marvelled that he had failed to remark the infatuation of his own daughter, and the even more sinister attachment of Rachel to Alastair. Typical man, she thought. Only sees what is pushed under his nose.

But here was an opportunity deftly to introduce the Stella question.

'Oh yes. And Rachel isn't the only one. Stella dotes on him too. Of course, she makes a bee line for anything in breeches. I'm worried about her, Roddy. Especially after what Farquhard obviously suspected last night. It seems I have acquired more than I bargained for there.'

His face darkened in a frown. 'Aye, you have that, and I'm afraid I can't say or do much to help you. Some slaves are incorrigible, cause trouble everywhere they go, and Stella and her mother are prime examples. When they worked here it was as if the place was accursed. There were mysterious outbreaks of fever. Farquhard was at his wits' end and consulted me about it but I was unable to help. Poor Chloe, the cook who died last night, got it into her head that poison was going into the food: she became positively obsessed with the idea, and went into a decline. It was only recently, after Farquhard decided to get rid of Stella and her mother, that Chloe began to bloom again. And now… Oh, I can't believe the kind soul has gone!'

Flora watched him struggling with his grief, saw his effort to explain a point of view which he clearly thought it important that she understood.

'My theory is that mulatto slaves are particularly feared because they're a constant reminder to colonial women of their husbands' philanderings – though in this case you only have to look at the overseer down at Farquhard's other plantation, where old Thea used to serve, to see who Stella's father was. I'm sure there's nothing in the rumour that Cornelius Harnett fathered her, rake though he is. Yet while we all know in theory that the girl's mixed blood is not her fault her undoubted beauty and come-hither attitude breed distrust. The women see her as a symbol of Satan's power, and associate her with voodoo, obeah, all kinds of sorcery.'

Flora felt her skin crawl, but was determined to stay outwardly calm. Above all, she felt inexplicably bound to support Stella.

'But it's all so unfair! It's laying all their prejudices and fears on to the girl's shoulders! As for her mother, when she conceived her, would she have any say in whether she slept with a white man or not?'

Roddy looked thoughtful. 'No. She would have to submit to her master, or the overseer, or whoever else lusted after her. But something you must learn, Flora, and that right now. Slaves have no rights. They are mere chattels, like tables and chairs and fields and ploughs. If they feel as we do, which is doubtful, these feelings count for nothing. So I'd advise you to rid yourself of this Stella girl as soon as you can – which won't be easy locally, for nobody wants the responsibility of her. You could always send her back to Wilmington, of course, and have her sold there.'

Flora remembered the lecherous roughnecks who had congregated at the slave market and shuddered. 'But I can't do that to her! Can't you see?'

And Roddy, for once, disappointed her. 'No,' he said, with a shrug of resignation. 'I don't see. You haven't taken in the full gist of what I have been saying. These African slaves are not like us. You would sell a troublesome horse, wouldn't you? Well, this is just the same.'

He spoke with dismissive finality, as if reproaching a recalcitrant child, and Flora knew the subject was closed. So she swallowed her frustration and returned, chokingly, to the immediate issue of the fire damage.

'Look at the devastation! It's heart-rending! Wasn't it a mercy the rain came on?'

The building that had been the kitchen was an empty shell. Its open rafters, blackened by the flames, stood stark against a blue, rain-washed sky. There was a foul smell of smoke, mingled with the foetid stench of burnt flesh and foodstuffs. Slaves were scrabbling inside, trying to salvage what they could from the ruins: the odd usable metal cooking utensil, china dishes and crocks, pots and pans and fire irons. But they had to work with caution because there was an all-too-present danger of falling beams and every so often one would come crashing down, setting up an avalanche of ash and debris.

She was deep in thought, mourning the fate of the innocent dead, when the sound of hoof-beats broke into her reverie. Allan, already in the saddle, and alongside him a riderless horse which he was leading by the reins. A mare it was, pure white, of medium height and with a gentle but alert look in her eye.

'She's for you, Florrie. Like her? Name's Delilah.'

Allan's eyebrow went up enquiringly, and he smiled that smile she had rarely seen recently, the one that she had found irresistible long ago, in their courting days.

'I thought it was time you had your own horse. Bob Schaw will be taking the phaeton and four back with him, and Annabella's carriage is really just big enough for herself, Anne and the children. So Farquhard agreed to sell this mare to me. He's a great lover of horses, it seems. I tried to persuade him to exchange the beast for that Stella wench but no such luck. He says his overseer would kill her. Not that that would be a bad idea, in my opinion.'

It was all too much for Flora. Running up she buried her face in the mare's neck, determined that Allan would not see her tears. And for once she was speechless.

III

November–December 1774

The time with the whole family together was all too short, but then the Mount Pleasant house, though large by back country standards, did not have elastic walls. The youngsters had to sleep in the stable and the men in the raftered attic rooms under the eaves. Then old Hugh became so worried about the frost coming and the work that still had to be done at his twin plantations of Mountain Creek and Cheek's Creek that he began to chafe after a day or two. Flora was further dismayed when Anne and Alex decided to go west with him and get settled at their own place before the worst of the weather set in. Alex's cousin, Morrison of

Skinidin, had already negotiated the purchase of land for them some twenty-five miles away, at MacDeed's Creek, and Anne's advancing pregnancy was of course a consideration.

It was hard to say goodbye to Anne and Flora clung to her, bravely trying to keep the tears at bay. 'I so wanted to be with you when the babe comes! You'll take care of yourself, won't you? You must keep warm and not work too hard!'

'Of course, Ma! Now don't fret! It may well be that you'll find somewhere near us, and that soon! And Alex will be down this way often. There will be farm implements and seed and all kinds of merchandise to be collected at Cross Creek, and wagons are going down there every day. So be assured you won't go for long without word from us.'

And with that the little procession of carts and horses was off. Flora stood at the door with a heavy heart and watched it wend its way up the valley before vanishing into the pine trees. She gulped back the emotions that wellnigh overwhelmed her then. Another part of her wrenched cruelly away! Of her seven children only Jamie and Sandy left with her now! And it was all very well being told that Anne was not too far away: the trouble was that she could not imagine her daughter in her home surroundings, going about her daily tasks, because she had little idea what life would be like at their new farm.

Annabella was sympathetic. She assured Flora that Anne would feel far from isolated up country.

'The Morrisons are at Crosshill, on McLendon's Creek, not far from where Anne and Alex will be. And Sandy Morrison's flourishing. Although he has opened a store he's still doctoring, and will be there for Anne when her time comes. Then there's Kathie Campbell, Donald Roy MacDonald's sister. Donald Roy's dead, may the Lord bless his soul. A pity you missed seeing him, just by a month or two: how you would have talked of the old days!

'But didn't Kathie's husband, also a Donald, shelter the Prince on Scalpay? They came out just last year – a brave pair, for they're in their seventies – and they live up that way too. Their son John and their four daughters emigrated with them. There's Barbara, and Isobel, and Christian, and Peggy. John has his own place now, and has built a dam and a grist mill along with Barbara's husband, Alex MacLeod of Pabbay – who's kin to the minister, of course.

The other three daughters are up nearer Hugh. Isobel married Alex MacLeod's brother, and is at Mountain Creek. Christian was widowed at home and her son John Bethune, who's a minister, came with her: he's organising the church up at Carmel. And Peggy's on Cheek's Creek: she married Duncan Campbell... Then of course there's Flora. My own sister. And yours too. You must remember that. Never feel for a moment that we are not full kin. No, my dear, Anne will not be without friends up country.'

Annabella's great long litany of Highland names and inter-relationships would have amused Flora had she not been feeling so much in need of reassurance. And there indeed was a certain measure of comfort in hearing about those folks, though what she did not realise was that Annabella was discussing people who lived miles from one another as if they were near neighbours: probably she did not quite appreciate, even now, the distances involved. What was important, however, was that Flora knew all these people intimately, had not needed Annabella to explain them, and gratefully recognised her half-sister's motives for what they were – a game effort to take her mind off her grief at Anne's going, and to assure her that if all those recent settlers were happy and prosperous there was no reason why the MacLeods should not do well too.

The evidence of prosperity was certainly all around. The Mount Pleasant plantation covered two hundred acres on the south side of a gentle slope some six hundred feet high. When Alexander had first taken it over, two years before, the land had been covered in pines. He and the indentured servants who had come with him from Skye had laboured long and hard. There had been thousands of trees on the concession and they had started by clearing just enough land to accommodate a basic log house. Other trees had then been killed off more gradually: rings of bark had been removed from them, making them shed their foliage and let the sun in. So eventually fields of Indian corn, oats and sweet potatoes had taken the place of the original virgin forest.

'It was hard work,' Alexander conceded, 'felling trees and burning off the undergrowth, but very satisfying in the long run. 'The soil's mainly light and sandy, and easily worked with the cas-chrom.'

He pointed to where a field worker was using the little manually-operated plough generally in use in the Highlands. 'Remember how hard it was, shifting the peat on Skye? This is child's play in comparison! Only problem is tree roots. We can't do anything about them, I'm afraid. But when one lot of land's exhausted we can always move on. We work a kind of crop rotation system. Indian corn for a year or two, followed by a year of peas and beans, and then wheat…'

In those two years Cuidreach had also built a separate kitchen, a smoking shed, and servants' quarters, and had considerably extended the house. What had begun as a simple cabin chinked with clay was now a handsome dwelling of squared logs, with a deeply overhanging gable roof of pine shingles and two brick chimneys, one at each end. The windows were tiny, the largest being only two-and-a-half by one-and-a-half feet square, which meant that very little light got in, but at least they were glazed.

'Farquhard Campbell got the glass up from Wilmington for me,' Alexander said proudly. 'We don't need it in the summer but it's a boon in winter: those shutters swing about in the wind and would let the cold in no matter how well made they were.'

Allan was full of admiration, and Flora suspected he was a little apprehensive too, realising what might be in store. He listened with something approaching awe to Alexander's expositions about local house-building practices. He had obviously made quite a study of them.

'You'll see a lot of 'dog-run' houses, where you get two identical buildings spanned by one roof, with a passageway in between: quite big they can be, with a stair in the open passage leading to the upper storey. The locals sometimes call them 'breezeway' or 'possum-trot' houses. Then there's the 'saddle-bag' style, where the two units are closer, with a chimney in between. It's all a matter of taste and family needs, I suppose.'

He went on to expatiate about saddle-notched joints, the pegging of lathes and the corbelling in of chimney sides, and Flora saw Allan's eyes glaze over. He had not envisaged the building of a home from scratch.

Finding land was Allan's affair, however, and Flora realised that the only contribution she could make was a domestic one. She marvelled at how comfortable life was at Mount Pleasant, and Annabella assured her that even the most modest Highland tenants in the Piedmont found their conditions better than at home.

'Remember the crofters' cots, built of peat sods, with no windows and a hole in the roof for a chimney! And even the tacksmen's houses often had muddy dirt floors, whereas here there's so much timber that wooden floors are just taken for granted. It's all so much cleaner and more spacious. Healthier too, I'll warrant, in spite of the mosquitoes and seed ticks in the summer.'

Flora looked around her, at the huge central room that was all of twenty-four feet square, and had to agree. Alexander was an exceptional person, of course. He had brought a whole cultivated life style with him when he emigrated. Here were the mahogany dining tables and leather-seated chairs, the silver cutlery and exquisite punch bowls, that had graced Cuidreach. Annabella's spinning wheel stood in a corner, and there were mirrors and paintings on the walls. Then there were the books, not just the three hundred Alexander had brought with him but many more new ones. Turning them over one day Flora noticed that a lot of them were about flowers.

'Oh, yes,' Annabella laughed when the question came up. 'You can't help being interested in horticulture here. Just wait until you see the dogwood and magnolias, in the spring! It's orchids that have captured Alexander's interest, though. He shares the passion with his great friend Roddy Boyd. That, and the study of bird migrations. It's all so beautiful, Flora. You'll see. Difficult at first, though, when your mind's still half at home…'

Difficult indeed. While Allan and Sandy helped Alexander in the fields, the stables and the outhouses Flora did her best to help with household chores. The hogs had recently been slaughtered and she helped render and dry the lard from them. Annabella was almost obsessive about using every single part of an animal, even insisting that the skins and old rancid grease went into the lye hopper for soap-making.

The long, arduous process of preparing the soap fascinated Flora. Wheat straw and hickory ashes were left for ten days to set, water was filtered through the ashes to produce lye, then after the unsavoury old fat had been added it was all drained and boiled up together.

She also learnt to make candles from myrtle berries.

'Too many of the folk around here ignore the riches that are all round them,' Annabella said. 'They insist upon buying lightwood or whale-oil candles when there the berries are, under their very noses. An idle spendthrift lot they are. And it's all so easy! Kate Boyd showed me. You put the berries in boiling water and boil them till they nearly melt. The surface goes solid when the mixture cools, and it's this that you use to make the candles. You just keep boiling until it's transparent and ready to pour into the moulds.'

Anne Schaw and Elizabeth Martin might have recoiled at the idea of getting their hands dirty but not so those thrifty Highland farm women. They laboured unceasingly and even when the day's work was done their hands were occupied with spinning and carding, knitting, darning, and quilting.

Flora's life soon settled into a not unpleasant work pattern as certain tasks became habitual. Drawing water at the nearby spring was one chore she became very possessive about. She would sling the carriers over Delilah's back and together they would penetrate deep into the woods. She remembered the day in late fall when Annabella had first taken her to the spot. The path had been almost hidden by thick undergrowth then, but her guide had told her that as long as she located the big maple there was no fear of getting lost, and so it had turned out. And each day she had watched the maple leaves change colour, until they flamed to crimson, fell, and eventually covered the ground in a crisp shining carpet of red and brown.

She used to attach Delilah's reins to a tree trunk and steal some quiet moments, sitting on the bank beside the clear, swift upsurge of water. Small animals came to the dell and she would gradually learn to recognise them from Alexander and Roddy's descriptions. Possums and chipmunks and – she came to dread the smell – skunk. Even a deer one day. Then there were the birds: bobolinks, dark grey with white and cream markings on the neck and back; white-throated sparrows; brilliant scarlet tanagers and blackpoll warblers migrating south from their breeding grounds in Canada. Everything was so new.

Contemplatively she would light her pipe – she had recently been presented with a corn cob that tasted cool and pleasant – and let her mind wander wherever it would. Until now she had resisted thoughts of home as too painful, but she knew she must cultivate the habit of calm communion with her family and what better place than here, in this arched cathedral under the trees?

It was impossible to visualise what Charles and Ranald were doing as they served the King in foreign parts. Johnny and Fanny were easier, however. She imagined them threading the narrow wynds and closes of Edinburgh or walking down the High Street with its castled crag at the top and the royal palace of Holyrood down below. She heard the bells of St Giles' and St Cuthbert's and Greyfriars, the sound of revelry from the Assembly Rooms, the cries of 'Gardy-loo!' and the shouts of oyster sellers and Musselburgh fishwives. Lawyers and physicians, caddies and pedlars, grand ladies with their maids and trollops with their pimps... all a world away from this tranquil wilderness.

Sometimes, with a tentative, almost unbearable longing, she let her mind drift back to Skye, to the changing sea below Flodigarry, the gulls crying, and the swirling mists over the mountains. Common sense told her that there had been no choice. They had had to leave. But the human soul does not live by common sense alone. Some days the act of memory brought on tears and she was glad that there was nobody there to see.

At other times, inevitably, her thoughts were of the here and now, and they were not always soothing. Her most pressing problem was Morag and her relationship with Stella. She told herself that the maid was pining for home. Presumably she had not yet recovered from the rigours of the voyage, the changes of scene and the climate. And Morag had a douce, Presbyterian morality about her that recoiled from the rough indiscipline of your typical everyday North Carolinian. Yes. That must be it. She was homesick. Needed lots of attention. Flora would make a point of indulging her. Particularly now that Anne had gone.

If only she could rid herself of this corrosive suspicion that Morag's malady sprang from some malevolent supernatural source, and that Stella was at the bottom of it! She lectured herself for being so credulous but the notion would not go away. Because of Annabella's strongly-expressed aversion to Stella, and Morag's understandable jealousy when she suspected the slave-girl of usurping her rightful place at her mistress's side, the MacDonalds had taken what they were convinced was the only course of action:

they had banished Stella to the outside servants' quarters. Flora had known that she would bitterly resent the demotion but Alexander and Annabella had insisted that it was the best solution. She would get up to no mischief there, under the shrewd eyes of their ghillies. And though she would be the odd one out – there were no slaves at Mount Pleasant, only indentured servants from the Highlands – she could speak Gaelic when she cared to and might well become one of the team if she behaved herself.

They all heaved a sigh of relief that she was out of the house. Out of sight, out of mind. But Flora was not so sure. Stella was sly. She had recently been manipulating chance meetings with Morag, when she would commiserate with her in her languishing state and suggest remedies. And Morag in her simplicity was only too ready to try the recipes out. Not that there was anything poisonous, Flora reckoned, about a tea made of mashed cow dung and flavoured with mint, but dogwood and crushed peach stones might not be so advantageous...

Sometimes Flora wondered if Stella transgressed simply to draw attention to herself. Old Neil had come on her in the stables one day. The yard cat had just had kittens and he had found Stella torturing one of them, holding a lighted spill to its tail.

'I couldn't believe it, Mistress! The cruelty of the jade, doing that to the poor wee helpless beastie! I'm afraid I took my hand to her! I'll be in her black books now, I'll wager, and a candidate for her witch's spells and potions! It's overstepping myself to say so, I know, but the sooner she's gone from here the better. Nothing has been the same among us since you bought her!' And he had gone off shaking his head.

Flora had another, more subtle and personal reason for wishing Stella gone, one that she could not reveal to anyone because it was so embarrassing. Twice she had happened to encounter Roddy on these forays to the well, and twice they had had the misfortune to be spotted, or possibly spied upon, by Stella.

It had all been so innocent. As Alexander's nearest neighbour Roddy came often to discuss matters of mutual interest, and the first time Stella had come snooping he and Flora had simply been talking together outside the stables: he had just arrived and she was about to mount Delilah and go to the spring. The second time had been equally guileless. He had simply asked if he might go with her and help her fetch the water. She had accepted with mixed feelings, glad to have his company but reluctant to forfeit those precious moments of privacy the errand afforded.

As always he had been so easy to talk to. He had just had a letter from his friend Phineas Bond of Philadelphia, who had studied with him in Edinburgh, and was eager to talk about it. Both doctors were aware of newly-developed techniques of experimental observation and research and frequently compared notes, while Roddy sent home regular reports about the effects of climate on health, the prevalence of small-pox, yellow fever and diphtheria, and the possible medical applications of the exotic plants he found so fascinating.

It seemed perfectly natural then, as they rode back side by side to Mount Pleasant, that Flora should describe Morag's mysterious illness and the doubtful remedies the girl had been credulous enough to swallow. She had expected him to shrug the whole matter off but instead he had looked grave.

'A distillation of peach stones, indeed! But that's highly suspect! Enough of that and your Morag will waste away! You must be vigilant, Flora. Remember that those Africans came here with a whole background of plant lore that we know nothing of. And 'tis not just herbs they know about. They dabble in witchcraft and voodoo, and frequently to terrifying effect.'

He paused, seeing how alarmed Flora was.

'Oh lass, little did you realise what a Pandora's box you were opening, when you bought that girl! Would you had just left her to the tender mercies of whosoever on the Tidewater might want her! There's really only one thing I can suggest. Hire her out to us for a while, and let Alastair take her in hand. He could do with extra help to get the seed planted. And I assure you he will suffer no nonsense. He'll see that she gets no chance to corrupt the other slaves as she did down at Farquhard's.'

Flora remembered the aqueous foxy eyes and cruel mouth of Roddy's stepson and recoiled. She would not commit a dog to his care, far less a human being.

'I shall think on't,' she said noncommittally, and promptly changed the subject. 'Annabella's making a pumpkin pie with lots of cinnamon and nutmeg in it, and she'll be roasting the turkey the boys shot in the woods yesterday. Oh, these American dishes are all so new, and quite delectable! You'll be staying to eat with us, won't you?'

So they rode companionably on and were almost back at Mount Pleasant when Roddy suddenly stiffened in the saddle and said under his breath, 'Talk of the devil! She makes me grue, the creature!'

And there was Stella standing at the roadside with an expression of sly contempt on her face. In spite of her anger Flora felt herself blush, for it was clear that the girl was putting a salacious interpretation on her superiors' togetherness. And suddenly the happy, innocent companionship they had known was spoilt. Yet – Flora had to admit it – there had indeed been a certain leavening of sexual attraction in those encounters, just enough of a frisson, an edge of danger, to lift them above the commonplace. But where had been the harm, as long as the mutual appeal stayed locked in their hearts?

Being on horseback now, and some feet above the mulatto, she was able to maintain her dignity and pass Stella with a mere curt nod. She vowed nevertheless that she would be more circumspect from now on, and as it happened the opportunities for clandestine assignations were dwindling, even had she been seeking them. For fate took a hand. Next day she met the bear.

It had been a particularly pleasant morning, with the sun filtering warmly through the tracery of branches above her, and it had been difficult to pull herself away from her gentle musings by the spring. A family of chipmunks had been playing about her feet and she had watched entranced. One, a particularly perky, inquisitive little thing with exquisitely etched brown stripes down its back, had stuffed its cheek pouches with nuts and looked so comical that she laughed out loud. So she had let the time tick on and realised with dismay that she had lingered far longer than usual. Sighing, she rose from her log and the chipmunks vanished.

She had just replaced the pipe in her pocket and was retrieving the water bottles when she was aware of an alien presence and a rank animal smell. Delilah, just a few feet away, let out a bray of alarm. And there it was, a shaggy black brute of an animal with powerful hunched shoulders and mean, burning little eyes. It was obviously on the alert, for it had raised its dun-coloured muzzle and was sniffing the air suspiciously. She thought fleetingly that she might have disturbed it as it was composing itself for its winter sleep, for its eyes were blinking and it was lurching forward with a curious oscillating movement.

What to do? Of course the family had discussed such a possible confrontation, talked with horror and a ghoulish fascination of what they would do if it happened. Frantically she went through the options, while she stood rooted to the spot. Run over to Delilah, jump on her back and ride away? Climb a tree? Or – she had heard this was the best option – stare the creature out while slowly, slowly walking backwards away from it?

But she could consciously do none of them. She was as if caught in a nightmare, her ankles chained and her whole body petrified with terror. They told her afterwards that her very immobility had probably saved her – that, and the fact that winter had not quite come and the creature was not starving – for one minute it was there, its baleful eye considering her, and the next it was gone, skulking back into the shadows.

She might still have plucked up courage and returned to the glade but as it turned out her nerve remained untested, for winter suddenly came sweeping through the valley

IV

November–December 1774

They did not have those brutally abrupt seasonal changes on Skye. Snow lying light on the ground, yes, and lots of clear frosty days when the sea sparkled and the grass went crisp with hoar, but rarely snowfalls six feet deep and never those devastating ice storms. The Piedmont had no mild Gulf Stream caressingly to to lave it with its warmth, but only a snell wind that came whipping through, bringing with it hailstones that stung like arrows and a cold so penetrating that it found every chink and cranny in a building.

Flora looked out at the mauve-tinted sky, thick with snow clouds, and sighed. Every pine needle was frosted as if with icing sugar;

raspberry canes and huckleberry bushes were fringed with ice; every tuft of grass had its little cap of snow.

Old Neil came in rednosed and shivering, his hair and beard encrusted with rime.

'It's that bad I must have peed icicles when I got up this morn,' he gasped. 'Ye'll need to let the milk stand by the fire, if ye want it for your porridge. It's frozen solid. As for the creek, I reckon the ice is that thick a bear could cross it.'

The severity of the weather alarmed Flora, whereas established colonists seemed to take the sudden transition to winter in their stride. 'How long will this last, Bella?'

'There's no knowing. Some years are worse than others. Not long, usually. A few weeks maybe.'

As it turned out, it was a season of short sharp cold spells alternating with sudden thaws. Contemplating a journey, no-one knew from day to day whether the roads would be ice-bound or deep in mud. Given a measure of caution, however, short expeditions were rarely impossible. Alexander and Allan even went down to Cross Creek during a clear interval to trade salt beef and cattle skins for tobacco and snuff, sugar, coffee, new axes and saws, and a range of sewing supplies for the womenfolk. They returned so bursting with news and rumour, none of it good, that Flora wished they had not gone.

'Everything's in a ferment. Those damned Committees of Safety are effectively ruling the colony. They're threatening now to boycott merchants who refuse to sign their non-importation agreement, and even the ones who are most loyal to the Crown are having to knuckle under. John Slingsby, for example. Evidently the brig *Diana* has just brought in over a thousand pounds worth of goods for his store at Cross Creek and he has been obliged to hand the lot over to the Wilmington Committee! Isn't that scandalous! They have the merchants in a cleft stick. The way things are going they'll be ruined, for they want to keep credit with their sources at home, yet here are folks refusing to trade with them if they have any truck at all with Britain!'

'It's almost as if battle lines were being drawn up,' Allan continued when Alexander paused for breath. 'We met Farquhard Campbell and according to him Martin's being downright pigheaded, still refusing to see any justice in the so-called patriots' case. And for their part they're becoming more and more aggressive, agitating for people to sign those declarations of support. Articles of Association, they're calling them. We saw Roddy too and he's worried that once the common sort get involved they'll go beyond logical discussion and start baying for blood. Thank God we're away from it all up here.'

But the more Flora came to know the back-country people the more she realised how divided they were. She had thought to find peace and harmony in the homely atmosphere of the local church, where the services were conducted in Gaelic and the old familiar Presbyterian values prevailed, but Alexander's warnings about the minister proved all too true. James Campbell was an ardent patriot. It soon became obvious that despite the opprobrium that might be heaped upon them for staying away many loyalists were boycotting services on the Sundays when he was officiating. They would plead illness, or blame the bad weather. Sometimes, defying distance and discomfort, they would attend whichever church John MacLeod was preaching at, and this Flora soon came to understand and even condone.

But she had grown to love the little Presbyterian church at Barbecue Creek and did not wish to worship anywhere else regardless of who was preaching. Even by Skye standards it was by no means pretentious, just a basic log building with rough pews and scarcely any adornment, but its stark simplicity represented everything Flora had been brought up to respect. Had not her grandfather, 'the strong minister' been one of the Outer Isles' most eminent Presbyterians? Here she could thrill to the measured tones of the old psalms, recite the catechism which she had learnt by heart as a child, and be reminded of the way she should go. The Sabbath service was a ritual never to be foregone.

Those Sundays had an atmosphere all their own. The whole Mount Pleasant household – master and mistress, family and servants – travelled the six miles to church in a tight convoy. The men usually chose to go on horseback, the women and children rode in the carriage or on one of the short-bodied, two-wheeled carts the local people favoured, while the servants used the wagons. The road, mainly through deep forest, was little more than a bridle path and sometimes hazardous but there was still a sense of occasion about those journeys. It was the only day in the week that the women wore their best finery and while they might pretend that the dresses were meant as a compliment to God – how else to come before Him, but looking one's best? – they also knew, particularly if they were young, that on Sundays the eyes of the whole neighbourhood were upon them.

Flora always marvelled at how many graves there were in the tiny churchyard, although the church had been standing for only ten years. The headstones were heart-rendingly simple, many of them carved with strange Celtic symbols and all of them bearing testimony to the families who had come to settle in the locality. Most of the names were Highland. On the very first day they attended the church Annabella had pointed out the stones that might be of particular interest. There were Camerons aplenty, and MacNeils and MacQueens, and one particularly poignant grave that she said she had taken it upon herself to tend.

'The folks can't come up this distance very often, you see. They're Campbells that live down on the Tidewater. And when they lost their babe — he was just six months old – they couldn't bear to bury him down in the swamps. They wanted him to be among the hills. So their twelve-year-old son came up here on horseback, carrying the wee corpse.'

Her voice had trembled, and it was brought home afresh to Flora that all of them had elected not just to live in this remote place but to die here too, and spend eternity in a foreign land. She had scarcely had time to consider the implications of emigrating, but Annabella had. And far from being sentimental, Annabella was essentially practical, even brisk: which made this glimpse of tenderness all the more significant.

Suddenly unutterably sad, Flora had reached for Annabella's hand in a gesture of love and sympathy. 'At least,' she said, 'we are all together here, and shall be so in death, when the time comes. And I hope that the Campbell child's parents will one day be buried here too, so that their child is not alone for ever.'

But come December it was as if some evil influence were abroad, determined to undermine the Highlanders' feeling of solidarity. It was no longer the kind of feuding that used to split the clans in their home territory – squabbles about land between Campbells and MacDonalds, MacLeods and MacLeans – but a more complicated alignment, depending largely on how long a person had lived in America and how strongly his allegiance to his chief, and especially to the Crown, had persisted.

The minister, James Campbell, was a case in point. Matters came to a head one Sunday when he waxed particularly bellicose, preaching an openly political sermon that was designed to last for the usual full hour. Its proclaimed subject, 'The last shall be first and the first shall be last' sounded an innocuous text enough, and Flora, in common with most of the congregation, let herself lapse into a day dream: there were few such opportunities in the busy daily routine of Mount Pleasant. Today her main preoccupation was the disappearance of one of her most treasured possessions, the rhinestone brooch the Prince had given her. She could not fathom what had happened to it, for she always kept it well hidden in a little box in her bedroom drawer. Desperately she recalled when she had last worn it – at Schawfield, maybe? – and her mind went back to those days on the Tidewater and all the people they had met. Surely those kind and cultured people, the Drys, the Quinces, the Moores and even Farquhard Campbell, could not possibly be contemplating rebellion against the King?

Then the minister's bellowing voice broke in on her consciousness and she realised that there was one such firebrand right here, in the pulpit of Barbecue Church. Already he was rousing the most somnolent of the parishioners with his passion. She saw old Maggie Stewart wake with a start and look dazedly around her, while those who had come for a lesson in doctrine frowned, bewildered by their mentor's contentious tone. Gilbert Clark, Duncan and Archibald Buie and Daniel Cameron, sober-suited elders all, were looking distinctly uncomfortable. The four of them were the recognised pillars of Barbecue Kirk, and were renowned throughout the area for their piety and knowledge of the scriptures. Flora saw a deep red flush of rage creep up from Gilbert's neck to suffuse his whole face. Was the man going to succumb to a seizure, right there in the front pew?

Seemingly impervious to the impression his words were making, or perhaps determined to ignore it, Campbell was raving on.

'Who should have dominion over us but the Lord Himself?' he roared, his eyes burning like coals. 'We came to this fair land to find freedom from want, freedom of thought, and freedom from tyranny, and those, praise the Lord, we have found through no-one's efforts but our own. Therefore we are determined that no human force, be it a parliament at Westminster thousands of miles away or a man who calls himself king, shall divert us from our course. Just think of it, my brethren! An America that stands alone, a stalwart and independent nation, its people subject to no laws but the ones they have fashioned with God's help! And in this nation no-one will have precedence over another by reason of birth or privilege. Everyone will prosper through his own labours, his own merit as an individual, and his own vision of what is good.'

As he warmed to his theme the minister strained and stretched over the pulpit, his long stringy neck, black vestments and grey tie-wig emphasising his resemblance to a bedraggled heron. At first what he was saying was received with a kind of surprised respect, and then as his utterances became even more extravagantly republican the more politically sophisticated grew decidedly uncomfortable.

Campbell probably appreciated, of course, that the ideas he propounded were completely novel. Anti-Royalists were a new breed. Even the original Jacobites amongst the Highlanders could not grasp those radical Philadelphian theories. True, they had taken up arms against the English king thirty years before but they had fought not to banish kings so much as to establish a different and possibly even more absolute monarchy. There were restless murmurings among the douce Highland farmers then as they noted the reaction of their elders, and the ripple of disapproval spread until it was clear that Campbell's privileged position as preacher was not going to guarantee his immunity from challenge.

Sensitive to his every mood, Flora felt Allan stir beside her and knew his hackles were rising. His anger grew like a storm building up, the mere suspicion of a current rising to a full tempest of rage and indignation.

Fearfully she laid her hand on his and said in an urgent whisper. 'Wheesht now, Allan. Remember where you are!'

But she might as well have been addressing the shades of the Highlanders in the graves outside, for all the attention he paid her. A low growl and then he was in full spate.

'You scurrilous blackguard, daring to use the church of God as a pulpit for sedition! I for one refuse to listen to such traitorous tirades, whether they issue from a man of the cloth or no!'

And with that he flung himself out of the church, to be joined immediately by Alexander.

Flora wondered if she should follow them. She knew that as Allan's wife she ought to show herself at one with him, but for a crucial moment she hesitated. And James Campbell was quick to use that moment. Few, he guessed, were likely to walk out now if he decided summarily to close the service. So clutching his dignity about him and dropping his voice to a snivelling incantation he launched into the benediction.

'... And may the blessing of God Almighty, Father, Son and Holy Spirit, rest upon you and your loved ones, wherever they may be, both now and always. Amen.'

The words usually united everyone in thoughts of those they had left behind in Scotland, but not today. The exodus from the church was hasty and irreverent. Flora came out to find a crowd of people gathered around Allan. The men were thumping him appreciatively on the shoulders, the women shaking him by the hand.

'Well done, man! Somebody had to stand up to him!'

'Spoken like the soldier ye are!'

And one fellow whom Flora had heard addressed as Munn said simply, 'Ye're the man we've been waiting for. A true leader come amongst us.'

She knew she ought to have felt proud of him then but instead she felt the weight of an ineffably ominous sadness. And she could not help noticing that no-one from the Mumrills came to shake his hand. Kate and Roddy, Alastair and Hannah and Rachel, all hurried away without a word. Only Jenny remained, staunchly stationed at Sandy's side.

By tacit mutual consent, though, they did not discuss the incident in private afterwards. Flora wondered if Allan felt almost ashamed of his outburst, or perhaps he resented her failure publicly to endorse his views – in which case, alas, another taboo subject had reared its ugly head between them. For her part, she was determined to disregard the whole affair as irrelevant to their present way of life, for she devoutly hoped that very soon they could be settled even further away from all those wranglings that did not concern them. Allan had heard of an established plantation that might be for sale near Hugh in Anson County, up Cheek's

Creek way. It belonged to one Caleb Touchstone, and there were two tracts, one almost five hundred acres in size and the other fifty acres. The more Flora thought about it the more obsessed she became with the idea of moving there. She hated to nag but became increasingly fearful that Allan would let the chance slip. She wanted to distance her family from politics. She craved escape from those dismal, claustrophobic pine forests. And it would be a good time to shed Stella.

V

January 1775

At home in Skye Hogmanay had been the social highlight of the year. Whatever the weather the islanders would wander from house to house, carousing with friends and neighbours until dawn. A certain degree of licence had prevailed then and the douce respectable women were expected to indulge their menfolk's lack of self-control – which they did, the men maintained, in an infuriatingly patronising, sanctimonious fashion. The wives would resignedly console themselves with the thought that it happened only once a year, and if Hamish had failed to come home that night his wife could be confident it was an excess of drink that had detained him and not some shameless trollop in the village.

But in the Valley of the Cape Fear it was a different story. First footing was impossible if you lived miles from your neighbour and the road between was through dense forest, home to ravening wolves and bears. Difficult enough in daylight, when you had all your wits about you, but plunge drunk into those labyrinthine pines in the dead of night and you were lost for ever.

So the Boyds and the Cuidreach MacDonalds had agreed that they would visit one another on alternate years and stay the night. This year was Alexander and Annabella's turn.

'I hope the men don't get too rumbustious,' Annabella laughed. 'I'll have to have the beds aired and see that there's a good supply of linen but chances are they'll never sleep in them, and if they do they'll scarcely notice if it's straw they're lying on instead of duck down. Let's get those tankards washed, Flora. And if you'll maybe see to the black bun in the oven there…'

They and the servants worked for days preparing food. Mouth-watering aromas drifted around the house, redolent of steak pies and venison stews, boiled ox tongues, baked hams and enormous pans of broth. Turkeys and chicken, duck and goose lay ready for roasting on the big pine table. Never any shortage of game: the men simply had to spend a few hours hunting and back they would come with enough food for weeks.

Annabella was a dab hand at concocting desserts and Flora watched as she whipped up the filling for her famously spicy pumpkin pie. Then there were syllabubs and jellies, tarts filled with apple, peaches and cherries, and whole basins of clotted cream. And the drink. Of course the drink. Jamaica rum. Madeira wine. Gallons of ale and whisky.

'They'll never eat all that! And as for the drink, you'll have us all stotious!' Flora protested, but Annabella insisted that the fare would vanish like snow off a dyke.

'I just wish Alastair didn't have to come,' she added, bearing out Flora's distrust of Kate's son. 'Maybe Hannah will suffer a miscarriage and we can enjoy ourselves without them. Not that I'd wish harm on the poor lass; she has enough of a cross to bear already, with that brutish scoundrel for a husband. But I only hope that when midnight strikes 'tis Allan or Roddy who crosses our threshold first. It has to be a man who's tall and dark. If it were Alastair, with his carroty hair and pale skin, I'd feel that our year's luck had flown out the window.'

Morag looked up from her task – she had been chopping raisins – and asked provocatively, 'And what happens to us servants and ghillies? Do we get to join you?'

Annabella refused to be ruffled. 'We usually find the ghillies want their own ceilidh. We give you all the run of the kitchen from midnight on. It's your holiday too, after all.'

'Aye. So I'd heard,' the girl responded doubtfully. 'But we've a wee problem. The mulatto. It seems she feels hard done by. The slaves down at the Mumrills got presents at Christmas, and clothes and shoes for the new year, and she got nothing. Christmas is celebration time down there. The slaves get to barbecue hogs and chickens and the big house hands out pies and candies, no' to mention whisky and ale. Then there's cock-fighting, and wrestling, and games for the bairns, wi' dancing and fiddling and a' kinds o' merriment. Seems she wanted to go down there at Christmas to see a lad she has ta'en up wi', one Hannibal that's a stable boy, and old Neil wouldn't hear of it. There's a lot o' ill feeling there. She's out to make trouble, I tell you.'

And she wandered off shaking her head in a don't-say-I didn't-warn-you kind of fashion.

The Boyd contingent arrived before dusk on the evening of Hogmanay, the women in two phaetons and Roddy and Alastair on horseback. They had brought two slaves with them, and Hannibal was one of them. Flora noticed that he still walked with a slight limp but seemed otherwise quite hale. Oh well, she thought, that will keep Stella happy. No point in depriving her of the lad's company. And we can depend on Neil and Deirdre to see that they don't get out of hand. It's a holiday after all.

At once the mulled wine started to flow. Then they all made short work of the gargantuan meal and the dancing began, with old Neil playing his liveliest reels on the fiddle. Flora tried to stifle her disapproval as she watched young inhibitions being shed. Jenny's behaviour was impeccable as always but even she had a glazed look about the eyes by the time the singing started, whereas Alastair and Rachel seemed not to care who saw their antics. Flora felt they ought to be exercising more self-restraint in the presence of Alastair's pregnant wife and tried to meet Kate's eye in the hope that she might intervene. But as always Kate was determined to ignore her presence.

But at that very moment Alexander consulted his pocket watch and stopped the reel in mid-fling. ''Tis mid-night, everyone! Happy New Year! And may Flora and Allan and all their family find 1775 a year of peace, prosperity and fulfilment in their new home!'

Everyone hugged everyone else then, and Flora could not but note that Rachel had purposely disarrayed her clothes just as she and Alastair met to exchange the customary greetings. Her low-cut gown had fallen suggestively from her shoulders – one tiny tug, Flora thought, and the nipples would show – and as she tilted back her head to be kissed the point of her tongue came out and licked her lips in a predatory, provocative gesture. And Alastair made no secret of his interest. His eyes gleamed with ill-concealed lust as he drew the girl to him and kissed her long and hard, one hand caressing the back of her neck and the other slowly kneading her bottom. There was no tenderness in the kiss, nothing of the chaste, shy devotion that irradiated Jenny and Sandy's embrace. Only sex. Sex at its cruellest and most basic.

Kate and Roddy didn't notice. Kate could never see wrong in anything her son did, and besides she was waxing maudlin by this time, uncharacteristically clinging to Roddy and wailing about someone called Maisie who had died one New Year. Flora knew the memories would mean nothing to her but could not help listening all the same.

'She was that bonnie! Why did she have to die? And not only she. There was Lord Boyd, that you claim was your father, felled on the scaffold, and the brave Lady Anne, that outwitted Hawley and befriended me and mine. To think that they're all gone and forgotten, as we shall all be soon!'

Her outburst trailed away to a sob and Flora guessed that only a life-time's restraint had prevented her from including young Alastair's father in her litany. In similar circumstances Allan would gruffly have told Flora that it was the drink talking. She would feel better in the morning. But Roddy was soothing his wife with platitudes. New Year was always an emotional time, he was saying. She had to be strong and live life in the here and now, never regretting times that were irrevocably gone. Come. Better perhaps that she go to bed. He would fetch her a posset.

As the Boyds detached themselves from the company Hannah's eyes followed them, full of helplessness and pain. She hadn't missed a moment of the charade enacted by Rachel and Alastair, and was sitting now like a trapped animal, valiantly trying to hide her chagrin. Flora's practised eyes noted the blueness beneath the normal sallow hue of the girl's skin and the hurt, haunted look on her face: she even thought she saw a flutter of movement under Hannah's waist as the unborn child stirred. Anger welled up, all the more vehement for its very impotence. How she would feel if Alex did that to Anne! Or if she found Allan behaving so! Did none of them care about Hannah simply because she was racially different? Here she was, far from her own people in Salem at the one time of year when she should be surrounded by love, and they were all spurning her, her husband flagrantly so.

On impulse she sat beside Hannah and took her hand in hers. 'Come with me to the kitchen and let's have a dish of tea. You look all in.'

She was rewarded by a wan smile. Hannah's glance was still yearning towards the corner where Alastair was leaning over Rachel and flagrantly fingering her ringlets. What the pair intended was clear even to a totally disinterested spectator. What Hannah must be feeling could only be guessed at.

'Forget them, lass. 'Tis nothing. Just the drink. See you fetch a shawl. The rain's teeming down out there.'

Together they gingerly negotiated the mud of the courtyard, guided not just by the candle light that glowed and flickered in the kitchen premises but also by a cacophony of shrieks and heuchs and voices raised in raucous song. Flora tentatively pushed the door open to find herself in a scene of bacchanalian revelry surpassing anything she had ever experienced. The whole room was vibrating, the floor thumping and groaning and the very roof creaking, so that it seemed that the whole building could collapse about their heads. One fellow was playing the bagpipes, and not very well at that: the sound, best heard as it slides down distant mountains, seemed at close quarters no more than a tuneless skirl of farts and belches. There was a strong stench of ale and whisky with a distinct underlay of sweat, vomit, tobacco and the miasma of unwashed human bodies – most of which, Flora realised with a shock of disgust, were in various stages of undress.

'Hold your nose, Hannah,' Flora cautioned, thinking that the girl was probably feeling squeamish already. 'And see that nobody knocks you down. Folks are flinging themselves about in those reels as if Auld Nick himself were after them. If you thought that was debauchery back there you have yet to see what 'tis like when the common sort besport themselves. Why, Master Hogarth himself would baulk at it!'

Deirdre was at her elbow in a trice, her face a study of shame and apology.

'Oh, Mistress, why did ye come? I'm black affrontit that ye should see this! There was naught I could do to stop it, I assure ye! The Cuidreach servants are in charge here, ye see. Neil and I have had to learn that we're here on sufferance!'

'It's all right, Deirdre. I know you're not one for the drink. And I'm not here to pry, nor yet to stay and spoil the fun. All I want is a dish of tea for Mistress Boyd here. She's feeling poorly.'

Deirdre cast a look of sympathy in Hannah's direction. It said, as clearly as if she had spoken aloud, 'Aye, and I'd feel the same gin I were wed to that monster.' All she did say, however, was, 'Of course, Ma'am, I'll fetch you some tea. Both of you could be doing with some, I'm thinking. How you're going to find a place to sit in this den of iniquity is unbekennt to me, though.'

Somehow Flora found a bench quite close to the door and Hannah managed to squeeze in beside her, her bulk overhanging the seat and severely testing its strength. Only now could they just distinguish separate identities in what had initially been a seething mass of bodies. Flora's eyes strained through the veil of pipe smoke. There was Colin MacArthur, acting the goat as usual, swinging his partner so sorely that it was a wonder her arm was still in its socket: and she screeching with laughter, not caring if she landed in the middle of the next set. Duncan Anderson was there too, and well on in drink. He had left Skye because his wife had died and with her all his ambitions. Flora suspected that the whisky was his chosen route to forgetfulness, and it was evident that if he took much more he would be unable to stand, far less dance a reel. Then over yonder was Effie Murdoch, her coarse laugh ringing above the music. And Dan Fernie with his shaggy hair and raggedy clothes: could the man not find something decent to wear for the New Year ceilidh? And away over there, at the back of the room…

Flora's heart missed a beat. Yes, it was Stella. Stella standing tall and proud, with white egret feathers in her hair, and wearing a gown that was all too familiar because it was Flora's best, the green one she had worn at the Wilmington reception and had eschewed this time because there was a bad wine mark on the hem. And there on the girl's shoulder, the final effrontery, was Flora's most treasured possession, the rhinestone brooch that had been the Prince's gift! Beside Stella stood young Hannibal, gazing at her as if she were some angel sent from heaven, and at the very moment when Flora's eyes rested on him he actually dared to put out his hand and finger the brooch, as if he were burning to remove it.

A whole host of suppositions and speculations filled Flora's mind then. To steal the clothes Stella must have left the kitchen premises and infiltrated the main house, which she had been forbidden to enter. She must have rifled through drawers and trunks and generally regarded Flora's possessions as hers for the taking. It was unconscionable, just not to be countenanced!

'Stay there, Hannah. I have something to see to,' she said grimly, and skirting the frenzy of the dance she marched to where the unsuspecting pair were stationed and approached them from behind. Stella started, feeling the hand snatching the back of her bodice, but Flora clung on.

'You're coming with me, you ungrateful little thief! I refuse to shelter you any longer!' And taking advantage of the girl's astonishment she frog-marched her back round the kitchen to the door, where she assured Hannah she would not be long, and then out into the rain.

After the rabelaisian din of the servants' ceilidh the revelry of the main house seemed positively staid but Flora had neither the time nor the interest to notice. By great good fortune Allan, Roddy and Alexander had settled by the fire with their tobacco pipes and ale and were deep in conversation. They turned as one when Flora came in, banging the door behind her and causing a blast of cold air to penetrate the room.

'Good God in heaven, what's this, Flora? You're like a bat out of hell!'

Allan's voice started on a note of irritation but lost its edge as he took in the scene before him: the mulatto wearing Flora's best dress, the brooch and the feathers. 'Oh, I see. So this is how your slave girl repays your compassion. With robbery and guile.'

By this time Stella had found her tongue. Her eyes flashed.

'Ah don' mean no stealin', Massah MacDonald! Ah jes took a li'l loan ob de dress fo' de occasion, seein' as how it was a special day an' Ah dinn hab no new clothes like de odder slaves down at de Mumrills. Ah wis gonna put dem rait back in de trunk fust chance Ah got. Oh I be real sorry! Ah no gib you any more reason to be mad at me!'

But Flora had had her fill of the girl's duplicity. 'Be quiet, wench. Your prayers and protests no longer cut any ice with me!'

Then she turned to Roddy. 'Does your offer to hire this incorrigible jade from me still stand? If so, have her and good riddance. You can take her away with you tomorrow. Meanwhile I hope Alexander and Annabella have some safe place to keep her under lock and key. I wash my hands of her.'

Roddy looked thoughtful for a moment but seemed to come to a decision. 'Aye. I shall hire her, at least until you and Allan move west. She'll go to Alastair, though, and work as a field hand. Kate and I don't want her about the house. We've heard too much about her antic ways from Farquhard – aye, and from you folks too. Evil walks with her wherever she goes.'

Stella's eyes darted from one to other of the speakers as the discussion went on, and with each decision they grew rounder and more frightened. Watching, Flora saw the last vestige of confidence fade from the girl's face and unmitigated terror take its place. A strangled cry issued from her, like a kitten mewing.

'Aw, Miz MacDonald, hon!' she ventured, and gradually found her tongue again, Flora suspected out of sheer desperation. 'You no gawn do stuff lik dat to dis slave gal dat lubs you! Young Massah Alastair, he de very Debbil incarnate an' Ah don' care who Ah sez it to! He worse dan de oberseer at Campbell's, an' dat's sayin' somethin'!'

'Less of that, do you hear!' This from Roddy. 'Alexander, is there perhaps a wee closet where we can lock this creature away for the night? And maybe Annabella or Flora here has an old shift that she can change into, for she'll have to shed that gala robe. The audacity of it, thinking she could get away with filching her mistress's finery!'

Somehow the jollifications lost their zing after that. Hannah returned somewhat cheered from the kitchen but declared herself ready for bed, where Flora feared she would not find Alastair waiting: ominously, there was no sign either of him or of Rachel. Sandy and Jenny were still in the parlour but were totally engrossed in one another, while Kate had retired long since. As one by one folks crept to bed there should have been only the usual night noises to lull them to sleep – an owl hooting, the rain pattering on the window, a horse neighing in its stall, wolves howling from the forest – but Stella was determined that they would not sleep. She kept up a constant screeching all night, from the closet by the stairs. Flora was reminded of a terrier they had once had at Flodigarry, that had shown its indignation at being kennelled outside by yapping nonstop till dawn, every night for a week. Eventually she stuck cotton in her ears, pulled the bedclothes over her head and insisted upon shutting the noise off from her consciousness. It did not quite work, for the keening echoed in her dreams, but at least she was not tempted to go and offer comfort. She knew that this time she had to harden her heart.

There were a great many bleary eyes and aching heads at breakfast next morning and few could stomach the vast amounts of food that Annabella had prepared. Kate, Jenny and Roddy did manage to polish off bacon and eggs, sausage, black pudding and coffee, but Rachel was very subdued and only pretended to eat, while Alastair had an air of furtive triumph about him. Flora wondered how many others at the table had noted how unusually flushed his face was and how, while ostensibly paying scant attention to Rachel, he every so often cast a look of sly complicity in her direction. Flora wondered if he had joined Hannah at all the night before. It was certainly obvious that he and his cousin had not stopped at mere foreplay. It crossed her mind then, in one of those flashes of intuition that carry a perverse kind of certainty with them, that despite her seeming forwardness Rachel could well have been a virgin before last night. The Strachan woman, she remembered, had been fanatically strict with her daughter. It could well be, then, that given freedom and an ample supply of drink Rachel had succumbed all too readily to Alastair's blandishments. Too late to regret it now! Anyway, whatever the situation it was Hannah Flora was sorry for. She had not appeared at table, and when questioned Kate looked unconcerned and said offhandedly, 'Oh, 'tis but a touch of the vapours. Too much sack last night, I'll warrant.'

Flora was tempted to retort that the girl's trouble was grief, not drink, but bit back the words: no point in further fuelling Kate's resentment.

The other subject she knew she did not dare broach was the fate of Stella. After screaming for most of the night the slave had fallen ominously quiet. Had she suffocated in that closet, or did she realise, with that uncanny insight of hers, that the eeriness of her silence drew people's attention all the more?

Roddy perhaps read Flora's mind. 'Great breakfast, Annabella. Sorry none of us did justice to it. But it's time we got a move on.

Alexander, maybe you can lend us a dog collar and some chains, to transport that half-caste safely? She's the kind that needs restraint. Would run away given an inch.'

Alastair meanwhile had opened the door and yanked Stella out by the scruff of her neck. She had been lying curled up in the foetal position and continued to crouch, cowed and terrified, at his feet. The sounds she uttered were like the squeaks of an abused puppy but far from arousing his pity they seemed to prompt him to further excesses of cruelty.

'Get up, you scheming, thieving black bitch, or I'll make you crawl on all fours to the Mumrills, like the animal you are!'

Pity wrenched at Flora's heart. She could not help comparing this degraded creature to the defiant reveller of the night before, with the feathers in her hair and her body moulding itself to the fluid contours of her mistress's green gown. Now her black matted hair stood on end from fright, the star on her forehead seemed to flash silver in the morning sun, and the ragged shift she wore was so pitifully short that had she not been clutching it to herself and pulling it down over her knees her whole uncovered pubic area would have been visible.

Alastair was all too aware of that. 'Cunt!' he hissed. 'Did I not say get up on your feet?'

At that Flora made to run forward but Allan held her back. His grip was like a vice. 'The wench deserves whatever treatment she gets. Let the Boyds do what they will with her. No need to watch this if it makes you squeamish.'

Feeling so helpless and chastened that she was dangerously close to tears Flora took herself off then to the tiny room that Allan and she had been sleeping in, and stationed herself at the window while the Boyds assembled to begin their journey home. Whether he had done it by accident or design was not clear, but Alastair had assigned the job of supervising Stella to Hannibal. The lad had to stand and watch as a leather collar was clamped around the girl's neck and attached by a long chain to the back of the Boyds' cart. Then her hands were padlocked together and she was blindfolded. Flora found herself praying under her breath that Hannibal would not be so besotted by love that he would try to free the captive: one such move, and he would suffer a similar fate. Hatred of Alastair boiled and burned in her, and she marvelled that otherwise civilised, kindly people like Roddy and Alexander should condone such barbarity. But they were all piling into the carriage or mounting their horses now, as if nothing untoward were taking place.

She knew she had to go to the door and see them off, or she would be open to a charge of churlishness. But the phlegm rose in her throat as she stood waving, outwardly calm, and watched Stella being hauled along behind that trundling vehicle. How long could she stay upright, and how long until Hannibal felt forced to succour her?

A gulp of anguish, and then tears of guilt and futility began to flow.

VI

February 1775

Mid-February, and already there were subtle signs of spring. The air had lost its bitter edge and there was a haze of fresh green appearing.

'There'll be a drift of thorn blossom first,' Annabella said, 'then the dogwood and crocus and jonquils will appear in the yard, to be followed by the flourish on the fruit trees. It's beautiful, the spring here. Far gentler than at home. Oh, there's a robin! First you'll have seen, Flora. You don't get them down at the coast. That's a male of course, and he won't sing until the females arrive, probably in a week or two.'

Flora gazed fascinated at the brown bird Annabella had indicated, which had just settled on a hand cart by the back door. To her eye it seemed larger than life, at least four times as large as a tiny, homely Scottish robin, and its breast was a brilliant red. Annabella clearly saw it as a symbol of the return of spring, but to Flora it was yet another instance of the new nomenclature she had to get used to. Even the birds were different, and more confusingly so than ever if they bore the very names that filled her with nostalgia.

The new calves were as vulnerably tender as they had been at home, though, and she relished their appearance in the fields, with their big pleading eyes and tottering spindly legs. Sandy and Allan spent a lot of time helping Alexander with the calving and Jamie insisted on being there too. He hated to be left out of anything the older men were involved in, and always came in in the evening round-eyed with wonder.

One night he was particularly excited and came running in ahead of the others.

'Sandy shot a bear! It was nosing around the cattle and would have carried off a calf given half a chance! Uncle Alexander's real pleased. Says it has been snooping around all winter when it should have been hibernating, and has been getting too bold for his liking. He knew it was there from the way the bark of the big hickory yonder had been slashed to shreds, but didn't want to alarm us. Oh, isn't it exciting, Ma! See, they're bringing it in now. Uncle says they'll use every bit of it. The skin for clothes, and the fat for lard and grease, and even the meat!' His freckled face wrinkled in disgust. 'Imagine eating bear!'

'We may have eaten it already, without knowing it,' Flora smiled. 'We'll have to get used to eating all kinds of strange things in the wilderness and may well find them good.'

Shouts echoed from the yard. Sandy's voice. 'Where shall we put him? Auntie won't want him in the house, will she, and I can't see Morag welcoming him in the kitchen!'

And Alexander replying. 'Put him in the toolhouse until morning. We'll skin and section him then.'

She looked out to see them dragging the great shaggy carcase through the yard. The beast looked strangely pathetic in death, despite the savage teeth and the lethal claws: its lacklustre eyes held no menace now and a trail of blood slithered in its wake. The men might be triumphant but she could not help a pang of pity. Better stop thinking that way, though. Out here nature was a force to be reckoned with and if people did not confront it with all the determination, ruthlessness and cunning they were capable of the wilderness would never be tamed.

Having seen the bear safely deposited in the tool shed Jamie lost interest in it and launched into his next piece of information.

'And there's an owl in the barn! Uncle Alexander says it lives there. A barred owl, he calls it. Oh, and Ma! I helped birth a wee calf! The cow was bellowing as if Auld Nick himself were after her, and kicking so hard it took every one of us to hold her still. Then suddenly there the bonnie wee new beastie was, up on its feet right away, all wobbly.'

'Aye, that must have been grand, Jamie. But look at you! You can't sit down to your supper like that. Go and clean yourself up at the pump.'

The lad was indeed filthy. Muck streaked his face, his jacket and breeks were encrusted with mud and dried blood, and he reeked of the midden. But she was proud of him. His body was filling out, he was clear of mind and steady of eye, and she could see that he was happy.

So was Allan. He was in his element caring for the beasts. It was what he was good at. Night after night he came to bed smelling of cows. That she did not mind, especially as his contentment combined with fresh stirrings of sexuality and he came to her hard and urgent, responding to the life force within him. But she realised too that he did not dare indulge himself to the extent of forgetting their need to find land.

One night as they lay replete with pleasure, his hand lying languid on the damp mound of hair at her crotch, her own gently caressing his slackened penis, she decided she simply had to remind him of it.

'My dear, is it not time you sought out this Caleb Touchstone and arranged to view his plantation now that the weather's mild again? We want to find our new place before summer and give ourselves a chance to get settled. Kind though they are we cannot be beholden to Alexander and Bella for ever.'

She sensed his irritation and feared for a moment that she had misjudged both her timing and the extent of her influence, but he seemed to swallow the tetchy reproach that was on his lips and said instead, 'Aye, You're right as always. I've been putting the journey off. Fear of the unknown, maybe, and not wanting to leave you, and enjoying the work with the kye. But I know I must bestir myself. I thought I'd contact Farquhard, or James Hogg, and have our furniture brought up from Wilmington. Sandy and Neil can go down to Cross Creek and bring it up while I go west to see Touchstone. Don't fret, lass. 'Twill all turn out.'

Sensibly Flora said no more, just snuggled into him and tried to sleep. She could not explain even to herself this recent feeling of being irretrievably trapped. She was every bit as frightened of the back country and its dangers as Allan was, yet somehow staying within reach of a town kept them too close to political upheavals that could only worsen as the better weather improved communications. And though Allan could protest his neutrality till doomsday she could not see him resisting Martin's flattery and his own lifetime's inclination to support the House of Hanover through thick and thin. The sooner she lured him away from trouble the better.

If only each expedition did not involve long absences of a week or more, for she missed her menfolk when they were away. They eventually left towards the end of the month and she settled down to helping Annabella on the farm, knowing that the harder she worked the more quickly the time would pass. Jamie was a great consolation, young though he was. He had been desperate to go with his father but Allan had been adamant. 'You're needed here, to look after your mother,' he had said firmly, and Jamie, bless him, had accepted the ultimatum without protest.

But she never slept well without Allan beside her, and made a practice of getting up at dawn to attend to the fires, collect the morning's eggs, and set the breakfast table. Chilly and dark though it was there was a freshness to the air then. She could sense the sap rising in the pastures. The new calves called plaintively for their mothers and birds were beginning their tentative twitterings. If life continued as pleasantly when they moved up country she would have nothing to complain about.

But as she was going about her tasks on the fourth morning she was aware of unusual noises outside. It was not yet light. Not a bird or barnyard fowl had been stirring but the subdued clatter set them all squawking. She found herself shrinking with fear. Instinct told her that the intruder did not belong here. Outlaws and robbers? Some deranged Indian or disaffected slave? A bear maybe, come from the forest to carry off the young hogs?

'Psst! Miz MacDonald, ma'am! You in dere? Dis here's Hannibal! Ah be needin' yourn help! Dey've buried Stella!'

She opened the door then to a breathless and bedraggled Hannibal. His eyes were staring in his head and he looked fit to drop from exhaustion.

'Good Lord 'a mercy, lad! Whatever's that you're saying? You mean the wench is dead?'

'Better for her an she was, lady. Dat young Massah Alastair hab de debbil in him, an' he gits mad an puts Stella in dis big hole, an' cubbers her up to de neck in de mud, an' leabs her dere wid two big white men keepin' guard. An' me, Ah cain't do nuttin' to help. If Ah try, he be mad at me an' eider gib me a beatin' or bury me too, an' a lot ob help Ah'd be to her den. So Ah decided in de night to ride up here an' ask you to help. Ah kin guess dat for all you hired Stella to dat Beelzebub you kind at heart. An' she still belong to you, don' she? Ah set to thinkin' dat maybe if you spoke to Massah Alastair he'd hab to dig her up agin.'

At first it was impossible for Flora to take in the enormity of what she was hearing. She could hear Allan's voice in her head, telling her that Stella was no longer any concern of hers – could hear Roddy too, insisting that Ashantis belonged to a different species that did not experience pain as we do. But still her reaction was one of unmitigated horror. And Stella was half white; so did that mean that she was not entirely immune to suffering? Anyway, it was inhuman to treat even an animal that way!

'How long has she been there?'

'Since yesterday morn, ma'am. 'Twas more dan ma life was worth to try comin' here by day, when dere was work for me in de stables. E'en so Ah'm likely missed a'ready... Aw, Mistress, don' you be standin' dere a-wonderin' an a-hesitatin'. Wid ebery minute we lose we bringin' Stella closer to her death!'

His voice trembled with urgency and desperation and Flora forgave him its sharp, disrespectful edge. Quickly she pulled herself together. Absolutely no question of her denying the boy's plea. She had already made up her mind. After all, when had she ever failed to give succour, no matter what the likely outcome? But she had to stay practical.

'All right. I shall help. But five minutes will make no difference now. Sit down while I change into riding clothes and get some food for the journey. See, there's some bread and ale on the dresser yonder. Eat your fill of it. You look half starved. Where's your horse?'

'Ah tied him to a tree down the hill, 'longside the creek, so's not to disturb nobody. Dere be some here, namin' no names, dat hates

Stella. An' den Ah jes creeps up, quiet as a possum, an den Ah
sees you in de candlelight dere an' Ah tinks to maself, bless ma
soul Ah tinks, dere be dat good kind Miz MacDonald dat rescued
Stella from de bad people down Wilmington way. She de very
pesson Ah wanna see...'

As the hysterical explanation went on and on the boy's teeth
began to chatter. Flora was reminded of the lacerations he had
suffered that day by the river, when the alligator had savaged him.
Poor fellow, he seemed to be destined to suffer for misdemeanours
not entirely of his own making. At least, she thought, he was
Roddy's slave rather than Alastair's, and surely Roddy would find
other punishments for this present breach of discipline, rather than
burying him alive.

'All right. I understand. Now eat what you can and we'll be off.'

They found old Neil in the courtyard, wielding a broom by
lantern light. He looked up in dismay, his eyes registering sheer
astonishment at Hannibal's appearance. 'And what might you be
doing here at this time o' the mornin', young fellow?'

Then seeing Flora he tried to inject an element of respect into
his voice but still could not contain his curiosity and disquiet.

'Oh, 'tis you, mistress. And where might ye be thinking of going
with this young jackanapes here, afore 'tis even daylight? Ye'll ken
the master has put his trust in me, to see ye come to no harm while
he's away.'

Flora considered briefly and decided to take the lighthearted
line. 'Och Neil, 'tis a matter of no consequence. I'm wanted down
at the Mumrills in a hurry, that's all. Will you saddle Delilah for
me? And tell the others where I've gone.'

A knowing look flashed across the old man's face. ''Tis young
Mistress Hannah's time, maybe?'

Flora had forgotten that possibility as an explanation, but it
seemed quite a valid one. She could always tell them afterwards
that the call had been a false alarm. So she simply nodded, stood
patting Delilah's nose as Neil prepared her for her early ride, and
jumped on the mare's back with panic beginning to stir in her at
the thought of the task ahead.

'Jes you ride along back o' me, Miz MacDonald,' Hannibal
whispered encouragingly. 'A good ting dat ma horse Sammy
knows ebery inch ob de track between here and de Mumrills. He

bin doin' it, eben in the dark, many a time dis winter. Ah be tellin' you as shouldn't, but Stella and me, we be lubbers you see, an' she jes be done tellin' me she carryin' ma chile. Ebber since dat day by the ribber...'

Flora didn't know which emotion was uppermost in her then – alarm at the slaves' clandestine meetings and Stella's subsequent pregnancy, reassurance because the lad was so familiar with the terrain, or amusement at the ridiculous coincidence of the horses' names. Sammy and Delilah, indeed! But Hannibal had already turned and was stumbling down the hill towards the creek. Flora dutifully urged Delilah down in his wake and waited while he retrieved Sammy. The horse was just a moonlit shadow in the darkness under the pines but she sensed a touching rapport between the boy and the animal: there was a whinny of welcome when Hannibal approached and a murmured soothing word as the boy mounted and confidently turned the horse's head towards the east.

It was a treacherous track at the best of times, and the hour before dawn on a damp morning in February was by no means one of those. Flora felt the cold drizzle enter her bones and shivered. Slave or not, Hannibal had a masterful way with him that belied his youth, the limp that was the legacy of the alligator's attack, and his lowly status in North Carolina's social hierarchy. Determined to ignore his companion's misgivings he spurred on his steed, simply shouting over his shoulder to her.

'Ah tied a piece ob white linen to de back ob de saddle, ma'am, an' dat way you can see where Ah be, in dis half-light. Ride like de lightnin'! Dere be no time to lose!'

Flora would not have referred to the prevailing gloom as half-light. Mighty trees crowded menacingly in on them, home to the prowling beasts of the night. Occasionally, looking up, she was aware of moonlight piercing the canopy of pines, and the outline of the horse ahead would shimmer briefly like a ghost: then the branches overhead would consolidate again and she had to put her trust in the sound of hooves in front of her, the faint gleam of white from Sammy's saddle, and Delilah's instinctive ability to keep to the path.

Fortunately most of the track was flat and the creeks they had to ford, though swollen by the rain, were passable. They stopped once in a glade to rest the horses, relieve themselves and eat the bread and cheese Flora had hastily flung together, but Hannibal was clearly so agitated and determined to make time that the pause was scarcely refreshing. Ten minutes, and they were off again, Hannibal digging his spurs into Sammy's sides and promising him all kinds of treats when they reached journey's end.

It came surprisingly quickly, and Flora marvelled at how light the eastern sky was when they emerged from the forest and gazed out over the fields and buildings of the Mumrills. Certainly one of the region's finest plantations, she thought, with its neat row of slaves' huts, its mill, barn and outhouses, and that handsome mansion house set in well-tended park land. Over to the left there stood a second house that had been built for Alastair and Hannah, not so opulent but still impressive by the standards of the area, and she wondered whether the young couple were yet stirring. Someone was, for candlelight gleamed in one or two windows.

Hannibal had reined in at last and she urged Delilah on to draw up alongside him, meanwhile breathing a congratulation to the mare.

'Good lass. You've done well. What way, Hannibal? I take it the young master's fields are over yonder? Take me to where Stella is!'

He grunted and started off at a gallop in the direction she had guessed at, stopping eventually by a huddle of low buildings overlooking a fenced field that seemed to have been recently planted, for tiny shoots were just beginning to push through the mud.

'She be round de back dere. By dat shed.'

Flora dismounted. She ached all over. Her riding habit was drenched with the light rain that was falling and her body with perspiration. Beads of moisture streamed down her face, making it difficult for her to see in the dawn twilight. Nothing had taken on definite colour yet: everything was a uniform grey. When, sick with apprehension, she crept behind Hannibal to the side of the shack, all she could make out was a scattering of old stinking gourds that had been missed at harvest time and left to rot. The scene at the back was much the same, just a muddy patch with a few blackened pumpkins strewn about, except that two kilted men carrying pistols were standing guard over one of them. She sensed

Hannibal's body stiffen with fright beside her and then break into a frantic lopsided jog. Her own immediate reaction was sheer sick-making horror. Could that obscene globular excrescence possibly be a human head? She felt her limbs move of their own volition, slow and painful as in some ghastly nightmare. Oh dear God give me courage. To faint now would help nobody.

The head was slumped forward so that the chin had settled in the mud. The features that were visible were of a glaucous hue, like a dead slug. Even the hair, which had been been black and lustrous and less frizzy than that of full-bred negroes, had the appearance of some straggly, fibrous vegetable matter – sisal perhaps, or the fetid filamental growth on a decaying turnip. The stench of putrefaction hung in the air.

Flora MacDonald had seen many ghastly sights in her time. On the *Eltham* and the *Furnace* she had seen young men flogged until the skin on their backs was flayed off in layers and the bone showed through. She still remembered those severed heads on Temple Bar, a livid reminder of the fate that awaited all who dared challenge the might of the House of Hanover. Then on the *Ulysses*, just weeks before, she had watched helplessly as starvation, sea-sickness and disease had turned people she knew into walking skeletons.

But she had never witnessed anything quite like this. Despite herself she gagged and felt the bile fill her mouth, rough and acerbic as wormwood. Her recognition of the two armed guards as Skye men did not help. One, from Armadale, was of her own clan, while the other, a mere boy, was a MacLeod from Dunvegan: she knew that it was through Alexander's exertions that both men had found a livelihood as indentured servants at the Mumrills.

It was this realisation that turned her disgust into rage. She saw the men cower as she vented the full volley of her scorn upon them, spitting out a string of invective in Gaelic.

'Callum! Malcolm! How can you stomach this gruesome scene? Have you no Christian compassion in you at all? You will fetch four spades this very minute – yes, two for yourselves and one each for myself and Hannibal here – and together we shall unearth this poor unfortunate creature!'

The men were regarding one another fearfully but making no move. At last Callum stammered what amounted to a refusal.

'That we cannot do, Mistress. Master Alastair's orders. Nobody gets to dig her up without his say-so.'

She sensed the tension in them, their fundamental decency at war with their dread of reprisal, and summoned all the resources of persuasion and authority she was capable of.

'But the slave belongs to me! Did you not know that? She is but on hire to the Boyds! Where is Master Alastair, anyway? If you will not obey me I bid you fetch him herewith, for there is no time to lose!'

At that the two held a muttered conference. Flora made out only the odd word here and there but it appeared that Alastair was at the big house. Some kind of crisis had arisen – Flora thought she heard the words 'birthing' and 'mid-wife' – and the men were clearly wondering whether they might be justified in freeing Stella since it looked as if she had been forgotten in the general hubbub.

'Aye, we'll do it,' Callum said eventually, and Flora felt a wave of relief surge through her. 'Ye'll take the responsibility for it, though, will ye?'

'I will that, and gladly. Now let's get to work.'

The tools were fetched from the shed. Hannibal was first to launch into the grisly task, and did so with such a touching mixture of impatience, tenderness and apprehension that Flora's heart went out to him. He fell first to his knees in the mire and began scrabbling around the head, feeling for the back of the neck so that he could support it and preserve it from any inadvertent blows.

'Ah be here by you side, darlin',' he crooned. 'Ain't nobody gonna harm you now. See, here's dat good Miz MacDonald come to rescue you. Now you jes stay real still. We all gonna dig like hell to get you outta dere. Me, an' Callum, and Malcolm, and the mistress. An' we'll dig real slow but sure. Dat's a promise. Hold on honey chile. We'll be real gentle.'

Flora was certain that his words of comfort fell on deaf ears. She could not see Stella's eyes but was sure they would be closed in death.

Fortunately the ground around Stella, though heavy and wet, had not had time to become firmly compacted. They had to resist the temptation to sacrifice care to speed, for it would have been all too easy to hurt the girl by delving into her flesh. Flora shuddered when the point of a shoulder blade was suddenly revealed: the skin was the same colour as the fuscous earth and just as lustreless. Then gradually, as the hole around the body was dug away, it was borne in upon her that Stella had been buried stark naked. She felt her own spade edge down towards the girl's belly and stifled a cry of incensed desperation. There was an unborn baby there, and for twenty-four hours it had been buried in that cold wet earth. The stab of realisation made her work all the more frantically. She hastily rubbed away the tears that threatened to blind her view of the task.

They had reached the crotch now and the full beauty of the pregnant female form they were uncovering was there for all to see. Hannibal's pace was slowing and Flora realised with a pang that the lad had to be at the end of his tether. He was crying, straining for all he was worth to control the great gulps of grief that racked his body. Stella's rounded contours had affected Callum and Malcolm differently, however. Flora sensed the frisson of sexual excitement that made them double their efforts to exhume each hand, and then to dig carefully inwards towards the thighs. Their prurience revolted her. They were continuing to dig not out of pity, nor even because she had told them to, but simply out of lust.

There was a great pile of earth around the hole now and had Stella been able to move and control her limbs she would probably have managed to pull her feet and ankles away and free herself. But she had fallen over on her side against the bank of soil and lay awkward and twisted like a rag doll, with her feet still rooted in the earth. A voice in Flora's head whispered that the only feasible line of action now, the only humane thing to do, was to enlist the men's services yet again and have them rebury this pitiful shell of a woman who showed no signs of life.

But Hannibal had other ideas. Quick as a flash he darted forward, grabbed Stella by the waist and wrenched her forcibly away. Then cradling her and murmuring endearments he lifted her in his arms and disappeared round the side of the shed to where the horses were waiting. It was a spectacular feat of strength for a lad who had been through so much, but sheer, desperate determination fuelled his resolve. Callum and Malcolm were caught off guard. Callum lifted his pistol and fired, but too late. Probably can't shoot straight anyway, Flora thought grimly. These fellows are but crofters after all, not soldiers.

It was the kind of occasion when instinct dictates one's reaction. Flora had not consciously considered what her line was to be after Stella was disinterred but she had probably intended to ride over to the Mumrills, tell the Boyds what had happened, and insist that, if the girl still lived, she be treated with kindness until she was well enough to be returned to Mount Pleasant. She would also have pleaded that Hannibal and the two Highland servants guards be exonerated, or at least let off with a light sentence. She had known that her interference would not inveigle her into Alastair's good graces but she cared not a whit about that. If he saw Stella's release as a declaration of war so be it. And she knew that Roddy would undoubtedly be on her side: that was a great encouragement and consolation.

But in the event she forgot all about the Boyds. Her only thought was of Stella. Those burly Highlanders might be hopeless shots but they were still a threat to the two runaways. She knew that if absconding slaves were apprehended the master could do what he liked with them, and punishment by torture or even death was not unknown.

'Callum MacDonald! Malcolm MacLeod! One of you move an inch from here and I'll see you hang!'

It was a ridiculous threat but it worked. Wild and forbidding though the Highlanders looked they were not well endowed with brains and still nurtured a healthy respect for the folks who had been their social superiors at home – the clan chiefs, the tacksmen, the doctors and ministers. They received Flora's outburst with open-mouthed humility and she gave them no time to reflect but darted away through the field, flung herself on to Delilah's back, and rode off in pursuit of Hannibal.

It did not take long to catch up with him, for both horse and rider were thoroughly exhausted and the additional load of Stella's body slowed their progress down. She had been afraid that in his terror and uncertainty Hannibal might already have left the worn track and plunged into the forest, but he had obviously decided to follow the path at least temporarily, perhaps careless now of whether he were apprehended or not.

When she came on him he had just stopped by a creek to water his horse and pay some attention to the limp bundle that had been draped over the saddle. He had taken Stella in his arms and was carrying her tenderly to the water's edge when he heard the thud of hooves behind him and looked back, his eyes wide with terror.

'Aw Miz MacDonald ma'am, y'all done gib us a scare, comin' on us like dat! But dere's nuttin you can do now. Y'all has a'ready done more to help dan we could hope for. Y'all must leab us be now. We gwine manage. Yeah, ma'am. Now that we's free from dat terrible Mumrills place we gwine manage somehow.'

She wondered if the boy had lost his wits. Certainly it would not have been surprising, given what he had been through and was still experiencing. It was as if having remonstrated with her he had dismissed her presence as irrelevant to the task in hand, for he laid his burden gently on a grassy mound and continued to address it.

'Now you jes settle dere a minute, hon. Hannibal gwine fetch you a drink.'

And he stumbled to the creekside while Flora dismounted and, swallowing hard, steeled herself to confront Stella at close quarters. At least the girl was no longer completely naked, for Hannibal had removed his thin cotton jacket and covered her breast, stomach and genitals: but her mud-coated limbs still looked grotesquely disjointed and her eyes remained closed.

Flora knelt, took the girl's wrist in her hand, and was astonished to feel a faint, fluttering throb at the pressure point. Her heart leapt. 'Hannibal! Come quickly! She's still alive!'

She tried to master her exultation, to tell herself that this trace of life was like the last glowing ember of a dying fire, but there was always the faint hope of its being nursed to a lambent flicker, and then to a flame. Then when Hannibal came running and excitedly raised Stella's head in a bid to help her drink, to be rewarded by a long, steady puzzled look from her large yellow-tinted eyes, they had to make a determined mutual effort to restrain their delight, for fear of frightening their patient back into unconsciousness.

'She will recover now, I'll warrant! Praise the Lord! See, let's get some warmth into her. I have more clothes on than I need. Leave us, Hannibal, and I shall make sure she is decently and warmly clad for the rest of our journey. Back to Mount Pleasant.'

It was Flora's way to make decisions, especially where servants were concerned, and it came as a flabbergasting shock when Hannibal drew himself up and replied firmly, 'No way, Miz

MacDonald. No disrespect meant, ma'am, but dat not a good idea. I know dis Stella here be yourn. You done buy her wid your money an' you hab de power to claim her. But dere be udder reasons dan money dat decide where a pesson otta be, an' her place be wid me, ma'am. If she die, wid ma chile in her, den I grieve sore an' gib dem both a decent Christian burial, for we be Christians both no matter what de white folks say 'bout her bein' a witch.'

It was flagrant insubordination on the lad's part but Flora saw the logic in it. She well appreciated that the heart has reasons that defy rational analysis, and could not but admire Hannibal's courage in gainsaying her.

'But where will you go? You may be sure that Alastair Boyd will waste no time in having you hunted down, and with the added burden of a sick woman on the point of death …'

'God will look after us. God, and some folks I know in de forest down Wilmington way, dat's all runaways like us. Da likes ob you be unaware ob dem people but dey dere, an' Stella's mudder be one ob dem. Dat's where we go, an' de sooner de better. We rest by day deep among de trees, far away from de track, den trabbel by night. Der be traders on de ribber too, dat harbour runaways an' buy tings from us widout askin' no questions. You not to be anxious for us, Miz MacDonald. We try to get word to you somehow, when we safe and sound. Now Ah want you to go home, lady. You done all you could an' we grateful to you for eberyting. All I ask now is that you pray for us, for de prayers ob de likes ob you must allus be heard, you bein' an angel an' all.'

She knew that she had no argument. The boy's simple faith in himself and his God was irrefutable. So she knelt again and took Stella's hand in hers. A brief pressure on the wrist ascertained that the pulse had strengthened to a steady beat: if it could do that in a mere ten minutes the chances of the girl's surviving had improved twofold.

'Bless you, child,' she whispered, 'and the bairn you carry.'

It was like a miracle when Stella's lips moved to shape a reply, but the only sound that came was a low croak as the vocal chords strove to function and failed.

'Take care of her, Hannibal. She's still mine, you know!'

This time he did not contradict her, but just nodded, and she realised that emotion had got the better of him: so without another word she mounted her mare and turned back on to the path again. Her heart was heavy. What chance of survival did a sixteen-year-old boy and a half-dead pregnant girl have in those forests, with wild beasts and even wilder white men lying in wait? But at the same time she experienced a little thrill of exhilaration. Chances were the world would never hear of this, her latest selfless bid to succour a fugitive victim of violence, but then Hannibal was no prince. At least, not in the worldly sense.

VII

Apart from her brief forays to the well Flora had not been accustomed to riding alone in the forest, and the harrowing events of the morning had unnerved her. The thick resinous smell of the pines hung heavy in the air, mingling with the sharp tang of leafmould and fungi. Once she smelt an unbelievably pungent odour that made her choke and gasp, and recognised it for skunk: even Delilah reacted to that with a whinny of disgust and seemed to quicken her pace, anxious to escape the overpowering stench. Flora resolved then to stop at the first glade she came to, preferably by a creek, so that she could drink her fill and wash away the vomit that had risen unbidden to her throat.

Her mind was in a whirl. Why had she agreed to abandon those young people to the terrors of this uncanny wilderness? Should she not have insisted that they return with her to Mount Pleasant, where Stella might have been cared for and the fugitives could have been hidden until the search for them was abandoned? For surely Annabella and Alexander, bound though they were by the mores of their slave-holding neighbours, would have been as shocked by Alastair's brutality as she was, and as anxious to help. But it was too late. She had allowed Hannibal to talk her out of it. So now she simply had to gather her wits and think what her strategy was to be. How much should she tell the others, if anything? If only she had found out whether Hannah had had her baby, for that had been her pretext for her hasty dawn departure, but then everything had happened so quickly!

She could not be quite sure but she thought that the clearing she came to at this point in her deliberations was the very one she had stopped at with Hannibal on the way over. She had been aware then, even in the early dawn, of arching branches, the kinder contours of live oak and chestnut and sycamore, and alders by a stream. Water, pure and cleansing like the forgiveness of God. She wanted to plunge into it, feel it trickle into her hair and down her neck, washing away the grime of delving, the sweat of the journey and the subtler, more pervasive foulness of the evil she had seen. Then sleep, calm and innocent.

She knew one did not deliberately court sleep when alone in the forest, but a bath in the creek? Why not? Doubtless there were leeches and she shuddered at the thought of those lurking water moccasins, but they were a risk she was prepared to take.

Having tethered Delilah to a tree she divested herself of the few clothes she had been wearing – Stella had been more in need than she of warmth – and left them on a grassy verge. Then she braved the icy waters of the creek. The impact of the cold was devastating. First it took her breath away and then she felt it creep into her limbs, cramping them inexorably. But she almost welcomed the physical challenge when she suddenly found herself totally immersed in a deep pool, for she recognised that the morning's events had left her curiously detached, numb to external influences of weather and temperature. Perhaps now, through the body's torment, she could find catharsis.

She did not know how long she lay there in the freezing water. It certainly was not a pleasurable time though the pain of it effectively prevented her from confronting the problems that had piled up in those last few hours. Afterwards she was to wonder whether she might have let the cold take over: at one stage she had indeed felt almost disembodied, and to have succumbed would have been all too easy.

But Delilah suddenly whinnied a warning from the bank. There was a clatter of hooves, a braying of dogs, a crash of activity through the undergrowth, and Roddy's voice sounded through the glade.

'That's Mistress MacDonald's horse! We've found them, lads! Well done!'

Flora had scarcely been contemplating anything as deliberate as an Ophelia-like suicide, but even if she had she would have preferred not to be discovered naked. As it was she managed painfully to pull herself in under the trees that overhung the bank and sit there, shivering. Pulling the willow branches aside she watched Callum MacDonald grab one of the dogs and plunge into the forest ahead, while Malcolm MacLeod branched off in the other direction. But Roddy's dog was not so easily side-tracked. Horrified, she watched him sniff out her clothes some hundred yards downstream from her and stand beside them, barking commandingly.

'You've found something, boy? Let me see!'

The silence that followed spoke worlds, and would have been funny had it not been so compromising. For there she was, covered in shame and goose pimples, gazing into Roddy Boyd's astonished eyes.

'Flora! Whatever are you doing?'

'What do you think I'm doing? Dancing a minuet? Just call your dogs off and then let me get out of here and get dressed. And turn your back while I'm doing it.'

He raised one eyebrow and grinned. 'But of course, ma'am. You know I'd never dream of looking. See, I'll tie this kerchief over my eyes and then maybe you'll let me give you a hand to get out of there. The bank's quite steep and slippery.'

She realised then that he was right. It wasn't going to be easy to clamber up without help right there, especially as her whole body was freezing. Gingerly she grabbed his sinewy outstretched hand and willed herself to find a foothold in the layers of mud at the water's edge. Since her feet lacked all sensation it was a mercy he was there to encourage her, for it was only with immense effort that she heaved herself up beside him.

'Oh Flora, you're incorrigible! 'Tis winter still, in the mountains up there. You've been laving yourself in melted ice! 'Tis as well I came this way. See, this will revive you.'

He produced a flask of brandy-wine from his hip pocket and she gladly drank from it, feeling its life-giving warmth trickle down her throat and penetrate the furthest visceral recesses of her body. She was doubly aware now of her nakedness, of how her nipples had reacted to the cold by standing up hard and erect. She knew too that her face was flaming with embarrassment. No man but Allan had ever seen her like this. It only added to her confusion to realise that she was disproportionately conscious of her body's shortcomings, of a stomach slack from child-bearing, pendulous breasts and podgy calloused feet.

It was a huge relief to see that Roddy's eyes were indeed covered, as he had promised. He was a man of honour, after all, and perhaps, being a doctor, nudity meant little to him? He certainly had adopted a brisk, almost professional manner.

'I brought a blanket, not knowing how long I'd be away. Give yourself a good rub down with it and get dressed. You'll be in agony for a while, of course, thawing out. And serves you right if I may say so. That was a most irresponsible thing to do.'

The next few minutes, while she dried herself and dressed, were indeed torture. Sensation returned to her limbs only very gradually, and came in the form of an excruciating, tingling pain which took complete control of her, reducing her to helpless tears. But eventually she scrubbed her wet cheeks with her sleeve, squared her shoulders and ventured out from behind the trees.

He had lit a fire and the sharp odour of burning pine cones filled the glade, mingling with the homely, more than welcome aroma of toasting corn bread.

'Come and eat,' he said. 'You'll feel more human then and readier to face the rest of your ride home. For I can't go with you, Flora. You have to understand that. Runaway slaves have to be apprehended and punished. They can't be allowed to run abroad, terrorising the countryside.'

'But that's preposterous, Roddy! The very idea of Hannibal and Stella terrorising anyone! It will take them all their time to stay alive, considering the state that poor girl was in! You know what that stepson of yours did to her, don't you?'

His face clouded. 'Aye. The bondsmen, Callum and Malcolm, told me. You put them in a right awkward position, Flora, making them dig the wench up. '

'But she was mine! And even if she had not been it was a barbaric, monstrous thing to do! Surely you, a doctor, could never condone that kind of punishment!'

'I'm not saying I do but as I've told you before slaves have to be disciplined according to the severity of their crimes. Alastair tells me that Stella was sullen and disobedient, which only bears out her previous reputation. We could not have her spreading insubordination. And now she has got Hannibal, one of my best slaves and a damn good stableboy, into all kinds of trouble. Just wait till I lay my hands on him! He'll wish he had never been born! Where are they, anyway? Did you not keep them with you?'

He was addressing her as if she were some kind of obstinately disobedient child and she felt anger and defiance boil up inside. His attitude increased her determination to give nothing away.

'Just as well that I did not, 'twould seem, if doing so would have delivered them to your tender mercies! I can swear with my hand on my heart that I haven't the slightest idea where they've gone, or even in which direction. But of one thing I'm wellnigh certain. Even without your dogs on their heels and your halloos echoing through the forest they have little chance of survival. The girl was near death. A miracle it was that she had survived at all.'

By this time Flora's teeth were chattering with cold, the accumulated shocks of the morning, and the effort of challenging Roddy's disapproval. But she could not resist one last bitter recrimination.

'I... I must say that I had expected a wider humanity from you, Roddy Boyd! Why I cannot quite explain. Maybe I had thought there existed a certain affinity of thought and sentiment between us. But I see that I was wrong. Any man who pursues blameless human beings like animals through the woods deserves nothing but contempt. What kind of country is this America, that reduces its servants to the status of pigs?'

She felt the sting of tears return. One reason was physical: the fire was not really warming her, only intensifying the torture of the thawing-out process, and a sudden wave of weakness was making her feel faint. But Roddy's curtness had hurt her more than she was prepared to admit. Cheated of his sympathy she felt isolated and abandoned and her distress was all the keener for being, on the face of it, totally unjustified. Yes, he had been quick to tell her of his past, but that, far from being the intimacy she had imagined, had merely been meant after all as an explanation of, and apology for, Kate's rudeness. As for those times he had accompanied her to the well, they must have been mere courtesies, neighbourly expressions of a willingness to help. She had been crazy to read them as any kind of compliment to her own charms, either of person or of conversation.

She swallowed the tell-tale tears and commanding her voice to betray not a tremor of frailty or disappointment said firmly, 'Annabella and Alexander will be worried for me. Thank you for the food, and the brandy-wine, if not for your gratuitous advice about how to treat fugitive slaves in this godless country.'

The words came out cold and polite, with an edge of sarcasm that she knew was not typical of her, but she scarcely regretted the tone. He thoroughly deserved it.

She had got up and hauled herself away from the fire, determined to master the tremors that were still racking her body, when she felt his hand on her arm.

'No, Flora. I can't let you go from me in anger. I have too much affection and respect for you for that. And you see, someone had to track those fugitives down, or at least make a show of doing so. Had Alastair been available, he would have followed more wholeheartedly than I, but with the new babe and all his attention was elsewhere.'

'You mean, the babe is born?'

'Aye. A wee lass. A bonnie wee thing, though of course, being a new grandfather, I could be prejudiced.' His voice thrilled with wonder and pride.

It was the kind of news that delighted Flora's heart. Vividly remembering how she had felt when Anne had produced little Allan – the sense of fulfilment, almost as if she herself had done the labouring; the lightness of spirit and assurance of family continuity – she immediately forgot her previous displeasure and impulsively threw out her arms to hug him.

'Oh, Roddy, I'm so glad for you!'

His lips were in her hair and he was murmuring softly, 'You see, we can't be enemies for long, you and I.'

Then he kissed her on the mouth and she felt her whole body ache with longing for him. It would be all too easy to indulge their mutual passion here in the woods. It would be their secret, the physical expression of the strong attraction they felt for each other, something totally outside everyday life. Allan and Kate need never know.

But he was pushing her gently from him and saying in his normal voice, 'There now. Better go and take the glad tidings to Mount Pleasant. We shall be summoning you all right soon, no doubt, to wet the baby's head.'

'And you? You intend to carry on this search?'

His face darkened. 'Aye. I do that. Hannibal's mine, and valuable. Better too that I should find him myself than that he should be at the mercy of any gun-happy dolt of a farmer that might chance upon him in the wilderness. Sorry, Flora, but that's just the way it is. Now off you go.'

He walked across with her to where Delilah was tethered and helped her mount. Then he whistled to the dog and together they cut back into the trees while Flora gave the mare her head and sent her thoughts winging through the forest to wherever Stella and Hannibal were. She might be white of skin and considered gentry in these parts but she knew, when the pursuit was on, that her every sympathy was with the hunted. It had always been so for her, and no colonial, no matter how persuasive, would ever change her.

VIII

March 1775

Flora spent the days until Allan's return in a state of tension. As she had feared, Annabella and Alexander had not applauded her expedition to rescue Stella. She had arrived back late in the day soaked to the skin by a torrential rain storm, having allowed Delilah to wander off the bridle path and get the pair of them thoroughly lost. Had they not come upon an isolated cabin in a clearing and discovered that the occupant was a MacNeil they might never have found their bearings, for the forest canopy was so dense that even on fine days the sun was rarely visible.

'You mean that you forced Alastair's bondsmen to dig the mulatto up? But if she deserved it, was insolent and disobedient...' Annabella's voice trailed off, uncertain.

Weary though she was of this endless discussion Flora could not but note her questioner's hesitation, and take advantage of it.

'Aye, and knowing yon Alastair you know as well as I what kind of thing she was being thrawn about. She herself is a product of her mother's being forced by somebody just like him, I'll warrant!

But I would ask you to let me be now, Bella. 'Tis clear we shall never agree on't.'

Despite being dank and dismal the early spring weather was amazingly mild, which gave her hope that Stella and Hannibal might have survived, but there was an ominous lack of news from the Mumrills.

Even Annabella remarked upon it. 'I'd expected some kind of word from Roddy and Kate. I hope nothing's wrong. Hannah's tough, like all the Indians, but they say the savages fall prey to infection and the bloody flux more readily than we do. And having that Alastair for a man would make any woman ill. She was all right when you were over there, Flora?'

'Aye. But the babe was just new born. I heard only that 'twas a girl.'

For obscure reasons that she could not explain even to herself she had made scarcely any mention of her encounter with Roddy. Why could she not just be natural about it and tell them the truth, for after all it had been a perfectly innocent and totally accidental meeting? Her vague, unjustified feelings of embarrassment and guilt annoyed and disconcerted her. She needed Allan. That was it. Needed him beside her in bed, his body cleaving to her own. Somehow, she was sure, when he and Sandy got back everything would fall into place.

And to some degree it did. They returned just two days later, amazingly just within hours of each other. Sandy arrived first, bringing one wagon laden with sacks of flour and sugar, barrels of spirits, tools, and bolts of cotton for the women to sew into garments, while the other was stacked with furniture and household effects. He also brought the mail, which he had intercepted quite by chance on its journey from New Bern to Mount Pleasant.

'You'll never believe it, Ma! There's a letter from Ranald! I'm afraid I couldn't resist opening it, especially when I saw that it's from Boston, of all places. Seems he's been posted there. Says they're reinforcing the garrison in case of trouble. Funny, isn't it, to think he's on the same continent, yet so far away. Here. Read it for yourself.'

The letter, written in Ranald's characteristic scrawl, had been sent to them care of Alexander and was very brief, but it at least assured them of his love and concern, and that, coming from Ranald, was a significant blessing. Maybe there would be word from Charles too, soon. So far she had heard only from Johnny. So different from Johnny, the other two were. Johnny the conscientious scholar never put a foot wrong, while Charles and Ranald were always getting into scrapes. Johnny loved cerebral things, was particularly interested in plants and geography, while the others revelled in change, physical challenge, the pleasures of the flesh. Flora loved all her sons, Charles and Ranald, Sandy and Johnny and Jamie, for what they were, the fruits of her body, but in her dreams it was Ranald who came to her most often and he was there beside her in spirit now, weather-beaten and grinning, with his curly brown hair ruffled by the wind and his pleasant voice teasing. Reading his letter she tried not to cry and Sandy, understanding, swept her attention away elsewhere.

'And 'twould seem you have a secret admirer in Governor Martin,' he joked. 'Either that, or for some reason he wants to stay in your good books! There's a large parcel from him here, addressed to you. Got his seal on it and everything.'

Mystified, she opened the package and discovered five packets of fragrant Indian tea. It had been impossible to get hold of any palatable stuff recently and the gift delighted her. 'It's for all of us. Kind of Josiah to remember us, and to realise that it won't be easy for us to get decent tea, out here in the wilds.'

Then, partly to take her mind off the Governor's possible political motives but largely because she was consumed with curiosity, she blurted out, 'But none of this matters! Tell us about what has been happening at the Mumrills! You stopped there on the way up, surely?'

'Oh aye. And the new babe's fine. So is Hannah. You heard nothing to the contrary, did you? Alastair's chagrined that it has turned out to be a girl – sees its femaleness as a reflection on his manhood, or something of the kind – but everybody else is delighted. Too bad that their celebrations have been marred by that Stella woman, yet again. There's a full-scale hunt going on for her and yon Hannibal, the young slave that was mauled by the alligator. Seems there was some kind of intrigue going on between them and they've vamoosed, the young varmints.'

All the time he was thinking, if I talk about other things Ma might not mention Jenny, but of course she did, having cause herself to change the subject.

'And Jenny?'

'Oh, she's fine. Asks to be remembered to you.'

His face was flaming. He did not tell her about the old-fashioned Celtic troth they had plighted, there by the creek, and how Jenny had shyly allowed him to loosen her bodice, fondle her breasts, and move on to wondrously new explorations of her trembling body, so smooth and white that touching her was like handling a new spring flower. Yes, the minister may not have sealed their union with a blessing but that would happen in time, of course. What really mattered was that they were totally committed to one another now.

But Flora did not need to have it spelt out. She knew, and was wondering whether to pursue the subject when a clatter of hooves, a rush of footsteps and a barking of dogs banished it from her mind. Allan's voice shouted through to her and in an instant he was there, his face hale and ruddy and his eyes triumphant.

'I saw Caleb Touchstone! He has decided at last that the back country's no place for a man of his age – he's seventy if he's a day, and his wife's dead – so he's living with a daughter up there, but she can't wait to get back to Cross Creek. She has my every sympathy, poor lass, for he's a dour one. You'd almost think he didn't want to sell, he was that churlish. A big rangy man he is, with a black beard. Must have been right fearsome when he was young. Like that bear Sandy shot, with mean wee eyes that have a squint to them.'

Flora could not contain her impatience. 'Och, Allan, don't keep us on tenterhooks. We're not interested in what the old man looks like! Tell us about the farm!'

Aware then of the circle of curious relatives waiting with bated breath he puffed out his chest like a self-important alderman and proceeded.

'Well, 'tis a long way west, as you know, up beside Hugh. He'll be just about five miles away I reckon, about the distance between here and the Mumrills.'

Annabella's face went pale. 'But Hugh's all of fifty miles from here, Allan! We'll never see you! Och, Flora lass, I wish you didn't have to go that far!'

But Allan brushed the protests aside. 'Wheesht, Bella. We'll see you all right. There's the clan gatherings, for one thing, and a family has cause to unite now and then for all kinds of reasons. Weddings, and funerals, and christenings and the like.'

Each listener had his own private thoughts then. There would be a christening soon, please God, for Anne's babe. But after that? Flora and Annabella both remembered old Hugh, bent and frail, and wondered whether his passing would be the next event to bring them together. But Sandy had caught the word 'wedding' and he visualised Jenny as she had been last night, with her corn-coloured hair spread out on the straw in the Mumrills hay-loft. There was a stirring under his kilt, as if his cock had a life of its own and was determined to assert itself. Yes, he would sacrifice his soul for the sure knowledge that the next family occasion would be a wedding. His wedding. But what did he have to offer Jenny at this stage? Why, his parents and he were virtually homeless! Besides which, he could not rid himself of a vague but undeniable suspicion that Kate did not approve of him.

'I fear your mother doesn't like me,' was the nearest he had come to discussion of it, and Jenny's answer had been unsatisfactory in the extreme.

'Fiddlesticks, Sandy! You imagine things! I guess she wishes that your folks were not so – how shall I put it? British? – but 'tis nothing personal. Except that, should it ever come to a fight, our families would be on different sides, I'll warrant. We'd be for the colonials and you for the King.'

Her cold, blunt analysis had shocked him, coming as it did in the midst of a tender exchange of kisses, but it added another dimension of uncertainty to their situation. He sensed that the relationship between their two families was complicated enough without his making it worse.

Flora was still pressing Allan for details. 'So if this Touchstone place is near Hugh we won't be all that far from Anne?' She was desperate to have her daughter near, just to be able to talk about the daily vicissitudes of domestic life that men might see as trivial but which to women were of vital importance.

Allan grinned. 'Wheesht, Flora. Let me tell you the rest. I saw Anne. 'Twas a bit out of my way but I spent a night at Glendale. She's well, just impatient for the babe to be born, and Allan and

Norman are flourishing. But don't imagine you'll be able to visit
regularly, from Cheek's Creek. It must be at least twenty miles.
Not that we'll never meet gin we make the effort, but we won't be
able just to ride over to Glendale as easily as we can go to the
Mumrills from here, for example. And of course the further west
we go the wilder and more dangerous the country.'

At this Jamie's eyes opened wide. 'Red Indians you mean, Pa,
with feather head-dresses and totem poles and tomahawks? They
cut your scalp off and then eat you, don't they?'

'Nay, lad. Any Indians that's left are away beyond the mountain
they call the Blue Ridge, in country that's yet unexplored. They
have their own lands and are quite peaceable if left alone and
unprovoked. What I meant was that the roads aren't so much used
and the creeks are often unforded, because there are fewer people.
And there's always the danger of attack by wild animals. Bears
and wolves, catamounts and rattlesnakes. You don't wander there
unaccompanied or unarmed.'

Flora was feeling the icy hand of fear gripping her guts but was
determined that it would not be reflected in her voice.

'You said there were two tracts, didn't you? One of five hundred
and one of fifty acres. What's the land like? Is it cultivated at all,
or must we tame it?' She waited for his answer with her heart in
her mouth. She relished a challenge, but please God, let it not be
too rigorous!

''Tis comely land, else I would not have clinched the deal. The
dwelling house overlooks a creek that cuts through the hills behind.
There's meadow land in front, and an orchard. Open country,
green and wholesome. And the house is big enough for all of us,
and has a kitchen and outhouses and space for the servants. There's
a good cottage to the back for Neil and Deirdre, too. A lot of hard
work to be done, of course, but we can cope with that.'

Allan's reservations did not quite register with Flora. She had
already made up her mind as soon as open country was mentioned.
To escape from those menacing, unhallowed pine forests and
inhabit the fertile fields of Anson County was her idea of bliss. All
kinds of ideas took shape in her mind. Maybe they would spend
a few days with Anne on the way west. Maybe this was the
beginning of a honeyed phase in their lives, blessed with sunshine
and prosperity. Maybe her children and her grandchildren would

be the start of a new dynasty here, stretching away into the broad smiling uplands of centuries to come. Maybe...

Then Sandy's voice broke in, bringing a sudden breath of harsh reality.

'You may not have heard, Father, that the news from Wilmington gets graver by the day. Those self-styled Committees of Safety are effectively ruling everything. The Slingsby business was only the start. If you refuse to sign their association against British trade you can even be declared unworthy of the rights of freemen. Everybody's really worried, it seems.'

Seeing his father's immediate concern he could not resist embroidering the sketchy information. 'Aye. They were distributing handbills down in Cross Creek, published by the Wilmington Committee. I have one right here. It lists all the folks that have refused to sign. John Slingsby's name's on it, and a Thomas Orr, and John Cruden, and the planter William Whitfield. Oh, and I see that Tom Cobham's on it, the doctor that looked after you when you were ill o' that fever, Ma.'

Manfully Flora tried to hide her distress. 'He must feel strongly indeed, to go that far. I admire his courage, but what good will it do? Better to keep his head down and let the stoushie pass.'

Allan flashed an unguarded look of scorn in her direction. 'Try telling Roddy that,' he countered. 'You'll mind that he and Cobham have been friends ever since their Edinburgh University days. Cobham even has a stake in the Mumrills. Roddy must be shattered. His sympathies are with the rebels, as you know, yet he hates confrontation. Says that if things get any worse we're going to have a full-scale war, with family and friends divided like in Jacobite days. Terrible it is.'

Flora felt the blood drain from her face, but fought off the presentiments that came crowding in. She knew what caused them. They were but irrational fears, left over from the anguish of Culloden and its bloody aftermath. Years ago she had vowed that she would never again let herself be embroiled in politics, and the decision still stood.

'Ah well,' she said, 'thank God none of this affects us. They can bicker to their hearts' content, in Wilmington and New Bern and Edenton. We intend to live our lives in peace and to hell with their wranglings!'

She felt the words stick in her throat as she flounced from the room, both surprised and angry at the venom in her outburst and the tears that were running unbidden down her cheeks. Then determinedly she pulled herself together and vowed that she would mention neither Stella nor politics as long as Allan did not.

And to her great relief he seemed to have made a similar decision for that night their secret talk was only of their need for one another.

'Oh Florrie love, I've missed you sorely and that's a fact. Come to me, bonnie lass.'

He folded her to him. His lips were on her breast, his hands hungrily stroking the contours of neck and waist and thighs, then gradually seeking the inmost recesses of her. His animal need was so urgent that he came almost at once, leaving her with a sense of disappointment, almost of violation.

Then he lay back and gave out a great sigh of contentment. 'That was for me. I'm sorry if I hurt you. Now 'twill be my turn to pleasure you, mo ghaoil.'

The homely Gaelic endearment had a world of tenderness in it and as he proceeded to suit his actions to the words she felt all her senses come together in a rush of overwhelming emotion. God, he was beautiful, this man of hers! The sharp planes of his face and his long limbs gleamed white in the moonlight, while the smell of his maleness and the tantalising, ever-so-slow movements of his hands combined to drive her, uncontrolled and trembling, to regions beyond the limits of time and place. Their souls joined in a shattering explosion of love and passion and semen, familiar with the habit of years yet still essentially different on every occasion.

'There, now. Happy?'

She buried her face in the springy black hairs on his chest. 'Do you have to ask? Wasn't it obvious, from the noises I was trying so hard to stifle?'

A giggle was called for then, she knew, to defuse their cataclysmic emotions. That was how she had always reacted in the old, carefree days. But levity was somehow inappropriate that night and in spite of herself she wept – bitter-sweet, post-coital tears that had a lifetime's joy and sorrow in them.

PART FOUR

I

April 1775

Allan had set his heart on the Cheek's Creek site and events moved with breathtaking swiftness now. For the most part Flora was pleased and relieved – hadn't she been urging him for months to take positive action? – but as always his impulsiveness left her cautious and doubting.

'You're absolutely sure this is the land you want? You haven't let that Caleb Touchstone talk you into it?'

'Nay, Florrie. I'm sure deep in my bones that this is the land for us, and I have it all worked out. We start tomorrow. You and the maids may as well come with us, for I reckon there will be no shortage of work for all of us. The house will have to be cleaned and made habitable, and the roof needs some new shingles. Then there's a well to be dug and fences to put up. Donald says he wants to come with us too, for Hugh could do with him on his farm. Can you be ready to leave at dawn, do you think?'

The words tumbled over one another. Typical Allan, scarcely giving her a moment to draw breath now that he had made up his mind. At last he had a project to sink his teeth into and everything had to be done in double quick time. Flora felt the electrical current of his energy as an almost tangible force, and would fain have responded wholeheartedly to it.

But her scepticism persisted. 'Tomorrow? So soon? Can't we wait a few days more, give ourselves time to gather our things and say farewell to our friends here? The Boyds want us over for the new babe's christening…'

Why had she said that? Alastair Boyd was the last person she wanted to see, and Kate had ignored her every overture, while she had to confess she found Jenny rather vapid for all her sweetness and Rachel nothing but a trollop. It was only Roddy who drew her. He and Hannah. She would hate to go without wishing them goodbye.

She knew at once then, from Allan's rising colour and beetling brows, that she had said the wrong thing. It was almost as if he had read her thoughts.

'Do I hear you right, Flora? Is a shindig at the Mumrills more important to you than getting settled in our new place? I wonder sometimes what matters more to you, the Boyds or your own family! You harass and harry me all winter for my dilatoriness and now, when I finally come to a timely decision, you would hold me back! All right then, stay if that is what you wish. But don't expect me to change my plans to suit your whims. Someone else can see you safely up to Cheek's Creek, when your ladyship decides to honour us with your company. Roddy Boyd and his patriot cronies, most like.'

The bitterness of his tirade stung more sorely than she was prepared to show. Normally she would have turned away and said nothing, leaving him to simmer down, but she sensed that she was not the true focus of his resentment. Something had happened between Allan and Roddy and she guessed, from that acid reference to 'patriots', that the argument was political rather than personal. What her husband craved was reassurance that she supported him, but she was equally determined to behave as if the colonials' quarrels were irrelevant, quite on the periphery of their bid to make a new life in America.

So she moved closer to him and put a trembling hand on his arm. 'Let's not begin this new phase at loggerheads, Allan. Of course I will come with you. You know that. You know too that the Boyds don't matter a jot to me, compared to you. 'Tis just that sometimes you remind me of a runaway horse, uncontrollably sweeping everything before you, and I feel I have to rein you in, pull you back to reality. If you insist upon leaving tomorrow, so be it. I shall tell Deirdre and Morag straight away and we'll be ready, never fear.'

She knew that she did not now dare bring up the other subject that was close to her heart, the possibility of seeing Anne en route. She would keep that for the right moment: perhaps Allan was considering stopping by at Glendale anyway.

Mollified by her surrender he had stomped off and she heard

him calling to Neil to start collecting the stuff they would need for travelling, as well as basic provisions to sustain them when they got to Cheek's Creek, for they were still unsure what they would find there.

True to her word Flora was ready before dawn, and the little equipage assembled in the yard just as the rising sun was turning the blue spruces by the gate to a deep, improbable shade of burgundy. The whole Mount Pleasant household had gathered to see them off. Flora felt the onset of quick tears but Annabella, though equally affected, hastened to reassure her.

'Cheer up, Flora. Just six weeks from now and we shall all be at the Mount Helicon gathering together. Our love meantime to Father, and to Anne and Alex when you see them, and may God go with you on your journey.'

The two women clung together until Allan touched Flora's shoulder and gently prised them apart. 'Come now. No time to lose. An hour in the morning is worth two later on.'

Once on the wagon trail that wended west they were immediately swallowed up by the trees. Flora looked back to wave goodbye only to find that the house was totally hidden by a wall of greenery. Their little procession felt suddenly detached in space and time. She was reminded of pictures she had seen illustrating an old poem she had read when under house arrest in London. The Canterbury Tales. That was it. They must look for all the world like a particularly bedraggled and colourless group of pilgrims.

Certainly they could belong to any century, she thought. Here were the horsemen riding on ahead, making sure the way was clear for the mule-drawn wagon to trundle on behind with Jamie and Deirdre, Morag and the other maids perched upon it. How that wagon creaked and groaned as its supplementary load of pots and pans, iron cauldron and cooking utensils clashed and clattered together. Then there were the three pack-animals, so heavily laden with panniers it was a wonder they could move. One was carrying the tools Allan had bought on his last visit to Cross Creek: a barking axe and felling axe to keep encroaching trees at bay; a plowshare; a saw, planes and chisels for wood-working; hammers and scythes, bolts and nails. Another carried blankets, extra clothes, candles, Flora's medicine chest and her large basket of sewing materials. The third was piled high with foodstuffs and the kind of luxuries that might not be readily available in the back country: precious tea and salt; brandy, sugar and tobacco.

Flora was acutely aware of how different this journey was from that earlier trek to Cross Creek from Wilmington. Then she had been a semi-invalid cocooned in a comfortable carriage, insulated from harsh reality by the attentions of slaves and servants whose whole purpose in life was to indulge and pamper her. The forests they had traversed had felt remote and frightening, yes, because the flora and fauna of this new country had been so alien to them, but the commerce of the river and the network of plantations had given the terrain a semblance of domesticity. Besides, Bob Schaw, their host and guide, had known the road intimately. This time they were simply following the dirt track, depending on the sun and their own instinct and common sense for assurance that they were going in the right direction.

At first it was bitterly cold under the pines, the morning air crisp and frosty. Delilah's breath exhaled in a shimmering mist and Flora was glad to be wearing her heavy cutty sark and an extra pair of thick hand-knitted stockings. Then gradually as the day lightened she forgot her discomfort. Even her fears about the journey subsided to become just a vague persistent thread in a densely-textured weave of preoccupations and impressions. Delilah did not have to be pressed beyond a steady trot because the wagon restricted the general rate of progress. The path was slithery with mud one minute and encrusted with rime the next, according to where the sun penetrated, and every so often the steady clatter of the wooden wheels would change to an agonising, grinding wrench as they encountered tree roots or rocky outcrops. Then she would hear Neil yell out, 'Gee up, ye lazy galoot ye!' to a recalcitrant mule, the crack of a whip would echo out, and she would be glad of her sure-footed mare and the chance to let her senses be seduced by the pleasures of the spring morning.

The abrasively clean, invigorating scent of pine sap filled her nostrils, overlaying the smell of hot horse and saddle leather, and the birds were singing, loudly enough even to drown out the sounds of human voices. Not that she could honestly call all of it singing. Some of the calls were liquid and harmonious enough – she recalled being told, in the fall, about mocking-birds and whippoor-wills – but there were also aggressive screeches that grated on the ear-drums, the maddeningly insistent tappings of woodpeckers, and a constant fluttering of unseen wings. And above it all, ever-present, was the feeling of breaking in upon a secret, undisturbed world of countless strange, primeval creatures. Everyone seemed to sense the alienation and said little. Only the younger ghillies, Jamie, and the ever-ebullient Donald were determined to defy the woodland, but even they fell silent at last, their heuchs and laughter swallowed up in the general cacophony of the heedless wildlife around them.

All the time, though, they had been imperceptibly but steadily climbing farther into the foothills, and come the afternoon they burst into a new landscape of ridges and hollows crisscrossed with streams and rivers. The pungent, heavy fragrance of hemlock and cedar gave way to the tang of grass and herbs, and instead of the pines there were areas of scrub oak, stands of chestnut, scatterings of dogwood and persimmon, all freshly green under a sky washed by the recent rains to a startlingly brilliant blue.

'See!' Allan exclaimed, pointing over the valley to where a red ribbon snaked up the hill on the other side. 'It will be easier now that we can see our road!'

And so it was. They were all heartened by this emergence into open country, and trudged doggedly on. At mid-day they stopped to eat on a wooded bluff overlooking a broad, nameless river.

''Twill be but a wee bit burn come the summer, that river,' Neil volunteered, 'but the winter rains frae the mountains have been swelling it to a very torrent. Nae shortage o' water anyway.'

Gazing at the panorama unfolding below Flora could not but be overwhelmed by the sheer bewildering immensity of it all. To think that this wild, fertile, amazingly beautiful tapestry of mountains and forests, rivers and meadows was theirs to tend and make bloom! She thought her heart would burst with joy and gratitude.

Only one thing niggled. So far they had not set eyes on a single soul. Surely there was a settlement somewhere in these hospitable valleys? They had seen cattle roaming around but she knew it was the custom to leave the beasts to graze at will: they came back to the byres of their own accord, for salt. So while there would be scattered farms there was no knowing how far they were from human habitation. Surely Allan did not expect her to survive in an unpeopled wilderness, far from the comfort and commerce of her own kind? Not she, to whom gossip and laughter were the very stuff of living! She tried to banish her misgivings as she enjoyed the picnic food Annabella had packed for them: little loaves filled with goat's cheese; smoked ham and tomato pickle; the strong, fruity applejack that was one of Mount Pleasant's specialties.

So they continued on their way, threading the maze of woodland and watermeadow, fording creeks and labouring up ever-steeper hillsides, until in a forest clearing they came upon an abandoned log cabin. The hungry woodland growth had almost reclaimed it, for there was an elder bush sprouting vigorously out of the chimney, the moss-furred walls were crumbling away, and large chunks of the roof were open to the sky.

Allan dismounted briskly, negotiated the front step with gingerly caution, and kicked the door open, releasing a rancid stench not just of wood-rot and fungus but of animal droppings, human sweat and candle-grease, all overlaid with even stronger exhalations of alcohol and vomit.

Flora poked her head into the only room. The rafters were so blackened with soot and the unglazed windows so overgrown with vegetation that at first she could make out little detail, only piles of dry leaves in a dry-stone hearth, and at one end of the room a rough wooden dais with a heap of smelly straw on it, which she supposed had been used as a bed. Then her feet sank into what could only have been cow-dung.

'Phew! It looked like good shelter but I'd rather sleep in the wagon tonight! The rest of you can go in there and welcome but give me good fresh air!'

And so it turned out. The servants decided they would be content to give the place a cursory clean and lie down there wrapped in their blankets, well removed from the unwelcome attention of catamounts and bears. Deirdre even managed to light a fire. Gradually the scent of pine smoke neutralised the other more obnoxious odours and soon the chicken broth Annabella had made for them was simmering fragrantly. An old, blackened girdle was unearthed from the depths of the saddle-bags and heated to cook flapjack-style corncakes made of cornmeal and lard. Accompanied by ale and brandy-wine it was a very adequate supper, shared in the green glade around the sheltering wagon.

'Well done, Deirdre,' Allan said, wiping his mouth approvingly.

The older woman's face glowed at that. She loved to have her efforts appreciated, especially by the master.

'I thank you, sir. They may not be like our Skye oatcakes but they will suffice to keep body and soul together in this wilderness. 'Twas the Mount Pleasant servants who taught me to make them. Useful for travelling, they said. Like ships' biscuits. 'Tis an Indian receipt but the darkies make them too.'

By now they were all beginning to feel mellow and replete. Soon it would be dark. Purple shadows were insinuating themselves into the clearing, heralding night. Someone began to hum an old Celtic air. It was the signal for Neil to fetch his fiddle and get the ceilidh started.

Flora couldn't say, afterwards, precisely what alerted her to the presence of a stranger in the group. Certainly the intruder smelt abominably, of turpentine and tobacco, stale sweat and unwashed clothes: but then, which of them didn't? Maybe she got an oblique glimpse of his skewed features over her shoulder – the long matted hair, grease-caked beard and small foxy eyes glinting in the fire-light – and sensed that they did not belong to anyone in their household. Certainly she would remember that her initial reaction had been one of revulsion and fear.

Until she heard him sing, and her instinctive distrust was immediately allayed. Clear and sweet-toned, his voice was responding to the fiddle, framing the lilting Gaelic words with a loving felicity that brought tears to her eyes. No-one who could sing like that could possibly have evil in his heart, no matter how he smelt.

So she turned, braced herself against his rancid breath, and addressed him directly in the Gaelic. 'I fear we did not see you come, in the gloaming. You are welcome to join us and share what is left of our food. Have you travelled far?'

'Aye, I have that. I'm a pedlar you see. 'Tis my trade to wander the country.'

He waved a ragged arm in the direction of a large chestnut tree where he had hobbled his mule. 'I'm used to stopping here when I'm down this way. 'Tis good shelter, like.'

That last speech had a hint of reproach in it, as if he regarded the deserted homestead as his property and was defying anyone to find fault with it.

'Used to be a fine cabin, this, not so long ago, in old Paddy O'Rourke's time. A fine upstanding Catholic gentleman, was Paddy. Aye ready wi' a welcome and a wee dram. Looked after the place fine. But he went away sudden, like. Some said a bear got him. Anyway, he never came back, and his wee house has fallen into rack and ruin.'

He paused reminiscently and then suddenly changed tack. 'But I forget myself. My name's Jock McIvor. An' you'll be Flora MacDonald. I'm sure glad to make your acquaintance, Ma'am. No true Highlander but would want to shake you by the hand.'

While Flora stared at him in puzzled surprise he launched then into a complicated explanation of how he knew she was on the road. This one he'd met had heard of Allan's purchase of Caleb Touchstone's land: another, out herding his cattle, had spotted them from afar and guessed who they were: and – most wonderful of all – he had spent the previous night at Glendale! Anne had entreated him to look out for them and pass on the news of a new baby there. A girl. To be called Flora.

Flora's first impulse on hearing all this was to embrace the messenger, but the rotten miasma that emanated from him held her back. She at once shouted out the glad news to the others, however, and Jock was eagerly summoned to join them all in a toast to the newborn Flora MacLeod. He ate heartily of the remaining corn biscuits and then produced a brace of sorry-looking squirrels that had been dangling, who knew for how long, from a string round his waist.

'Maybe you'll be for roasting these, ma'am? I'd have had them skinned ere now, but what with meeting you and all...' And he held out the offering to a reluctant Deirdre.

Flora could read what the housekeeper was thinking. She had had her fill of cooking, and to start preparing the pitiful mangy creatures for the pot was not in her evening's programme. But her response was creditably diplomatic: maybe she too sensed that there was more to Jock McIvor than met the eye – or the nose?

'I'm afraid it's too dark to see right now, Jock, and the fire's low. You'd maybe like some broth, and some cheese maybe? The squirrels will keep fresh till tomorrow, willn't they? They'll be good stewed, or fried in cornmeal batter.'

'Oh aye. Aye. They will that, I reckon. I'll have them for my dinner the morn.'

And with that he happily subsided into a haze of applejack and brandy-wine. His singing became progressively more tuneless and maudlin until eventually, sozzled and exhausted, he wrapped himself in his plaid and fell stertorously asleep by the fire.

Sleep did not come so readily to Flora. The wagon bed was comfortable enough but inevitably the mattress was infested with fleas and she itched abominably. Then although the fires that the men kept going radiated companionship, comfort and a certain sense of protection from wild animals the air became colder as the night wore on and she huddled closer to Allan, to be solaced by the familiar male smell of tweed, woodsmoke and ale. His presence lulled her into a state of semi-slumber, waves of welcome oblivion alternating with spells of nightmare in which monsters emerged howling from the shadows and fell upon her.

Towards morning she awoke from one particularly terrifying dream and did indeed hear wolves howling. Through the overarching branches, not yet heavy with leaf, she could catch glimpses of the sky and realised that it was ablaze with enormous, steel-white stars. How close they were! Infinitely closer than at home. There had to be a moon somewhere, even more radiant and dazzling. This America was awe-inspiring enough in the daytime but at night its strangeness passed all her understanding. She could but stare and marvel at it.

Again she drifted off, only to be alerted by the subtle change in atmosphere as the rosy light of dawn invaded the clearing and a solitary bird began hesitantly to chirp. She realised with a start of dismay that Allan had left the wagon and was sitting by the dying fire, deep in conversation with Jock McIvor. She heard their voices as a confused murmur but there was no mistaking the intensity of their exchanges. Suddenly she found herself shivering uncontrollably, and knew it was not just from the cold of the early spring morning. There was something odd about this Jock McIvor. She could not quite put her finger on it but somehow the individual aspects of him did not add up to a credible, whole person. He was too full of contradictions. She was glad he was journeying in the opposite direction.

II

April 1775

It rankled that if McIvor had just come from Glendale they couldn't be all that far from Anne right now, and Allan must know it. She realised now that she had set her heart on the visit but had no reason whatever to assume they were going, for though Allan had celebrated the birth with the rest of them he had said nothing about actually going to see the babe. What if he had no intention of turning off and making for McDeed's Creek?

It did not help that he seemed particularly preoccupied this morning, even to the point of seeming to avoid her company. If he was not riding on ahead, ostensibly surveying the lie of the land, he was checking saddles and girths, ascertaining that loads were secure, or going off on short hunting forays with the boys. That McIvor fellow had to be the cause of it, she was sure. What could have kept the two of them talking so intently when everyone else was sound asleep?

Eventually he reined in beside her. 'Sorry if I seem to have been neglecting you, Florrie, but there has been so much to see to! Did you see the turkey Donald shot back there? My, but he's quick! They say even the Indians find turkeys hard to shoot. They fly in flocks, you see. But Donald caught this one off guard. It was busy showing itself off to the females, strutting about like a peacock with its tail all spread out. Served it right. It'll be a treat tonight, roasted with sweet potatoes and some corn.'

Then his brows knitted. 'Something bothering you, Florrie? You're not feeling fevered are you?'

An outrageous plan raced through her head. Could she feign illness and make it a pretext for cutting the journey short? Her longing for Anne and little Flora tugged at her, dividing her loyalties. What harm in a lie, if it brought them all together? Allan ought to have understood and agreed to the visit anyway!

But even as she schemed she knew she could not do it. In her head she heard the uncompromising voice of her Presbyterian grandfather declaim with mingled sorrow and condemnation, 'Thou shalt not bear false witness!' and cast the temptation aside.

'How far are we from Glendale? I had thought we might spend a night at least with Anne and Alex, and see this new grandchild.

Please, husband. It is very important to me. I so yearn to see the new babe and it can't be far, when the pedlar was with them but two days since.'

His reply, though considerate and regretful enough, was still a refusal, and her heart sank.

'I did think about it, but 'twas different for me those weeks back, travelling alone and unencumbered. One man, agile and familiar with the track, can make Glendale in a day from the O'Rourke cabin but it would be a different story with wagons and horses. We'd be adding days to our journey, lass, and I can ill spare the time. We have yet to plant seed, fell trees, clear fields, round up and buy cattle. Then we are faring well in this fine spring weather but I'm told it can change in the blink of an eye at this time of year and we can find ourselves contending with floods and swollen rivers. No, Flora. You'll just have to reconcile yourself to wait until the christening or the Mount Helicon Gathering, whichever comes first. Come now! We simply have to recognise our priorities and stick to them!'

People, and particularly her family, would always be Flora's priority, and Allan knew that only too well. Flora tried one last bitter protest.

'But the clan gathering's all of six weeks away, at the end of May! And couldn't the others carry on to Cheek's Creek with the wagons, while we went to Glendale alone?'

Even as she spoke, however, she realised it was no use.

All she wanted then was to hide herself away and sulk like a thwarted child, but experience had taught her that such behaviour cut no ice with Allan. She could use his guilt and discomfiture now, though, to find out what else had been worrying him.

'What were you and that McIvor fellow talking about so seriously, in the middle of the night?'

He looked startled. She could see that his instinctive reaction was to stall.

''Twas close on daylight, Florrie. Jock wanted to be on his way by dawn and I was anxious to get fresh directions from him. He knows the terrain well, says the rivers are fordable now and the hills not too steep. Two more days, he thought, and we'll be almost there. And he agrees with me about the property, says it's pleasant and airy, in a land of streams and water-meadows and that we couldn't have made a better decision.'

She tried hard to share Allan's enthusiasm but her disappointment at missing Anne still rankled and she could not believe that he and McIvor had talked about nothing but the local topography. After all, Allan had covered the country already himself.

'But I saw and heard you, Allan! Don't try to fob me off! There was something more. Something sinister. I could feel it. Is there someone or something we have to guard against, up there?'

She tried to keep the hint of hysteria out of her voice but he must have caught a trace of it for his hand closed over hers, where it rested on Delilah's reins.

'There is nothing to fear at Cheek's Creek, Florrie. Nothing. I promise you.'

He seemed to consider a moment, then added, 'If you insist upon knowing, 'twas but politics we talked of. The trouble among the merchants at Cross Creek and down on the Tidewater. Evidently there was some kind of unlawful convocation of patriot elements in New Bern at the beginning of the month, in defiance of Martin. He called the official Assembly for the 4th, with John Harvey as Speaker, but on its own initiative it met on the 3rd, with that very same Harvey presiding! Needless to say Martin was furious and tried to break up the rival assembly, but not before it had re-elected three members to the Continental Congress and approved the non-importation agreement. Seems they're forcing people to sign what they're calling a 'test', as a pledge of allegiance to the American cause.'

'And what does that mean?' She heard her voice, small and fearful.

'It means that Martin can fulminate to his heart's content but gets nowhere. He simply isn't in charge any more. Last month he wrote to General Gage, the commander-in-chief of the King's forces in America, asking for military support against what he called gasconading elements, and according to McIvor this latest upheaval has had him complaining to Lord Dartmouth in London that royal authority has been humiliated. But of course North Carolina isn't the only state that's in ferment, and by no means the worst.'

He suddenly stopped short then, seeing the anguish on Flora's face and realising he had said too much. 'But none of that need bother us up here. And gin it did, 'twould be men's work.'

Flora was about to retort that that was little reassurance when a shout suddenly rang out. All male hands were needed to dislodge a wagon wheel from a rut in the road. Allan turned back to supervise and Flora could have sworn she heard him sigh with relief. Her curiosity about McIvor was still unassuaged. How could a mere pedlar know and care so much about happenings as far off as New Bern? She struggled to sink her fear and frustration in the beauty unfolding around her, but the questions still niggled.

Fresh-scented and green, its contours varied and soothing to the eye, the countryside had a tranquil, Arcadian quality. The dogwood was past now, its delicate white blossoms sullied by rain and wind, but other shrubs, particularly redbud and azalea, were blooming prolifically and the grass was starred with wild flowers. Some, the ubiquitous buttercups and violets and ragwort, were familiar enough, but others were unknown in the old world, though Sandy seemed to know all their names, he who had never shown much interest in plants before.

Idly she extended a hand to touch a pretty shrub that grew profusely beside the trail. It had shining serrate green leaves with whitish undersides. 'And what's this? I've kept meaning to ask.'

'Don't! That's poison sumac! It causes fever and will have you covered in blisters!'

She recoiled then, alert to the danger but perversely fascinated, and also intrigued by her son's newfound knowledge. 'Where did you learn all this American botany?'

'Jenny. She couldn't help but know. Her father is something of an expert.'

It was the first time he had deliberately brought up Jenny's name in conversation and Flora knew what it meant. Probably he'd talk about nobody else now, having once made it clear how the land lay.

Strange that a landscape should look so peaceful and static, yet be full of movement and noise. Streams and waterfalls bickered and boomed, birds twittered and fluted endlessly, and there was a persistent background of animal sounds – the lowing of cattle, the chatter of squirrels, the scutter of innumerable tiny mammals and the drone of insects. Above it all a boundless sky of pristine cerulean blue. Dear God, she thought, just grant us peace to nurture this land as you would wish, for if it continues half as beautiful it will not be difficult to love.

She could see by the fourth morning that Allan was confident of reaching Cheek's Creek that day. Everything had conspired to ease the journey – the airy spring weather, neither hot nor cold; the optimism of the travellers; the wonderful sense of freedom. They left at dawn that day well rested, their bellies replete with the fried trout and cornbread pressed upon them by the Cameron who had given them shelter. The cold early morning mist whirled and eddied around them like smoke from a witch's cauldron. Everything was silent, as if even the birds sensed the strangeness. They were in a landscape of gentle ridges and indentations now, and the creeks were criss-crossed with waterfalls that arched crystal-clear and delicate over rocks swathed in brilliant emerald weed and ferns.

Then she saw the deer, and her heart stopped. There were four of them not a hundred yards away, a stag, a doe and two fawns, drinking by a creek. The stag was a twelve-pointer, his antlers encrusted with moss, his dark nostrils flaring and alert while the female and her young grazed fearlessly. The mist softened the delicate outlines of their bodies, so that they looked insubstantial as ghosts, blue shadows merging gently with the trees and rocks around them.

It suddenly struck her that these animals seemed to have no fear of man. Bear perhaps, and wild cats, but they had no cause to flee from people. For a moment she thought she was the only one in their group to have seen them, until she saw Donald and Sandy cock their guns simultaneously.

'Don't! Leave them alone!' she yelled, but of course it was useless: the temptation to shoot was overpowering. The animals scattered in sudden panic. All but one.

'Got it!'

Sandy could not contain his excitement. He had indeed felled one of the deer, but it was the smallest of the four, a tiny kid-like creature with spots on its back and enormous pleading brown eyes. Flora was appalled. She dismounted and was on her knees beside the animal before the others could get near.

Then Allan ran up. 'Let me put her out of her misery. She's wee, but will make good eating. Venison for supper!'

'No! let me see how badly she's wounded first.'

Tentatively she examined the beast. 'She'll live. The bullet has grazed her side, but that's all. You can't possibly kill her. She's scarcely weaned. And much too beautiful. Besides, I want her. I saw her first. She's mine.'

'Oh, Florrie... Will you never learn?'

The exasperation in Allan's voice made no difference. 'Give me ten minutes to staunch the wound, then we'll hobble the beast and take her with us. You said yourself that 'twas not far. She's my pet fawn now. I lost Beanie in that storm, remember. I'll keep her and call her Beanie, in memory of my wee hen.'

Allan muttered something under his breath, about a fawn being a different story entirely from a mere fowl. But Flora was adamant, and this time she got her way. Maybe she just imagined the look of trust and gratitude in the animal's eyes when she bathed its side with water from the burn, but she was convinced that there was a bond between them.

They reached Cheek's Creek that afternoon. Allan purposely did not tell them how close they were, so that they would come on it unexpectedly.

'There. That's it yonder. Just like I said it would be, isn't it?'

She gazed down over green pastures and gentle wooded slopes and there it was, a cluster of wooden buildings nestling under the hill, with a broad meadow in front and the river running nearby. The ground around was much more broken than at Mount Pleasant, and she could see that there would be wide vistas all round.

'Yonder's the house, in the centre, with the kitchen to the left. There's servants' quarters, and a barn, and a stable to the other side, and a crib for Indian corn. Those three stands of trees yonder, those are the orchards. We'll have cherries in a month or two's time, and then the peaches and apples and persimmons, enough to make our own cider and brandy. There's a spring there too, with a stone surround and water that I'm assured is pure as can be, and cool even in the height of summer. And see, that's the field where I'll plant the corn. And away over yonder by the creek, that's the grist mill. I mean to make that pay. 'Twas Caleb Touchstone's main source of income, so he told me... See!'

Even from afar the mill installation was impressive. The mill house appeared to be three storeys high – Allan explained that the top floor was used for the bulk storage of grain in bins – and the immense waterwheel towered almost to the ridgepole. Allan pointed out the long wooden channel carrying water over the farm lane from a diversionary dam that spanned the creek.

'That's where we'll get the water to power the wheel,' he explained. 'There's a lot of work to be done before we get every-thing back into working order, of course, but Touchstone assured me 'twas all sound enough. Said there's a local man, a McAulay, that's worked there since the place was started twenty-five years ago, and he knows every cog and belt and pulley in the place. I must seek him out. 'Tis a special craft, the milling. But what a challenge, lass! I can't wait to get started! We'll have it working flat out by mid-summer, you'll see!'

His eyes were shining. Flora could not help muttering a prayer to herself that his fresh, fierce enthusiasm would not be dashed by inimicable forces beyond his control – climate, or politics, or economic circumstances. She had seen so many of his dreams shattered. He certainly deserved good fortune now, after so much adversity.

Everyone in the little band seemed to be similarly affected by the feeling that this was a momentous day, one they would always remember. A new beginning. By common consent they had reined in their horses and were all sitting quietly, taking in the details of the farmland that was to be their home. Even Jamie was speechless, though Flora could guess how his thoughts were running. Meadows to romp in. Ponds to wade in. Rainbow trout, there for the catching. Then as if they had agreed one and all that closer inspection was called for they spurred on the horses and trotted down, with the cavalcade of wagons bringing up the rear.

Flora tried gallantly to hide her disappointment as they approached the house and its manifold imperfections began to show up. Must not let Allan see her dismay. For he had clearly bought this property for the land and the mill, and not for the dwelling house. This was no fine raised Tidewater mansion complete with tall windows and shining portico, but a plain low dwelling of unpainted peeled and notched logs. There was a long-galleried stoop running along the front and a mud-and-stick chimney built along one end. Little had been done to maintain the place. The shingles on the roof were badly broken and many were missing altogether. The wood of the walls was rotten, encrusted with weeds and fungus. There was no glass in the tiny windows: she assumed the beige-coloured squares that covered them were deer hides or cow leather.

In trepidation she let herself be led inside and here conditions were even worse than she had feared. Cobwebs festooned the rough, smoke-blackened rafters. Dust lay thick on everything. Worst of all, the floors were of packed mud. This in a country that positively groaned with timber! But at least the room was spacious, she reckoned about eighteen by twenty-five feet in area, and the fireplace projecting into it at one end was enormous. Her eye travelled from the ingle to where a narrow winding stair led up to the loft and she had a moment's brief vision of flames leaping in the hearth and a side of beef roasting on a spit. Yes, she could make a home of this place. She defied anyone to think otherwise.

'Get a fire going in the hearth, Morag,' she said, 'and make us a dish of tea. We all deserve a treat. We'll get started cleaning up this midden in the morning.'

III

April 1775

Nothing daunted she was up before daylight, determined to light a fire, start the porridge and organise the milking. She must also get some idea how many hens were laying, for weeks of neglect must have sent them scurrying away to roost in remote hideaways known only to themselves.

But early though she was Donald McAulay had been up long before, for when she opened the door she found him standing on the stoop, a vast, many-chinned and ample-bellied Gael with a diffident, somewhat sheepish smile. Even if he had stayed silent she would have recognised him for the miller by the nutty smell of freshly-ground grain that exuded from his every pore, overlaying the usual morning odours of the farmyard – hogs and cows and horse-shit.

'Mistress MacDonald? An honour to meet you, ma'am. My mother came from Mull, from down Bunessan way, and my father from Caithness. I'm the miller. I was wondering, could you maybe take me on? It has been powerful lonely around here since old Touchstone went, and I miss my craft.'

The voice was gentle and polite. No boorish colonial vulgarian, this.

'Come in, man. Come in. Sit down and have a plate of good porridge while I fetch Allan. He's in the byre.'

It took her a good five minutes to make Allan listen to her, he was so excited at the prospect of all he had to do.

'Just as well the weather's fine, isn't it Florrie? I want to clear that stand of chestnut yonder and get the corn planted. And Caleb Touchstone said he had about fifty cattle roaming the woods: we'll have to round them up, brand the calves, consider adding to the herd. And I haven't even looked at the mill buildings yet...'

That was her cue. She urged him into the house and soon the two men were deep in talk. She listened with one ear then as she busied herself mixing corncake batter.

Donald was convinced that the mill could be working again within the month.

'There's been a wheen o' leakage from the millpond the last year or two, ever since Caleb's health started to fail and he just lost interest, but if I can get a man to help me drain and repair it I'll soon get it tight again. Then the log cribbing on the dam needs shoring up, and I'll have to reinforce the planks of the spillway, but none of it's beyond fixing.'

Donald might be a quiet, gentlemanly sort of person but when he began to expatiate on the intricacies of his craft he was unstoppable. Flora's mind reeled as he went on to explain that some of the locust pegs securing the hand-hewn chestnut timbers of the giant millwheel were loose, and the furrows of the granite millstones would have to be recut and dressed if they were to grind efficiently again. Some of the split heart pine shingles of the millhouse roof had been lost in a snow-storm, besides, and would have to be repaired before the rains came or the joists inside would rot, but that could likely wait... She listened bewildered to the terms of this new vocabulary – hoppers and paddles, chutes and raceways, buhr stones and flumes – and wondered what Allan was making of it all. From what she could gather it was just as well that there was an experienced man ready and willing to take that department over, for Allan knew nothing about milling. He was not even an arable farmer. It had always been cattle with him.

But Allan's present state of near-manic optimism left no room for self-doubt. He would cope. Grist mill and cornfields, orchards and cattle, hogs and horses and poultry were all simply part of the day's work. His only problem was shortage of labour, and wasn't that why he had brought indentured servants from the old country? So, 'Can you spare me some of the women to work in the fields, Florrie?' was his cry as soon as he had arisen from the breakfast table. 'It won't be for long. Just a day or two. We must get on with the outside chores while this weather holds.'

She needed every one of the maids to scour and scrub, and almost told him so. She had just realised that the choking stour that lay thick on everything was only a surface layer: underneath were other, more stubborn abominations, the brown, greasy legacy of years of neglect. Had that Touchstone woman had no pride? But Allan seemed not to see the house's shortcomings. For him the land and beasts and the mill were paramount. She could see from the dismay writ large on their faces that Morag, Deirdre and Chrissie did not relish the prospect of outside work but they had to accept their master's word as law. So, for that matter, did she.

After the first day or two, when he grudgingly gave Flora a hand to set up beds, tables and dressers, Allan was scarcely ever indoors to see that the house left much to be desired. He worked like a whirlwind. The air rang with the clank of his harrow, the jangle of his harness and the scraping of his saw. In all the daylight hours he hardly allowed himself a moment's rest, and come night he simply collapsed exhausted in her arms. His skin, always ruddy, turned the colour of rich bronze and his hands became hard and calloused, the nails encrusted with dirt. All that mattered to him was the farm.

Emptying the chests and boxes that had contained their worldly goods was therefore a solitary task, and all the more bitter-sweet for that. Nine months was a long time without setting eye upon household effects that Flora had always regarded as essential parts of her. Now, as she removed them one by one and released a complex aroma of lavender and verbena, mustiness and damp, she felt a torrent of sensations overwhelm her. The sheet the Prince had slept in. The tartan bed hangings Dr Johnson had commented upon. Her precious red damask curtains, which she intended to put right back in the box until the windows were glazed and worthy of them. Tablecloths. Books. The Hogarth print. Looking glasses, a small carpet and the family portraits. Even a locket with a piece of Scottish heather in it, and a tortoiseshell snuffbox, a family heirloom, that Alan had given her as a wedding gift. The precious clutter of a lifetime, and in the business of those months she had as good as forgotten it! She blanched, realising that at the height of the storm it might all have found its way over the good ship *Ulysses*'s side.

The Flodigarry daffodil bulbs were right at the bottom, wrapped in a bolster cover, and exuded a strong stench of rotten vegetation. But only one had actually decayed; the other five, when she wiped away the festering liquid matter that clung to them, she found to be quite sound. What was more, each survivor had sprouted a pale, wriggling shoot that seemed to yell out for earth and water and sunshine. Hastily wiping away an insistent tear Flora carried the bulbs out to the yard and planted them under a redbud tree. Too late for blooms this year, she knew, but in the years to come they would speak to her of Scotland.

Gradually the house acquired a more lived-in feel. A fire burned brightly in the grate, taking the sharp damp tang out of the air. Armfuls of lilac and new greenery brought perfume and colour while the shapes of familiar furniture imparted a soothing sense of continuity and purpose. She could not help noticing how out of place such items were in this dismal hovel that was now her home but she must not despair. The harder they worked the more comfortable everything would be.

Sundays were their only respite, and Flora was thankful for the Sabbath balm they brought. Then they all trekked to the church at the nearby hamlet of Carmel, where John Bethune, Christian MacDonald's son, was minister. Here she was back among her own people, and might almost have thought herself on Skye. Here she saw her stepfather Hugh, her half-sister Flora MacQueen, and Flora's son James, who was a teacher.

It both amused and saddened her that nobody seemed to have

changed one iota. Her half-sister Flora MacQueen was still dour and withdrawn: it took Flora no time to realise that those old, irreconcilable personality differences were still there. Nor had the two Campbell sisters who lived nearby, Isobel MacLeod and Peggy Campbell, lost their skeery, jealous streak. A pity their kindly parents were not here, but down country beside Anne: Flora had been so fond of their mother, old Kathie.

But one sentiment united those new neighbours. To a man they all maintained that emigration had been their only hope of survival and that in coming here they had indeed found a land of promise. Rather to Flora's consternation, too, they seemed to regard the MacDonalds' arrival as a necessary completion of the circle. Allan was their acknowledged leader, the laird who would represent their interests in Anson County and beyond.

'Aye,' Peggy announced one day when she came round to Kingsburgh ostensibly to proffer a crock of freshly-churned butter but really, Flora knew, to see what the MacDonalds had done to the place, 'we're all real glad you're here, with all this trouble going on. Allan's a military man and a gentleman. He'll be the one to rally the clans gin it comes to a fight.'

Peggy had her mother's beady little eyes but whereas Kathie's were warm and affectionate the daughter's roamed critically over everything, eager to find fault. Flora was acutely conscious of the holes in the roof, the dirt floor and the as yet uncurtained windows, and vowed to herself to tackle Allan one day soon and have him devote some time to the house.

Meanwhile she just had to let Peggy speir. The woman had the knack of being parsimonious with information herself and yet of managing to winkle out details from others. Meanspirited and prying, that's what she was. Flora found herself chattering nervously, angry with herself for feeling at a disadvantage, for well she knew Peggy of old.

'Everybody that's newly come is for the King, you'll find,' Peggy went on. 'It's just the long settled ones and the folks that came up from the south or down from Virginia and Pennsylvania way that's firebrands. And a right lot of hotheaded rebels they are, with their oaths of allegiance and their refusal to trade with the home country. The cheek of it, defying the Governor! Allan must be right indignant, I'll wager.'

Desperately Flora temporised. 'We've scarcely discussed it, Peggy. We did not come here to get embroiled in politics, but to make a good living on the land. I'm hoping we can live in peace and get on with all our neighbours, loyalists and patriots alike.'

Peggy cast a sceptical look in her direction. We'll believe that when we see it, it seemed to say. Aloud she said grudgingly, 'That's the best dish of tea I've tasted in months. None of yon yaupon stuff for the Kingsburgh MacDonalds, eh? Where did ye come by it, Flora? Did Bob Hogg have it hidden away under his counter in that fancy shop o' his down in Wilmington?'

'No, 'twas a gift. From the Governor, sent to us when we were living down at Bella's.'

She knew immediately from the smirk of triumph that spread over Peggy's smug, porcine features then that she had said the wrong thing.

'And you try to tell me you are not committed!' Peggy grunted. 'You mark my words, Flora MacDonald, Josiah Martin is counting on Allan. After all, was he not an officer in the King's service, in the '45?'

It was as if she were casting up Allan's past allegiance during the rebellion on purpose to offend, and Flora bit back a retaliatory retort. No point in creating ill feeling. It was sadly obvious, however, that this close-knit Highland community, transplanted lock stock and barrel from beyond the seas, still had its small-minded, jealous and ignorant elements. Travel, after all, could only broaden the mind if there was a mind to broaden.

Fortunately Flora soon discovered who her real friends were. Her stepfather Hugh would always be there for her, and the third Campbell sister, Christian Bethune, who was a different kettle of fish altogether from Isobel and Peggy. And to Flora's incredulous delight she found a new, unexpected kindred spirit in Kathie's grandson, Christian's son John Bethune.

The first time she saw John was the very first Sunday they attended church. It was a sparkling April morning, loud with birdsong and fragrant with the woody scent of late daffodils. Even the church, which she guessed would usually smell damp and musty, felt freshly cleaned, as if an army of elves had descended upon it overnight and polished it with beeswax. She was aware too of colour crowding in from outside, pressing importunately against the window panes – the new iridescent green of a beech tree, the dazzling roseate hues of redbud and azalea and rhododendron: no need for extravagant stained glass here.

But young John, Carmel's minister, was more beautiful by far than these. She caught her breath when he mounted the pulpit, a tall, slender reed of a man with a mop of nut-brown hair that he had tried unsuccessfully to tame by pulling it back into a queue. Everything about him glowed, from his light, sorrel-tinted eyes to the spotless white stock he wore, and he exuded authority and confidence without seeming arrogant or overbearing. As the native Gaelic flowed from him he seemed to caress it, as something precious and irreplaceable. And that was the burden of his sermon that first Sunday – the need for this Gaelic-speaking community to hold fast to everything that was uniquely valuable in their heritage: their culture and folk-lore, their language and above all their faith.

'As the first generation of Highlanders to settle here in search of a peaceful, prosperous way of life, we must strive to keep our traditions alive. We can do this without cutting ourselves off from others as some have chosen to do' – Flora nodded in agreement then, realising that he was referring to Hannah's people, the Moravians – 'but must never compromise our beliefs or allow ourselves to be seduced by outlandish theories. In these troubled times many will try to sway us this way or that. Some would have us break away entirely from our roots and even envisage a separate nation, while others would keep us so tied to the old things that we stay blind to injustice and corruption. We must however continue clear-eyed and single-minded. Let us enrich this country with our ancient culture and work to bring God's blessings upon it, for that is what He has called us here to do.'

Flora could not help comparing this youth's earnest goodness with the provocative belligerence of James Campbell, down in Barbecue Church. She knew instinctively that John's sole purpose in life was to cherish his flock and keep them mindful of their heritage, not to goad them into disputes that they did not fully understand. Politics did not matter to him, only tolerance and peace.

Gradually, as the weeks passed, she began to regard John Bethune as one of her own. He had taken the spiritual welfare of

the whole community upon himself and clearly regarded Allan
and Flora as allies in his fight against evil. What was more, he saw
intellectual enlightenment as a means to salvation and upheld the
Classics as a valuable source of mental exercise and stimulation.
So he had gladly agreed to teach Latin to Hugh's seventeen-year-
old grandson Ian, and was delighted when Flora suggested that
Jamie might join his weekly tutorials. Some days the lessons were
conducted at Hugh's farm on Mountain Creek, sometimes at
Kingsburgh. Flora found herself looking forward to John's visits
much more avidly than Jamie, who was no scholar, did. Although
she did not understand a word of Vergil or Cicero there was
something infinitely reassuring about John's sonorous voice
construing the ancient texts. Surely, while people like John were
prepared to pass on their knowledge to the young, this new land
need never lose touch with the old solid traditions.

Despite his youth John was passionately interested in history
and regarded Flora as a repository of knowledge. What did the
Young Pretender look like? Was it true that the Prince of Wales
had sought her company, all these years ago in London? And
always, unspoken, there was the respectful but puzzled codicil –
how did she end up living obscure and poverty-stricken on Skye?
Had anyone asked her those questions at home she would have
considered them impertinent and fobbed them off as part of an
irrelevant past but John insisted that they were important. He
could not hear enough of her memories.

John lived by the ideals he proclaimed from the pulpit and
assumed that she would be his ally in propagating them. One day
he even went so far as to plead for her help. It was a close,
enervating afternoon, with ominous banks of cloud building up
over the hills and flickers of white lightning playing about on the
horizon, and much to the boys' relief Flora had bade them leave
their books and come and have some lemonade – whereupon Ian
and Jamie had scurried off on some esoteric ploy of their own,
leaving the adults to chat.

John soon guided the conversation from inconsequential talk
of mutual acquaintances to more serious matters and she recoiled
inwardly, marvelling that such a young man should be so
percipient.

'Whether you like it or not, Mistress MacDonald, and no matter what you do, your attitude is bound to affect the Highland folk here. You and your husband are close kin of the MacDonalds of Sleat and Clanranald, and of the Dunvegan MacLeods. You are natural leaders. And don't underestimate your own personal influence. The clans will pay heed to you. For many of them you're still the heroine of the '45.'

She heard his homily in silence. She knew what he said was true but did not want it so, for she preferred not to be seen to be even conscious of the controversies that were raging. She and John and Farquhard Campbell together would make a formidable trio, quite strong enough, she was sure, to keep the vast majority of the Piedmont Highlanders stubbornly neutral, but underscoring everything John said was his uncanny, intuitive reading of how matters stood between herself and Allan. John wanted her to shout her neutrality to the skies, to the point even of making a third political option of it, but she did not dare do that because it was not in Allan's nature to stand on the sidelines. He might profess detachment but he relished his new-found role as a potential leader of the clans, and there had never been any doubt about his willingness in a crisis to fight for the King.

John's voice took on an even more urgent note as he continued.

'You must beware, both of you, of the various people who will try to influence you at Mount Helicon. Some of these patriot agitators are vicious. There's one James Coor, a builder, that's working hard right now to win over the Regulators and deprive Martin's camp of support. He'll have spies at the gathering, you mark my words. Try to stay out of any controversy, I beg you. 'Twill all seem friendly enough – the gatherings always are – but this year I fully expect sinister undercurrents. Warn the others too. Better such counsel comes from you than from me, young and spineless as I must seem to them.'

She knew he wanted a pledge from her but she was still instinctively evading the issue.

'Och, John, I'm but a poor farmer's wife that's too busy milking cows and washing clothes to be found meddling in such matters 'Tis men's business, that. See, have more lemonade and then I must get on with scouring that table yonder. It's thick with grime. A disgrace, that's what it is. But I'm loath to begin again, it's that hot. Do you think this is the summer starting?'

As she spoke she mopped her brow. Then she hastily ran the kerchief round her neck, where her hair was hanging in heavy wet tendrils, and down over her bosom, where trickles of sweat ran down to soak her cotton bodice. The linen shift she wore underneath was clinging uncomfortably to her legs and the air around her felt static and suffocating.

'Aye, could be. I saw a red flash yonder. That's the dangerous kind. Could be in for a real bad storm.'

His voice was drowned out by a mighty thunder clap immediately overhead. The wooden house creaked and shook, and as if someone had turned on a tap a torrential downpour descended. Flora had not experienced anything like it since the tempest on the *Ulysses*. She was not surprised when Jamie came running to her, white-faced and shaken. He had not forgotten the trauma of those days at sea, and was still young enough to seek a mother's reassurance.

Then Allan and Sandy burst in, their clothes, hair and faces pouring water. They were attempting frantically to close the door against a third intruder, a drenched and draggled Beanie, but the animal was determined to find shelter and nosed past them to the fireside, where she lay down and curled up with a satisfied, proprietorial air.

'Just look at the creature!' Sandy laughed. 'Thinks it's a house dog!'

'Aye, but just wait till she's a full-sized deer,' retorted Allan tersely. 'Then she won't be so welcome. A bit of nonsense, encouraging her. Not that I blame the beast for taking advantage of folks' softness in this weather.'

Then having made sure Flora heard he called over to her, 'Is there maybe a wee dram for us two watersoaked fellows? Nobody could work outside in that downpour. We'd catch our deaths. Downright dangerous too, I'd imagine. I've never seen such lethal looking lightning.'

'Aye,' This from John. 'I've been trying not to alarm Mistress MacDonald and the lads, and Jamie here, but folks get killed regularly in lightning storms hereabouts. I never cease to wonder at the dramatic way the weather can change. It's like a curtain coming down in a theatre, marking the end of an act, when one season gives way to another. That's the spring over now, I'll warrant. Time for the heat and the mosquitoes. Not my favourite time of year.'

'How long is this rain likely to last?' Flora looked ruefully up at the low-raftered ceiling which was leaking in several places.

'Och, an hour or two, I guess.'

But John's sanguine estimate was away off target. The thunder continued to bellow and the rain to pelt down. Eventually Allan went off to help Neil and the servants tend the horses, which had been chomping and chafing in alarm ever since they sensed the electricity-laden atmosphere; Flora went back to her spinning wheel; and John returned the two reluctant boys to their tasks.

The storm had been raging for a good hour when there came a knock at the door. John looked up, startled and suspicious, and called over to Flora, where she sat at her spinning.

'Let me go. There are them that would take advantage of bad weather to beg shelter and then rob and harry new homesteaders.'

But the soaking, half-dead fugitive from the storm was no robber, though his appearance might have proclaimed him one. Iain MacRae stood on the threshold. His buckskin breeks were ragged and filthy, the soles of his rough leather shoes had detached themselves from the uppers, and water cascaded from the tattered old hat he wore.

'Iain mac Mhurchaidh!'

John Bethune's voice held a hint of exasperated disapproval, and it ran through Flora's mind that perhaps he feared being upstaged by the lively young poet. Not only that, but MacRae was far from being a pillar of the church: it was his wont, rather, to mock the unco guid, and frequently to effect. Flora's own reaction, though similar to the minister's, had necessarily however to be more charitable because this was her home and hospitality was her watchword.

'Come you ben, Iain lad,' she therefore said, 'and I'll fetch you some dry things to put on. Then you can tell us all that has befallen you and Siobhan since we saw you last.'

She was aware as she said it of a frisson of mingled fear, curiosity and excitement. What an evening this promised to be! For already the yard and the surrounding fields were awash with mud and Cheek's Creek, usually an innocuously chattering brook, was a raging torrent. No hope of anyone getting back to Carmel now.

And she knew that she had under her roof two people who were as different as they could possibly be – a chaste, temperate Presbyterian minister and a rip-roaring profligate poet who cared not whom he offended.

IV

April 1775

'Och, Mistress MacDonald, but that was grand!'

Iain MacRae did not stand on ceremony when he was eating. They watched him consume his third platter of venison stew and grab another chunk of corn bread to scoop up the last vestige of gravy. To wash it down he swallowed jugfuls of applejack but did not refuse ale and brandy-wine when Allan offered them. Flora remembered one of her grandfather's half-serious sayings – 'I'd rather keep you a week than a fortnight' – and smiled wryly to herself. Just as well venison was plentiful.

There was every indication that the revelry would go on and on. Allan and John Bethune might not be contributing much to the conversation but Sandy and MacRae were waxing garrulous, well oiled now by wine, usquebaugh and the euphoria of renewed friendship. The unique idiosyncrasy of the group was further heightened by the electric tension that sizzled in the air as the thunder and lightning continued to rage. Each in his own way was savouring the cosiness of companionship and the pleasure of simply being alive. The scene was set then for a taigh-ceilidh, when the men would sit round the table with a bottle and sing in turn: so nobody was surprised when Sandy, his voice ever so slightly slurred, urged Iain to start things off. At that Flora took herself off into the shadows and sat, quietly listening. This kind of ceilidh could be rowdy and was strictly for the menfolk.

All too eager to oblige, the red-headed poet took a swig of ale from his tankard and wiped the foam from his lips. His eyes, fiery and passionate in the candlelight, fixed on each listener and demanded full attention.

'Ye'll be minding the verse I wrote for my good friend and

patron Ruairi MacKenzie of Fairburn? Aye, well I mind the composing of it, lying on a bed of heather with a good drink in me.'

And he launched into the slow cadences of 'Ho ro gum b'eibhinn
liom…', while the others hummed the melody. Flora stole a glance
at John Bethune's face then, and was relieved to read a look of
rapt delight there. That was Iain MacRae's way, the way of all
true poets: he could charm the birds off the trees.

No sooner had the last note died away than Sandy cried out,
'Let's have 'Tha mi tinn, tinn, tinn' now! It's my favourite. We all
know it, so we'll each sing a verse and all join in the chorus!'

Iain cast him a doubtful, somewhat crestfallen look that had
Flora remembering the words of the song. In it the poet's wife is
reproaching him for his prodigal ways and though admitting the
charge he retaliates by declaring that his prowess as a hunter and
fisherman does much to compensate. Yet – and this is the refrain
– he is sick and in low spirits though he does not tell others the
cause of his complaint.

Listening to Iain singing Flora longed to hear more of what had
happened to him and Siobhan. She knew that they had gone
further up country to the Carthage area where life would be lonely
and hard; guessed that his convivial nature had rebelled, deprived
of the language and laughter of his own kind, and that that was
probably why he was here.

And as if in answer to her unspoken questions the young man
heaved a deep sigh when the last 'Tha mi tinn, tinn, tinn' chorus
ended.

'Let me sing you my latest,' he said simply. ''Twill tell you all.'

The words he intoned then were full of such poignant yearning
that Flora felt tears sting her eyes and was glad of the comforting
shadows that masked her presence. The crisp, march-like melody
with its insistent beat did not lighten the poem's message, but rather
emphasised its mood of doom-laden disillusionment. For Iain
MacRae had not taken to life in the wilds of North Carolina.

'It's in America we are at this time, beneath the shadow of the
wood that never ends: when the mid-winter turns to warmth,
apples and nuts and sweet fruit will grow.

'Little do I care for the people here with their drugget coats and
great hats, their short trousers split to the waists, the kilt-hose is
not, alas, to be seen.

'Truly we are Indians indeed: beneath the shadow of the trees not one of us will remain alive. Wolves and other wild beasts cry in every dark den; we are really in extremity since the day we deserted King George.

'Bear my greetings with a welcome to Kintail of the cows, where I was reared awhile when I was a little child. Handsome youths used to step it out there to the music of the dance and long-tressed girls with cheeks like the rose.'

The voice trembled with feeling. It was the timeless cry of the displaced, dispossessed Gael who hoped for better times yet could ignore neither the grim reality of life around him nor his painful yearning for the mists and heather of home. Iain had dared put the exile's agony into words, and the silence that followed when his lay ended spoke worlds.

Uncharacteristically, it was the minister who broke the spell.

'But we must not despair, man. 'Twill not do, to spend our time in nostalgic lament for a homeland that denied us a decent living. The Lord has brought us here for a purpose. Gin we work hard we will make this country blossom, and be blessed for it. Just provided, always, that we do not become embroiled in any of their wranglings.'

Iain flung him a look of disdain. All very well for you, it seemed to say. You can afford to be lily-livered. You're the minister. Folks expect you to be a pansy. All he said, however, was, "'Tis easier for you here, among your own. Over our way, we have naught but Sassenachs and trashy Irish, and they're an ignorant, belligerent lot. Would run you through as soon as look at you. Why, Siobhan was wellnigh raped one day. She was walking innocently by the river when a vagabond jumped out of the bushes and grabbed her by the bodice; did not help that he had a great hole where his nose should have been.'

Flora imagined the girl's terror and sighed. If the people up Carthage way were so savage why did MacRae stay there, and above all why had he left his young wife to suffer those indignities while he wandered around the country? For well she knew that the poet was not one to take insults lying down. He must have made enemies. Many of them.

But Iain was in full flood. 'Goes without saying, of course, that they all call themselves patriots up our way. They're spoiling for a fight, those turkey-cocks, running around with their flintlocks at the ready. When they heard about Lexington you'd have thought it was them that had fought the battle and not the troublemakers up in New England. We can't let them get off with this, I said to Siobhan. I must see Allan MacDonald and discuss what's to be done.'

He paused and a shocked silence fell, until the minister asked tentatively, 'Lexington, did you say?' Clearly the time of glad reunion had given way to a mood of suspicion and speculation.

'Aye. There've been two battles now. Concord and Lexington. Did you not know? The middle of last month it was. They say folks around here can scarce believe that it has come to war but 'twas inevitable in my view. You'll all be for the King, won't you?'

Full of dread Flora held her breath while Allan came in with, 'Of course, man, of course. That goes without saying. But we dare not rush things. We have to wait and find out what line the Governor and his loyal followers are taking. If it comes officially to war then we are here, but let's not be hasty.'

'And I'd go further still and resist the whole idea of fighting,' put in John Bethune bravely. 'We did not come here to disrupt and ruin our lives, but to save them. And there hasn't been any fighting here yet, has there? Nobody hurt?'

Flora sensed Iain MacRae's scorn then, felt the firebrand's impatience to face the foe, and shuddered. Too many of the Highlanders had that same pugnacious streak in them. Were they already forgetting Culloden?

Clearly MacRae had, for his eyes were flashing his contempt.

'Well no. Not exactly. But they're busy rallying recruits for the militia. You should see yon Colonel Spenser drilling his volunteers, down at Cross Creek. It's laughable to see – all those rawboned, slouching, untravelled boors with their flat feet and twitchy eyes, pretending to be soldiers! The air's full of commands – 'Present arms! Load muskets!' – and there they all are, the gomerils, fumbling away swabbing their barrels, ramming home the balls, patching and wadding with a charge of powder and pouring the rest into the priming pan of the flintlock, like bloody professionals. Och they're pathetic, with their bandy legs and brains like pumpkins.'

But Flora had caught a note of grudging admiration, almost of awe, creeping into Iain's voice as he continued. He was by no means as dismissive of the Americans as he pretended to be, and his next remarks bore this out.

'A week or two of being drilled, though, and every one of those bumpkins is a crack shot, shooting to kill, while we sit by and do nothing to stop them.'

Allan looked grave. 'I knew nothing of this until now, Iain. What are the folks in Cross Creek doing, the merchants and planters and timbermen?'

'It's hard to say. Most are bewildered, I think. Find it hard to believe that the New Englanders have gone this far. Aye, they're in a right ferment of indecision, I'd say. Take yon chiel Farquhard Campbell. He's a rebel at heart, I'll wager – has been on every accursed committee since the Battle of Alamance and maybe even before that – but he'd do a lot of damage to his business if he came out openly against England, and as you'll likely know he has a son-in-law, Walter Cunningham, that's a captain in the British army. Not to mention his famous predilection for your good self, may I say, Mistress MacDonald.'

He nodded over in Flora's direction and she felt her face flame in the firelight as he went on.

'You mark my words, though, he's a devious Campbell through and through and will stay uncommitted until he sees what way the wind blows and then come out for the stronger side. I can't be doing with his kind, that sits straddling the fence. Better by far to know where you stand with folks. Isn't that right, Kingsburgh?'

Flora noted the deliberate use of the title and cursed MacRae for so goading her husband. But all Allan gave him in reply was a non-committal 'Aye,' and she breathed again.

But when the others had wrapped themselves in their plaids and made a bid for sleep she plucked up courage and challenged Allan as they lay intertwined together.

'You knew things had come to this pass, Allan?'

For a moment he hesitated. She wondered if he was considering countering her curiosity with the usual endearments but he seemed to sense her determination.

'No, Florrie. I swear I had no idea they were this bad. The Lexington news is alarming beyond words. But I may as well tell you that yon McIvor fellow was no pedlar. He is an army officer come from up New York way, from my cousin Alex that lives on Staten Island. You'll mind Alex maybe, and how interested Roddy was to hear that his wife's grandmother was a Livingstone? Seems she was related to the Boyds in some roundabout way. But anyway, Alex has been enlisting Highlanders from the settlements along the Mohawk River, to fight for the King. And he wanted me to pledge my allegiance too, should the time come. Which I fear it has, my love.'

Flora felt a chill of fear enter her bones and tried not to shiver. The knowledge that Allan had deceived her about McIvor's true identity did nothing to ease her panic. No point in protest or reproach, though: he had been trying to save her worry.

'Promise me you'll keep out of this for as long as you can, Allan. I still think 'tis not our fight.'

But it was obvious that her husband had had enough of humouring her, and would countenance no such promise.

'Och, Flora, it has been a long arduous day. Turn over and go to sleep, and stop meddling in affairs that don't concern you.' And he deliberately turned his back on her.

After that her trembling would not stop. Gulping back her tears she struggled to compose herself. One question kept hammering in her head. Had they come to the other end of the world simply to find new dissension and grief? Oh, Lord, let it not be so. For hours she lay sleepless, gazing into the darkness with panic in her breast, listening to the roar of the thunder and the pelting of the rain.

* * *

Come morning other more pressing considerations took over. Scarcely had the merciless light of dawn wriggled between the chinks of the ill-fitting timbers than Donald McAulay was battering at the door, yelling that he needed all hands, and that right away.

No subservience this time, only a peremptory desperation that brooked no refusal or excuse.

'It's chaos out there! The dam's burst, we've got two muckle tree trunks balanced on the spillways, and ye'd better see to the horses! They're champing and neighing away there like to break the stable door down! Where's that Neil got to? I thought he was aye up first!'

Poor Neil. Flora sighed. It was the one reservation she had about Donald, his instant and inveterate dislike of their oldest and most faithful retainer. She must tackle him about it one day. But not today. There was too much going on.

Overnight the creek had turned into a boiling chocolate-brown torrent, its banks no longer clearly defined. Sweeping inexorably down, it had turned the normally placid mill-pond into a frothing maelstrom that flooded over the dam, bringing with it the fallen debris of the forest floor, uprooted saplings and drowned branches. The farmyard was awash, the lane ankle-deep in muddy water, the livestock bedraggled and forlorn-looking. The storm had sharpened the morning smells, creating a heady emanation as the tang of herbs, the spicy scent of wet leaves and the grainy reek of the mill coalesced with the odour of animals and the stench of damp mud.

But Donald assured them that the worst was over: the rain had stopped and the water level was going down. So everyone rushed to help put things to rights. Even John Bethune laboured all morning to repair the damage the storm had wrought.

Donald's face cleared with the sky.

'Thank the good Lord we can see to work now. I've never seen it that bad, I can tell you. The pond must have doubled its width last night and I guess the water on these spillways was all of three feet deep! Must have put our work back a good week or two. There. We can take a breather now. Is there maybe a wee drappie o' apple brandy yonder, Sandy lad? I could fair wet my thrapple.'

It was as she was laying out piles of cornbread and cheese to accompany the liquor that Flora heard Sandy put a proposition to his father.

'Could you maybe give Iain MacRae work, father? Siobhan's in the family way again and he's at his wits' end. They're totally out of their element up Carthage way – just can't seem to settle – and we could do with the extra help.'

Flora sensed Allan's deliberation and instinctively followed his thought processes. Yes, they needed help, but where was the money to come from and was MacRae the man he wanted, even if he could afford him? What skills did he have, apart from gamekeeping and versifying? Above all, what kind of influence would he have on Sandy and Jamie?

Her thoughts echoed his and then added what for her was a decisive codicil. MacRae's extreme loyalist sentiments might well sway Allan into actively taking sides, and that was the last thing she wanted.

Her relief therefore knew no bounds when Allan shook his head and said firmly, 'I'm sorry, son. He'll have to find work somewhere else.'

But Flora did not know that Iain's visit had had a deeply unsettling effect on Allan, enhancing his feeling of political isolation. The more people from outside whetted his appetite for news the more he chafed to be fully informed: he might be living in the back country but by God he was ready if Britain needed him. And hadn't Martin acclaimed him as the obvious leader of the Cape Fear Highlanders, should conflict come?

V

May 1775

As long as Flora refused to entertain memories of May on Skye she could open her senses to each new challenge as the semi-tropical summer unfolded. The sheer abundance and fecundity of flora and fauna dazzled her eyes and bombarded her ears. Each day began misty but no sooner was the sun up than its light streamed down relentlessly on an effulgence of colour and the air trembled with overpowering odours – the fresh green scents of trees and grass, the pungent tang of animal droppings and newly-cut straw, the overwhelming fragrance of lilies and roses and lavender. Wonderful, provided she could forget her inner visions of massed bluebells in a beech wood. She did not verbalise the ache, was unable consciously to attribute it to a harshness of the light, a lack of subtlety in the prevailing hues, a simple superfluity of richness, but there were times when she would have given her all for a burst of lark-song and a glimpse of the Quiraing. Then her thoughts would wander dangerously into forbidden territory – Fanny – and depending on where she was, or with whom, she would either allow herself the indulgence of tears or smile determinedly and bend her attention to yet another pressing task.

Allan did not seem to notice her inner struggle, or chose to ignore it because he feared it had to do with politics. To cheer her he talked at length about the forthcoming gathering at Mount Helicon, how Highlanders from all over North Carolina would be there and for a few festive days they would cease to be farmers from around the Yadkin or the Pee Dee or the Uwharie and would become again simply MacDonalds from Skye, MacRaes from Kintail, MacNeils from Barra, MacLeods from Mull or Campbells from Argyll. They would feel themselves back in the old days.

Much as she looked forward to the occasion Flora very much doubted this. In her recollection of clan gatherings in the distant days before Culloden the weather had always been fresh and sunny, her stepfather Hugh had invariably won the caber-tossing contest, and she had spent the day in a kaleidoscopic whirl of brilliant tartans and benevolent smiles. The pipes had skirled, young dancers had demonstrated their ability in a bewildering succession of sword dances, reels and strathspeys, and even the dourest of clansmen had ended up singing. That chapter of her life was closed now as surely as the Hanoverians had cruelly decreed the break-up of the clans. Mount Helicon could never recapture the long-lost delight.

Yet Christian Bethune assured her that the clans had indeed recreated the magic, here across the ocean. The gathering was a recognised institution now, a fair, a sports meeting and a ceilidh all rolled into one. Furthermore, Allan had promised that this time they would not bypass Glendale, but would go round that way so that all the family could journey together. Quite a cavalcade it would be, for of course Hugh and the Mount Pleasant folks would be there as well, and Anne was planning the christening for that time. It all seemed too good to be true, and Flora flung all her energies into preparations, knitting garments for the new babe, churning butter, manufacturing soap and candles as Annabella had taught her. She also gathered herbs and roots, having learnt from Stella which ones were of use, and made from them all manner of potent distillations and infusions to counter colic and malaria, rattlesnake bites and foul distempers. She found herself vowing that come next year when the farm was fully operative and she had lit upon her own specialities, she would be better prepared to barter her own homespun, farm produce and potions, but even as it was she was hoping she might exchange her little hoard for a few lengths of fresh muslin to make shifts, and she had set her heart on a copper kettle. Allan was hoping to make some money too; he had already rounded up his cattle, branded the new calves, and managed to enclose a few beasts for sale.

With all their necessary camping gear as well the MacDonalds almost looked to be moving house. The nights could still be chilly, so they had piles of quilts and blankets, and an axe to chop down tree-branches for firewood. They had sacks of corn and sugar; sides of ham and flitches of bacon; beans and cheese; tea and honey; the obligatory usquebaugh and brandy; and of course tobacco, both the chewing and the smoking sorts. You couldn't cook without pots and pans, the horses had to be fed, which meant supplementary bags of grain, and Flora insisted upon taking her medicine chest in case of accidents or illness. Add to all that a flintlock, powder and wadding in case some tempting game chanced by or a wild animal ventured into their camp; a change of clothes; a rope and some kindling, and there was scarce room on the cart for people.

Until the last minute Flora tried not to look forward with too much excitement, just in case something occurred to prevent the expedition. When had she last felt such delighted anticipation? Not since that day – was it only eighteen months ago? – that Dr Johnson had visited them at Kingsburgh.

But nothing got in the way. They rode to Glendale, where everything was as neat and comfortable as they had hoped. Anne and Alex had settled in their new home with resigned determination and optimism. If North Carolina was the fate God had decreed for them, then so be it: they would make the most of it. Alex, the paradigm of the cultured Highland gentleman, was already much respected locally, and surrounded with books, fine furniture and sporting paraphernalia he had brought from home he was in his element.

Anne, of course, was happy wherever Alex and her children were. She glowed, and seeing her with her new baby at her breast Flora was beset by an amalgam of feelings: a sense of self-congratulation on seeing her daughter so contented and fulfilled; an alarming broodiness that would have been amusing had it not been so strong; and an even more disconcerting emotion that she had to recognise as envy of Anne's youth. Through it all, though, shone the intense love she felt for her daughter, and the confidence that it was returned.

Anne and Alex had acquired a carriage and the womenfolk, along with grandsons Norman and Allan and the baby, were conveyed to Mount Helicon in unaccustomed style. Jamie meantime was feeling that he had been granted adult status because he was allowed to ride Delilah: he was a confident rider and Allan had it in mind to buy him a horse of his own that weekend.

The children squirmed and jumped with ill-suppressed excitement.

'Will we be sleeping outside? What if a big black bear came and snuffled round the fire, or even put his muzzle under my blanket?'

'You'd lie still and pretend to be dead. But that won't happen. There will always be one of the servants on watch, with a musket at the ready.'

'Can I have a go at the caber-tossing?'

'It's never too soon to try, lad, but you won't toss it far while your muscles are undeveloped. 'Twill not be long, though. You've the makings of an athlete.'

'How far is this Mount Helicon place? Will we be there tonight?'

'No, son. We go first to Mount Pleasant, to see Aunt Annabella and Uncle Alexander. We'll spend the night there and then journey to the gathering, which will take another day at least.'

And amazingly that was just how it turned out. For once everything fell into place. They arrived in the late afternoon of that last Friday in May full of good humour and magnanimity, largely induced it must be said by Cuidreach's liberality with the bottle. Clansmen were assembling from far and wide, each family choosing a convenient glade or clearing for a campsite in the accommodating terrain of sandy uplands, wooded valleys and grassy ridges.

'Scarcely a mountain,' Allan remarked. 'No Skye man with the Cuillins on his mind would have glorified these mere slopes with such a name. But it's a grand place to have found for a gathering, I'll give them that. And what a prospect, down over the river! Isn't that Rockfish Creek yonder, and the Campbell place? Farquhard and his brood will be around here somewhere, I'll wager!'

Flora followed his gaze, away over the rolling countryside, as a voice she knew proceeded to fill them in. John Bethune, knowledgeable as always about the local churches.

'Aye, and yonder's the old Bethesda Kirk, that was the first in these parts. Must be all of twenty years since it was built. Poor old Hugh MacAde the first minister had a job of it there.' He grinned ruefully. 'Had to give up on the Highlanders in the long run. Said we were a lot of devious hypocrites. Didn't have the Gaelic, of course.'

'John! But it's grand to see you! Your mother's here? And your grandmother? Oh, how I'd love to see Kathie again! Go and fetch them, and come and join us, all of you. Oh, isn't it a perfect evening!'

The meeting with Kathie aroused a multitude of feelings. Kathie was seventy-three now, and wept copiously as she folded Flora to her ample bosom.

'If only my poor brother Donald Roy had lived to see this day! I certainly thought I'd never see ye again, Fionnghal. Soon I'll be sleeping my last sleep in the kirkyard yonder but my rest will be all the sweeter for knowing you're near.'

Flora fondly scrutinised the plump, sharp-eyed little woman who was John Bethune's grandmother and laughed.

'Nonsense, Kathie! You're as fit as a fiddle and could well live to be a hundred. I do declare you're happier here than you were on Skye!'

Meanwhile the circle around every campfire was growing in like fashion. For miles around the Piedmont rang with delighted cries of recognition and welcome as people who had not met for months, and in some cases years, ran to greet one another. Snippets of family news were exchanged, usually harmless but occasionally malicious.

A favourite topic, it seemed, was the flagrant affair between Alastair Boyd and his cousin Rachel. One woman who lived near the Mumrills clearly took delight in embroidering the scandal with hostile insinuations.

'You mark my words, that wee buttered bun will be in the family way before the summer's out. It's right sorry I am for Hannah, for all she might have a dash of the Cherokee in her. It's a house divided, the Boyds, if ever there was one. It's taking the poor doctor all his time to keep the peace these days. You'll be knowing, of course, that Kate and her beloved Alastair make no secret of being all for the rebels. Yet Alastair has had the cheek to come here, you'll notice, and bring that wee bint Rachel with him. Come to spy for Abner Nash, I'll warrant.'

Her voice ran on, delighting in every salacious detail, but Flora had heard enough. Alastair Boyd here! And with Rachel! She prayed earnestly that she would not encounter them. She did not want her holiday spoilt by rancour.

Certainly that was the last emotion her own presence seemed to stir among those she was meeting right now. At first she wondered how Allan would react to all the homage she was receiving but he laughed it off with feigned exasperation.

'Come away and stop gossiping, woman. You'll have the whole weekend to catch up. Everybody's famished. I've sent Sandy and the boys to gather wood and we'll soon get the fire going. Then Neil's going to roast a haunch of venison and sweet potatoes. Anne and Bella have brought all manner of pies and puddings and some Atholl brose. It's going to be quite a feast, I can tell you.'

'You've put up the flag?'

'Aye. As if I'd forget it!'

He pointed proudly to the edge of the clearing that the MacDonalds had appropriated and there it flew, the clan banner with its crest of heather. Other family groups sported similar symbols – broom for the Murrays, wortleberry for the Mac-Queens, myrtle for the Campbells.

As they busied themselves preparing the meal they watched new fires springing up like blossoms in the twilight. Down below, in the bowl-shaped hollow where the games would take place next day, a larger, central bonfire was well underway. Sparks flew and the air was filled with the sharp scent of burning cedar and hickory. Then suddenly a hush fell.

'The ceremony's starting! I'll have to be ready!' Flora scarcely recognised Allan's voice, so choked and tense it sounded.

As the dusk thickened the fires flamed brighter. Then some smaller torches detached themselves and began to move, like giant fireflies flickering, as the chief of each clan plunged a faggot into his fire and carried it down the slope towards the great communal pyre below. There he threw his brand into the blaze, crying out the name of his clan as he did so.

'The McGregors are here!'

'The MacRaes are here!'

'The Campbells are here!'

When Allan's voice rang out, clear and confident – 'The MacDonalds are here!' – Flora thought her heart would burst with pride.

After this roll-call of the clans it was as if the whole hillside erupted in song and fiddle music, conversation and laughter. Flora and her family settled down to eat, pulling up logs to sit on and taking it in turns to skewer chunks of venison smothered in peppers and dripping with lard. Then they lit their pipes and passed the liquor bottle round. Flora felt the mellow warmth as the whisky penetrated her bones and knew that she had rarely felt so content. The clean, pungent fragrance of pine needles was in her nostrils, the tang of woodsmoke, roasting meat and tobacco. A soft mist filled the valleys and gradually the raucous voices died away to a gentle susurration.

Then suddenly, not far off, someone started to play the pipes.

'That can only be Donald MacCrummen,' Allan murmured. 'Him that used to be piper to the Dunvegan MacLeods.'

The eerie sound with its characteristic melancholy evoked a whole gamut of gut-wrenching memories. Flora knew that if she could penetrate each heart she would find the same feelings harboured there. Pride and thankfulness most of all, and a determined bid for fellowship, but through it all a wistfulness as people yearned for the Highlands and the folks they had left behind.

At last, one by one, the family came to say goodnight and she realised with mingled amusement and surprise that they were deferring to her, regarding her as a sort of matriarch, a source of solace and fount of wise advice. How very odd. She must think about it, try to live up to this unsolicited respect.

She and Allan sat in the twilight together then and gazed into the fire, serenely smoking their pipes. Gradually the sky deepened to purple, the lines of distant hills softened, melted into one another and faded into darkness. The moon rose, full and high, from behind the arch of trees and cast blue shadows over the ridges. Only Venus was bright enough to compete in that sector of the heavens, but away in the east the Milky Way shone white, a trail of star-dust scattered down the sky. The pipe music had ceased as abruptly as it had begun. The only sounds were the chirping of crickets, the occasional rustle of some tiny woodland creature, and the stifled, excited cries of lovers carried on a mere whisper of a breeze.

'There'll be many a bairn conceived this night, I'll wager.'

'Aye. Just as long as none of them's ours.'

She knew, though, that on a night like this she could never gainsay Allan, despite warnings about the vulnerability of women at the time of change. She felt his hands creep up under her shift and sighed with pleasure.

* * *

They woke to fog before dawn, to the smell of woodsmoke and damp clothes. Still warm as they lay huddled together under their quilts, they were resigned to an hour or two of dank discomfort before the sun would rise and dry off the dew. Reluctant to leave the nest, Flora cuddled closer to Allan. Then she heard a crashing in the undergrowth close to her head and all her senses stiffened. Bear? Had some drunken reveller thoughtlessly left food lying about to tempt animal intruders?

But bears did not have human voices. Still fuddled from sleep and aware of having overdone the whisky the night before she struggled to put a name and a face to this one.

She was not kept in doubt for long. She turned her head and saw a pair of thick-soled leather shoes, farmer's shoes with horn buckles, just by her right ear. Travelling upwards her eye took in a neat stockinged leg, a dangerous-looking dirk, and a plaid of MacRae tartan. Above it all, suddenly illuminated as pine-sap in the fire briefly flared, the familiar face of Iain MacRae.

What he had said was, 'Kingsburgh, I'm in trouble. I need your help. And Sandy's.'

Allan was quick to rouse himself. At first his hand had gone instinctively to the flintlock he kept beside him for emergencies: then she felt him relax as he realised who the intruder was.

'Och, Iain, what would you be wanting of Sandy and me in the middle of the night, man? Surely it can wait till morning?'

Iain's answer made her blood run cold.

'I fear I cannot, sir. I have had – what shall I call it? A difference of opinion, maybe – with yon galoot of a MacDonald they call Alastair of the Mumrills. He accused me of taking liberties with that Strachan lass, the one he says is his cousin. Ye'll maybe mind her from the *Ulysses*. A bonnie red-haired wee thing with a proud walk and roving eyes. Green eyes. I swear I wasn't insulting her, though. Just asked for a wee kiss for old time's sake, and mussed up her hair a bit. Och, but he's a right rogue, that one, and shifty with it. What's more, I know for a fact that he is no true Highlander, but a bloody American patriot that would have every Gael here that didn't sign their goddamned association hanged! Trouble is, I told him so and he has challenged me to a duel. Pistols at dawn. The whole caboodle. So you see I need a second, and somebody there in case I'm badly injured, or worse.'

VI

'You can't be serious, man. This is a friendly assembly, not an occasion for murder like the ancient Roman games. Be sensible. Work off your energies in the tug-o'-war contest, or the hammer-tossing, and you'll find your grudges vanish.'

Flora admired Allan's quiet reasonableness. She knew that inside he must be as panic-stricken as she was but he was managing to keep his tone dismissive, even light. All kinds of considerations must be chasing one another round his head. Alastair's very presence at the gathering, in itself a threat. The liaison, or flirtation, or whatever it had been, between Rachel and Iain on the Atlantic voyage. The possibility which John Bethune had hinted at, of spies and agents provocateurs infiltrating this year's company for their own political ends. All at once Mount Helicon ceased to be an idyll and took on a dangerous cast.

She knew that Iain was not one to be moved by common sense, and his reply, edged now with hysteria and a hint of menace, bore this out.

'Don't think to change my mind, Kingsburgh. You've come across this Alastair MacDonald, have you not? You understand, surely, that the Highland pride in me rebels at the thought of compromise or surrender? Why, when he came on Rachel and me he accused me of trying to swive her, wouldn't believe we were just having a laugh. As if I, a married man, would have taken advantage of the lass! Not, mind you, that she wasn't all for it herself, the wee blouzabella! But I refuse to be called a lowborn Highland tyke and other names too crude to mention. My honour cries out for revenge!'

By this time the commotion of voices had everyone around the campfire stirring. Consternation reigned. Iain had spotted a tousled Sandy wrapped up in his plaid not far off, and shouted, 'Hey, Sandy! Get up, man! You'll see things my way, I'll warrant. There's a duel startin' in a half hour and by God, when it's over it's either me or that blackguard Alastair Boyd will be with our Maker!'

In Sandy's case too the truth took a few minutes to penetrate, and when it did his instinct was exactly like his father's.

'But Iain, the whole thing's crazy! I'm sure Alastair didn't knowingly insult you to the point of provoking a duel! Besides, he's my sweetheart's brother. I can't support someone who wants him dead!'

If Flora had not known the two characters so well she would not have felt so desperate, but Alastair Boyd and Iain MacRae! If she had been asked she could not have thought up two people more likely to rile one another to the point of internecine hatred. But a duel! One of them could easily be killed. It was all too preposterously stupid to contemplate, yet she shuddered at the tragic inevitability of it.

She knew from Allan's silence that he too was weighing up all the dangerous implications of the affair, and could only feel relief when he said evenly, 'I'm sorry, Iain. I can't get mixed up in this. You'll have to find somebody else.'

Sandy took a similar line. 'Go and make peace with the man, Iain. It's the only sensible thing to do. Admit you were a fool, carried away by the wee drabag's beauty, or some such excuse. The number of times I've told you that your love of the women would be the death of you yet, and you'd never listen!' And he lay down again by the fire, dismissively burying his head in his plaid.

Iain sounded really desperate then. There was a catch in his voice and Flora thought she heard his teeth chatter as he made one last plea.

'Neither of you's willing to help me in my hour of trial, then? So much for the friendship and allegiance of my fellow Gaels. Well, at least promise me this. If I die, tell Siobhan it was because I would not let myself and my King be vilified by a rapscallion knave. And tell them I care not where they bury me, as long as there's a rowan tree planted by my head.'

With this melodramatic speech – Flora wondered how far its pathos had been deliberately orchestrated – Iain made to stride away, the picture of trust betrayed. Then she saw to her dismay that Sandy was on his feet again, spurred into action by his friend's appeal.

'Wait, Iain! Of course I won't let you face this ordeal alone!. Father, should we not at least go with Iain and try to smooth things over? These two will never see eye to eye if left to themselves to sort it out. They're both too damn thrawn.'

Yes, and in Iain's case the stubbornness was compounded by a mistaken, almost medieval, sense of chivalry offended. He just could not help carrying all his emotions to extravagantly poetic extremes. Flora was not altogether surprised, then, when Allan reluctantly gathered his plaid about his shoulders and followed the two young men.

Nor did she hesitate herself. Determined not to let them out of earshot she started after them.

'Come, Morag. And bring my medicines. We may well have need of them.'

Darkness was still filling the hollows as they worked their gingerly way down the slope. The heavy dew had soaked the grass and Flora felt her stockings wet through the thin pattens she wore. If it had been an ordinary morning she would have inhaled the varied scents of herbs, wild flowers and pine resin with gratitude, and thrilled to be alive, but an almost spastic quivering had seized her limbs. She struggled to control it, complaining to the maid of the cold but knowing that only fear could make her tremble so violently.

Eventually they emerged into the central clearing where the embers of last night's bonfire were still smouldering. Tentative rays of sunshine were beginning to penetrate the mist now and they could discern a knot of men standing just ahead of them. Instinctively she backed away.

'Stay in the shadows, Morag,' she cautioned. 'We don't want to be seen. This is men's business.'

One voice, almost hysterical in its vehemence, broke the silence. Its harsh nasal tone could only belong to Alastair Boyd.

'They Gawd! To think Ah caught that thar dirty shitten lout MacRae tryin' to wriggle navels wi' ma cousin!' Then a note of triumphant glee crept in. "Sblood, see who he's got wi' him! The sainted MacDonalds! If there's one other Johnny Ah'd gladly riddle wi' bullets it's that thar popinjay Sandy. You mark ma words, when the war gets a-goin' it's that nest o' vipers we'll have to scotch first.'

Flora had to strain to hear the words that came in reply, for they were spoken in the soft lilting tones of a native Gaelic speaker and were calculated to soothe.

'You have taken this matter too far, Alastair. Reconsider, I beg you.' And when no answer came the man added sternly, 'You should not have come here at all. The folks around here do not regard you as a Highlander. You do not belong. Forget this whole affair and go home.'

The response was an incensed growl. 'But Ah've every right! Ah'm as much a Highlander as any goddam clansman here. Have you forgotten Ah was sired by a MacDonald, Farquhard, and a Jacobite at that?'

Farquhard Campbell! But then, it followed. Wasn't he one of Roddy's best friends? It was natural Alastair should have turned to him, just as Iain had come to Allan.

By now the sun was almost up. Soon its rays would burn away the morning fog. Already the faint, eerie outlines of the hills were appearing on the horizon. Flora saw Alastair and Farquhard walk over to confront Iain and Sandy. Irrelevantly she thought how bucolic her men's muddy deerskin broghans looked beside Alastair's polished silver-buckled shoes. What a dandy the man was. Though the day was scarce begun he had dressed for this tussle with death in powdered wig and lace jabot, and she noticed with a momentary flash of anger that he had the nerve to flaunt a badge with the MacDonald crest on it. Then she remembered his reputation as a crack shot and her heart turned over. Dandy he might be but he was no nancy-boy.

It was immediately clear that reconciliation was the last thing in the adversaries' minds. Even with their seconds struggling to restrain them they were at one another's throats, yelling vituperations.

'Yew flash whippersnapper of a bung-eyed Gael, darin' to insult ma cousin! Full as a hog's ear yew are, stewed to the very eyebrows! No way can yew stand up, far less shoot straight, with that much liquor in yew. 'Tis a kindness Ah do yew, savin' yew from the hangman. Better a quick bullet than the hempen fever.'

And quick as a flash the reply came back. 'I'm as ready as I'll ever be for ye, ye misbegotten bastard skunk.'

Alastair's vulpine mouth twisted in a snarl. Flora guessed that that one word, 'bastard' had sealed Iain's fate. And she could not help suspecting that there might be some truth in Alastair's taunts. Iain was indeed staggering where he stood. Lack of sleep? Sheer terror? Or perhaps, right enough, the usquebaugh from the night before? She almost cried out in her agonised concern for him.

But Farquhard had stepped between the two men and forcibly pulled them apart. 'Calm down I say. Now myself, Sandy and Kingsburgh here, we all beg you to reconsider. You're brave lads both. Nobody will think the worse of you gin you shake hands and walk away. Many's the one around these parts that has had disputes with his neighbours, but heaven forbid that it should come to fatal blows.'

The situation had been so emotionally charged that Flora had not been aware of other bystanders circling the glade. Clearly word of the forthcoming duel had circulated swiftly around the gathering and everyone seemed to be here. John Bethune had stepped out now, hands raised in firm but gentle protest, and with an authority born of moral conviction was adding his plea to Farquhard's.

'This is not the Lord's way to settle disputes. Think on't, I beg you. Violence solves nothing, only breeds hatred and death!'

But his efforts at intercession evoked nothing but scorn.

'Sanctimonious hot-gospeller!' Iain spat. 'Bide by your Bible and keep your pious nose out of what doesn't concern you!'

Alastair was equally dismissive. 'Don't yew patronise me, preacher man! Ma mind's made up, to rid the world of this doggone upstart son-of-a-bitch. Stand aside, Farquhard, and let me have at him!' And he reached out to grab hold of Iain's plaid. 'Pistols at ten paces! My cousin's honour demands it!'

In exasperation Farquhard nodded.

'So be it. I wipe my hands of the pair of ye. Ye ken the rules.'

In the suspenseful moments that followed Flora felt her every muscle tense. The scene before her seemed to go into slow, choreographed motion, formal and stylised as a ballet enacted to a musical score of the birds' dawn chorus. It stamped itself upon her mind, a series of vivid, unforgettable impressions. The brash, contemptuous Boyd, who, if Sandy won Jenny, might well end up a relative one day – oh, heaven forbid! – and Iain, the rash infuriatingly lovable poet, heart-broken for home, whose temper matched his flaming hair. She prayed with all her might, as the two men paced out their distance and turned to fire, that Alastair would be the one to die.

But Iain's shot went wide of its mark, off into the bushes somewhere, and it was he who fell. She knew that the look of shocked surprise on his face as he sank to the ground would haunt her for ever.

VII

Alastair let out a whoop of triumph that had Flora's blood boiling. Then still carrying his smoking pistol he marched jauntily over towards Iain's motionless figure and poked it contemptuously with his foot.

'Lump of rotten meat! Ah caint say Ah'm sorry Ah've kilt him. An' from what Ah've heard tell his naggin' wife'll be well rid of him. Another Hannah she is, so they say.'

For a moment Flora wondered if he was on the point of kicking her as well, for she had immediately dashed over, beating Allan and Sandy to it, and had hunkered down at Iain's side. Kick me, she almost said, and you will be dead meat yourself: my menfolk will take only so much. But Alastair had clearly thought the better of it and was swaggering away, still snarling invective.

Glad to see the scoundrel go, Flora gently turned the motionless body over and steeled herself for what she would see. Iain had fallen on his left side, clutching his chest. Chances were the bullet had penetrated his heart. There would be blood everywhere. But to her puzzlement there was no bullet-hole visible in his clothing. He seemed strangely unscathed. Hope leapt in her. Perhaps there was yet a pulse, and the lad could be saved! Tentatively she stretched out a hand and made to grasp his wrist, and as she did so she happened to looked into Iain's face, whereupon one eye opened and winked broadly at her.

'Has the bugger gone? I can get up off this cold ground? Fooled ye all, didn't I?' And Iain sat effortlessly up, large as life.

Flora's first reaction was an angry retort.

'You should be ashamed of yourself, Iain MacRae, deceiving us all into thinking you were dead, and you just play-acting! Do you realise what torture you have inflicted on us all? We've been sick with worry!'

Then as the tension broke and relief flooded her she felt a wave of hysterical laughter ripple through her body.

'Allan! Sandy! He's whole! 'Twas all a ruse!'

As it turned out Iain's fall and feigning death had not been altogether a calculated hoax. The bullet had caught him a glancing blow on his right forearm and the superficial wound had to be cleaned and dressed – a duty Flora was all too happy to perform when they got him back to the MacDonald camp-site. Once there he could not stop talking – how he had wanted to give in when they had begged him to, but was too proud; how scared he had really been, for he wasn't ready to die for a long time yet and wanted Siobhan with him when he did; how the searing pain in his arm had come as an unbelievable reprieve, and with it the idea of faking death had taken shape: above all, how much he still hated that bastard Boyd for keeping him away from the games, for there was no possibility of his tossing the caber now.

Iain was garrulous at the best of times but his chatter was so obviously brought on by shock that Annabella set herself to concocting a calming infusion of cramp bark while Flora staunched his wound.

'An old Cherokee woman gave me the receipt,' she explained. 'She called it squaw bush, and recommended it for women's troubles, the monthly stomach pains and the like. I usually put skunk cabbage in with it, and some ginger, but no matter. 'Twill soothe the nerves, especially if we administer it in sack.'

Flora very much doubted if the sack was a good idea in Iain's case – would it not stimulate him to even wilder flights of loquacity? – but decided not to interfere, and was glad, some ten minutes after he had swallowed the dose, to see the patient turn drowsy and fall asleep in mid-sentence.

Allan meanwhile had been working out their next move.

'Better to put it about that Iain has been injured but not fatally. That will satisfy Alastair. It may mean that Siobhan hears tell of it up in Carthage ere he wins back home – bad news travels quickest – but we can try to get word to her not to worry. Meanwhile we'll keep watch over him here but carry on as if nothing untoward has happened. Sandy, go with the ghillies and find one or two straight young pines for the cabers. Then we'll get started on the stripping and smoothing of them. All this disruption has lost us two precious hours. Harebrained young rapscallions, bringing discredit on what should be a harmonious gathering!'

Allan's comments reduced the duel to little more than an unfortunate incident, to be gravely regretted but nevertheless forgotten, and Flora saw the wisdom in this. The more fuss that was made of it the more importantly it would figure in people's memory of the day, and they did not want that. So she pretended to be unperturbed as the lads around practised for the forthcoming games, swinging their arms and hefting imaginary cabers.

Amazingly, too, the succession of glad events that followed did much to cheer them. The MacDonald team, which included Cuidreach and Glendale as well as Allan and Sandy, gave a heavier Campbell side a run for their money in the tug-o'-war, and actually brought the Camerons to their knees. But Allan was so exhausted after his efforts that he decided against taking part in the more demanding caber-tossing competitions, which traditionally brought the games to an exciting climax. Flora could see the pain in his eyes when he declared himself unfit, for back in the old days few had been able to challenge him and he still had the broad muscular shoulders and powerful physique that the contest demanded, but she applauded his good sense.

'Good to see you're learning prudence with the years,' she

whispered, and added daringly, knowing it would cheer him, 'After all, I need a man with energy in my bed.'

Despite her preoccupation with Allan, however, she could not but admire the prowess and stamina of the sturdy Highlanders who took part in the throwing contests. This was where the more mature, physically developed men shone: it was no sport either for mere striplings or for the flabby. As it happened, it was a MacEachan from Cross Creek who carried off the laurels, a forty-year-old with not an ounce of excess weight on him, all brawn and sinew: someone said he was the blacksmith.

But rather to Flora's surprise Farquhard Campbell acquitted himself well too. Flora watched him crouch and heave, dart ahead with the tree-trunk in his powerful hands and catapult it expertly forward, and marvelled at his strength.

'He was the champion for years,' Annabella volunteered, 'much as Allan used to be in the old days at Portree, but they both have to bow out gracefully now, I reckon, and give the young ones a chance.'

Their own young ones did not exactly distinguish themselves. Donald was frankly too young, while Sandy, though keen to excel, was peculiarly unathletic. Brave, yes, and handsome, but not prepared to spend time limbering up and seriously honing his body to a pitch of sporting perfection. Idly Flora wondered what he was really good at. Writing and figuring, probably. He had a good head for money, would run the farm as a profitable business one day. So she found her mind drifting off into conjectures about the future and the caber-tossing became secondary to her thoughts, a mere blur before her dreaming eyes – so much so that she failed to grasp what everyone was jeering about when Alastair Boyd's caber landed a mere three feet from his toes and he stamped away scowling. He had fondly imagined that caber-tossing was something that could be accomplished without practice, had not appreciated the weight of the pole. Nor had he realised that Highland dress did not become him: he was not accustomed to the swing of the kilt, which looked manly on a true clansman like Farquhard but ridiculous on someone to whom wearing it was not second nature.

Flora found that she could not scoff with the others, however. Alastair's discomfiture was certainly deserved and gratifying to

see, but knowing his unsporting personality she feared it did not
augur well. He was the kind to harbour grudges, to nurse the
memory of defeat and make sure the victor suffered for it one day.
Premonitions stirred in her again and although the mid-day sun
was hot she felt a shiver run through her.

A sudden encounter with James Coor, the Cross Creek builder
who was reputed to be one of the leading patriots in the area, did
nothing to dissipate her sense of impending trouble. Coor was a
wiry, ferret-faced fellow with small, ice-blue eyes and hair like
straw, and he was collaring Allan now with the kind of cocky,
triumphant impertinence that would have had Allan drawing his
dirk had he been confronted with it in a similar menial at home.
But this was America. One had to watch one's step. Fearfully she
strained her ears to listen.

'Ah, Master MacDonald of Kingsburgh himself. Ye'll have been
hearin' the latest news frae New Bern, eh? That they've banished
yon rascally Martin to Fort Johnson at last? High time, I say! Him
and yon hoity-toity wife o' his, sitting in a bloody palace pretending
they're royalty and expecting the rest o' us to contribute no' juist
to his ain coffers but to a king on the other side o' the ocean that
cares not a whit whether we live or die! It gars ye boak!'

He paused for breath. Allan put out a hand and said something
in a small, strangled voice which Flora interpreted as a plea for
more information. She got the impression, however, that it would
not have mattered much what he had said, for Coor was determined to carry on.

'Aye, the folks o' Mecklenburg County issued a declaration o'
defiance that they style their Resolves, an' followin' on that Abner
Nash went to seize six o' the palace cannon and when wee Martin
refused to hand them ower Abner juist up and ran him oot o' the
toon. Should have run him through and all, I say, when he had
the chance. A big mistake to let him go. Botched it, that's what he
did. Could mean trouble later, when this war really gets going.'

Flora had a mental picture of the Martins as they had been at
the Wilmington reception – pompous and grandiose, perhaps, but
urbane and refined in a way that few colonials could even aspire
to be – and pulled her shawl more tightly around her shoulders to
combat the chill. Her voice came out small and fearful: she
reproached herself for the note of pleading in it but had to know.

'And Elizabeth Martin? And those poor bairns? They're at Fort Johnson too?'

'That bloated cow and her ailing calves, ye mean? Wha kens? Or cares?'

The gathering took on an atmosphere of suspicion and uncertainty after that. They found themselves reading insults and innuendo into the remarks of people they had regarded hitherto as friends, and try as they would to forget the Governor's plight they were forced to consider its grave implications. How could anyone possibly pretend, now, that the colony was not on the brink of war?

But try they did, for there was fun to be had and business to be done. Despite Farquhard Campbell's having seconded Alastair in the duel, for example, Allan still had to talk business with him, and Flora heard them arrange for Sandy to go over to Rockfish Creek and collect some horses.

'Aye. You tell the lad he's welcome. I have a fine chestnut I can give you for a good price, and a brood mare I'll be sorry to part with. As for your winter storage needs, just leave that to me. You say you'll want some whisky casks, and a big barrel of hickory wood for smoked meat? Aye, but I'd recommend some stonewear jars for your salted fish as well, else it will take on a turpentine taste. And if you want barrels for apples and squash you must see that they're seasoned right.'

All of which seemed amiable enough. The pair even shook hands when they parted.

Then Farquhard caught sight of Flora and signalled her over. 'My dear friend. I've been seeking the chance to talk to you.'

She immediately sensed the warmth between them. 'Ah yes, Master Campbell. 'Tis sorry I am that our day began so inauspiciously. Do please know that the duel was none of our doing. We would fain have stayed out of it.'

'And I too. But as you've doubtless heard there are more dangerous things afoot than young men's squabbles over women. I beg you, Flora, do everything in your power to keep your husband aloof from the troubles that threaten to tear our country apart. He is fiery and public-spirited, but that very nobility could be his undoing if he lets himself become embroiled in this fight. Let those of us who have been here all our lives, and know the problems, be

the ones to make the decisions. As you can well imagine 'tis hard
enough even for us merchants. We sympathise with the colonists'
rightful case yet must keep faith with our suppliers in England if
we are to stay in business. You see that, don't you?'

The beetling eyebrows quivered. There was no doubting this
man's sincerity. Flora found herself nodding her agreement.
Certainly she appreciated Farquhard's dilemma. But at the same
time her intuition told her that the events of the morning could
only have acerbated the existing antagonism between Farquhard
and Allan. Not only was the old resentment between Campbell
and MacDonald operating here, but Farquhard knew that Allan
was fast usurping his position as the leading Highlander in the
area. Whether this had come about inevitably, by reason of Allan's
family connections, or by design, made little difference. Farquhard
was jealous.

Yet she could not help liking the man and considering him a
friend, and as different responses to his plea fought for supremacy
in her mind it was good will and trust that got the upper hand.
Her hand reached out to touch his red hairy one.

'You may depend on me, Farquhard. All I want in the whole
world is peace and the wellbeing of my family.'

'Aye, and that's another thing I'd bid ye be mindful of. I wanted
Sandy down our way because it will give him the chance to stop
at the Mumrills on the way back and see Jenny. Roddy tells me
she's pining for love of him. Would have come here with her
brother had she not been all too aware of the scandalous goings-
on between him and Rachel. But if Sandy wants to see the lass
he'll have to be circumspect. Not that Roddy would gainsay him,
but Alastair and Kate – ah, that's another story. In their eyes an
alliance between Boyds and MacDonalds is as unthinkable as that
between Capulets and Montagues, in the play, and they'll do
everything in their power to stop it. And their patriot sentiments
only make it worse. So warn him, Flora, if you get the chance.'

Suddenly Flora felt that she had almost too much to cope with.
That evening, as they sat round the fire listening to the bagpipes'
haunting tune and singing the songs of the old country, conflicting
emotions tugged and churned. Every so often someone would try
to lighten the mood with a happy tune in reel tempo, but always
the mood reverted to elegy and the pibroch keening. Nostalgia

now was interlaced with dread and openhearted friendship with suspicion. Of all the people here they could trust only their own close family. Everyone said even Farqhuard Campbell was suspect, although Flora was sure she knew better, and as for the Boyds, there was little doubt about what side they were on!

She sat in the velvety shadow and vowed that she would not allow this new atmosphere to poison the happiness of the christening next day, and when they won home to Kingsburgh she would do all in her power to keep Allan there. Let them fight their war without him. She wanted nothing to do with it.

VIII

June 1775

Back at Cheek's Creek the routine of farm work re-established itself and the bickerings of firebrands on the Tidewater faded, becoming a mere irrelevant counterpoint to the call of the herders and the scrunch of the saw. While the family had been at Mount Helicon Donald McAulay and the farm workers had taken time to lay a pine floor in the great room of the house. Appreciatively sniffing the pungent, honey-gold resin that still oozed from the newly-sawn planks, Flora envisaged Kingsburgh taking on the patina of a desirable home. She could happily hang her curtains now, and scatter hooked rugs here and there, to give an impression of colour and cosiness.

Not that warmth was a consideration those days, for the summer heat was really asserting itself now. She had never experienced such oppressive, enervating conditions. A shimmering pall lay over everything. Come mid-morning Beanie and the dogs lay panting in the shade, Jamie spent all his time paddling in the creek and the maids vied with one another for tasks that would keep them indoors. Flora felt her hair cling in wet tendrils round her neck and every article of clothing was clammy with sweat within five minutes of putting it on.

Since her days on the Cape Fear Flora had developed a dread of mosquitoes but they were an inevitable part of the environment here and she had to school herself to live with them. They settled round her ears and nose, wriggled their way under cuffs and collars, insinuated themselves into every tiny aperture in her clothing. Where normally she would have gone barefoot she had to tie sacking round her ankles, wear slippers and petticoats and a bonnet – all contributing to her discomfort and exasperation. Rubbing crushed penny-royal or tobacco leaves on exposed areas of her body made no difference: the creatures still came in their carnivorous thousands. Gnats and horseflies, side-tracked from fields and stables, cared not a whit whether the flesh they devoured was animal or human. And bluebottles: wherever food was, there they were too, loud and voracious. She was convinced that when she emerged of a morning from under her tent of butter muslin they were lying in wait, hummingly agog to savour the stink of her chamber pot, the strong stench of her night-time sweat, the sweet clinging odour of Allan's semen.

The hum of flies was only one element in a cacophony of sound. Birdsong she had expected and revelled in – after all, they were used to it on Skye – but the unending pulse of the cicadas was new. A constant background vibration, it surged and fell like the sea, and sometimes she got the impression of differently-pitched noise to right and left of her, as if percussion instruments were playing in counterpoint, staccato drums on one side, metallic cymbals on the other. The air was never still, even at night.

Donald McAulay was constantly warning her to watch where she trod because the meadows were alive with snakes and by no means all were harmless. A two-year-old had just died of a rattle-snake bite down Campbellton way. The bairn had taken it for a toy and thought to play with it, when he disturbed it curled up by the corn-crib. Flora recalled Roddy's warnings then. One of his naturalist friends had counted at least thirty species of snake in North Carolina. Moccasins. Rattlesnakes. Banded water snakes. Pit vipers. 'Be careful, especially in summer, and in long grass,' he had said. 'They reckon only six species are venomous, but you have to watch out.'

Stay clear of deep pools, too, Donald cautioned, for water-snakes are among the deadliest. Flora almost fainted from shock when Jamie, hearing this, gaily came up with, 'Oh, that's what I must have seen in the mill dam yesterday! It came slithering out of a hole in the bank and I almost collided with it! There's a monster catfish there too, with the ugliest face you ever did see, and great long whiskers!'

It seemed that nature was teeming with terrors, slimy and venomous and primeval, on an unimaginable scale. Nothing occurred in moderation: it had to proliferate.

But to Flora's great delight there were new pleasures to counterbalance the heat, the insects and the lurking dangers of snakes and wild animals. In the weeks they had been away nature had exploded in a riot of colour. She would never forget her first sight of a magnolia tree in blossom. It was outside the church where the redbud had had pride of place six weeks before, and the pristine purity of the freshly-opened flowers quite took her breath away.

'Just look at it, Allan! I'd scarcely noticed it before. Looks just like a plain, leathery-leaved oak tree normally, yet here it is, covered in huge white blooms bigger by far than roses.'

Christian Bethune was there too and was quick to expatiate on the local flora. She had been a great one for her garden at home.

'Och, that's just a wee shilpit thing, that magnolia tree, compared to the ones down on the Tidewater. I brought a sapling up from there when we first arrived, and it's growing fast. You'll have to see it before the flowers fade. That's the sad thing about the magnolia flowers: they don't last long. But see that trumpet honeysuckle yonder. Did you ever see such a mass of bloom? I come round here every morning early, before the heat, just to smell it. No, there's no shortage of flowers to tend. Trouble isn't encouraging them to grow as much as stopping them overrunning everything once you get them going.'

And the flowers encouraged birds as well as insects. Flora found the humming birds most fascinating of all. They came in flocks on their summer migration to central America, a flutter of green and white plumage with here and there a flash of brilliant pink where the sun caught the ruby throat of the more colourful male, and she would never tire of watching their long tubular tongues sipping nectar through their curved, needle-like bills. Colour was the rule rather than the exception here: scarlet tanagers would come out from the forests, scissor-tailed fly-catchers with their long divided tails would swoop over the creek, the orange under their wings glinting: why, even sparrows had white throats and light striping on the head, blackbirds had red wings, and if a bird had to be black and white it carried the colour scheme off with dramatic verve. So much to learn about them all.

The crops were ripening too and already it was obvious that maize was grain of a totally different order from the oats and barley of home: already it towered to shoulder height and was developing long solid husks sheathed in silky green. Allan had burnt off great patches of forest to make field space for this Indian corn, and was jubilant about the prospects for cattle feed, bread-making and distilling. Flora had not exactly enjoyed the locally-produced liquor, found it too fiery and disliked its strange greasy aftertaste, but Allan maintained that his concoction would rival Scotland's best, given his home-grown corn and the clear mountain water from the well. His enthusiasm was boundless and whereas Flora flagged in the increasingly humid heat he appeared not to mind it, grew tanned and sinewy.

Randy too, to the extent that she wondered whether the climate might be to blame for the marked sexuality of so many Americans. Not that she minded, except for the stickiness of those June nights when sleep was slow to come, even after love.

On one such night they were wide awake until well after midnight. A full moon shone with unusual brilliance on a vase of creamy tuberose she had placed on the bedside table. The air was fragrant, the mosquitoes had gone, and the only sounds were the throb of tree-frogs and the occasional screech of a barn owl.

'Put something on and let's go down to the creek,' Allan said. 'The chill of the water will refresh us. Come, Florrie.'

His voice was thick with needing her, and as they crept down through the farmyard and past the mill buildings he drew her close and caressed her under her cloak, eliciting an answering shudder of anticipation. Somehow the primitive smells of byre and stable, the soft musky breath of sleeping animals and the pungent odour of their droppings, excited her even more.

'Wheesht, Beanie. Go back to sleep,' she whispered shakily when the gangly form of the fawn materialised out of the shadows and made to join them, and such was the magic of the night that the beast seemed to understand and lay down again on her bed of straw at the stable door.

Shafts of moonlight picked out Allan's strong features and

glinted blue on his white night-sark, so that his whole presence seemed to shine. Was this the man with whom she shared the humdrum routine of each ordinary day, eating and sleeping, labouring, worshipping and frequently disagreeing? She was intensely aware of his physical power, the muscles strengthened by his work in field and forest, yet tonight there was an almost ethereal quality about him. Wonder and love welled up in her and she felt she would burst with gratitude to the God who had made it possible.

Beyond the shadow of the farm buildings the night was studded with stars, and it was as if their innumerable lights were reflected on earth because the glowworms were out in their thousands. As clear and icy as diamonds, they flickered and twinkled from every bush and reed, enhancing the sense of novelty and strangeness. She smelt the musky fragrance of lavender, the sharpness of mint, the clean spicy tang of spruce and cedar. For the first time in weeks she felt cool and invigorated

Shedding their clothes just upstream from the dam they chose a pool that lay silvery under the moon and slid together into the silky, mountain-fresh water. It was cold enough to take the breath away on first impact but after the initial shock the benison of its cleansing balm both soothed and stimulated. Stimulated because Flora's every nerve was alive, responsive to the hard demanding body beside her. Allan seemed to sense that she did not need any further preliminaries and as he slid into her he let out a little strangled whoop of joy that might well have been mistaken, had anyone in the house heard it, for the hoot of a distant owl.

'Ah, mo ghaoil, but that was beautiful,' he sighed, and they lay together in the shallows, relishing the coolness. ''Twas as if ye were a seal woman, come from the Minch to give me back my youth, ye're that supple and shiny and yielding.'

His voice trembled. Normally she would have laughed and teased him then, making some light-hearted remark about folks of their age besporting themselves like irresponsible youngsters and imagining they were seals, but the spell was still working. The moon had set and the fireflies had gone but there was still a sprinkling of stars in the sky and his shadowy frame still glistened. They lingered, holding one another in companionable silence.

Then suddenly a little breeze ruffled the water. There was a rustle in the reeds and a bird chirped from beyond the meadow, plaintive and mysterious. Then the stars faded as a pearly crepuscular light crept tentatively over the hill behind them. Morning.

'You'd think we had no work to do, woman. 'Tis a witch you are, tempting me away from my good bed in the middle of the night, and dallying till dawn. A fine thing it will be if Donald McAulay comes down to the mill and finds us here, ye shameless hussey ye!'

'Och, he'd but smile and turn away, and well ye know it,' she laughed. ''Tis natural, after all, that folks should want to bathe in this weather, and choose the early hours to do it.'

'Aye, but not when they've scarce had any sleep.'

He was pulling himself up as he spoke and she followed him to the bank of the creek, conscious now as she had not been before of the sharp stones under her freezing feet, the need to find footholds on slippery rocks, the new sensation of actually feeling cold and shivery. Enjoy it, she told herself sternly, for come mid-day you'll be longing for respite from the steamy heat, the seed-ticks and the flies. And even then the night that was past was shaping itself in her memory as something separate and precious, to be cherished in times of quiet reflection, or loneliness, or sorrow.

As she had well known they would, things returned with the breaking day to humdrum normality, but only for an hour or two because greatly to their delight Sandy came home. He had managed to beat Farquhard Campbell down to a good price for the two fine horses and had brought fresh supplies of coffee beans, salt and imported spirits – all commodities that had been difficult to come by since the start of the troubles.

'Farquhard seemed right anxious to please,' he announced with some satisfaction, and then chuckled. 'Ye can only laugh at what's happened. Seems that when poor Governor Martin was run out of town he left his favourite horse and coach behind, and instructed yon secretary fellow from Dundee, Neilson I think his name was, to apply to congress to get safe conduct for their removal to Farquhard's house! Put Farquhard in a most embarrassing position, I can tell you, him that pretends to side with the patriots. Mind you, he's a right canny one is Farquhard. Must have given Martin cause to trust him, wouldn't you think, or is the Governor just a wee bit naive?'

Allan was all attention, could not wait to hear the latest news from the Tidewater, and Flora's heart sank as Sandy gave details of developing antagonisms. In Wilmington the rebels were stepping up their campaign to force people to sign the association, threatening those who refused with all kinds of punishment and humiliation. Sign the test, they were insisting, or we will not only boycott your business: we will burn your crops, shoot your hogs, harass your families and your slaves, have you tarred and feathered and make you wish that you had never been born.

'Field days have been appointed,' he went on, 'when all able-bodied men have to turn up to be drilled, or face the consequences. Already loyalists are terrified and a lot of them are planning to flee the country.

'Slaves seem to be causing the rebels a lot of problems. Evidently a rumour was put about that the King's government was about to give the negroes their freedom, so the Wilmington Committee ordered them disarmed, and announced that if more than four slaves were found to have strayed off their master's plantation they would be sentenced to eighty lashes and have their ears cut off. Of course they've been trying to tempt the slaves to their side as well, telling them that if they murdered their loyalist masters they'd be given their plantations. Terrible it is.'

'Heartless devils,' Flora breathed, and thought of Hannibal and Stella. It was fugitives like them who were bound to suffer in all this mayhem.

'Did you hear what has happened to the Governor's lady? I've been so worried about her. Nobody seemed to know anything.'

Elizabeth's plight had been constantly on Flora's mind but questions about her had elicited only indifference. Peggy MacQueen had put the general attitude into words when she said sourly, 'I don't see why you should bother your head about that one, Flora. She has never shown a hint of interest in us High-landers. Imagines she's a cut above everybody here, the besom.'

Even so Flora was infinitely relieved when Sandy reported that that same Neilson had helped Mistress Martin escape from Wilmington. She was now understood to be safely in New York but in poor health. Not surprising, Flora thought, and remembered hearing that Elizabeth had been pregnant, yet again.

So far the talk had all been of impending war and Allan could not hear enough, but other questions were hanging all the while in the air, waiting to be asked. For some reason she could not fathom, Flora felt that Sandy had been purposely postponing confronting them, and at last she could wait no longer.

'And the Mumrills folks? Did you see them?'

'Aye. At least, I saw Jenny. And her father. Her mother only briefly. I stayed but an hour or two. I did not feel welcome, I fear.'

His face suddenly flamed and took on an expression Flora had never seen on it before – a lost look compounded of hurt, anger and puzzlement – as he added, 'But I prefer not to talk about it. Must get the travel stains off me. Is there some hot water in the cauldron there, Ma?'

'There is that, son.' Flora had been steaming the dinner – beef stew, potatoes and beans all in the one pot – and taking it from the large hook over the fire she poured some of the water into a basin and handed it to him. With a mumbled word of thanks he took it and turned away, but not before their eyes had met and she had read the anguish there. She resolved then to bide her time before tormenting him with queries.

It was evening before she found him alone, in the stables tending the new horses. Under the low rafters and in the steamy heat the stench of male animals, their sweat and droppings, was almost overwhelmingly strong and for a moment she almost reeled as if against a tangible barrier, but gradually her nostrils got adapted to the odour and her eyesight to the gloom.

'Ah, there you are. You've been avoiding us, Sandy, and I think I know why. Come now. Talk to me.'

He did not look at her, just went on brushing, his head against the horse's neck. Her heart went out to him but she knew not to touch or hurry him. He would tell her in his own time. At first he talked trivialities. Wasn't this a magnificent beast? Look at the shiny brown of his coat. You could see why they called him a chestnut couldn't you? And how intelligent he was: you'd think he knew every word they were saying. He'd understand Gaelic, of course, having been Farquhard's...

Then he buried his face in the animal's side and sobbed. She saw the manly shoulders heave with grief as the words came out, barely audible. She sensed his exasperation and helplessness, the chagrin of a deep and violent passion frustrated. But though she burned to take him in her arms to soothe him as she had done when he was a child she still made no move, just let him go on.

'Oh, those Boyds! Talk about a family divided! I could kill that Alastair, Ma! And 'tis all Mistress Boyd's fault. She's the rebel one, has been all along. Why does she hate us so? We've never done her any harm!'

'But Jenny? You saw her, didn't you? She is the one that matters, after all, isn't she? You love one another – don't think we don't all know it, for it has been written all over both your faces since the day you first met – and if you marry 'twill not be her brother and mother you will take to bed, and thank the Lord for that.'

She gave a shaky little laugh, attempting a moment's levity, but saw at once that it was a mistake. Sandy groaned. His clenched fists pounded the horse's side. The animal reacted to the sudden uncalled-for bombardment with a startled whinny and a shudder went through its body, making Sandy's head jerk up. 'Steady boy,' he murmured, articulate and calm at last, and pulling himself together continued his tale.

'You must know that Jenny and I have managed to meet in secret two or three times since we moved up here, Ma. It hasn't always been easy but her father knew what was afoot and helped us. Last time we…'

He hesitated, and blushing an even deeper shade of red went on, painfully feeling for the right words. '… We pledged our troth yet again, Ma, in the old Scottish way, over the burn. And we're just like man and wife now, Ma. Nothing can separate us. No, this has nothing to do with Jenny doubting me, or loving me the less. It's just that – well, we decided to tell the rest of her family, make our commitment public as you might say, and her mother reacted with such venom that I just had to leave the Mumrills with the whole question of my marriage to Jenny unresolved. You see, if it comes to war there's no doubt whatever about what side the Boyds are on. They're patriots. Yon Alastair's downright dangerous. He's already drilling a company of recruits down there, against the time it comes to open conflict. A fine time to ask for his sister's hand, isn't it, with my own father itching to fight for the King!'

There was no mistaking the bitterness in his voice and Flora flinched, guiltily conscious for the umpteenth time of the long, significant shadows that stretched still from that summer evening thirty years before when she had found it in her heart to help a fugitive prince. If only she could excise that whole episode of the rescue, simply cut it out, and so secure her son's happiness and the good will of his intended's family. But for that hatred of Charles Edward Stuart Kate might well have harboured less extreme political views, might even have warmed to the idea of Sandy as a son-in-law. But the past was irrevocable.

'I'm sorry, son. Truly sorry, for I like Jenny. You make a fine couple.'

She did not add her reservations. Beautiful Jenny might be, with her corn-coloured hair and soft eyes, but there was a vapidity, a lack of self-assurance about her that augured ill for Sandy. The girl would be swayed all too easily by her mother's determined opposition to the Kingsburgh MacDonalds.

Her fears were borne out by Sandy's agonised response.

'Aye, that's as may be. But I'm so many miles away from her up here and can't go running over to the Mumrills every day, especially when I'm far from welcome there. The poor lass is distraught, Ma. She's torn between me and her mother, and with this war looming she just doesn't know where to turn. Besides, she's… Oh, Ma, I didn't mean to tell you, but I'm glad now that I have, because I love and need her that much!'

His expression, its mixture of pride and wonder, uncertainty and angry bewilderment, wrung her heart. Her hand went out to touch the strong, crinkly hair at the back of his neck, and she remembered with a pang the desperate physical intensity of young love, how it consumed every waking moment, set the heart racing and the nerves tingling. Felix O'Neil. That's how she would have felt about Felix O'Neil, had she gone to France with him. The sigh she let out then was for herself as much as for Sandy.

'I won't tell your father. He has worries enough, and only time and the Lord's good Providence will sort this out. Meantime try to be brave. And you know that both you and Jenny have my prayers.'

She left him still contemplatively grooming the horses and wandered down to the creek where only that morning life had seemed idyllic and love a continuing delight. A blue heron stood tall and stately in the shallows, ever alert for its evening haul of fish, and its priestly stance reminded her of James Campbell, the minister down at Barbecue Creek who had so infuriated Allan with his treasonous talk. Panic seized her. Hitherto political discussion had been speculative and theoretical but now those divisions were causing despair and irreconcilable rifts among the people she most loved and she could see no way of stopping it. Like a deadly avalanche it was gathering speed and threatened to overwhelm them all.

The heron sensed her presence, cast what she fancied was a baleful, irritated look in her direction, and with a flap of its bedraggled wings awkwardly lifted its bulk into the air. Its going left her feeling inexplicably bereft, and it was only then that she gave way to her tears.

IX

June 1775

The heat did not let up; if anything it intensified as June wore on, and Flora succumbed to an uncharacteristic languor which she tried desperately to hide from Allan. If only it would rain, and cool the air! Many a time she gazed hopefully towards the mountains and saw violet-coloured clouds pile up, fretted with flashes of blue lightning. A downpour seemed inevitable then, but nothing happened. Oh for the soft sweet gentle rain of home, for a west wind off the Minch and a cuckoo calling. Her longing for Skye and for the children she had left behind racked her almost to breaking point. There seemed little respite anywhere from exasperation and anxiety. Sandy's obvious unhappiness, those murderous mosquitoes, and a new, insidious questioning of even her nearest neighbours' political motives weighed heavily on her mind.

Allan did not seem to notice. He was enthusiastic to the point of ebullience because his work on the plantation was bearing fruit. The grist mill was a particular point of pride.

'Donald was telling me that it took all of three years to build, when Touchstone took over the land all these years ago. Evidently the state legislature was so anxious to attract grist and sawmill entrepreneurs that they offered fifty-acre tracts of land to such settlers, and exempted them both from taxes and from service in the militia. But you had to know just where to build. This is perfect, because over yonder the natural fall of the creek could be heightened by building the dam, and then the millrace could be created to lead the water to a spot where it could be dropped over a waterwheel.'

The mechanics of the mill did not really interest Flora but the waterwheel held an undoubted fascination, especially in the heat. She loved its spherical solidity and the cool, soothing swoosh of the water dripping over it. Her mind wandered away – it was doing that too often these days – but Allan was still in mid-lecture. Dominie-like he pointed towards the structure that was fast becoming the very heart of Kingsburgh.

'Think of all the blasting and digging they had to do, using horses and drag-pans, before they could even get started on the mill buildings! The work that went into it! Oh, Florrie, haven't we been fortunate, being able to buy a treasure of an installation like this, and to have someone like Donald to work it!'

Donald McAulay was certainly proving indispensable. He had tackled the damage which neglect and the recent storms had wrought, patching the holes in the roof of the main building with split heart pine shingles and replacing not only the massive door but sills and plates and broken floorboards. His skills were legion. When he wasn't hewing timbers he was dressing millstones or hollowing out sycamore logs to make storage barrels, all in preparation for the busy weeks ahead when the harvest was in and the neighbours started to bring their grain to be ground. Allan kept praising his diligence and Flora was forced to admit that he put their more easy-going Highland servants to shame: but then, unlike them Donald was used to the heat and the humidity.

Try as she would, though, she could not banish instinctive reservations about Donald. For all his devotion to his trade there was a loucheness about him that put her on her guard, and his curious antipathy to Neil, their oldest and most faithful retainer and a relative at that, was quite inexplicable. But perhaps this was all in her imagination, and voicing such suspicions would make a shrew of her. So she feigned interest, and while Allan expatiated on the milling process she contented herself with listening to the swish of splashing water. It was as close as she could get to rain.

Allan was down at the mill the day Jock McIvor showed up again. Seeing the loose-limbed barefooted figure trudge up the lane Flora shivered despite the clammy heat. His coming could not be accidental – not with rumours flying around about more and more loyal subjects being harried down on the Tidewater, and people like Alastair Boyd and James Coor drilling recruits.

As McIvor approached the stink of ingrained dirt and tobacco intensified. Clouds of flies circled his head, attracted by the runnels of sweat on his face. Not surprising, of course, that a travelling man would smell like a midden in these conditions, but Flora felt only revulsion.

'Ah, Mistress MacDonald, how glad I am to see you again. I fancy, in this heat, that you'll be needing some summer-weight stuff to make shifts and dresses? I have some fine plain muslin here, and a painted gauze that's bound to appeal...' He gestured towards the twin panniers slung over the back of his moth-eaten mule, and Flora marvelled at how easily she had been taken in by his disguise, that night at the O'Rourke cabin, for his voice was cultured and his whole bearing that of a military man, if not a particularly savoury one.

Usually she welcomed itinerant salesmen and ushered them in, for sometimes they brought news from Glendale, or even from Mount Pleasant and the Mumrills, but knowing McIvor's true identity she hesitated and was civil only with difficulty.

'I would have you know, Master McIvor, that I have my husband's confidence and am well aware that you are not what you seem. If 'tis really himself you seek I fear he is not at home right now.'

What had possessed her to be so churlish and inhospitable? McIvor was regarding her in a half-amused, reappraising way, as if realising for the first time that she was someone to be reckoned with.

'I guess I could wait for him then. He is working in the fields, or about the steadings?'

Her mind was working frantically. The forest. Yes, that was it. She would say Allan was out felling trees. Anywhere that would necessitate so long a wait that this unwelcome visitor would think twice about dallying.

But McIvor was unfazed by this information. 'Och well, in that case he won't be long. He may even arrive back before I've shown you the dress stuffs. See this striped taffeta here. The sheen on it.'

He was taking bundles from the pack animal's back and making to carry them into the house when there was a clatter of hooves in the yard. Flora's heart sank as Allan dismounted and running eagerly towards McIvor clapped him companionably on the shoulders.

'My, but it's good to see you, man! Come in! Come in! Flora, fetch us some lemonade, or applejack. I'm parched! God, McIvor, you must feel burnt to a frazzle in this sun! Now tell me, what news from the great world outside? 'Tis all rumour here. Scurrilous rumour with little substance, I trust.'

He was ushering McIvor into the house, leaving Flora to follow like a lame dog. Panic had seized her, a helpless, largely irrational fear that clawed in her belly like some tenacious cancer.

'My wife knows who you are, Jock. It's impossible to keep secrets from the woman, I'm afraid. But there's nobody else here, so you can talk freely. The servants are all outside in the kitchen premises, or in the fields.'

The officer had collapsed into a chair, stretched his long legs, and removed his slouch hat to reveal greasy hair tied back in a tight queue, soldier-fashion. Flora supposed it was naturally black, but he had powdered it with rice flour which had turned soggy and matted in the heat to give a speckled effect.

'I have something important for you here, Kingsburgh, and must say I'm relieved to have it off my person. It's from Governor Martin.'

So saying he laid down a canvas bundle that Flora had assumed contained assorted haberdashery, and continued. 'He wants you to take it into your safe keeping, hide it in a secret place. Quite an honour he's paying you, I should think. He assured me it's nothing dangerous in itself, of course. Just papers.'

Allan accepted the bundle as if it were some special jewel or royal accolade and it lay on the table in front of them, symbol of Martin's trust. 'Go and fetch that cold drink, Flora,' he said sharply, and Flora flinched, knowing that her presence was restricting the conversation. But as she busied herself in the adjoining room scraps of talk were quite audible and she listened unashamedly. After all this exchange affected all of them.

'No sooner was I back in New York after my last mission than General Gage sent me back to the Carolinas with yet more despatches. The General would have Governor Martin recruit forces here and send them north to swell a national army, whereas the Governor wants to rally the loyalists and keep them here to defend his own territory. But take it from me, Kingsburgh, little pockets of local resistance are not going to stem this tide. Martin is underestimating the danger. He thinks people like that Farquhard Campbell down in Cross Creek are with him, but they clearly are poised to come down on whichever side seems to be winning, just to save their own skins. Take my advice and go north, Kingsburgh. You're a military man. They could do with you up there and your services would be well recompensed.'

So it had come to this? Emissaries travelling hundred of miles to lure her husband away from her and off the land he was working so hard to cultivate? This pseudo-pedlar would stay in her house not a moment longer than was necessary!

'You mentioned some taffeta. You have enough to fashion a gown, and matching thread to sew it with? Then I shall have it, and I venture to suggest that you visit Mistress MacQueen, my half-sister, before dark. She was saying only yesterday that she needed some butter muslin to make a pavilion for her bed. The mosquitoes have been bothering her something awful.'

Flora would normally have pressed an invitation to supper upon such a caller, and might even have offered him a bed for the night: she knew that Allan would recognise the snub, but she did not care. This fellow spelt danger, a threat to her peace of mind and their new way of life. She felt smugly triumphant as she watched McIvor skulk away. She was almost certain he would not go near the MacQueens. Dress-lengths, indeed: such were just part of the camouflage.

She expected Allan to rebuke her for her crassness but he had other considerations on his mind. No sooner had McIvor gone than he attached a pistol to his belt and hurried out to the yard, calling urgently to Neil and Sandy. Something had to be done, and quickly. He was summoning all the leading Highlanders to a meeting right here, three days from now.

The orders were peremptory and unequivocal. 'Neil, I want you to go to Mountain Creek. Get Hugh and the Campbells. Sandy, I know it's a long ride to Mount Pleasant but Cuidreach has to come, and the MacLeods of Pabbay. And they might get word to Murdoch MacLeod: we could certainly use him. Go now. Don't tarry. I'm going to start for Glendale as soon I can, to alert Alex and Sandy Morrison.'

All briskness and resolution, he burst into the great room where Flora was pretending to busy herself with her newly-acquired length of taffeta.

'Don't look so disapproving, Florrie. If the colony is indeed at war we backcountry people have to discuss what to do. We must at least be prepared to defend ourselves and our property.'

Perfectly rational, on the face of it. His stance needed no vindication and she knew it. Then why the note of self-justification in his voice, and why her own angry determination to pounce upon it? It was fear that prompted her, fear that soon the creek down there might run with blood: yet her words came out not fearful but bitter and querulous.

'Why do you have to take the initiative in this matter, Allan? Why not leave that to Hugh, or to Cuidreach, or to someone like James Cotton who's in the thick of things already? We've just newly arrived and are yet to make our way!'

It was on the tip of her tongue to add that he would do well to heed the strictures of Farquhard Campbell or John Bethune, but realised in time that mention of those temporisers would simply fuel Allan's wrath. Already he was bristling.

'And what gives you the right to interfere? Why do you think that Martin entrusted me with those papers, instead of Hugh or Alexander? Tell me that! Because he regards me as the laird in these parts, that's why! Well, I don't intend to let him down. 'Tis time you recognised, Flora, that you are not the only person of note around here.'

The jibe hit home. She watched in stony, peeved silence as he turned irritably away from her and began scowlingly to gather together some food and a change of clothes for the journey. She almost offered to help him but her hurt persisted, the moment of possible reconciliation passed, and she watched him ride off, ostensibly careless of her vexation.

Alone, she looked out over the ripening corn where swallows dipped and butterflies danced blue and white and yellow. For once she was blind to beauty. So many tales, these days, about solitary riders being ambuscaded and set upon by ruffians using their so-called patriotic views as a pretext for violence. If that should happen to Allan, and she had let him go without as much as a goodbye, she would never forgive herself. But she had to stand her ground, do all in her power to convince him, even yet, that neutrality was the only course open to them.

* * *

As arranged, the prominent Highlanders in the district did indeed assemble at Kingsburgh three days later. They gathered round the big table and the brandy-wine flowed: no taigh-ceilidh this, though, but a serious conference in which the talk was all of war. At Hedgecock Creek, so they said, Samuel Spencer had just held a meeting exactly like this, except that those present had been Whigs and Spencer had insisted that local farmers be forced to sign the association. His Tory counterpart in the area, James Cotton, was under constant threat of arrest, not knowing when he might be set upon by unprincipled knaves.

Flora listened with her heart in her mouth. It was obvious from the start that the group saw Allan as their leader, and that he was both proud and glad to be so regarded. So it did not surprise her when he was appointed as an ambassador to Governor Martin, entrusted with the task of going personally to Fort Johnson to assure him of the Highlanders' loyalty and readiness to rise. They would, of course, need arms and ammunition, and above all commissions to allow them to raise troops by proper authority. Allan was the man to arrange it.

It had never occurred to any of these men that they might react differently. Some of them were army officers on half pay while others, especially the ex-Jacobites, feared that the rebels would face reprisals of the kind they had suffered after Culloden and were determined not to risk their necks again. All were born monarchists, brought up to believe in the Divine Right of Kings, and sought to preserve that doctrine in this new Scotland across the seas.

Overhearing their deliberations and decisions Flora felt she could read Allan's thoughts. At last he was getting the recognition he deserved, as a prominent tacksman and a soldier. One day, when the troubles had receded and the colonies were safely and rightfully restored to Britain, he would be honoured for having defended his king and upheld his country's laws. The name of Allan MacDonald, the hero from Skye who rallied the Highlanders of North Carolina against a vicious foe, would echo down the corridors of history.

She saw his eyes flash and his features set in firm lines. He revelled in a commission like this, did not seem to consider that Fort Johnson was a hundred and fifty steamy, disease-ridden, snake-and-crocodile-infested miles away; or that half the population of the country he would travel through would gladly see him dead; or that he was abandoning his home and family at the very time of year when the work load was at its most onerous. His king and country needed him. That was incentive enough.

X

June 1775

Now began a time of loneliness and depression the like of which Flora had not known since her arrival in America. Allan had gone, she knew not for how long, and Sandy had not returned from his mission to Mount Pleasant to summon Cuidreach. Well Flora knew where he was, of course. It would take more than Kate's disapproval to keep him away from Jenny.

In a desperate bid to ease her mental torment she pushed her body to its limits, labouring in house, garden and farmyard. Their little potato crop was ready, new supplies of strawberries and raspberries seemed to ripen by the day, and all this produce had to be preserved somehow, made into jam, or bottled, or rendered into brandies and cordials. All this on top of the normal household chores, the cooking and cleaning, laundry and mending. From dawn to dusk she drove herself relentlessly, eliciting no real pleasure from the tasks because Allan was not there to appreciate their outcome.

'Ye'll have to let up a wee bit, Mistress,' Deirdre ventured one day. 'Ye don't want the master to be coming home and finding you ill now, do you? Nobody can work in this heat the way you're doing and not suffer from it.'

And Morag, emboldened, had to put in her twopenceworth.

'Just what I was saying to Mairi only yestreen. She's wasting away, I said. Needs one of her own famous tonics, so she does.'

Flora's only respite from toil was her occasional visits to her stepfather Hugh, more bent and frail than ever now, and to her increasingly more enigmatic neighbours. Always dour by nature, their attitudes had been rendered all the more insular by isolation, and now that Allan's political stand was an open secret some of them were frankly hostile. A few of the older ones had retained their Jacobite sympathies – remembering the depradations of the redcoats after Culloden they could not bring themselves to support a Hanoverian king – while others seemed to be engaged in a purely personal vendetta, out of spite, or jealousy, or sheer perversity.

Peggy Campbell never stopped speiring.

'That's ten days Allan has been gone, isn't it? And I haven't seen Sandy either. He has a lady love maybe? They say he goes after that Boyd girl, down on McLendon's Creek. He'll no' have his troubles to seek there, I can tell you that. They're rebels to a man, the Boyds.'

'I know nothing of the Boyds' politics, Peggy. Only that they're friends.'

Peggy sniffed: she was a past mistress at delivering a particularly dismissive, scornful kind of sniff. 'Aye, and a lot of good friendship does when it comes to war. You of all people should ken that.'

Only John Bethune was totally trustworthy and supportive, but even he, whether unintentionally or by design, could compound her doubts and misery. He never came to tutor Jamie without detailing the Committee's latest efforts to force known loyalists to sign the 'test'. Their most recent victim had been James Hepburn, an attorney-at-law who had been accused of trying to raise troops in Cumberland County. John was most indignant about the extravagant terms used to denounce the man.

'Called him a false, scandalous and seditious incendiary who endeavours to make himself conspicuous in favour of tyranny and oppression, and told all friends of American liberty to avoid all dealings and intercourse with such a wicked and detestable character! Poor man had no choice but to recant and sign the association!'

Flora sighed. 'But surely, John, if we but lie low…'

John's fist came down on the table with an almighty clatter, as if he were preaching hellfire to a dozing congregation. She had never seen him so angry, and was suddenly reminded of Christ's righteous wrath when he banished the money-lenders from the temple.

''Tis past the time for lying low, as you put it! Well you know that, Flora! We must speak out for neutrality, actively recruit people as pacifists, and refuse to align ourselves with either side! We have been lukewarm in the cause of peace, Flora, and see where it has brought us!'

His voice quivered with angry reproach, but while her reason told her that he was right in feeling she had let him down she still felt bound to justify her inaction.

'You have your pulpit to spread your message, John, and most applaud you. 'Tis the Christian way you advocate. But I am but a farmer's wife …'

'No, Flora! No, I say! Didn't I tell you before that you could sway this whole decision, gin you but realised your own power? Only you can persuade Allan, and it is Allan the folks around here look to to lead them!'

With desperate sincerity he went on to explain that the course he would follow was not a line of least resistance, and certainly did not rule out danger.

'Already I have made enemies, even in the Church. That rebel minister James Campbell has been pouring contempt on what he sees as my wishy-washy stance. But it is not a sign of weakness, Flora. It is the third way, and the most difficult of all to follow. We must be prepared to speak out, though. So far we have been too passive.'

'Passive? Can anyone be passive these days?'

The voice came, firm but thoughtful, from the doorway, and Flora looked up to see Sandy standing there. Dishevelled and red-faced though he was after his journey he yet conveyed an instant impression of strength and masculinity, and she marvelled afresh at how those past few months had changed him. He had broadened out, but without adding an ounce of fat to his frame. His bronzed features had fined down and his hair, which reminded her of her own in her youth, had been burnished by the sun to a coppery sheen. She ran to his embrace, and a wave of relief washed over her as the two men shook hands. Now, with Sandy here, she felt less vulnerable to John's censure.

'I'll fetch some apple brandy. And you'll stay for your dinner, John? It's good to have you back, son. So many tales of rebellious factions looting homesteads and burning crops. No word of your father?' Her fears had come rushing out in spite of her attempts at calm.

'No. Not yet. But you're not to fret, Ma. He can look after himself.'

Knowing every vibration and cadence of Sandy's voice Flora could read the anxiety in it. They all three knew that Allan was somewhere between here and the coast. Even in October that wilderness of impenetrable pines had been a place of menace, haunt of alligators and poisonous snakes, spiders and wild animals, where even the plants could be deadly. Add to those the threat of attacks by human predators in the mosquito-ridden, blistering heat of mid-summer, and you had hell on earth. She had a sudden momentary vision of him lying helpless in a swamp, racked with fever or critically wounded, and frantically shut out the thought. If she dwelt on it she would go mad.

'You stopped by at Glendale?'

'Aye. All's well there. The babe's flourishing and Anne's blooming. Thinks she may be in the family way again.'

Yet another child, so soon after the last, and with things so uncertain? Flora did not know whether to rejoice or not.

'And Jenny?'

A light seemed to go on behind Sandy's eyes. 'As lovely as ever.' By way of explanation he turned to John and said without a hint of embarrassment, 'You'll know, I'm sure, that Jenny Boyd and I are betrothed? There are obstacles to our union, though, for her brother is more active than ever in the rebel cause and she is torn in two.'

Then greatly to Flora's astonishment the son who had never uttered a political statement in his life launched into a thoughtful analysis of the situation as he saw it.

'There is justice on both sides, John, isn't there? It's true of all wars, I suppose: some fight for a cause because they believe passionately in it, others because they follow their leaders blindly or are so inspired by hate and the urge to violence that they care not what a battle is about. You see, the Boyds have been in America a long time. Alastair and Jenny were born here. They cannot feel the same loyalty to an English king. They see themselves as Americans. A new people.'

The speech was clearly quoted from the political gospel according to Harvey, Harnett and Hooper, by way of Kate Boyd, and Flora felt as if someone had dealt her a body blow. For Sandy to speak this way, when he had hitherto echoed Allan's views on everything! 'Better not let your father hear you,' she gasped. 'I warn you now, lad. We want to live in America, yes, but we will never cease to be Scottish. So keep those rebellious ideas to yourself. We did not come here to see our family rent in two by wranglings that don't concern us.'

It was the minister's cue.

''Twould seem that the Lord ordained that I be here in this house at this very hour, to show you the danger of taking sides. Your mother and I were discussing this very subject when you arrived, Sandy. I was insisting that she should actively champion the cause of neutrality. Do nothing but say much.'

He spoke with such quiet, Christian integrity that Flora acknowledged his rightness in her heart, but she could not match his courageous singlemindedness. She had a husband who, though far from bellicose, had a strong sense of duty and also – she admitted this to herself with reluctance – of his own self-importance. To support John openly would be to invite further conflict into her marriage.

'Go and have a wash, Sandy, and I'll fetch that pot of rabbit stew. You must be famished. Then I fancy Neil could use your help. There's a cow having trouble calving, in the out field yonder.'

She tried to sound brisk and in control as she veered the conversation away from politics but her heart was pounding and the debilitating heat was like a tangible weight pressing down on her. Every movement was agonising, sending trickles of sweat down the crevices between her breasts and thighs. As she dished the stew she heard the drone of a mosquito at her ear, languidly forced herself to swipe at it, and triumphantly crushed the long fragile corpse between her fingers, drawing blood. Her own? The insect had probably bitten her but the evidence would just be one more red swollen weal in the rash that already peppered her body.

* * *

Although Sandy's presence somewhat soothed her nervousness she still could not relax. Her senses were constantly on the alert, so that even the pleasantest tasks, like collecting the daily stock of eggs from the hen-house or feeding Beanie and the dogs, were done with only half her mind. The ripening corn, mellow in the sun's slanting rays; the meadow starred with wild flowers; the cool green ferns around the well and the warm sweet breath of cows and horses – none of these could distract her completely from her anxious waiting. It was as if all joy and anticipation were suspended, against Allan's coming home.

So when, late one afternoon, she looked beyond the fields and saw a cloud of dust materialise into the shape of a horse and its rider she ran excitedly out, only to face the bitter realisation that this was someone else, a big, burly bearded man with a mass of black hair that kept getting into his eyes. He had been riding fast: his horse was in a lather and he was slumped exhaustedly in the saddle. No threat here, she realised. Just a neighbouring farmer from down the creek, Sam Williams, come on some casual errand. Then why had her stomach knotted in dread? And why did Sam look as if all the hounds in hell were after him?

'Kingsburgh's at home? I would speak with him on the Governor's business.'

He was gulping the words and looking furtively around as if he feared being overheard. His abruptness, the total lack of any neighbourly greeting or pleasant social chit-chat, brought all Flora's fears rushing to the surface.

'No, Sam. He isn't back.' And without realising her own lack of logic she proceeded to bombard him with questions.

'You've heard something? He has been wounded, or ambuscaded, or imprisoned? If so don't beat about the bush, man! Tell me, for I'm sick with worry!'

Sam dismounted painfully, and as he did so she was remembering what she knew of him. He was not all that young although

his son Dave was but thirteen. Allan had always had a good word
for him, praising him as a staunch loyalist whose only fault, if such
it was, was his obsessive devotion to his pretty, vacuous young wife.
For all his bulk and facial ferocity he was kindness itself. A gentle
giant, Allan had called him, and it was that consideration that
prompted his actions now, for he came over and impulsively took
her hands in his huge, capable horny ones.

'Wheesht now, Mistress Flora. See, ye're all keyed up! I'm real
sorry if I scared ye! Allan's well, the last I heard. On his way back
to ye now I reckon, and will be with ye any day. There has been
a battle, is all. Up Boston way. At Bunker Hill. Seems each side's
claiming victory. And I bring good news. I'm to tell you your son
– Ranald's his name, isn't it? – came out whole and has been
promoted to lieutenant. Ye're not to listen to tales that he was
wounded bad in the last skirmishes. Some scratches maybe, but
not bad enough to keep him from his duty. Now isn't that cause
for rejoicing!'

She tried to smile. The news of Ranald was indeed consoling.

'Come away ben the house, Sam, and let me get you a drink.
It's getting late. We can give you a bed for the night if you want
to stay.'

Her welcoming monologue ran on, nervous and disjointed, but
her thoughts were off on a track of their own. Why had Sam been
so harassed and hurried, if all he had to report was a far-off battle
and word of Ranald? Did those items of news merit a special
journey, at breakneck speed and with the evening coming on? Her
sixth sense told her that Sam was holding something back.

He was hesitating now, weighing up her invitation. 'A cold drink
would be nectar, Ma'am, but I can't linger. I daren't leave Jessie
on her own too long. Like you she's restless and fearful these days,
and I've been away a lot. But is that your Sandy I see yonder? I
guess I'll have a word with him.'

Before she could protest he was off, loping down the lane with
his long farmer's stride. She saw him engage Sandy in earnest
conversation and then surreptitiously hand over something white:
some kind of missive, she surmised. Unaccountably, the gesture
both puzzled and irritated her. Those damned colonials! In some
ways they were gallant towards women and frequently allowed
them more freedom than at home, but why were they so

overprotective and patronising? For she was certain that Sam had decided to keep the letter's contents from her, and that could only mean one thing. It had to do with Allan.

Eventually Sandy brought Sam indoors and they sat down to cornbread and applejack. But the atmosphere was still tense and apprehensive, with an underlying secretiveness that put Flora's nerves on edge. She was just about to thrash out at them, to declare that she was no simpleton and well able to sustain whatever blow fate had dealt her, when a clatter of hooves cut her protest short.

'My Gawd! It's our Davie! If something has happened to Jessie I'll never forgive myself!'

The boy had slid from his overwrought pony and was stumbling blindly through the farmyard. His face was a distraught mask of white terror banded with what looked like soot, his teeth were chattering uncontrollably, and he was bleeding from a wound just behind his ear. The smell he exuded was an acrid mixture of woodsmoke, blood and sweat and he was on the verge of fainting.

Appalled, everyone strained to understand what the lad was trying to say. His words were a disjointed succession of sounds, blurred and distorted with sobs and running over and into one another so that only his father could make full sense of them. But Flora followed enough to understand why Sam turned the ashen grey of old suet, grabbed his pistol, and shouting, 'Look after the lad, Flora!' ran towards his horse and galloped off. A mere split second's hesitation, and Sandy had followed him.

Flora did her best then to calm the boy. At first he clung to her, convulsed with sobs – he was but a child, after all – and she cradled him until the tears and tremors began to subside.

'Hush, son. See, I'll bandage that cut. Then I'll get you a drink that will help you calm down, and you can have a sleep on the bed yonder.'

Mercifully the wound was superficial and did not need stitching. She applied a salve of hog's lard and mashed burdock root before dressing it with lint and clean linen. Then she fetched some blankets and a posset of rum spiced with ground raspberry root, but it was obvious that the boy was still too distraught to settle. He kept babbling about his recent ordeal and Flora had to accept that the only way to soothe him was to let him talk about it. So gradually the tale came out.

'A gang of men came to our house, looking for Pa. They had long flintlocks and pistols and said they were from down the Cape Fear, from a Colonel Ashe's regiment. They didn't seem like real soldiers, though – more what my Pa calls white trash, all hairy and smelly, in tattered breeches and greasy hats. There must have been thirty of them, and oh, they were that fierce, mistress! But Mom told them Pa was away. She's brave, my Mom…'

He gulped. His eyes dilated with fear and then filled with tears again as he plucked up the courage to carry on.

'They didn't like that. The one that was leading them got angry. He… lunged at her, and pulled off her bodice and threw her to the floor and… Oh, I can't say it! They did terrible things to her! There was only one man that wouldn't. Said he didn't join the patriots to rape innocent women.'

Flora felt the quick onset of nausea and almost choked. Her hand tightened on young Davie's and she had to force herself to pull it away when she felt him flinch. She willed him to stop speaking but clearly he needed this painful catharsis.

'Those that weren't hurting Mom started going through the house, pulling everything out of drawers and closets. They took all the food and drink they could find, and when I tried to stop them one of them took the butt of his pistol to me. That's how I got this cut.'

His hand went up pathetically to the bandage and he fingered it with a gesture of surprise, as if he had just remembered it.

'I ran and hid in the kitchen press then, until they went away. They had set fire to the corncrib before they left and it took me all my time to put it out. That's why I'm all smoky. Then I helped Mom into her bed and came here to tell Pa. Oh, Mistress, I'm that scared to go back, but they'll need me there. Let me go. Please. I can't stay here drinking cordials with them ruffians abroad and my folks in danger.'

With this he made a feeble effort to get up, but Flora restrained him with all the firmness she could muster.

'No,' she said gently. 'You stay right here. 'Twould but make matters worse, you riding off alone at night, and in this condition.'

Then she realised she was weeping, and it was as if all the pressures of the last three weeks had coalesced and burst the floodgates. It was not only for the Williams family that she wept, for if this could happen to Sam and Jessie, a decent, law-abiding farmer and his douce wife, what might be in store for Allan and herself?

While the lad slept, snuffling and moaning every so often when a memory stirred, she gazed out over the darkening meadows and suddenly they were full of menace, a menace so loud that her mind was deafened by it. The evening lowing of cattle was an ominous bellow, the crickets screamed, and the pricking stars overhead seemed to emit a shrill, ear-splitting shriek. Even the perfume of roses, usually restful and balmy, was obtrusive and threatening. It's because they're dying, she thought, that's why there's something fetid and festering under the usual heady aroma. Nothing can survive in the heat here. And there crept unbidden into her mind the fragrant memory of a rose bush that had grown by the door at Flodigarry. Deep red cabbage roses, dewy and sweet after the rain. Her head swam. Succumbing then to grief and loneliness she fell to her knees in a crumpled heap and prayed with all her heart for Allan to come home.

XI

July–August 1775

Come morning young Davie had sufficiently recovered to insist upon going home, and Flora, a mother herself, knew all too well how relieved Jessie would be to have him back. She suspected too that Sam would be so incensed at the rebels' treatment of his family that he would be out seeking revenge – a suspicion that Sandy corroborated on his return late that night. Grim-faced and weary, he was too shocked and angry to consider sparing Flora the details.

'Oh, the state that poor woman was in! Call themselves soldiers! They're just a bunch of lawless marauders with naught in their minds but killing and violence! No need to fear that I'd favour their cause now, Ma. Not after what I've seen.' And after wolfing down some bread and cheese he took himself off to bed.

And it was in the grey dawn of that very morning that she was aware of Allan creeping into the bedroom. It was his smell that first alerted her – a rancid stench of horse and ale, body dirt and unwashed clothes. Overjoyed though she was at his safe return she still had to brace herself to have him close, until a wave of tenderness flooded over her and washed out every sensation but love. In the tenuous light his face was gaunt and bony, almost spectral, and when he held her to him she felt the sharp angles of his bones dig into her flesh.

'You've been riding all night?'

'Aye. And every night for the last ten. A hundred and fifty miles it was. I've had to hole up through the day. But oh, Florrie, I'm too tired to talk! I could sleep for a week!'

'Then do so, dearie. I defy anyone to disturb you.'

But she doubted if he had heard her. He was lying stretched out on the bed, still fully clothed, and his breathing was deep and even.

It was late afternoon when he awoke, rested but ravenously hungry. She fetched water for him to wash in, and as he laved away layers of grime she noticed with mounting concern that his face and neck were speckled with insect bites, his arms and legs scratched and bruised, his movements stiff after fifteen nights in the saddle. She longed maternally to spoil him with her ministrations, to soothe away the torment of the journey and make him whole again. He fell upon the food she had prepared like a vulture upon fresh carrion.

'Ah. That's better, Florrie. I've been feeling like a hunted animal these last few days. My, that tripe's good. You know to put lots of milk and onions in it.'

His voice sounded relaxed now and Flora ventured a question.

'But did you not bide with some of the Cross Creek and Wilmington families? Surely they fed you? And Governor Martin? Does he not have epicurean tastes?'

Allan let out a bitter laugh at this. 'To be honest, my love, I kent not who was friend and who foe, down Wilmington way, so 'twas best not to expect hospitality from any. The friends I might compromise and the foes – well, 'tis better not to rankle them. I carried a bag of meal, some fatback and porter, and there were wild strawberries by the track. Meagre maybe, but a better diet than poor Martin's. There on the *Cruizer* he has to be content with biscuit and wild cabbage, with only occasional fish and oysters for variety.'

'The *Cruizer*?' You saw him on the *Cruizer*? That rusty old wreck we passed at the river mouth?'

'Aye. Did you not hear? He had Fort Johnson stripped of its guns, then he and the garrison moved out. Just to be on the safe side, you understand. 'Tis a rough life for him, with only that arrogant rogue Collett for company. Maybe that's why he was so delighted to see me.'

He gave a wry grin. 'But don't look so shocked, Florrie. ''Twill not be for long. Josiah is confident General Gage will soon come to the rescue and take control of things.'

'So he doesn't think we have any reason to fear, up here in the Piedmont?'

Her voice came out small and tentative. She wanted passionately to believe him when he wiped his mouth with his kerchief, nodded briefly, and said placatingly, 'Of course we're safe here, lass! All those tales you hear, of folks being harassed and travellers ambuscaded, are but isolated incidents, and as often as not embellished. And in the unlikely event of outright war the mother country would never let us down. You can depend on that.'

Flora was about to protest that the tribulations of Sam Williams' family could not be shrugged off as either irrelevant or exaggerated, but Allan's hand had come up and gently removed the mob-cap she was wearing. As he fondled her hair and stroked her neck she felt the familiar frisson of sexual excitement that unfailingly forced the demands of the insistent present to take precedence over everything.

'Come, lass,' he was murmuring urgently. 'I have other things on my mind right now than Josiah Martin and those damned Americans. Sandy and Jamie are working outside?'

'Aye.'

'Then come to bed. 'Twill not be dark for a good two hours yet. Just think, mo criodhe! We can pretend that we are but twenty again.'

They shut the curtains at the windows and round the big four-poster bed and abandoned themselves to a blissful hour of precious privacy that neither the stifling heat nor the droning flies could spoil. And for the first time in weeks Flora was supremely happy, her fears banished by the knowledge that her man was home again, and that he loved her.

Come evening, with the men in from the fields, Jamie and Sandy were full of questions. Flora listened with only half an ear to their chatter as she served venison stew, sweet potatoes and carrots.

For Jamie, wild animals were the most fascinating part of travels downriver. 'Did you see any bears, or snakes, or alligators, Pa?'

'Aye. A few snakes, writhing about on the path ahead of me, and one day, down by the river, I accidentally trod on an alligator a foot long, a mere babe, that in six months' time would have been big enough to devour me. There were bears about too, of course, but any I disturbed loped off into the forest. Same with the wolves. I was glad to be on horse-back though, riding as I was through the night.'

Then Sandy came out with the question that Flora had dreaded to ask.

'And did you get matters straightened out with Martin? If this is indeed war, where do we come in?'

Allan's voice dropped to a near whisper and he looked cautiously over in the direction of the side table where Flora was dishing cherry pie and cream. She had to strain to hear him but his gist was clear enough.

'Josiah is sanguine about loyalist support, and I have authority to unite the Highlanders with the Regulators, to form a fighting force.'

Flora felt herself blanch. A wild hysteria born of fear and despair erupted in a querulous protest.

'I trust to God you did not let yourself be talked into danger, Allan! Had we not agreed 'twas best to keep out of their squabbles?'

Later she reproached herself for speaking right then. He was newly home, physically sore and mentally overwrought: but it was as if the words spoke themselves.

Allan's eyes blazed. His answer came back like a whiplash. 'Let me decide matters of policy, madam. This is none of your affair.'

And she found herself answering, calmly but tersely. 'But it is, Allan. I have thought long and hard over it, and I do not choose to let my family be involved. 'Tis madness, truly.'

This sent Allan into a lather of blustering rage. 'You would question my sanity, woman? 'Twas for you I risked my life in the swamps, for you I went to hell and back, to ensure we could defend ourselves gin it were necessary. Well, I would have you remember that I am master in this house and shall go the way that I alone decide. Let us have no more recriminations, Flora. You hear me?'

He had got up from the table and was towering over her, his fists clenched and his deep voice rising to a bawl. Had she not detected an undertone of pleading desperation in it she would have collapsed in tears or retaliated with a hissing vituperation, and either response would have been inappropriate.

As it was she was able to hold her ground and say levelly, 'As you wish, husband. But my opinion is a valid one, and it holds.'

This defused his temper enough to have him lower his voice and Flora felt Sandy and Jamie let out their breaths with relief: they were not used to hearing their parents quarrel.

But Allan was still scowling. It was not his way to let a woman get the last word, and when he delivered his ultimatum they all knew he meant it and would stick by it.

'The subject of politics is now closed between us, Flora. I will not have you and your pacifist cronies dictate to me where my duty lies. You understand?'

And he proceeded determinedly to demolish the cherry pie.

XII

August 1775

All through the remaining weeks of summer Flora replayed that quarrel in her mind, over and over, while Allan thought and acted independently of her. They still worked and worshipped and made love together; still discussed the problems of family, maids and ghillies; still marvelled as nature's bounty unfolded in this luxuriant, exotic land: but just as Charles Edward Stuart had been a forbidden topic in the past the new subject of political and military developments in Anson County and beyond was never raised. It hovered there between them, ominous as a thunder cloud, and she dreaded the day it would burst and inundate them all, but when he was with her Allan behaved as if it did not exist.

She did not realise how forlorn and excluded she was feeling until she discovered that her daughter Anne was similarly troubled. All the family had been summoned by old Hugh because he had decided to give his grandson Donald, Cuidreach's son, a tract of land on Mountain Creek, and wanted everyone to be there to witness the deed of conveyancing. Not having seen Annabella and Alexander, Anne and Alex and the various children since May, Flora was delighted. There was nothing she enjoyed more than a family ceilidh, and while she saw her stepfather frequently there was something soothing, almost blessed, about being with him on a special, relaxed occasion. Now in his eighties, stooped and white-haired and still mourning the loss of Flora's mother Marion, he was yet agile in mind and body and took great delight in showing off the fruits of his labours in field and orchard. He was also clearly proud of young Donald and confident that the lad would prosper on his new fifty-acre farm, with its dwelling-house and outhouses and fenced fields of wheat and Indian corn. The boy was such a general favourite, so prepossessing and modest, that Flora felt a sharp stab of remorse, recognising how much Fanny would have glowed had she but seen her manly cousin so honoured.

But from the start Flora also sensed an unease. It was indeed only to be expected that the men would take themselves off after the enormous meal and leave the wives and children to amuse themselves with play and gossip – nothing new there – but there was an undercurrent of undue haste in their departure this time, a furtiveness, that she could not help noticing. Finding her daughter in floods of tears compounded her complexity.

'Fegs, Anne, but this is not like you. What ails you? I'm your mother. Tell me.'

'It's Alex, Ma. I know I'm no longer pretty and there's another babe on the way already, but I had always thought he loved me just the same. But it seems he doesn't any more. He's scarcely ever at home. He says he's off buying hogs, or rounding up cattle, and has talked recently about having been appointed a land agent, but – oh, Ma, I hate to say this about my Alex but I fear he has another woman! I imagine him with a darkie slave, or somebody like that Rachel Strachan down at Mount Pleasant, and I'm just eaten up with jealousy! Sometimes I feel I shall go mad with it!'

Her heart full of love, Flora folded the girl in her arms. Reviewing how those past few weeks had been for herself, she

realised with a start that had she been young like Anne, and
vulnerably pregnant, she might well have suspected Allan of
infidelity. For he too had recently taken to staying away on flimsy
pretexts.

'Shush, lass. You are but overwrought and tired, with all the
work you do. 'Tis nonsense you talk, doubting Alex. Come now.
You are just at the difficult time when the babe's not showing yet
but the changes in your body make you moody and easily upset.
Try talking to him. Share your fears. I'm sure he'll understand.'

Even as she spoke, though, she was reflecting wryly on the irony
of her advice. For the last thing she could do herself, right then,
was discuss her own fears and preoccupations with Allan.

Anne had let out a long sigh. 'Yes, ma. I know you're right. I'll
try not to worry. I wish I could be calm and trusting like you,
though. Not that Pa's one to go astray' – she let out a little giggle
at the idea: why did one's children always think one immune to
the charms of the opposite sex? – 'but when Alex told me all that
had happened to him down Wilmington way I thought you'd never
let him out of your sight again.'

'You mean the snakes and alligators?'

Anne regarded her with baffled disbelief. 'You mean he didn't
tell you about being roughly set upon by a posse of patriot militia
who yanked him off his horse and hustled him to Bob Howe's
house? Seems his every move had been monitored, ever since he
left home, and they were determined to find out what he was up
to. Cornelius Harnett and that ruffian James Coor were there and
Coor would have had them extract the information they wanted
by force, but Howe and Harnett, lechers though they are, were
too gentlemanly for that. Oh Ma, did you not know? They let him
go when he protested that he knew nothing of the loyalist plans,
but the whole business unnerved him. That was why he didn't
dare travel by day afterwards, or call on anyone he knew. Even as
it was, on the eve of his return some bandit took a pot shot at him.
The bullet came whizzing out of the bushes and barely missed his
ear. Ma, are you listening? Oh, I'm sorry! I thought you would
know!'

With a supreme effort Flora managed to hide her hurt.

'No. He didn't tell me about that. Didn't want to worry me, I
suppose. It would seem that we women are purposely being kept

in the dark about much that is going on. But be reassured on one point: harlots don't come into it.'

Yet the certainty of some deliberately hidden agenda made Flora feel exactly as she would have done had she suspected Allan of being unfaithful. She tried to behave naturally but the sense of betrayal and insecurity persisted. It deepened even further when Alexander began to talk about recent developments on the Tidewater. So the Wilmington Committee of Safety had burned Fort Johnson to the ground, and everyone knew all about it but Flora!

'Just as well Martin had the sense to move out to the *Cruizer* when he did. A pity, mind you, that he hadn't just cleared out and gone to New York with his wife and children when he had the chance, for a fat lot of use he is to us here, sitting on a rusty old hulk in the middle of the river. A clever strategic move that two-pronged sortie was, mind you, with Ashe coming down-river from Wilmington and Howe up from Brunswick. Ashe brought three hundred men with him, so they say, and it was mere child's play to land above the fort, charge the gate, and burn the whole lot to the ground. Just as well you got home when you did, Allan, or you might have got caught up in it and still be a prisoner down there in the pocosins.'

Flora saw Allan cast a sharp glance in her direction before replying.

'Och, it won't be for long, man.' He then added dismissively. 'Martin's sure General Gage will relieve him soon. We mustn't be pessimistic. Just as long as we're prepared to help if necessary.'

Then pointedly changing the subject before the full implications of what he had said could sink in he turned to young Donald.

'Now tell me, lad. About this grist mill you're considering building on the creek. I hear you've got Daniel Betton to manage it for you. I hope he's as good a man as my McAulay. Not that I intend to let you take my business away, mind you.' And he laughed good-naturedly. Everyone knew that the area could easily take another grist mill, with new tracts being cleared and cultivated all the time.

In fact, there was more than enough work for Allan as all the cornfields round about seemed to ripen at once, and it alarmed Flora that he was rarely around to supervise the farm servants.

She had watched fascinated as the grain-stalks grew higher by the day. Totally unlike the knee-high oats and barley of home, the cobs were on a level with her head. Each one presented serried rows of luscious golden kernels sheathed in pale green silk, and clamoured to be harvested.

Then she began to see neighbouring farmers coming lumbering out of the forest towards the mill with bundles of grain on their backs, or leading laden mules, and that was when Donald McAulay came into his own, in his juddering world of gears and grindstones where the dust-filled air stifled and choked. As often as not Allan wasn't there to oversee the milling process, collect the dues and see that nobody was cheating: so Flora would go down regularly to the mill, her shrewd business sense savouring the prospect of exacting toll for every bushel of grain

Most of the farmers were well known to her and invariably decent and polite. To a man they were relieved to have the milling facility at Kingsburgh restored.

'There's nobody quite like Don McAulay for getting things just right,' old Davie Cameron maintained. 'He's a real wizard when it comes to gauging just how much water to let into the wheel, and what the ideal space between the grinding stones should be, and how much grain should be fed to them at a time...'

'Aye', Ewen Cameron concurred. 'I could go to Colin McMaster – he's nearer – but there's nobody quite like Donnie when it come to adjusting the stones. He kens that the top stone has to be set higher for corn than for wheat, because ye need a bit o' coarseness in your corn bread and hush puppies.'

So after a day or two Flora found herself looking forward to her ritual visit to the mill. It was a welcome respite from digging sweet potatoes, cutting briars and baking bread. She usually chose early afternoon, the time of day when the heat was at its most oppressive and all creatures – men and cattle, cats and dogs and horses – existed in a state of drowsy suspension. Then she would join the farmers by the millpond while Jamie and the other youngsters stood under the spillway and let the cool water splash over them. A chance now to enjoy a pipe, or just to gaze mesmerised at the rush of water splattering over the wheel. A chance, too, to catch up with the latest gossip, for as the men waited for the grinding to be done they sat together ineffectually dangling fishing lines and talking. Flora soon realised that if she said nothing they would forget she was there and lapse into that lackadaisical kind of exchange that is almost a series of soporific, flow-of-consciousness monologues.

It was all so spasmodic, so full of tantalising pauses when they seemed almost to have forgotten what they had been talking about, that Flora had to curb her impatience, but she knew she had to be quiet if she was to learn anything.

'You'll have heard that Bob Hogg and Sam Campbell refused to go with Ashe to burn Fort Johnson. They're to be tried for desertion.'

Bob Hogg? Flora almost cried out in her distress for the kind Wilmington merchant who had befriended them scarcely a year before. So Bob had joined the rebels. Even if the allegiance had been but temporary the news was still a shock. What sort of a quarrel was this, that made folks turn on their own kind?

A long, sleepy hiatus, then a voice said, 'Aye. But they'll likely get off. I'm not so sure about James Cotton down in Cross Creek, though. Ye'd hear what happened to him, when he ignored the rebel summons? A company under yon ruffian Davie Love burst into his bedroom one morning and carried him off to the Committee at Mack's Ferry. He was fly, though. He treated them to rum, then stopped at a public house and got them that stotious on cider that they let him escape. Rumour has it he's wi' Martin on the *Cruizer* now'

'Good for him! Yon Davie Love's naught but a drunken galoot, right enough. Serves him right he was tricked.'

Another long, infuriating silence, then a deep sigh from Donald. 'Aye, but was it no' terrible, what the patriots did then. Ye ken I've never been a Hanoverian, Ewen – heaven forbid – but what thae rebels are doing in the name o' freedom is terrible indeed. Aye, so it is.'

The old man shook his head and said, wonderingly aghast, 'They laid waste Cotton's cornfields, and threatened to burn his house and mill and drive away his cattle. So he came back at last, and was taken to Hillsborough. Sam Williams and his brother Jacob too. 'Tis said they were all three set free, but only after they had recanted and taken the test.'

Flora listened horrified. She imagined what James Cotton's wife had gone through, left helpless and alone, not knowing what fate had befallen her husband. And how degraded and defeated Sam Williams must have felt, forced to take an oath of allegiance to a gang of thugs he despised, the kind of people who had ransacked his house and raped his wife.

But there was more to come, closer to home.

'Ye'd hear they're investigating Allan? He's suspected o' recruiting for the King.'

The words were spoken soft and low, but Flora heard and felt her throat go dry. She did not recognise the hoarse croak as her own voice when she called over to Jamie.

'Rest time's past. There's fruit to pick and corn to cut.'

'But Ma, we've only just got here!'

'Do what I say and come!'

She had not meant to sound so shrewish – young Jamie had so little fun these days – but the youth obeyed, and laboured with her in the searing heat as they helped the ghillies with the harvest. Frequently, as the weary day wore on, she felt the dazzling yellow of the corn dance and shimmer before her eyes and her head throb painfully. Her heart fluttered with frantic palpitations and her whole body ran with perspiration. And all the time the words rang in her head. You would hear that they're investigating Allan...

She felt so feverish and was so preoccupied with her thoughts that when a strange crackling filled her ears she scarcely registered its deadly implications. Then some warning instinct made her look down and she saw her first rattlesnake there at her feet. Some seven feet long, it had a black and gold diamond pattern on its back, a wild, arrow-shaped head, and malevolent eyes that were fixed on her with cold-blooded concentration. She saw it poised ready to strike, the huge fangs of its forked tongue swaying independently of one another, and was transfixed with horror.

So was this how her life in the colonies would end, bitten by a serpent in a cornfield? Vaguely she thought that all her life ought to be passing before her eyes, but all she could think of was how someone, Roddy probably, had once told her that a rattlesnake's tail clicked at the rate of fifty rattles a second. That, and this awful fear about Allan being suspected by the rebels.

But at the crucial moment one of the ghillies sneaked up from behind. A knife flashed and with the impact of the blow the snake crumpled in death, all its awe-inspiring resilience gone.

'That's the only way to treat a rattlesnake, eh? Just in time, weren't we ma'am?'

For the labourers the killing was an occasion of great rejoicing and triumph. With self-congratulatory bravado they fell on the creature and proceeded to cut it into steaks – just like chicken, they said – while Flora thought she would surely keel over with shock, relief and disgust.

Her escape from certain death was bound to cause tremendous excitement and comment among the family but she was determined it would not take precedence over this newly-discovered danger to Allan. How to find out more? To ask Allan himself would just invite his wrath. Sandy would seek to shield her, and to admit her ignorance of her husband's activities to anyone else would be demeaning. No: all she could do was keep her eyes and ears open.

The other time that she met the neighbours in the course of her work was on wash-days. Laundry seemed to pile up endlessly. Not that the family wore many clothes in the heat, but what they did wear became drenched in sweat so quickly that washing was imperative. So she and the maids would lug great baskets and bundles of linen outside, where some garments were washed directly in the creek and others, the ones that called out for hot water, were scrubbed with lye in great troughs made of hewn-out logs. An arduous process but companionable.

Of course, wherever the women were gathered, there was Peggy Campbell. Adept as ever with the snide comment and belittling gesture she would sit on her boulder by the creek and wash the same garment over and over, pretending absorption in her work but really only there for the gossip. Shifty and devious, she would invariably leave her post and seek Flora out if she spotted her nearby, while Flora, immediately on the alert, would caution herself to put a guard on her tongue, knowing that her every word would be analysed, given Peggy's own chosen interpretation, and then turned disparagingly over.

'So Allan's away again. How long has he gone for this time?'

Flora winced. It was not often that Peggy was quite so direct. She sensed trouble.

'Och, he's not away for long. Just a day or two. He's off with

Glendale helping him look over some property. You'll have heard, of course, that Alex's a land agent now?'

Safe enough. Everyone knew that by now, surely.

But Peggy gave her a long, level look that bristled with scorn and Flora felt her knees go suddenly limp as the malicious busybody let out a low, humourless cackle of triumph.

'Flora MacDonald, ye're a great one for the prevaricating, and that's a fact! Pretending ye don't ken what your own man's up to. Glendale a land agent, indeed! A likely story that! It's recruiting for the Hanoverian the pair of them are, that's what!'

Flora turned away in silence. Then, her face flaming, she gathered up the clothes she had been washing, carried them to some nearby bushes, and spread them out to dry. All the time her heart was thumping as a turbulent throng of emotions raged and seethed – humiliation, futile rage, a hopeless sense of betrayal and above all fear. How could Allan do this to her? Why had he refused to tell her how deeply involved he was in the colonists' troubles?

In her heart she knew the answer. He had known that he did not have her wholehearted support, but had gone his own way regardless. Sadly she left the little knot of women and wandered back to the house, to find comfort with Beanie the fawn and the farmyard hens.

PART FIVE

I

September 1775

At first it was just a whisper of coolness in the mornings, a little breeze that ruffled her skirts as she gathered in the last of the apple harvest. Then she noticed streaks of colour appearing on the trees – spectacular hues of red on dogwood, sourwood and blackgum; brilliant yellow on tulip trees and hickory; dashes of vivid russet and crimson on maples and oaks – all superimposed on and mingling with the evergreen uniformity of white pine and hemlock, spruce and fir. All so sensationally beautiful, and normally she would have been entranced by it, but she was dead to such pleasures.

She knew she was no longer welcome at the mill because it was now Allan's military headquarters, the loyalist stronghold where he drilled his two companies of clansmen. Wee Willie MacKenzie stood sentry at the door and a line of armed men patrolled the lane, on the lookout for patriot scouts. She heard the tramp of feet, the clank of weapons and the ring of sharp commands – 'Present firelock! Lower firelock!' – and shuddered, contemplating the ultimate purpose of it all. War.

After their exercises the leading clansmen would come back to the farm kitchen for oatcakes and ale and a jug of fresh milk, cold from the springhouse, and it was then that she gleaned the information that Allan was still stubbornly withholding from her. Some of it, dramatic phrases like 'The Third Provincial Congress' and 'The Fiery Proclamation', made her feel like a child who overhears an adult conversation and strives in vain to interpret it.

Some wisps of information she did understand, though. It seemed that the Whigs thought Josiah Martin might indeed arm the negroes, and give them their freedom if they agreed to fight for the King. Such rumours, she knew, could only cause hysteria and incite the mob to violence. Already terrible measures had been

taken against any stray slaves who had been apprehended away
from their masters' lands. Eighty lashes was a commonplace
punishment. Such tales of the patriots' barbaric cruelty sent
shudders down her spine.

Most alarming of all, she realised that the conflict was no longer
purely a political one, to be resolved by diplomatic means. The
patriots talked about North Carolina contributing two battallions
to the 'Continental Army', with James Moore and Bob Howe as
colonels of the first and second respectively. The thought of James
Moore, so wealthy and prominent a citizen, being actively
committed to the enemy cause gave Flora much food for thought.

Nor, she realised, was this fight local. General Gage had decided
to bypass Josiah Martin and post a military man, another Boston
general called MacDonald, to control North Carolina. He had
refused to restore Martin's old rank of colonel and had only agreed
to captaincies for Allan and Alex – a circumstance which caused
much resentment among the loyal Highlanders of Anson County.

But Allan did not share their pique, or if he did he was prudent
enough not to show it, which brought home to Flora yet again
how mature and confident those past months had made him. She
watched him there at the table, his solid neck square on his
shoulders, his raven-black hair gleaming and his muscles taut, and
for a moment all she felt was the maleness of him. If I could but
agree with him about this fight, she thought, what a formidable
team we would be!

Masterful now, he insisted that his rank was of no importance.
"'Tis more important from now on that we have regular troops
to back us, and a dependable professional command. Now, about
this recruitment drive. We must be prepared to knock on doors,
engage the folks we meet on the road in conversation, debate our
cause in store and tavern and aye, in the very kirk. Ye ken the line
ye have to take. Remind waverers that they owe their land to King
George, and that success for the rebels means spiralling prices,
fields laid waste and livestock lost. And above all remember that
our worst enemies, to be most of all reviled, are the cowards that
imagine they can avoid taking sides!'

Aware that the jibe was directed at herself Flora worked on in
silence but felt colder and more defenceless than ever. Just how
irrevocably Allan had become involved was brought home most

forcibly to her the next day, when Kenneth Black, a fanatical loyalist farmer from down Nick's Creek way, appeared with two strangers in tow. Kenneth, she remembered, had leased Glendale to Alex and Anne. What on earth was he doing up here?

She watched as the three engaged Allan in earnest conversation, and sensed her husband's excitement as he invited them inside. His manner was uncharacteristically respectful, almost obsequious, and indeed the two visitors had a cachet about them that proclaimed them no mere country bumpkins. The elder, who must have been nearing seventy, was tall and military-looking, with a pallid, seedy complexion, while the younger, though shorter, was wiry and bursting with energy.

'You'll have a dram, sir?'

That 'sir' of Allan's had Flora doubly curious, and she hurried through to the great room to proffer the drinks.

'Ah, Florrie. See who we have here! This is a distant cousin of mine, Lieutenant-colonel Donald MacDonald, come all the way from Boston to help rally recruits to our cause. And this is Colonel Donald MacLeod. We can give them beds for the night, lass?'

The two men clicked their heels and each bowed over her hand.

'Honoured indeed to meet you, Ma'am. There's no true Highlander would be otherwise.'

All perfectly courteous and in order, so why did she feel so wary?

Only gradually, as the conversation unfolded, was her unease explained. Here in the persons of those professional soldiers was the very proof of the direction the conflict was taking. They talked of having been waylaid by patriots at New Bern and forced to take vows of non-alignment, which they had taken without a qualm of conscience despite having no intention of keeping them. But around the Cross Creek area enemy scouts had become suspicious and Kenneth Black had decided to bring them into the back country until the hunt died down.

Most alarming of all, their talk was all of recruitment and plans for the forthcoming confrontation, which they regarded as simply a matter of time. Allan's participation they clearly took for granted. She bristled when the older officer turned to her and with what she saw as a condescending presumption of intimacy called her 'Fionnghal' and said,

'Allan here is one of my most prized captains. I intend to work for his promotion to major, by the time this campaign is properly under way.'

Her instinct then was to jump, wife-like, to Allan's defence, and to protest that had General Gage given Governor Martin proper support Allan would have been a major ere now, but suddenly the whole enormity of what was happening overwhelmed her. These men represented the military might of an empire threatened, and they were here in her house, in the wilds of Carolina. What a coup for those rebel scoundrels should they smell them out! Fresh terror seized her as she realised afresh that nobody would be safe in bed that night. The officers were up and away at first light, and watching them ride off left her mightily relieved, but a flash of cognition told her that until this crisis was over the dread would never leave her.

Who to turn to, to explain her inner struggle? Her stepfather sympathised but man-like begged her to put her marriage before her religious scruples and give Allan support. How else could they defend this way of life, he would argue, if not to fight for it? Only John Bethune understood her fully, but he would have her forfeit her marriage for her principles and that was the last thing she was prepared to do. Gradually, too, she was coming to recognise a sea change in her outlook, a hardening of attitude that owed nothing to Allan's persuasion – he had gone his own way regardless of her, after all – but much to admiration for his fortitude and a weighing up in her own mind of the justice of his cause.

She did try, on one last desperate occasion, to pull him from the brink. Three men in filthy buckskins rode up to Kingsburgh one day when Allan was up at Hugh's. Fearful she opened the door to them, to have a letter flung in her face and a rough voice cry, 'Read that, mistress, and tremble! Your daughter down at Glendale's got one too!' And with a wild whoop they cantered off.

The day was hot but she shivered, as if a piece of melting ice had slithered down her back. Fear for Anne and a dreadful fascination overcame any scruples and she found her shaking hands tearing at the parchment. The message was from the Wilmington Committee of Safety, and warned Allan that if he continued in the Government's service he and his family would suffer. Stifling a scream she hastily folded the paper up, doubly conscious now of this conflict that was pulling the clans apart and plunging her whole family into mortal danger. And to think that

Allan was at the very hub of it all! Surely she could stop him.

She was already in bed when he got home that night, exhausted as always but with a strange, scarcely suppressed tension about him – the kind of tension, she acknowledged wryly, that would have had her suspecting a woman had she not known that he was too preoccupied with his military activities to have time for such frivolity. To her amazement, too, he began to tell her, as he got his tinder-box and lit a candle, about the armaments situation in Anson and Cumberland counties. It was hoped that the government would supply rifles to those Highlanders who had none: if not, he and the other leaders would have to do it.

She listened to him in appalled silence, aghast that she had almost come round to his point of view, and then screwing up her courage said flatly, 'You must give up this whole venture, Allan. You are in grave danger. So are Alex, and Anne, and all of us. See. This came today.' And she handed him the letter.

But all he afforded it was a scornful perfunctory glance before holding it to the candle flame and reducing it to ashes. His face in the flickering light was thunderous. 'A pox on their empty threats! How dare they try to scare me and mine with their blusterings!'

Determined nevertheless to ignore his fury she persisted. 'Why can't we plant and harvest our corn and tend our cattle in peace? That's why we came here! Even our own clansmen are divided, Allan! Don't you see that many of the older settlers don't want to be involved, but if they have to choose they'll go the rebel way! Please husband, don't be the one to tear us apart!'

Perhaps he realised how genuinely panic-stricken she was, for although his sentiments did not change his features softened. 'But if we let them cut ties with England, Florrie, we'll be at the rebels' mercy, without law, or security, or title to our lands!'

'We could still get away. Isolate ourselves further west. We are used to the hard and solitary life. Please, Allan.' She felt the tears in her voice.

''Twould make no difference, Florrie. Our farm would still be pillaged. Please don't fight me. I am doing what I must. Oppose me and we are simply the more vulnerable.'

He drew her to him. She lay listening to the night noises, the crickets clicking, a dove cooing, the neighing of a horse in the stable, and knew that he had won. Or rather, her love for him had.

Nor was it only love. In those past months he had found new strength and conviction, and she respected him for it.

Then, from a totally different and unexpected quarter, came the catalyst that would confirm everything. Hannibal.

Flora was feeding the hens one morning, unselfconsciously calling them by name and congratulating herself that even the cock, magnificent in ruby-red crest and gleaming metallic feathers, no longer saw her as a threat to his harem, when she was aware of a movement by the water-butt. The slave emerged then, silent as a shadow and seemingly as insubstantial. His whole person was an unrelieved grey, from his torn, foul-smelling breeches to his sickly pock-marked skin: she had not realised that ill health could rob a negro's complexion of its indigo glow. But most alarming of all was the dirty, blood-stained band of cotton swathed turban-wise round his head.

'Hannibal?' The name hovered in the shimmering air, instinct with doubt and terror.

'Ma'am.' The lad swayed and he keeled forward, to land sprawled in the dust at Flora's feet.

'Quick. Into the house.' She did not consider implications or consequences. Another human being needed her. That was enough. 'Morag! Deirdre! Bring hot water and towels! And some brandy! And be quick about it!'

But though Hannibal let himself be guided indoors his agitation mounted as he summoned up enough strength to talk. 'Leave me be. Jes go help Stella. Ah dinn hab de strenth ter carry 'er no furder. Ah done left 'er in de woods yonder an' she hurtin' bad, wid de babe comin' an' all. 'Tis near 'er time, Ah reckon.'

'But whatever happened to you? Tell me. Then we'll go fetch Stella.'

For a brief moment Hannibal's old fire flared up.

'Dey done cut off ma ears. Dat Massah Alastair and his militia men. Jes de outsides, o' course. Ah kin still hear a li'l. Woulda done worse, Ah reckon, were threatenin' ter tar and fedder me and den hang me on a tree, but Massah Boyd, de fadder, he angry an' made 'em let me go. He good man, dat Massah Roddy. We owe our lives to 'im an' to de good Lord above, Stella an' me.'

The bile stood thick and sour in Flora's mouth and she felt her stomach heave.

The boy was weeping now. 'Please, Ma'am. You be a kin' Christian lady. I know you not one to leave ma Stella to die.'

All the while Flora was weighing up her options. 'Where is she?'

'Down past de mill, jes inter de forest. Dere be a clearing ba de path, where yer can see ober ter de mountains? Dere be a big live oak, an' some maples an' hickories…'

His voice trailed off, overcome by weakness, but Flora could visualise the place. It was about a mile off, too far to make carrying feasible.

'We'll need Delilah,' she concluded after a moment's quick thought. 'Morag and Deirdre, you come with me. Jamie, stay with Hannibal. Don't let him get up. He has to rest. And give him all the liquor he wants. 'Twill do him no harm.'

They found Stella lying on the moss in a corner of the glade, where the clean fecund smells of cedar and fresh grass were overlaid and interlaced with the sour fumes of her vomit and the musty exhalations from her clothes and body. It was immediately obvious from her anguished cries that she was well advanced in labour. The contractions were coming in quick succession and sweat stood on her brow.

'Get her on to the mare's back. Easy now.' As she helped lift the moaning girl Flora muttered assurances to her and simultaneously gentled the animal. 'There now, Delilah. Go quietly. 'Tis a fragile cargo, this.' And she walked beside the animal, guiding it by the reins back to the farm.

Deirdre, the experienced one, had been quick to anticipate everything that would be needed: hot water, old sheets, an infusion of cramp bark. But Flora was quick to see the look of futility on the old woman's face, and suspected that had this patient been a dog or a sheep, or even a cow, it would have been left to die. Stella's emaciated body was grossly misshapen. Her shoulder-blades protruded through the threadbare sacking of her meagre shift and her limbs were dry and brittle as sticks, so that the swollen belly looked obscenely, pathetically distended.

Flora's mind teemed with questions. Had Stella ever felt the child move? Where had she been, these last four months? Had they found that community of runaway slaves down on the Tidewater, where the mother was? But she did not voice them. It was more important to encourage the girl, to exhort her to effort:

she and her maids were not equipped for heroic surgery.

And certainly the girl was in no fit state to take in questions, far less answer them. She was off in her own personal hell, where demons stretched her on the rack and fed the flames of her torment. Flora's voice must have penetrated her consciousness and kept her sane, however, for in response to the women's encouragement she made the supreme effort and disgorged a tiny, dead blood-stained scrap of bone and tissue on to the towel between her legs. The body was scarcely recognisable as human but two features were immediately obvious – it had been female, and on its forehead was a livid birth-mark in the shape of a star.

Hannibal, who had refused to stay away, let out a yelp of anguish and rushed to Stella's side. The women were for shooing him away, insisting that the girl's travail was not done, but Flora restrained them. She had overcome the wave of nausea that had engulfed her and summoned up a new fortitude from who knew what atavistic store of self-discipline.

'Courage, Hannibal,' she said now. 'These next moments are crucial. We may yet save her, gin ye don't despair.'

After some time, too, it did indeed begin to look as if Stella was going to survive. Flora marvelled at the slave's resilience. She remembered the horror of the pumpkin field, imagined the terrors of the chase and the couple's sufferings in the months past, and found that her main emotion was not pity any more, but sheer unmitigated rage that any human being should be subjected to such tortures.

If she had had any lingering doubts about giving Allan her support they certainly vanished now. She had to fight, not only to preserve this plot of ground she had come to love but to ensure that the Alastair Boyds of this world never got their cruel way. The truth came to her with all the force and certainty of revelation. Saul on the road to Damascus.

She was surprised at how empowered and almost carefree she felt then. The sense of isolation had gone and she even plucked up enough courage, while the women tended Stella, to go herself to the mill with the men's mid-day dinner of bread and cheese.

The new recruits were lined up in the mill yard, a motley lot of assorted types and ages, wearing ragged knee breeches and long linen shirts. Flora steeled herself to approach them, but soon realised they were nearly all neighbours, and well known to her. To a man they greeted her with sheepish grins.

All but Allan, who stopped drilling with a peremptory 'Stand easy!' and looked daggers in her direction. 'What's this, woman? Haven't I made it clear that I don't want you meddling here? 'Tis Jamie's job to bring our dinner.'

'But I must speak to you, Allan. Come with me to the waterside yonder. 'Tis pressing.'

Some new firmness in her manner must have alerted him, for he followed her without protest down to the dam and they sat on the grass together.

'Well?' He squinted at her, the mid-day sun in his eyes.

'I – I want to say I'm sorry. For doubting you and – and all this.' Her gesture took in the courtyard and the sad little apology of an army. 'At last I see you have cause, and promise to do all I can to help.'

He gave her a sideways look, puzzled and incredulous, as she went on.

'You will be angry, no doubt, when you hear what it took to change my mind at last.'

And she told him about the two slaves, hearing her own voice rise hysterically as she recounted the melodramatic events and Alastair Boyd's part in them. Someone in London had told her, once, about the format of ancient Greek tragedy, how a chorus described the action to the audience and reflected upon it. She suddenly saw herself as such a narrator, an emissary of horror. Surely Allan would respond now as those listeners did so long ago, with pity and terror?

She said as much. 'Be merciful, husband. Let them stay.'

But Allan was made of sterner stuff. 'You hope to inveigle me into harbouring the scum of the runaway slave population, by pretending at this late stage to support the King? You who have made it your business to obstruct my every effort in the loyalist cause? You must think me soft-headed, Flora! Now be off with you, woman, and see to it that that thieving trollop and her troublesome swain are clear of my premises before sundown!'

'I shall do as I see fit. And as for my sincerity in the loyalist cause, you will see the proof of that anon. I am not one to go back on my decision.'

The words had come tumbling thoughtlessly out but she did not regret them, and having voiced them she turned on her heel and walked away, leaving him gazing thoughtfully into his ale.

II

October 1775

She installed Hannibal and Stella in the hay-loft that afternoon, with instructions that they keep themselves well out of the master's way. Their presence, after all, was little different from housing two extra beasts, and as long as they had food and a roof over their heads they were content. Stella, once so proud and spirited, lay thin and pathetic on her bed of straw and vowed eternal gratitude to Flora. All her obis she would give her – the amulets of chicken's blood and feathers, compounded with grave dirt and eggshells; the alligator's teeth and parrots' beaks, so potent in their spelling; and, most valuable of all the sorcerer's armoury, the deadly seven-boned tail of a rattle-snake. Flora listened to her ravings and muttered thanks, marvelling all the while at the girl's credulity. Much good her charms had done her.

Hannibal meanwhile tended his young wife and did all he could to help about the yard while the men were occupied elsewhere. There was much to do at this time of year. Flora had brought Murdo McMillan the blacksmith into her secret and Hannibal was a regular visitor at the smithy when scythes needed sharpened, wheels mended or horses shod. Despite the continuing summer heat he did not seem to mind the forge, where charcoal blazed and the great leather bellows pounded.

As he regained his strength he also proved a valuable timberman. His muscular body shone as he wielded the axe in regular flashing strokes, to produce squared logs for buildings or chunky pieces for the winter fires. He helped get in the barley, harvest pumpkins and squash, gather peaches and fashion storage barrels, and during Allan's frequent absences Flora wondered how she would have fared without him.

For she was openly loyalist now. True, she came up against a lot of bitter criticism, particularly among some old Highlanders who remembered the '45. 'Turncoat!' they would snarl. 'Ye were our heroine once, the lass that saved Bonnie Prince Charlie. And now ye'd have us fight for the Hanoverian!'

But she was ready with her answer. 'Times have changed. And so have circumstances. Can't you see, those Americans would have us do away with kings altogether? We are fighting for the old Scottish way of life that we would keep alive here. The Stuart cause is irrelevant now, a part of history. We are fighting for the right to farm our lands and bring up our families under British law, in a part of Britain beyond the seas.'

Some would nod and seem mollified, others would shut the door in her face and that would sadden her, but knowing in her heart that she was right now she did not temper her message. And at last Allan was realising that she was serious. He began to share information with her and something of the old trust crept back into their love-making.

Greatly to her relief, too, the fall brought a respite from hostility in the immediate area, as if folks realised that with winter on the way there were other life-preserving considerations to see to. Allan spent more time at home, making the farm work easier but Hannibal and Stella's situation untenable. They eventually slipped away into the woods again, protesting life-long devotion to Flora but insisting that they would just make trouble for her if they stayed.

Autumn was rich with new sights and sounds and smells and because her uncertainty and fear had almost receded Flora found herself savouring them again. Added to the usual bitter-sweet nostalgia of the waning year, however, there was a desperate need to cherish each sensation, to stamp it on her memory so that in less joyful times it would be immediately recollectable. A harvest moon hanging red over the stubble fields. Wide swathes of golden rod, brilliant in the sun. Hairy caterpillars, white with jet-black lines down their spines or black with brown stripes: the locals declared that the width of the bands indicated how hard the winter was going to be. The smell of wood-fires, scented with drying venison, and the comforting fragrance of warm pumpkin bread. Above all, because right there on the farm, the strong, acrid aroma of grain being made into whisky.

Allan's devotion to this task amused Flora, and she teased him. 'Yon John Barleycorn will be the death of you yet! It's well seen you'd rather make usquebaugh than sausages or black puddings! And all these hogs newly slaughtered, waiting to be smoked!'

But as always he had an answer for her. 'Och, Neil can see to the hogs. Everybody tells me that up here the most productive way to market corn and rye is to make whisky out of it. I can distil ten gallons of whisky from a barrel of rye flour, and when you think that a packhorse can carry only four bushels as grain, but twenty-four when it's made into whisky, you've got to agree that it makes good commercial sense.'

She did, of course, and returned to her own tasks more contented than she had been for months. The weather was cooler now. Mosquitoes and gnats no longer tormented her. Her pantry bulged with food – hams and haunches of venison, an abundance of sausages, bags of grain, bushels of apples, jars of tender young pickled cucumbers. She also spent time in her simples room, concocting poultices, distilling herbs, infusing roots and bark, against the inevitable winter's ills and the vague, disquieting menace that hovered constantly on the brink of her consciousness but which she had taught herself to live with.

She did not quite know why, but she drew a strange comfort from the knowledge that Hannibal and Stella were not far away. Sometimes she heard Roddy's voice in her head, telling her sternly that nobody could trust negroes, and then she would remember how recalcitrant, thieving, and maybe even murderous Stella had proved: but then she would take cider and loaves to the young couple in their hide-out in the woods, and their gratitude always had her returning. They said they had found a cave in the hills where they were sure they could survive in the winter, given occasional help from her, and this she gladly pledged.

She suspected that she might never be free of recurrent bouts of that fever that had plagued her on the Tidewater but now that the flies had gone she rarely succumbed to those enervating attacks. She even found physical labour peculiarly satisfying. How different chopping dry pine was from the wet, exhausting task of cutting peats: the splintering wood light and aromatic, unlike the foetid, heavy glaur of a Scottish moorland.

Then she would feel almost a renegade for making those

invidious comparisons, and her thoughts would turn inevitably to her family back home. Letters assured her that Fanny and Johnny were well and happy and she prayed that it was so, but it worried her that Allan no longer talked of fetching them over to America. She suspected that the reasons were not financial – thanks largely to Sandy's sound management of the stock and profit from the mill the farm had prospered – but there was an unspoken consensus that in the prevailing political climate the time was not right.

Josiah Martin had certainly not let up in his efforts to keep the Highlanders loyal, and even wrote personally to Flora, pleading for her help. 'The people respect and love you,' he insisted. As always, she responded to such assurances with mingled gratification and dread – dread because the Committees of Safety had adopted new resolutions to the effect that anyone who received letters from Martin would immediately be branded an enemy of the liberty of the people.

The Provincial Congress, the patriots' main policy-making body, kept up a constant barrage of propaganda. They had appointed a special committee to try to persuade recently-arrived Highlanders to join them, and Flora was sad to learn that not only was Alex McAlister a member of it – that was to be expected – but Farquhard Campbell as well. One Lachlan McIntosh had come specially from Georgia, too, and even contacted Flora in the hope of gaining her support.

Determinedly she dismissed their overtures as impertinent. She knew that most Highland settlers were too unsophisticated to be swayed by those new revolutionary ideas. They were by tradition inveterately loyal to their daoine uaisle, the tacksmen they had depended upon at home and whom they still regarded as their feudal superiors.

It was a different story, however, when the church became involved and the rebels put forward their case as derived from God. James Campbell was not alone in his revolutionary preaching. Two ministers, Elihu Spencer and Alex McWhirter, were paid forty dollars by the Congress to go to North Carolina, and at Joseph Hewes' instigation four Presbyterian clergymen from Philadelphia wrote to their fellow churchmen defending the right to revolt.

Allan was furious when the letters were printed and distributed, and especially when a tract appeared penned by someone calling himself Scotus Americanus, who took the line of 'If we cannot be of service to the cause, let us not be of injury to it'.

'We mustn't let up and let those blackguards steal a march on us! They're just taking advantage of our clansmen's natural respect for the clergy. They think they can come here and talk folks round with pious platitudes and flowery oratory? Well, they're wrong!'

Much to Flora's relief John Bethune thought the same. 'I have made it a rule to avoid politics in my sermons,' he insisted, 'but they force me to it with their false philosophising. Oh, Flora, to think we came here only to be divided again! I've been hard put to it to talk my mother over, for like us she would have stayed aloof gin it had been possible. As for Peggy...' His face darkened and he sighed. ''Tis aye hard to guess what Peggy's thinking. She's deep, that one.'

At least Allan no longer withheld any news that came his way. 'I have Josiah's assurance that the men I raise will have arms and pay like regular troops. Lord Cornwallis is bringing seven regiments from Ireland and Sir Henry Clinton is coming from Boston with two companies. The Carolina loyalists are not alone you see, Florrie, but part of a grand master plan. Everything's falling into place. Come next summer this whole crisis will be over. The rebellion will be crushed and we'll all be able to get on with our lives again, our animosity forgotten.'

He sounded so irrepressibly confident that Flora almost believed him. She listened to details of how Alex had spent all of fifty-five pounds personally recruiting in Anson, Cumberland and Guilford counties, and how he hoped that even the Orange County Regulators would come and swell the loyalist ranks: but her thoughts then were not for the success of his recruiting drive, but of her daughter and grandchildren's welfare. Poor Anne, she thought. She must scarcely see her husband these days. Just as well winter is coming. The frost and snow will surely put an end to all these wanderings of his.

So when the land grew hoary and sere and the leafless orchard trees turned grey she almost rejoiced. Gladly she would close her crimson curtains against the view of dun fields under a vast starry sky, and light grease lamps to supplement the glow of the firelight. Then she devoted her time to domesticity. Her spinning wheel whirred and her knitting pins clacked, while under her breath she prayed that the cold would last for ever.

She did not give up on her efforts to help Allan recruit men, however. She knew instinctively that an appeal to the Highlanders' Celtic consciousness was vital, and on a special visit to Lachlan MacFarlane asked him to go out into the forest at nightfall and play the pipes. There was nothing like the skirl of the pibroch to fire folks' blood. Nor was she averse, on occasion, to exploiting her own celebrity status. Even on the coldest days she was a familiar sight as she rode the woodland paths, a latter-day Boadicea in a green riding habit, a tartan plaid draped round her shoulders. Confidently she would dismount in farm courtyards and go knocking on doors, or searching around byres and stables for potential recruits.

Her lilting Gaelic would echo in the frosty air. 'Jock! Meg! Catriona! Are ye about? Did ye get our summons to the ceilidh at Kingsburgh, on Hogmanay? Everybody's coming! See ye're there!'

That was one thing she knew she excelled at, giving parties, and what was more natural than a celebration of their first New Year at Kingsburgh?

'We've been that busy in house and fields since we came that we've never had all our neighbours together but now everybody's welcome. Open house, and there'll be kegs of whisky handy, as much as ye can stomach.'

She knew that few would resist her invitation. When the word spread they would come from all around. Perhaps Anne and Alex and their children would come though Anne was very pregnant now, but this shindig was not only for her nearest and dearest. Her underlying motive was to lure the unsophisticated, often shiftless and in most cases uncommitted, clansmen, get them stotious, have a list handy for them to sign their names in, and so enrol them in Allan's army.

III

January 1776

So while all too aware of the approaching conflict Flora determined temporarily to ignore it, apart from that one overriding preoccupation of gathering fresh recruits. She would not let worry spoil the preparations or cool the warmth of her welcome. Everything would be perfect, from the polish on the silver to the spices in the sauce.

And so it turned out. As Allan and she greeted their guests she knew that everything had been done to make her belated house-warming a success. The great room had been hung with evergreens. Fires flickered and candles glowed, their light reflecting the brilliance of crystal and silver. A linen cloth, pristine white, had been laid on the table and on it stood a huge punch-bowl full to the brim with potent liquors in which, jewel-like, bobbed fruits of every hue. Sweetmeats and nuts graced the dresser and numerous side tables, while in the kitchen, waiting to be served later, were the more substantial dishes – turkey and venison, beef steaks and pickled tongues, fish and shellfish, a whole range of puddings, jellies and syllabubs.

She also knew that she and Allan looked the perfect Highland hosts, presenting as neat and stylish an appearance as was possible in this back-of-beyond terrain. Her green taffeta gown was trimmed with tartan while he was in full dress – kilt, frilled jabot, brooch, dirk and buckles gleaming with silver. Rather to her surprise she found she could not keep her eyes off him: her gaze kept returning for reassurance to his clean, towering figure, and each time she felt a surge of pride and affection. Desperately she fought off the persistent, premonitory fear that tempered it, telling herself firmly that this was no time for pessimistic speculation and elegiac misgivings.

But try as she would she could not rid herself of it. If Allan had been of the isolationist persuasion total complacency would have been perfectly justified. But he was not that kind of person: his feeling of political responsibility was too strong for him to want to cut himself off from the region's sufferings. So Flora's euphoria was not absolute: she even found herself wondering whether they would have considered such a ceilidh at all, without an ulterior motive for it. Nor could she help recalling the Hogmanay of only a year before, spent so amicably with the Boyds and the Cuidreach MacDonalds. So much had happened since then: a new home, burnished and furnished to her liking; a host of new friends; a life physically hard but full of promise. Why had it all gone sour? Knowing that it had not been her fault did little to cheer her.

She was also worried about Sandy, who had taken advantage of the recent dry spell to ride down to Cross Creek and had not yet come home. His errand had been innocent enough: he was to order uniform coats and crimson sashes from Donald McDougald the tailor, for both himself and Allan, as well as collecting the usual supplies of tea and coffee, salt and sugar and tobacco at Campbell's warehouse. Salt in particular had suddenly become scarce – maybe Sandy had had difficulty getting a supply of it? – but Flora knew that nobody from Kingsburgh was safe on the roads these days, knew too that though he had said he would spend Christmas at Mount Pleasant with Alexander and Annabella, and then look in at Glendale on the way home, he had another more pressing priority than paying a visit to an aunt or a sister. Jenny.

Determinedly she dragged herself back into the here and now, realising that Christian Bethune was just at her elbow. This whole party had been thought up for the likes of Christian: extra fuss and graciousness were therefore called for.

Not that the kiss she bestowed on the withered cheek was any the less sincere for that. 'Come over and get a dish of punch, Christian. Or would you rather have some mulled port? Fegs, hasn't it been cold? See, this'll put some heat in you. And I hear the fiddler tuning. Everything will warm up when the dancing starts.'

Certainly, although midnight was still a long way off, the noise level was rising: snorts and guffaws of laughter; sudden bursts of conversation; loud belches as the viands were digested; the roar of singing and the squeaks of dalliance. The noses of the more bibulous had taken on an even rosier sheen than usual and many a carefully-curled wig sat comically askew. Flora noticed with some satisfaction that Allan, Alex and Hugh had already begun goodnaturedly to propel the more sodden revellers towards the recruitment list, probably to make sure of their signatures before they were too drunk to stand. Not without amusement she watched her stepfather approach daft Hamish McKechnie and slap him heartily on the back.

'Come on, Hamish! Ye're not going to leave our Flora in the lurch, are ye? Shame on ye, hanging back when our country needs ye! Sign, man, or gin ye cannot write just put a cross and I'll see your name goes alongside.'

Sheepishly the young simpleton did as he was told, scratching a cross on the parchment. Flora knew she ought to pity him – what right had she to trick a half-wit into service? – but hardened her heart. Put him on a battle-field and Hamish's sheer brawn would more than compensate for his lack of intellect.

But how many of those pressed volunteers would remember their pledge, far less be willingly on hand when the time came? Surely quite a few of them would have swithered, or even refused outright, without the fuddling effect of the rum.

A raucous voice interrupted her thoughts. 'A reel, Fergus, and let the Deil tak the hindmost!'

Simultaneously a group of stalwarts swooped upon rugs and furniture and in no time had the room cleared for dancing. The drink stayed, of course, relegated to the sideboard to be indulged in whenever refreshment was called for.

First on the floor as the fiddle began to scrape out the measures of a randy reel was Phemie Cameron, the closest thing to a scarlet woman that the neighbourhood could produce. 'Heuch!' she yelled tipsily, her supple body frenetically eager for the dance. Then raising her hands easily above her tousled head she pas-de-basqued on the spot and called to the more reluctant guests to come and make up the sets.

It was all froth and laughter after that. The steps of Highland reels came to these folk as instinctively as breathing. Even the heaviest of them moved with a swift, assured lightness. They leapt in the air, they linked arms and birled their partners about, they side-stepped and swerved and pranced. In to the centre, turn; away from the centre, turn; up and down, turn; back to back, turn – by this time sweat poured freely from every brow and the room reeked of smoke and none-too-clean humanity, but nobody cared. It was Hogmanay. They would think about their troubles another night.

Then, just when the reel was at its most frenzied, the door opened and Sandy came in, his arm held protectively around the waist of a clearly terrified Jenny Boyd. Fergus the fiddler's mouth dropped open and the movements of his bow slowed down to strathspey time. Alerted by the change in tempo the dancers tried to adjust their steps until they too saw the reason for it and almost stopped in mid-figure. It was only when Phemie Cameron – bless her for once, Flora thought – tossed her head and shouted, 'What's wrong wi' the lot o' ye? Can ye no' stand the pace? Back to reel time, Fergus!' that the company's attention was drawn back to the dance.

Even with the music thrumming, the dancers heuching and the feet clattering, however, Flora felt the undercurrent of excited curiosity. They all knew who Jenny was. Douce and comely she might be but she was yet sister to the notorious Alastair Boyd, likely the most fanatical patriot of them all. She looked fearfully over at Sam and Jessie Williams and saw the shock in their faces. Sam's fists were clenched and a thunderous frown sat on his features.

It was the signal for Flora to take the initiative. In a flash she was at the young couple's side.

'Thank God you're here, Sandy! We thought something terrible had happened to you, that you weren't here to bring in the new year with us. And you, lass. You know you're welcome. Come ben the house and you can have a wash and something to eat.'

Jenny came without a murmur. Briefly touching the girl's shoulder Flora felt the bony, freezing cold frame and was reminded of Stella. Of course, Kingsburgh was fifty rain-sodden miles from the Mumrills. The ride must have been a night-marish ordeal: it was no wonder Jenny was wet through and debilitated. But even as she considered this Flora knew that there was more to Jenny's apathy than mere physical exhaustion. It was in her eyes, a brainsick wildness that made the heart turn over.

Ushering Jenny through to the back bedroom she decided on briskness. No questions yet. 'Let's have that riding habit off. It's caked with mud. You can undress while I fetch a ewer of water and then I'll find you a nightgown. Ignore that drunken rabble through there. Your plight is more important than any new year ceilidh.'

Even as she spoke she realised that the din in the great room, the singing and thumping and yells of 'Slainte!' and 'Bliadhna Mhath Ur!' could mean only one thing: it was midnight, the dawn of 1776, and here she was, apart from them all. No matter. She turned back to Jenny. 'Come now, lass. One more last effort now and you can sleep as long as you like.'

But Jenny continued to behave like a disorientated puppet. Her movements were jerky and automatic, as if she had no idea where she was or what was being asked of her. Tentatively she lifted her fingers towards the buttons of her jacket and began, all thumbs, to fumble ineffectually, so that Flora was forced to take over the task. It was like preparing a child for bed but infinitely more harrowing.

Nor had a child ever been known to fall asleep so fast. Vaguely aware perhaps of the benison of bedclothes Jenny had simply let out a long sigh and collapsed into slumber. Gazing then on the still, white face Flora saw lines of suffering that had not been there a year before, and a maturity that sent her mind spinning into a vortex of speculation. Jenny was in a helpless, traumatised state and she could not wait to know why.

Meanwhile all she could do was return to the party and pretend that nothing untoward had happened. Kissing her, Allan told her that Sandy had gone to bed in the hayloft, adding under his breath, 'Everybody has signed up. Well done, mo ghaoil. Now the sooner they go home the better.'

Flora thoroughly endorsed the sentiment. She had almost forgotten about the list of volunteers and longed for peace and quiet. But while the women were beginning to take their leave the men lingered, most of them too sozzled to be aware of the time. They had spilled over, as the night advanced, into the kitchen, the barn, the outhouses, and would doubtless stay there, pixilated, till morning. No point in staying up now, though. The squalid aftermath of stale tobacco and vomit, spilt liquor and mangled food remnants could wait until tomorrow to be seen to. Not that the general disarray was her main concern as she drifted off into a tremulous sleep. Jenny. Whatever had happened to Jenny?

It was Sandy who enlightened them, late the following morning when all but Jenny were awake and attending with laborious reluctance to a bare minimum of essential tasks.

'Alastair had his spies out – yon traitors Callum MacDonald and Malcolm MacLeod I'll wager, Ma: they've had a grudge against you ever since the Stella episode. They heard I was at

Mount Pleasant and started following Jenny every time she came to our secret trysting-place, an abandoned log cabin in the woods. Oh, we were that happy there! It was like being man and wife and we felt no shame in it – why should we, when there's such love between us and we're hurting nobody? – but the brother seems to have thought his sister's honour was threatened. He told her parents and they put her out!'

His voice rasped with bitterness and hate as he went on. 'Her mother was the worst. She behaved like one demented, saying she'd rather see her daughter dead than wed to a son of Flora MacDonald's. She was that fierce that my poor Jenny says she even feared for her life.'

'But Roddy? Did her father not intervene? It's monstrous, to disown your own daughter!'

Sandy's brows lowered. Flora realised with a spasm of dismay that the furrows his ordeal had etched on them were there for good. 'Jenny's father, for all his strengths in other ways, is but putty in that woman's hands. 'Tis as if he gave up fighting her and Alastair long ago just to achieve some kind of unstable domestic harmony. Jenny did say, though, that he sought her out when she was bundling up her things and pledged a father's love. Said too that he thought she'd be better off here with us, and that he trusts you to care for her now, Ma, more kindly than her own mother would.'

'He really said that?'

'Aye.'

All through Sandy's account Flora had been nursing her bitter, puzzled disappointment at what she saw as Roddy's hen-pecked weakness, but now a message was emerging that made sense. He was confidently entrusting his daughter to her, and silently she vowed that she would not fail him.

IV

January should have been a quiet month for the Anson County settlers, with bad weather restricting outside work, but 1776 defied the rule. Governor Martin, now existing precariously on the sloop *Scorpion*, issued a proclamation on the 10th, calling on the King's loyal subjects 'to put down this most horrid and unnatural rebellion that has been excited by traitorous, wicked and designing men'.

Flora sensed Allan's pent-up tension as the farmer in him retreated before the trained military man and he awaited the final call to arms. It came, couched in stirring if bombastic terms, on February 5th. Though she could not find it in her heart to prick the bubble of her husband's jubilation she still could not stifle the essentially female misgivings that stirred in her at the thought of all she loved being flung into the arena like pieces on a chess-board.

'The time has come at last!' Allan enthused. 'Seven regiments of British regulars on the sea, making for Brunswick! We shall crush the rebels right here in the Carolinas! No need to go north!'

He went on to explain how Martin had undertaken, under oath from Lord Dartmouth in London, to unite the North Carolina loyalists into a provincial corps that would march with horses and wagons to the coast, there to meet the British regulars from Ireland under Lord Cornwallis, and Henry Clinton's two thousand troops from Boston. The combined forces would then fan out to take the Carolinas while British armies from New England, New York and the south would crush resistance in the central colonies. The government was confident that loyalists would rally in their thousands, especially as various incentives were being offered to newly-settled Scots : their arrears of quit-rents would be cancelled and new grants of land would be exempt from rent for twenty years.

It was all high drama now. Allan's own locally recruited battalion, some three hundred and fifty strong, was detailed to stand by while Neil, Sandy, Jamie and a ghillie were despatched on horseback to the furthest corners of the county, each bearing a fiery cross.

Allan's order was deliberately histrionic, for well he knew the effect his impassioned appeal would have on those emotional Gaels.

'Lift high the cross, so that all can see it! Say little, but to name the meeting place: Cross Creek, under the oak tree in the square. And stress that they have but ten days to repair to the banner!'

Beacons burnt on the hills. Lachlan MacFarlane piped the ceòl mor and Highland blood stirred, throbbing to the memory of time-honoured rituals. Youth responded to the lure of adventure and even old men who had hoped never to experience the carnage of war again found themselves caught up in a swell of fervour. They did not stop now to consider that it was the hated Hanoverian they were defending: this was a fight for a new and precious homeland, a Scotland beyond the seas.

Never had Flora seen her husband so purposeful and virile. His energy erupted in feverish military preparations by day, while at night he needed but three or four hours' sleep and seemed to resent her exhaustion, pressing his attentions upon her whether she craved them or not. Loving him she could not find it in herself to deny him, but the emotional and physical toll was mounting. Surely even now some influential figure – the King himself, perhaps? – would step in and forbid this folly! But the eve of the muster came and brought no reprieve.

For many months afterwards she would recall the details of the last night before they marched. The sounds of it stayed with her, sharp and distinct as an etching – a fox barking, the sough of the wind in the pine trees, the rush of the creek after the recent rains. Smells, too: the odour of burnt wax when the candle was snuffed out; the mustiness of leaf-mould and moss in the dampness outside; above all the strong stench of the man beside her, a compound of tobacco and snuff, sweat and whisky and excitement.

He had wanted to talk, and she later reproached herself for falling into a doze despite her determination to stay awake.

'At least I know I've done everything possible to recruit and train those men,' he had said. 'I have a viable fighting force there. The rest is in the lap of the gods.'

Eventually she fell into a shallow, tortured sleep, his arm about her shoulders and his limbs interlaced with hers; he must have extricated himself with great tenderness and care, for when the darkness lightened to grey she was panic-stricken to find him gone.

An impenetrable mist shrouded the garden and outhouses, but she heard the rat-a-tat of a drum and the ugly opening belch of a bagpipe sounding from the direction of the mill and shuddered, all too aware of what it meant. Oh, why had she let Allan's passion for his cause persuade her to promote violence and bloodshed? Rousing battle-cries and martial tunes were not music to her ears: her soul responded to the gentler, feminine sounds of bird calls and the soothing lullabies of Gaeldom.

But knowing Allan was already in the thick of things she hurried to saddle Delilah and join him. Riding along the lane she urged herself to exude confidence but could not throw off the memory of a dream from the night before. Culloden. She had imagined herself at Culloden, among the gore and anguished cries, the gunsmoke, confusion and grief. How many of Allan's men, she wondered, felt the heavy shadow of that tragic battle yet lying upon them? Ironic that those very men who had been deprived of weapons by their Sassenach victors should now be rushing, virtually unarmed, to defend the interests of an English king.

For while Allan had done his utmost to make soldiers out of this First Battalion of the Anson Highlanders it was clear even to Flora's unmilitary eye that the little force was poorly armed. True, most of the officers carried pistols and long, straight, basket-handled swords, many of them family heirlooms like Allan's, but the commonest weapon was the farmer's fowling-piece, a flintlock musket some six feet long. Nor were the men adequately dressed for a stroll in the rain in peace-time, far less for an arduous military march: a few wore tartan plaids or trews; some of the officers on half pay sported ancient, green-moulded uniform coats that were much the worse for wear and exuded a foetid smell; but most were in buckskin breeks and home-made shoes of untanned hide stitched with leather thongs – the famous broghans of the Highlands.

Determinedly Flora pulled herself up in the saddle and willed herself to banish the phantoms of nightmare and doubt from her mind. Was the battalion not marching to reinforce professionals? And in the matter of courage who could hold a candle to the Gaels?

Some of the womenfolk had come already. They stood in a disconsolate huddle, shivering with cold. The indomitable Isobel MacLeod was there, and Peggy Campbell, as sour-faced as ever but staunchly determined to stand by Duncan now that he had decided to join Allan. Flora too. Her own kin.

But the air around them trembled with something other than the natural chill of the morning. Their hostility was almost palpable, and one by one they turned their backs on her when she greeted them. What had they hoped from her, she wondered – that she would somehow be strong enough to talk their men folk round to staying neutral where they themselves had not been able to?

Only Christian Bethune came over to her, took the hand she proffered, and murmured a gentle blessing before turning her gaze back to the tall straight figure of her son. John had finally agreed to act as chaplain to the troop – he could not let his spiritual charges down at a time of crisis – and Flora marvelled at how his calm gaze mirrored his mother's serenity.

John had just come from comforting Deirdre, who was inconsolable, muttering incoherently about impending disaster and death.

'My Neil has the sight,' she was moaning, 'and can see naught but trouble arising from this venture. Not that he would dare gainsay the master, but many a time he has told me of his fears.' Then, seeing Flora, 'Oh mistress, can ye not stop it yet? We know ye could, given the will to.'

Flora shook her head sadly. 'Forget these old superstitions, Deirdre,' was all she could bring herself to say. 'Concentrate instead on raising a smile. For Neil's sake.' And she rode over to where Allan was busily engaged in marshalling his men.

'Where's Papa Hugh? Has he not come yet?'

Allan laughed in disbelief. 'Not come? He was here before anybody! Wouldn't be surprised if he has been here all night. Slept in the mill, maybe. Takes his command too seriously, I'd say, but that's the way he is. He's over there, lass.'

Hugh was just a few yards distant, and was calling out commands in a weak, rasping voice that Flora scarcely recognised. In the half-light his face looked pinched and spectral, the face not of a military officer but of a man close to death. He had dismounted and she noticed he was limping badly.

The sight of him pulled Flora up short. 'Is he fit to go, do you think? He doesn't look able to ride from here to Cross Hill, far less to be in command!'

Allan let out a wry laugh. 'You just try to hold him back, Florrie, and you'll invite a fusillade of scorn, as well as causing him pique. I've suggested already that he might consider backing down but it's difficult for me, remember, as second in command. I daren't be over-forceful or he'll think I'm trying to oust him from his rightful rank. He is essentially a military man, proud to be known as the greatest swordsman in the Isles, and tends to see me as a mere cattleman, just incidentally a soldier. Any decision to resign command must come from him, and there's nobody in the world I'd more happily take orders from. He's a legend, lass.'

It was then, as Allan veered off to superintend the loading of a wagon, that she saw young Jamie approach his grandfather and engage him in conversation. Edging closer she was just able to hear scraps of it.

'What did your father say to it?'

'He said no. That I have to stay with Ma. But I don't want to. I'm nearly eighteen. Old enough to go, and you all know it.'

'Don't make trouble for me, lad. He's your father. He knows best.'

Flora heard the weariness in the old man's voice, the longing to be free of the burden of making decisions.

'But you're in charge, Papa! You're the colonel. You can override my father if you want to enough! Please!'

A sigh of resignation from Hugh, then a relieved lift to his voice when he spotted Flora behind them.

'There's your Ma yonder. We'll see what she says.'

Flora felt her blood run cold. No need to guess what the conversation had been about. That Jamie, a mere stripling, should contemplate going to war! Squaring her shoulders she affected the air of the domineering matriarch, knowing all the while that the pose fooled nobody: the tremor in her voice betrayed her fear.

'I'm surprised at you, father, condoning such a thing even to the point of seeking my permission. No, Jamie! I absolutely forbid it. You stay here!'

To her surprise they seemed to accept her verdict. Jamie looked crestfallen while Hugh, after a swift, knowing glance, bowed his head in feigned humility and changed the subject. It was only much later that she would realise that the debate was far from over.

'So be it then, Florrie. But I was talking to Allan a while back and 'twas suggested that you and Jamie might come with us as far as Cross Creek, gin it please you. 'Twould cheer the men to have you with us.'

So the partings could be postponed and the vexed question of Jamie's recruitment be left in suspension for a few more days. She could have her menfolk's company, the chance to doctor their ills and nurture them. It was what she had been put on this earth to do and for a brief moment her heart almost sang.

The light mood mercifully stayed with her as the little army moved away from the mill, down the lane, through the farmyard and past the house. She rode beside Allan and Hugh, Sandy and Jenny and Jamie, all six of the family group on horseback. The servants followed on foot, leading the pack horses laden with the woefully meagre supplies of arms, blankets and food. Drums rattled and the pipes played.

Passing Kingsburgh's door she was on the alert for good omens, and was quick to notice the green spears of daffodil leaves pricking through a lingering patch of snow.

'See, Allan! the Flodigarry bulbs! They're up already! It's a sign of hope. I know it!'

Usually such comments elicited an exasperated growl but to her surprise he shook his head fondly. 'You are incorrigible, woman! Here we are, marching off to war, and you prate to me of daffodils!'

It was said with a wondering affection that made her want to lean over and kiss him right there and then, but Delilah suddenly neighed, disapprovingly she fancied, and broke into a trot. It was only then that Flora realised to her dismay that it was pouring with rain and Kingsburgh had vanished behind the trees.

V

On February 10th the Kingsburgh contingent arrived at Cross Hill in Cumberland County, home of Sandy Morrison of Skinidin. As a scion of the nineteenth chief of MacLeod Sandy had brought three hundred clansmen from Skye in 1771, and had had no compunction about pressing them into service in his friend Glendale's Second Battalion. Alex's recruiting drive had also borne fruit and brought in new volunteers from far and near. Some of those were 'country born' men and their arrival had been totally unexpected. Alexander Legate, a member of the Committee of Safety in Bladen County, had defected to their side, as had Thomas Rutherford, although the dyed-in-the-wool patriot Alex McAlister was his wife's cousin. They had both brought welcome companies of Regulators to swell the Highland ranks.

Again those pathetic gatherings of women and children with their familiar blend of stoicism and dread. Here were the redoubtable elderly couple Kathie and Donald Campbell from McLendon's Creek, and their daughter Barbara MacLeod. Barbara's eyes refused to lose sight of her husband Alex as he rode among the men issuing orders, while her parents clung to their son John, fearing they would never see him again. They also found themselves greeting their two newly-arrived sons-in-law whom they had not seen for many months, and their grandson John Bethune.

'So you'll be seeing to the men's souls, John.' There was a noticeable catch in Kathie's timmertoned voice.

'Aye, Granny. 'Twas against my heart's wish to go to war but the Lord would have me where I am most needed.'

It was spoken with quiet dignity. Flora saw the folds of the old woman's face quiver and wondered if she was going to give way to tears but she managed a watery smile and said simply, 'We're proud of you, laddie. See you come back safe.'

But Flora's own Anne had to be the most broken-hearted of them all. In six days' time she would be twenty-two, and was heavily pregnant with her fourth child. For many months now she had existed in an agony of loneliness and worry while Alex ranged the country in the King's cause, and now here she was, gamely trying to smile as she took her leave of him.

Allan and Norman stood solemnly by her, clearly sensing that something of consequence was afoot.

'Where's Pa going? And Granpa? And Papa Hugh?'

'They're off to fight the Americans. But they'll all be home soon. Never fear.'

'But are we not all Americans now?'

'Wheesht, Allan. See. There's Granma.' And she had turned to embrace Flora, her eyes full of tears.

The boy had fallen silent for a moment and then said gravely,

'Don't worry, Ma. I shall take Pa's place while he is gone. Just as I'm sure Jamie will look after you, Granma.'

Flora felt as if a knife twisted in her chest then, but quickly drew the boy's attention to all that was going on around them.

'See how busy your Uncle Kenneth is.'

'Yes. Pa says he's the aide de camp. What does that mean, granma?'

'It's a kind of assistant to the officer in charge, who's your father of course.'

The boy's eyes were shining with pride. 'Oh, how I wish I were old enough to go too!'

But by now Torquil MacLeod the drill-master, who had served in the regular army, was exhorting the men into something approaching marching order. The pipes had started to skirl. Allan favoured his daughter and the children with a last brief embrace but clearly his mind was elsewhere. He was fuming at the cowardliness of some Regulators who, having agreed to join them, had turned and fled when they caught sight of a party of Whigs.

'Lily-livered louts! They're reported to have said that since Tryon disarmed them nobody had the right to expect them to fight! We're better off without such unruly scum, I say! Give me my own people, clansmen I can trust, and to hell with cowards!'

* * *

So by the 15th, the appointed day, they were established in Cross Creek, where their numbers were again augmented by recruits from all over the area. This was to be the final test of local loyalists' allegiance, and Allan was immediately caught up in the task of allotting ranks and positions in his battalion.

'Hugh has at last seen sense and decided to resign his command to me, and I must say I'm glad of it. Glad too that I did not press him. It was his own decision. He comes with us, of course, but only in a voluntary capacity.'

'Thank God. I was not happy seeing him with all that responsibility on his old shoulders. How many are we, all told?'

'Around three thousand I reckon. Not as many as Martin had hoped for, of course, but doubtless many will still join us on the way. Murdoch MacLeod will be our doctor, and they say Tom Cobham's coming as well.'

Ah, Tom. Flora wondered grimly what the good doctor from Wilmington's friend, Roddy Boyd, would have to say about that.

'Aaron Vardy is wagon-master-general,' Allan was continuing. 'Malcolm MacLean's the recruiting agent, and each battalion is to appoint an adjutant, and a quarter-master to find lodgings and tents, and a commissary to be in charge of food and clothing.'

He broke off abruptly then, his brows knitting in concentration. 'What's that infernal racket yonder? I can't hear myself speak! I trust they aren't ours, these drunkards! Fegs, but we need some discipline around here!'

Flora looked over to where the group of rowdy Highlanders had gathered and let out a sigh of mingled exasperation and indulgence when she spotted Iain MacRae's red head in the midst of them. Trust him to see the occasion as a blend of the cavalier and the carnival, and himself as the fount of martial fervour. As ever the life and soul of the party, he was yelling out the words of the current rallying song.

'Haste Donald, Duncan, Dugald, Hugh!
Haste, take your sword and spier!
We'll gar these traytors rue the hour
That e'er they ventured here.'

'We have too many like that Iain MacRae,' Allan said tersely. 'They drown their fears in usquebaugh, then can't see to draw a sword when the time comes. But let them roister. I have my own men to see to, and I've arranged to meet Caleb Touchstone. He has a superlative rifle. Says he'll let me have it for £7.'

'We must be very wealthy all of a sudden.'

Flora could not resist the jibe and found it hard to keep an element of bitterness out of her voice. In this matter of spending money Allan seemed to have thrown caution to the winds. He had already paid over £30 to Messrs Marshall and Miller for nine stands of arms to equip his men, and George Miller had persuaded him to buy a silver-mounted rifle as well, which had set him back another £9. Blankets, shoes, shirts, a cask of rum to maintain the men's health and morale on the march – all those were being met out of Kingsburgh's fast-diminishing personal resources. The demands on him seemed never-ending.

She had half expected Allan to fly into a rage at her snide comment but instead he went on the defensive.

'Now don't quibble, Flora. Please! Some officers have had to pay out even more. Take Alex yonder. He has had to pay £85 on thirty guns for his men, and £6 for swords and pistols, and Donald MacDougald is making colours for him into the bargain.'

For an unguarded moment a treacherous thought sidled into Flora's mind then. While Alex, like Allan, was sparing no expense in the King's cause, poor Anne and her children were the ones who suffered. What if – it was the mere wisp of a possibility, certainly, but it kept brushing like a butterfly's wings against her carefully-fostered certainty of victory – what if something went wrong?

Determinedly she thrust the disloyal doubts aside and concentrated on what Allan was saying.

His voice had taken on a note of wheedling self-justification.

'The government has promised to return all our expenses in full when the revolt is put down. And 'tis necessary, lass, as you must see. You would not have our kin and ghillies march to war garbed like those pitiful Regulators yonder?'

Admittedly those newly-arrived recruits were a sorry-looking lot. Shambling, unschooled peasants for the most part, they had glum bucolic faces and walked hen-toed, like Indians: indeed Flora wondered if many of them had native blood in them. What was more, their attitude towards the newly-settled Scots was far from friendly. They saw her as a foreign incomer and her husband as an upstart who had helped foment trouble. She had seen knots of Regulators gathering in the square, had heard the gist of their conversation and felt the chill of their scorn as she passed.

'There's that Flora MacDonald,' one had shouted, loudly so that she was bound to hear. 'Hey, Miz MacDonald ma'am, when's Governor Martin comin' wid them thousand troops he promised? For if he don' come soon we's hiein' us home to our farms. 'Tis nearly seed-plantin' time.'

So she was scarcely surprised when two days into their stay Allan came to her and complained that many of them were filtering away homewards. Indeed of the three thousand Regulators Martin had optimistically believed he could rally to his cause only two hundred would take part in the march.

'We march tomorrow, no matter what the weather. We cannot afford to lose any more men to rumour and unrest, and to the temptations of the town. Discipline breaks down when country folks that haven't met for months find themselves all of a sudden close to whorehouses and taverns and rollicking roosters like Iain MacRae.'

Then a note of pleading came into his voice. 'I know you don't court the limelight, Florrie, but the campaign has reached a stage where it needs a rallying voice to focus it. They would see you as a symbol of Highland unity. You will speak to them, and perhaps remind them of the gravity and rightness of our loyalist cause?'

Well she knew that for many here she was far from being a heroine. Many of the older Lowlanders remembered her only as the rebel who had befriended the Pretender, and not everyone was a friend of the 'new Scotch'.

But every straw had to be clutched. 'If you think 'twould do an ounce of good, of course I shall do what I can.'

So next morning the bugle sounded to summon the army. Flora had stationed herself under the oak tree, a small but uprightly defiant figure on her white mare, and at the sight of her blue bonnets were flung high and the square echoed to shouts of triumphant greeting. She started her speech of exhortation but her words were drowned in a clamour of cheering. No need for her to say anything: her very presence was enough.

So successful had she been in boosting morale that the march to Campbellton started off on a wave of optimism and national pride. Banners waved and pipes skirled – not to the satisfaction of Donald MacCrummen, though, whose officer rank precluded him from piping. Few paused to register the shortcomings of the hastily-convened, essentially disparate force, or to consider that the vast army Martin had predicted consisted of but fifteen hundred men, more than a third of them unarmed.

Certainly Allan MacDonald felt nothing but pride as he scanned the ranks and noted the predominance of his clan tartan.

''Tis a MacDonald rising, Flora, or so they say.'

And she, for once infected by his exuberance, called confidently back, 'That pleasures me well. Let them see how MacDonalds can fight.'

VI

It continued to rain, a persistent misty drizzle that would not have been out of place on Skye, but Flora rode doggedly on, determined to be part of this incohesive clamjamfry of an army. As they approached Campbellton, however, Allan manoeuvred his horse alongside and begged her to turn back and make for home.

'This march is not for women, Flora. You have played your part, and that nobly and to good effect. Now your place is at home, running Kingsburgh. The corn seed has to be planted and the cattle seen to, and you know how important it is that the remaining servants be supervised. Please, Florrie. I need to know that you are in charge while we are gone.'

'And Jenny?'

'She will go with you. Sandy insists upon it. But Florrie' – Flora's heart began unaccountably to beat like a fist against her ribs – 'Jamie is determined to come with us and I must give him his head in this. We have cosseted him for too long, I think. He is not a boy any more and certainly no pansy. So I have asked Alexander to take him under his wing. Better he be with his uncle.'

Flora was reminded now of the '45, when family members had served in different units to provide some measure of insurance against the possibility of a whole male line being wiped out: for the same reason some had even chosen to fight on opposite sides. Suddenly the enormity of their situation struck with all the force of a physical blow and she almost cried out in anguished protest. None of her menfolk left! Not a single one! And today was Sandy's twenty-first birthday! He ought to be celebrating with his friends and family at Kingsburgh or marrying Jenny, not marching off to war!

She felt tears running down her cheeks, mingling with the concentrated downflow of raindrops from the pine trees. Then it was as if an oppressive weight descended on her head and a hysterical scream took form there, vainly beating against the indifferent void. She swayed helplessly in the saddle in a moment of total blankness.

Then Allan's voice came from a great distance. She felt his arms round her and his comforting presence steadying her.

'You see, Flora, you are not strong enough to ride these paths in winter. Please obey me in this.'

The deciding factor, though, was not Flora's compliance or Allan's insistence but the approach of Donald MacDonald, who peremptorily claimed Allan's attention in a brief, incisive exchange after which Allan returned with resolve writ large on his features.

"'Tis an order now, Florrie. Farquhard Campbell has turned up. He has scouts everywhere and their latest word is that James Moore's regiment is encamped at Rockfish Bridge, just six miles away. Lillington and Caswell's militia and minutemen are marching to join them. So Farquhard advises us to outflank and outmarch them by crossing the river and marching to the coast down the east side, by Negro Head Road. 'Twill mean a forced march, Flora, fording swollen rivers with wagons and horses, crossing swamps and keeping a constant watch for enemy sorties that would encircle us. You women have to go. Your very presence would exacerbate our problems.'

Flora felt herself blanch. Was Allan exaggerating their plight, or had the campaign indeed crystallised into a pell-mell race to the coast? A chilling, treacherous thought stole unbidden into her mind: if the Highlanders reached Wilmington safely only to discover that the British fleet was still at sea, what then? They would be marching to nowhere! Angrily she brushed the intrusive misgiving aside as she would a troublesome mosquito. Of course the British would be there. They had to be. They had promised.

Meanwhile Allan was adding yet another argument to his plea. 'There are rumours, too, that Whig troops are marching on Cross Creek, from Hillsboro' under Colonel Thackston and from Salisbury under Colonel Martin. You must be out of town before they get there.'

His reasoning was incontrovertible, and when the army halted for a brief rest stop at Campbellton the command's policy of shedding its every encumbrance became doubly obvious. A motley, rain-drenched group of camp-followers had already gathered – women, children, and old people – and were being herded into wagons. In their midst, patiently helping, was Farquhard, and seeing Flora he rode up and doffed his bonnet.

'I hear you were an inspiration back there, Flora. It's a true heroine you are still, and no mistake. But you must get back to Kingsburgh now, lass. Your work is done. See Peter yonder? I suggest you give your mare into his charge and we'll see to it that you and Jenny get safely home in my phaeton.'

What an enigma this Campbell was. Impossible to disentangle his complex motives or ascertain where his political loyalties really lay. Why was he befriending her and Jenny when he had sat on countless Whig committees and was one of the Boyds' best friends? Was he for a new evolving America or did he favour even stronger ties with Britain? Or did politics not really matter to him at all, as long as he protected his own wealth and the security of his family? Puzzlingly ambiguous he might be but right then Flora scarcely cared. His very presence, affectionate and reassuring, was a godsend.

Everything – the pressure under which the army marched, the worsening weather, the need to avoid those enemy forces heading for Cross Creek – demanded haste, so that their farewells, while not exactly perfunctory, were necessarily brief. So many things left unsaid, Flora thought, as she clung to Allan in a last poignant embrace and took her sons to her bosom in an agony of desperate, soul-searing love.

Frenzied with grief, her pale blonde hair suddenly haloed by a vagrant shaft of sunlight, Jenny sat in the carriage wringing her hands and weeping copiously.

'I don't want to lose Sandy!' she sobbed. 'Oh, it's too cruel that he should be leaving us on this day of all days, when we should all be rejoicing!'

Flora's distress, though equally deep, was beyond tears now. Her wretchedness lay like a stone in her heart. Lost, cold and alone she felt herself hovering on the brink of some hideously yawning pit and did not have the will to draw back. As Allan helped her into the carriage she felt a weak protest on her lips but knew resistance was hopeless. There was a scraping of hooves, a squelching of wheels in the mud, and they were off. A last lingering look behind afforded only a dismal blur of shambling men in buckskins and dirty tartan, the depressing rearguard of the loyalists' fragmentary army. Then even they disappeared into the ubiquitous pines and all that remained was the thin wail of the pipes, a melancholy counterpoint to the juddering rattle of the phaeton.

VII

The rain persisted for days after Flora's return home and she moved, dull-eyed and dispirited, in the limbo of fear Kingsburgh had now become. She longed for the clarity of frost to bring some sparkle to the landscape but every outward scene lacked definition, existing only in shades of grey. The weather prevented all but the most necessary and routine outdoor tasks and so she forced herself to work at her spinning-wheel, or in the kitchen, simples room or dairy shed. She knew that without something to divert her mind from its nightmarish imaginings she would descend into total despair.

Living as she did in such relentless misery she knew that her efforts to cheer Jenny rang false. The nausea of early pregnancy and a succession of tormented nights had reduced the girl to a silent wraith, impervious to comfort. Unnaturally pale and thin, she jumped nervously whenever anyone came near her, ate next to nothing, and seemed to collapse exhausted after attempting even the least demanding domestic tasks.

'You must make an effort to help me, Jenny,' Flora would plead. 'There's so much to do, without the men.'

And indeed there was, for the servants who remained were on edge too, waiting for word. They were ingenuously credulous of every rumour that wafted, ultimate source unknown, through the settlement, and listening to them Flora could not but be affected by their insidious pessimism. Dread fretted the floor of her stomach as if some cancer had lodged there.

For every one of the rumours was bad. 'They' – that amorphous, omniscient entity that controls the mechanism of hearsay – spread tidings of deceit and disaster, slaughter and mayhem for General MacDonald's army. They spoke of a rout at Widow Moore's Creek, said that the cream of the Highlanders, some fifty of them, had been killed or wounded as they tried to cross a bridge that the Americans had previously greased with tallow and partially dismantled. The remaining loyalists, so they said, were scattered throughout the colony, and even now bands of them were being picked off by Moore's scouts and carried away as prisoners to Hillsboro', or Halifax, or even Philadelphia. For the loyalist cause there was now no hope, no hope at all.

Morag's hysterical outbursts always irritated Flora, however, and after one particularly gory litany her anger flared. 'I forbid my maids to listen to this pernicious gossip! 'Tis but a tissue of foul lies put about by those who would dishearten us! Now dry your eyes and get back to cleaning the silver! I will not have the master returning to find his home a neglected midden!'

Despite her exasperation, though, the circumstantial detail of the reports worried her. She had not been to Widow Moore's Creek – it was on the north-east Cape Fear and she was familiar only with the north-west branch of the river – but she could visualise the typical dismal landscape of stinking, stagnant pocosins and dark, dripping pines. She came then to dread the nights, when sleep brought no solace but only gruesome nightmares in which Allan, Sandy and Jamie floundered and sank in an alien wilderness of glaur. Facing each new day hollow-eyed and unrested she tried to remain even-tempered and sympathetic in her dealings with the servants but their unmitigated gloom irked her beyond measure. She tried to recognise that their illiteracy and gullibility made them the natural prey of rumour-mongers, that it was just their way to delight in superstition and feed upon syllogisms, and the more she scolded them the shiftier and more sullen they would become, but one day her patience snapped.

Entering the kitchen unseen, she had found Deirdre and Morag absorbed in a macabre conversation, the details of which sent her stomach heaving.

'They're dead, every one, their bodies lying black and bloated in the swamp. Malcolm Cameron saw it happen. He alone, it seems, has won back home to tell the tale.' Morag's voice had a remote, keening quality, as if she were reciting some ancient ballad about bloody battles long ago.

Flora felt herself shudder but even as her flesh crept some residual logic told her that Morag was revelling in her recital of horrors.

Not so Deirdre. She had clapped her work-worn hands over her ears and was rocking back and forth as if hypnotised. ''Tis as Neil said 'twould be. He saw it in a vision, long ere we came here. I aye said we dare not spurn the prophesies of them that have the gift. Eeeeeee ...'

That last high-pitched cry came from a time before words. It

For Promised Joy

was the lamentation, pure and elemental, of a woman abysmally bewildered and bereft, and hearing it Flora flew into an uncontrollable rage.

'Quiet, both of you! Just see what you've done, Morag! You would drive us all mad with your melodramatic lies!'

She had always made it a point of pride never to strike a servant; even Stella, who had provoked her to exasperation and beyond, had never felt her hand. But the slap that she delivered now to Morag's pasty cheek left the outline of finger-marks and sent the girl reeling back in a second of appalled disbelief. Then the bovine face flamed in an outburst of retaliatory anger and humiliation, and she launched into a long string of Gaelic vituperations the like of which Flora had not heard since that far-off April day at Flodigarry – could it be just two years before? – when Marion Martin had showered her with curses.

''Twas you that made them go! You that sent them all to death and perdition! A pox upon you, Mistress Flora MacDonald!'

The sarcasm and hatred in that one word, 'Mistress', the shock of being so reviled by a mere servant, the unconscionable impertinence of it all! The whole bombardment of insults merited only one response from Flora and she was quick to voice it. 'Get out of my house! I have no wish to set eyes on you ever again!'

Frozen-faced the girl made for the door and Flora realised that she could not stop shaking. Deirdre lifted a tear-stained face and said, respectfully but firmly, 'Did you need to do that, Mistress MacDonald? We're that short of help about the place, and I greatly fear that dismissing Morag will cause feeling among the others.'

'Then so be it. Better a few that are faithful than a nest of viperous, insubordinate troublemakers.'

Seeing Deirdre's genuine distress, though, Flora felt her anger evaporate. Her hand came out to touch the older woman's trembling shoulder in a gesture of silent sympathy.

'You really think the men will be back, Ma'am, that 'tis all rumour, what we're hearing? Oh, I'm that afeared for my Neil! Say they will come home, that the stories are but wild surmise!'

Flora summoned all the conviction she could into her answer then. 'Yes, Deirdre, they will be back. They are in the Lord's hands. Why not go now and make some tea? We deserve it, I think.'

'Tea?' Deirdre's eyes lit up. 'There is yet some left?'

They sat then in the blue shadows, no longer mistress and servant but friends reconciled to waiting, and drank the fragrant brew. While offering temporary comfort, however, it did not banish their fears. Flora knew that Morag's defection was symptomatic of a simmering resentment not just at Kingsburgh but throughout the whole neighbourhood. She had been noticing that few greeted her with open, welcoming smiles any more. Some, her own half-sister Flora MacQueen among them, even ignored her presence. She sensed their antipathy but was determined to endure. She had to believe, absolutely had to, that the march to Wilmington had gone on unhindered.

VIII

March 1776

It snowed at the end of February just when they were expecting signs of spring, and as so often happens with unseasonable weather the freeze was as intense as it was brief. Cruel, swirling winds rattled the black dead branches of the trees and penetrated every cranny, curling sneakily into Kingsburgh's living space and chilling its occupants to the bone. Flora saw the brave green spikes of her daffodils vanish under a blanket of white and felt her thoughts smothered with a sadness as relentless as the snowdrifts. Time and distance no longer held any perspective for her. Nothing consoled, not the fire that burnt daily in the hearth, nor her morning porridge, nor yet the clean clothes that appeared freshly laundered as if at some magician's behest.

It was only as the mists of her despair gradually dissipated that she identified her benefactors and blessed them. Deirdre had never left her side, a penitent Morag had returned on hearing of her mistress's depression, and she had had two staunch helpers in Stella and Hannibal.

Deirdre was unstinting in her praise of the negroes. 'Just emerged from the woods one morning, they did. Said they were perishing with cold and would do anything I asked of them in return for a bed of straw in the stables. To tell you the truth, ma'am, they weren't in that bad shape. Wouldn't be surprised if they'd been robbing white folks to keep alive. Not that I was going to hint at that, mind you, I was too glad to have their young able bodies to help about the place.'

Flora was all contrition. 'Well, you have me firmly back in place now and I promise not to let you down again.'

She looked out over the bleak, featureless landscape, wondered what she could say to sound a note of cheer, and actually dredged up some words of assurance. 'At least the men won't be facing this kind of cold down Wilmington way. The winters are never so severe, so they say, down on the Tidewater.'

She heard the tremor in her voice, knew she could not sustain the tone of conviction, and quickly cast about for some subject less fraught with emotion. 'Tell me, Deirdre. How are the others? Christian, Peggy and Isobel, and Flora? I have not heard a word from them.'

She rightly suspected that Peggy, Isobel and Flora were silent because they blamed her for their present distress, but surely Christian was with her in spirit?

Deirdre's reply confirmed this. 'Mistress Bethune, so they say, refuses to believe that her son is dead, and bears her worries with a courage that does credit to her name. The others' – her face clouded over and she hesitated – 'the others are not well disposed towards you, and are all too ready to fear the worst. They say Flora MacQueen's sick. A wasting illness. She pines for her father.'

Flora felt a petulant protest rush to her lips and almost blurted out, 'And so do I!' as she had a sudden, unbearable mental image of Hugh's black eye-patch, the stooping gait and shock of white hair. Where was the gentle old man who had brightened her girlhood with his kindness? Would she ever see him again? Then remorse hit her. She had been so consumed with her own grief that she had neglected her neighbourly duties. Normally she would have met the other women regularly at church, but services had been suspended during the minister's absence and the prayer meetings she had held instead in the great room had been restricted to her own household. She vowed to rectify the situation as soon as the snow stopped. It was her duty, the least she could do for the missing menfolk.

And the weather did indeed change, though not immediately.

The thaw only came after three disconcerting days when rain and frost, sunshine and fog, seemed to fight for dominance. Then suddenly she realised that the snow had vanished and it was spring. On a wave of optimism she decided to make those calls. Where to go first? Christian, who lived furthest away, it might be wise to leave until another day, and Isobel and Peggy were so close by that visiting them presented no problem. Flora it would be then. She would take a jar of cranberry jelly and maybe even a packet of precious tea from her fast-dwindling supply: Flora was known far and wide for her enjoyment of a good cup of tea.

The unaccustomed sun dazzled her eyes as she saddled Delilah. Her peripheral vision took in great swathes of blue sky, green fields and the distinct, heart-lifting outlines of the distant Uwharies, scarcely visible in summer when the forest trees were in leaf and the air less clear. She noticed that the Flodigarry bulbs had survived and the shoots had thrust higher, their tips thickening to buds. A bird sang somewhere. It was an afternoon designed specially to foster hope, and Flora felt the first surge of physical wellbeing she had experienced since Allan's departure.

The mare seemed to sense her purposeful optimism and chafed impatiently, anticipating the ride. The last dregs of a lingering doubt about the wisdom of her mission filtered away from Flora's mind. Surely the track would be passable between here and Mountain Creek. It was only a mile or two. Delilah and she rode it regularly, and they could always turn back if they met a snag. As for the object of her expedition, she knew in her heart that she was doing the right thing, calling on Flora MacQueen. Even if her gesture elicited only the usual dour irritability she would at least have the personal satisfaction of having made it. The woman was her half-sister after all. High time they banished the tacit resentment that had existed for too long between them.

Her wishful thoughts of sisterly reconciliation kept her mind quite pleasantly preoccupied as Delilah, undeterred by the mud, trotted easily along the open path that skirted Cheek's Creek. It was only when they cut away into the trees and came on a section of bridle path where the sun had not penetrated that the mare suddenly stumbled and alerted Flora to the change in conditions. Here under the canopy patches of unmelted snow were still treacherously rimed with frost. Sternly she told herself to exercise extra care and concentrate on her riding, and it was with considerable relief that she eventually emerged from the gloom and saw the tumbling waters of Mountain Creek ahead. The MacQueen house, a substantial two-storey building of white-painted logs, gleamed a welcome just over yonder. Flora gave Delilah a little spur of encouragement and they cantered hopefully towards it.

But that expected welcome was slow to materialise. After dismounting and tying Delilah's reins to a tree Flora stood for fully five minutes on the threshold, feeling cold and increasingly uneasy. Of course, she thought, Flora might not be able to acknowledge her knock, for wasn't she reported to be ill? Better then just to open the door and shout through. So with sisterly confidence she raised her hand to the latch and was on the point of opening the door when someone pulled it violently from inside and there stood Flora MacQueen, her face flaming with feverish indignation.

'And what might you be wanting, coming poking around my house when you haven't been invited?'

The accusatory tone caught Flora totally unawares. 'I ... I just came to see how you were,' she stammered. 'I heard you weren't keeping too well and thought I'd bring you some jelly, and a wee bag of tea.'

For a moment the little blackcurrant eyes glittered with greed and Flora reflected grimly that perhaps her half-sister's love of tea, one of the few traits that marked her as human, would persuade her to open the door wide and invite her in. But instead the jaundiced face screwed up in a paroxysm of hate and a torrent of pent-up bitterness came spitting out.

'You would dare to bring me tea! Governor's tea, the stuff he used to bribe you to his way of thinking! 'Twas Martin's flattery that swayed you and Allan to his cause and brought us all to the sorry pass we're in this day. A pox on your tea! 'Tis poison! Take it away!' And ignoring Flora's feeble protest she banged the door shut.

For a moment Flora stood incredulous on the doorstep, shaken to the core by this unprecedented display of hostility. This was the first time she had openly quarrelled with any of her step-relatives, and while Flora had never been her favourite she had always attributed the antipathy to a mutually acknowledged difference in temperament: as long as she handled the MacQueens with kid gloves they had all rubbed together quite amicably, until today. The gauntlet was clearly down now, however, and all she could do was leave with all the dignity she could muster. So knowing that Flora was probably watching from behind the kitchen curtains she gulped back her humiliation, squared her shoulders, and walked back to where Delilah was waiting.

But a wedge of pain had settled in her heart and even the day's brightness could not dispel the hurt. Blinded by tears of frustration and bewilderment she forgot the exigencies of the road and left its negotiation to Delilah. Her head teemed with questions. How was she to heal this festering resentment? Did everyone in the neighbourhood feel this way, and if so how was she to continue to live among them? Above all, where were the men who would pooh-pooh all this petty cattiness, Allan and Sandy and Hugh and Jamie, not to mention Alex and Alexander and all the others?

When they entered the glade where the terrain had been slippery earlier in the afternoon a retrospective word of caution whispered in her mind, but it was soon crowded out by the far more pressing considerations of the war and its devastating consequences. When Delilah completely lost her footing Flora was caught unawares and was appalled to feel herself being pitched from the saddle. Instinctively she thrust out an arm to break the fall and landed awkwardly with the limb twisted under her body. There was a sickening crack as a rending pain shot up her arm, so commanding that she could not even attempt to haul herself out of the frost-encrusted slush of the track. She heard Allan's voice in her head: idiot, he was saying, riding abroad in this weather to visit someone who doesn't care a docken for you. I thought you'd have had more sense, Flora MacDonald. The words were vibrating, jumbled and senseless, in her inner ear as she blacked out.

She would never know precisely how long she had lain there unconscious but it must have been some time because when she came to a shaft of pale watery sunshine was penetrating the glade at a low angle and she was rigid with cold. She felt as if her clothes were being frozen fast to the hoary bridle-path and it suddenly struck her that she might well perish here, as inertly insignificant as a tree-branch randomly tossed to the ground in a storm.

Tentatively she made to pull the injured arm out from under her, only to experience another wave of nausea and stabbing pain. Then she heard a sharp snort at her right ear and swivelled her eyes round to see that Delilah was a mere ten feet away from her. The animal had righted herself and was now patiently cropping an isolated patch of grass she had found on the forest floor.

'Delilah. Come closer, lass.'

The mare looked mildly up, abandoned her snack with a resigned toss of the head, and clomped over to her mistress's side, seemingly regarding it as quite normal that Flora should want to mount her from this ridiculous prone position.

Pulling herself on to her feet was sheer agony but Flora knew she had to do it or die. The shooting pain darted up her arm with each tentative movement and every muscle in her body seemed locked in a crushing cramp, but she gritted her teeth and somehow dragged herself on to the animal's back. The rest of the journey home, though only three miles, was an excruciating blur of pain. Handling the reins to steer Delilah in the right direction was quite beyond her. She had to depend entirely on the beast's instinct and experience to carry her, slumped helplessly in the saddle, back to Kingsburgh.

Deirdre had been out collecting eggs in the farmyard and when she spotted her injured mistress the surprise on her face turned to the scarcely-disguised exasperation of a mother reproaching a wayward child. 'Lawd-a mercy, woman, whatever's happened to you?' she called, her voice harsh as she rushed to help.

Flora felt too weak to summon up a retort. She slid painfully from the saddle and would have fallen in a crumpled heap had the housekeeper not been beside her, steadying her. Hannibal also materialised from somewhere in that almost uncanny way he had, and together the two of them half-carried Flora into the kitchen, Deirdre still clucking her concern.

'Morag! Hot water and a flannel! And hurry! I don't have all day! The mistress is hurt!' There was a peevish edge to Deirdre's voice. She and Morag had not been seeing eye to eye since that bitter altercation with Flora: all right for a housekeeper to harbour private reservations about the war and the missing men but for a mere minion like Morag to air her views was insolence itself. Now Flora wondered whether she was just imagining that Morag took an unconscionably long time to fetch the water and bandages, and sighed at the disharmony that was affecting her household.

'Now sit you down here at the window where there's still some daylight left, and I'll get this arm bound up. I fear you've broken it.'

'Yes. All you can do is apply a hot fomentation to ease the pain and then wrap it up in a sling. 'Twill doubtless knit together in a week or two.'

The very effort of speaking seemed to compound the pain and tire her out, and with the weariness came black despair. She knew it would take much longer than a week or two to heal this break which she sensed was more than a simple fracture. And as for that other aching lesion in her heart, until she heard from Allan that could only get deeper.

IX

March 1776

Flora's descent into total despair was relentless and steady now. Whole days when she could do very little work on the farm. The injured arm ached perpetually, robbing her of sleep and torturing her waking hours. She took to sitting, deliberately isolated, in her favourite seat by the fireside with Beanie stretched out at her feet. Hating her own incapacity she felt herself wax irritable and had frequently to curb her tongue when she was tempted to lash out at the servants' shortcomings. She thought she read a resentment in their eyes, as if they suspected her of having purposely engineered her disability to complicate their lives. Only Stella and Hannibal remained properly respectful.

Had Jenny been of a different temperament she might have helped but she had succumbed to the apathy that always seemed to come on her when Sandy wasn't there. Though physically there was nothing amiss the girl had long since resigned herself to disaster and took in every ghoulish rumour with an acquiescent nod of the head. Normally this lumpish indifference would have angered and irritated Flora but she herself was too deep in gloom to react. The two women would therefore sit silently in different corners of the great room, Jenny pretending listlessly to sew, each wrapped in her own morbid thoughts. Fears that should have brought them together had only, it seemed, severed them irrevocably from one another.

But strangely enough it was the lethargic Jenny who first smelt danger the day Alastair Boyd came. Like snakes and animals growing restless ahead of lightning strikes or earthquakes she seemed to possess some preternatural antennae, programmed to respond to the clatter of distant hooves and the ring of menacing voices long before her normal senses apprehended them. Flora had just been aware of a low growl from Beanie, a pricking of ears and a shudder running through the animal's tawny hide, when a blood-curdling scream shattered the uneasy peace of the room. Jenny had rushed towards the window and was standing in a lather of demented agitation, her arms flailing and her eyes staring wildly. Her mouth opened in a speechless 'O' of terror and then the strangled words came out.

'They're coming! They're coming I tell you! They're going to murder us all!'

In the old days Flora would have put the outburst down to hysteria and would have argued that approaching horsemen did not necessarily mean an impending attack – why, it could be their menfolk coming home! – but the urgency and suddenness of it, coupled with the doe's jittery behaviour, forced her into a state of alertness.

'Quick! Out the back yard and down to the mill! Allan always said that was the best place to go!' As she spoke she was clutching at a bag of valuables she always kept beside her, containing the Prince's sheet, the brooch he had given her, some family jewellery and silver. But she threw the precious horde aside when the din outside precluded all thoughts of escape, and clutched the fireside poker instead. When Deirdre appeared at her side armed with the meat cleaver from the kitchen she reflected wryly that if this represented Kingsburgh's line of defence they might as well be wielding feather dusters.

But the thought had no sooner entered her head than the marauders burst in, bringing with them a blast of cold air and the reek of maleness and horse. There were three of them – Alastair

Boyd, Callum MacDonald and Malcolm MacLeod. All of them wore mudspattered homespun hunting shirts and deerskin leggings, and all three carried weapons.

Right away it was obvious that whatever damage Boyd was contemplating his first business was with Jenny. He strode up to where she had tried to hide, cowering, behind the heavy damask curtains and in one swift sweeping movement dragged the drapes from the wall. Then he put himself to battering her systematically, raining blows on her face and head until her features were unrecognisable and the floor around her drenched in blood.

When she eventually lay still he wiped his hands down his breeches and called over to his henchmen. 'Take this worthless strumpet that used to be my sister away. Rid us of her where you will. She is not of our kin any longer.'

His foxy green eyes swept the room then, taking in Flora and Deirdre's huddled forms by the fireside. The women's pathetic efforts to arm themselves were just the spur he needed to display the cold, contemptuous sarcasm that was his stock in trade.

'Ha! So yew thought to confront us, did yew? Well now, in't that real brave? But best take ma advice if yew want ta go on breathin in an' out real regular like. Ah'll be havin' that there poker for a start, ma'am.'

So saying he yanked the poker out of Flora's hand with a deft flick of the basket-hilted sword he was carrying. The steel did not touch her but she flinched, expecting to feel its point, knowing full well that he had no intention of sparing her. Nor had he. He was merely turning his attention elsewhere, to her pathetically-swathed arm.

'Aw. Now in't that a shame! Come on. Let me hiv a look at it, see if it's hurt bad enough to keep yew quiet, yew thrawn Highland bitch yew!'

As he spoke he moved the sword in little exploratory circles round the linen bandage, gradually tearing away the successive layers while Flora willed herself not to cry out. This man must be mad, she thought. How else to explain the slavering foam at his mouth, the savagery in his eyes, the brutal snarl that pretends to be laughter? As he drew close she tried not to gag at the rancid brandy-and-sweat smell of him, and to avoid those eyes she concentrated on the moon-shaped silver badge on his hat, with its

vainglorious legend, 'Liberty or Death.' Strange, she thought, how
both sides make the same claims and flourish similar slogans:
maybe they both think they have God on their side.

'Pay attention, woman!'

So her apparent impassivity was rankling. Perhaps that would
be her weapon. With a great effort she pulled her eyes downwards,
skirting his glare, and for the first time her gaze rested on the long
sword with its intricately-chased handle. Allan's sword, the very
one he had inherited from his father! The one he had been carrying
as he rode off to war that wet February morning!

'Aha! So yew recognise it, do yew? Aye, 'tis indeed your man's,
wrenched off him at Moore's Creek. A trophy of war, and all mine
now. Ah jes wish Ah'd had the pleasure o' running him through
wid it, the bastard, but he got away. Somebody else would track
him down though, that's for sure, for few o' the runagates got very
far. Ah guess yew all can jes get used ta the notion that he ain't
comin' back here no more.'

Each stunning declaration was timed to coincide with another
jab of the sword, until on the final words the last shred of material
fell away and a searing pain shot up Flora's arm. Looking down
she saw a long bloody gash where the sword-point had slit her
flesh. Nor was her tormentor finished. He was continuing
sadistically to run the blade up and down the wound, savouring
her agony. She felt the room sway. Noises jangled in her head –
Alastair's measured mockery, horses whinneying outside, pleading
sobs from the servants.

And something else that she found hard to identify at first, a
mordant, snarling cough that was somewhere between a horse
braying and a dog growling. Glancing down she realised then that
Beanie had sprung up from her station by the ingle. She felt the
rough texture of the animal's tongue against her free palm, saw
the pale pelt bristle aggressively. No roaring stag this, no wild
denizen of mountain and crag prepared in the fullness of its might
to take on all comers, but a half-grown domesticated doe, gently
nurtured and unacquainted with violence. Beanie knew however
that her mistress was being threatened and an atavistic impulse
sent her into self-defensive mode, head down ready to butt and
small cloven hooves stamping.

Distracted by the doe's intervention Boyd let out a fiendish guffaw. 'In the name of Satan, if 'tis not a bloody deer! Quite a menagerie, is Kingsburgh! Ah well, this here animal's gonna make a good meal for me an' ma men tonight. Better than horse, wouldn't yew say?'

And suddenly the sword was not probing Flora's arm any more. It had found another target, deep in Beanie's heart. The doe let out a bellow of pain which subsided within seconds to a defeated whimper as she crumpled up and sank, eyes glazed, to the floor.

'Devil!' The word was a distillation of horror, grief, and a hatred that burnt clear and bright in Flora's heart.

But Alastair seemed to have done with her now. He had turned his glittering gaze upon Deirdre. 'And here's the other old harridan. Another MacDonald, Ah guess. Ma own daddy's clan. Jes fancy that!'

The taunt jolted Deirdre out of her terror, as it was doubtless designed to do. 'Aye, an' 'twere better had ye ne'er been born, ye bastard spawn o' Satan.'

For Boyd it was the ultimate insult. His powerful fist lashed out at his victim's jaw, which broke with a nauseating crack as Deirdre fell. 'Ah'll teach yew to sass me, ye skinny old fustilugs! Yew'll soon shut up when yew see what Ah've brung fer your inspection! Hey! Callum! Malcolm! Go fetch that there l'il old gift we brung up special for Mistress MacDonald here.'

The two men hesitated, looking with mingled doubt and fear first at one another and then at their young master. Flora remembered that back in the old country Malcolm MacLeod had been a friend of Neil's son, Colin. Clearly he had reservations about what he had been commanded to do.

Icy fingers of terror crept up her spine. She knew instinctively that her household's harrowing ordeal, far from being over, was about to reach some kind of apocalyptic climax. The baneful seeds of it were in Alastair Boyd's tight mouth and furious demeanour as he yelled, 'Go, I say!' at the two retainers; in the men's reluctant compliance; in the premonitory hush of dread that settled over Boyd's wounded victims.

What happened next was the stuff of nightmares. Only a monster of cruelty could have devised the horror that now transfixed the little group as Boyd's two roughnecks reappeared carrying a filthy log-like bundle which they flung with studied nonchalance upon the floor. The thing was some six feet long and was wrapped in holey flannel sheeting, and at first the whole of Flora's being resisted the grisly knowledge that it was a corpse. Then she saw a horny, skeletal hand protruding from the makeshift shroud, a lock of white hair and a grey foot, and just as realisation dawned Deirdre let out a long, agonised screech of grief. The bile stood harsh and bitter in Flora's mouth, then, as she watched the old woman rush over, fall on her knees, and take Neil's rigid body in her arms. The initial frenzied shriek gave way to an eerie keening and then to a gentler, distraught crooning, as if the bereaved woman imagined that by some miracle of wifely tenderness she could bring her husband back to life.

The whole episode had so far been acted out with all the stylised inevitability of Greek tragedy – good and evil counterpoised, Deirdre as an elderly Antigone; Alastair the tormenting archon who gave no quarter. But one humane gesture did break the pattern: Malcolm MacLeod bent forward, gently touched Deirdre on the shoulder and whispered something in her ear. She shrugged him away as if he had been some troublesome gadfly, but not before Boyd's quick glance had taken in his subordinate's almost involuntary lapse into kindness.

'Leave her be, yew weakminded fool! Ah'll brook no show of sympathy for foul loyalist scum! Git movin', man. We ain't finished here yet.'

Nor were they, but by now everything was swimming before Flora's eyes. The stench of blood and death assailed her nostrils and the pain in her arm was so overpowering that she welcomed the oblivion of unconsciousness. Why fight it? There was nothing left to live for.

But just as she gladly gave in to the blackness a new smell forced itself in on her awareness, and mentally fuzzy though she was she was quick to identify it as smoke. At the same time she felt herself being dragged bodily along the floor while a familiar coaxing voice pleaded and soothed.

'Try to stay 'wake, Miz MacDonald. Help me git ya outa here. Dese debbils, dey've fired de house.'

Desperately she made to get up but pain forced her to rely wholly on her rescuer: she knew, however, that it was easier to move a sentient person than an unconscious one. Frantically she took in the horror of the enemy's final bid at her destruction. Flames had already overwhelmed her precious curtains, the carpet covering on the table, some linens that Deirdre had been about to sew, and as they gathered momentum they were leaping up towards the walls and rafters. Their steadily growing rumble was punctuated by sharp crepitations as they attacked the dry wood of chairs and dressers and then snaked relentlessly up to the attic and under the eaves where they fell to consuming straw pallets, bales of hay, barrels of carefully-stored flour, oatmeal and sugar.

She heard herself choke as the reek filled her mouth, eyes and nose. Tears ran unchecked down her face, mingling with lumps of soot and the blood that seemed to be everywhere. Then suddenly the blessed spring rain, Hannibal handing her over into Morag's care, and his calm voice, reassuring her in the midst of chaos and heartbreak.

'Now ya be a' right, ma'am. Ya away from de fire now.'

She felt herself sinking gratefully back into unconsciousness as pain reasserted its hold, but one question cried out to be answered.

'Deirdre?'

She felt rather than saw Hannibal shake his head. 'Ah rait sorry, Ma'am. Ah done try to git her but she wouldn't be moved. Said she wanted ta be where he was.'

X

For days afterwards Flora existed in a world of shadows. Frequent doses of laudanum kept the realities of shock and pain hovering at one remove, so that the ghastly truth of all that had happened mercifully entered her consciousness only gradually. Stella and Morag ministered to her assiduously, their old animosity towards one another still simmering but now tacitly acknowledged as trivial compared with their mutual desire to make the mistress well. Adversity had turned them into partners, however reluctant.

Slowly Flora's mind began to focus on the visions that kept flickering in the maelstrom of her memory, vague recollections of events so loathsome that she recoiled from them in horrified disbelief. Piecing the fragments together she at first rejected them as the stuff of nightmares. Hadn't she dreamt it all – Boyd's diabolical brutality; the firing of Kingsburgh; and then, more confused and hazy but still startlingly insistent, a sombre double funeral in the bleak rain-soaked meadow yonder, with all the neighbours weeping?

How haunting it was, this nightmare. As it had receded it had left ringing in her head the howling of a dog and the sound of tuneless voices intoning the Auld Hundredth. 'All people that on earth do dwell, sing to the Lord with cheerful voice.' The voices, she remembered, far from sounding cheerful, had been choked and broken with grief.

And there had been another solitary voice keening a Gaelic dirge from another, even older time. So women bereft might have lamented their loss at the dawn of history.

'Hark the whirlwind is in the wood, a low murmur in the vale. It is the mighty army of the dead, to bear them away through the air.'

Fearfully she confronted the awful truth that what she had experienced was no figment of her overheated imagination but raw, immutable fact. Neil and Deirdre were gone. What puzzled her most, however, was that as she had emerged from the darkness her own overwhelming emotion had not been grief, or terror, or even the solace of sorrow shared, but a sad, self-centred sense of shame and rejection. The feeling had been powerful and unadulterated, and still lingered like a bad smell even after the daylight brought other emotions and memories to mitigate it.

Then the truth struck her with the force of a body blow. Not a soul had talked to her, that day at the graveside. Peggy Campbell had even gone so far as to spit in her face.

Her whole body ached. The injured arm throbbed incessantly and she could not move it. Through eyes that streamed with tears she gazed round the upper room of the mill, where Hannibal had installed her after the fire. She was surrounded by sacks of grain but its rich malty aroma was overlaid by another more sinister stench, the acrid miasma of burnt timber. A rat scrabbled. She reflected dully that Donald McAulay would have to get a ferret to it, then remembered that the miller had fled weeks before, having aligned himself with the rebels.

'Y'all be 'wake, Miz MacDonald hon? Hannibal, he be up at de house, seein' what he can find in de ashes o' drink an' vittles. Dere be li'l left Ah fear. Dese debbils burnt de lot.'

The feline eyes flashed with hate and indignation, and Flora understood afresh why this half-breed woman had aroused such fear and hostility among the white colonists. Harm me and mine, those eyes said, and you lay yourself open to all manner of cabalistic vengeance.

'The whole house is gone?' The words came out weak and despairing.

'Purty well so, Ma'am, but tanks ta ma Hannibal 'twas jes de main wing dat was burnt total-like. Dey'll build it agin good as new when dey gits home, you'll see.'

The girl then embarked on a eulogy of her man that presented him as a Hercules and a St. George rolled into one all-conquering, ubiquitous hero.

'Dat Hannibal o' mine, he done show dem cut-throats a ting or two! Y'all heard dem horses a'squealin', when de men was inside tormentin' y'all? Well, dat be Hannibal a-cuttin' at der fetlocks wid a scythe! Den he jump out on Massah Boyd an' catch 'im unawares wid it. Oh, Ah be rait proud, when Ah hears how he weaved dat scythe fra side ta side, all de time a-parryin' de blows fra dat big sword, an' de pistol shots an' all, den sent de ruffians scamperin' away, runnin' scared. Dey 'fraid ob him, ya see, he dat fierce when he be roused. Dey tink he be possessed ob de debbil.'

And she cackled mirthlessly, a laugh that made Flora's flesh creep

Flora would learn later that Stella's saga of superhuman bravery was scarcely accurate, for a group of farmhands and herdboys had helped Hannibal banish the marauders, but the picture the girl painted of the incensed negro singlehandedly tackling Alastair Boyd and sending him packing gave Flora a sense of shuddering satisfaction

'How long have we been here at the mill?'

'Sebben days, Ma'am. Hannibal an' me, we look abter y'all, keep ya fed an' warm, an' Ah bin seein' ta yer arm.'

'Nobody else? Where's Morag?'

'She be here wid us, but she ain't doin' much.' The yellow eyes blazed contemptuously. 'Jes sittin' a-starin' into space, she is. Ah been the one dat's been doin' de cookin'. Ah been makin' de ash cakes ma mammy used ter make, outen meal or flour, an' water fra de creek, an' a pinch ob lard. Mammy, she done show me how ter rake all de ashes out de fireplace den kivver de cake wid de hot ashes an' let it cook till it was done. Dat kept us goin' dese days ob trouble, yea ma'am.'

Much as Flora suspected Stella of lying in the matter of Morag's lethargy she did recognise then that her plight was desperate. Here she had been, holed up wounded and helpless, for a solid week, virtually homeless, her family gone, her friends and neighbours turned against her. If Alastair Boyd had indeed been wounded, she reasoned, he would not be satisfied until he had wreaked his revenge. He could be riding in their direction right now, with a more formidable posse of rogues this time. A scintillating panic filled her mind, blinding her to all other considerations than escape.

'We have to get away. I'll manage if you can find a wagon. If we stay here we die.'

Stella's eyes opened wide and for the first time since the delivery of that still-born child Flora read stark terror there.

'But where kin we go, Ma'am? Hannibal an' me, we do a' rait in de woods, stealin' fra white folk's yards when we hungry, but y'all caint survive dat way. No Ma'am. No way.'

She spoke with resigned finality and Flora looked up to where shafts of spring sunshine penetrated between the flour-encrusted rafters and sighed. Life no longer held out any hope of joy or pleasure; all she could see ahead was grief and pain. In a vain effort to hide her tears she turned her face to the wall.

Stella did not leave her, but sat hunkered by the straw pallet in an attitude of stoical calm, her mistress's hand in her own rough one. Then all at once she flung the hand aside and jumped to her feet, transfixed with terror.

'Hosses! Dey be here! Oh, where dat Hannibal when we be needin' 'im? Dey be comin' up de lane!'

Flora watched the girl creep away and look fearfully through the inch-wide space between the log timbers of the mill structure. Her whole person seemed to shrink and the sun caught the star on her forehead, throwing it into vivid prominence.

'Dere be jes two ob dem,' she gasped. 'De leader, he be wearin' dat damned rebel badge…'

Then a little strangled whoop of amazement burst from her.

'Miz MacDonald, y'all not ta faint now! Dat be Massah Boyd, de fadder, and he got yo papa wid 'im!'

Flora felt her heart leap on a wild carousel of gladness. Her impulse was to rise and run to them but weakness overcame her and she submitted to Stella's restraining grasp.

'Y'all caint get up. No way. Dey wid Morag now. Dey knows y'all's here.'

Then suddenly it came to Flora that her euphoria might be misplaced. Was not Roddy Boyd on the rebel side? Had he come here to take her into some kind of custody? And what of Hugh? Was he Roddy's prisoner? Horrifying speculations chased one another through her mind in pell-mell confusion, but all she could do was wait helplessly as footsteps echoed on the wooden stairs and voices rang.

The conflicting claims of joy and doubt were so intense that she did not notice Stella's furtive removal from her bedside to the darkest recesses of the attic room. Had she read the girl's mind she would have summoned her back, for she was never to see her again. Trusting that they would not be missed in the excitement of this strange reunion the negroes were about to slink back into the woods, because much as they respected Roddy they knew he would regard them as nothing other than runaway slaves deserving of the harshest punishment he could devise. Besides, their work was over now. The Mistress had someone to care for her.

XI

'Florrie! What have they done to you? Och, but they have a lot to answer for, the devils!'

Hugh was kneeling by Flora's makeshift bed, his voice all love and concern. She tried to smile, to make light of her own predicament and focus on her stepfather's own ill and bedraggled state, for he seemed inches shorter than when he had left, and his face was ash-white and wizened, as if he were close to death: but all she could summon up by way of sympathy was a rush of tears.

'Allan? Oh, tell me, Pa, where are Allan and Sandy and Jamie? Are they…?' She swallowed hard, unable to complete the question.

But Hugh knew what she meant. 'Wheesht, now Florrie. Don't fret. Aye, they're alive, or were the last time I saw them, some two weeks since. We were all captured when we scattered following the disaster at Moore's Creek. Allan and Sandy – aye, and our own Alexander, and John Bethune and even Farquhard Campbell, serves him right for his duplicity – were with us when we were all marched up to Halifax. A terrible march it was, with the folks in the villages spitting at us and yelling curses, but Major Rutledge, that was in charge of the prisoners, was a decent sort. They're not all fiends, the rebels. Come to think of it, you should have got word from the major long ago, that your men were well: he tried to notify relatives through folks like me, that were too old or hurt or ill to be a threat.'

'And Jamie? My Jamie?'

Hugh's face clouded over. 'Nobody knows, Florrie. All I can tell you is that he and Alex escaped. Chances are that they're still in the woods somewhere, or trying to get downriver and away to the likes of Charleston where they can join the British. But oh, Florrie, you'd be that proud of Jamie gin you could see him! Going to war has made a man of him. I'm confident, somehow, that he's safe. He and Anne's Alex together are a formidable pair, you know. They won't give up without a fight.'

'And how have you chanced to come here with Roddy Boyd, an enemy? I would have him know that no-one of that name is welcome here. His family have brought naught but grief to me and mine.'

Her voice quivered with bitterness and a pathetic dignity. Hugh's return had strengthened her spirit. If he was Roddy Boyd's prisoner the gaoler would get no cuttings from her. But even as she spoke the memory was stirring of Jenny's fate at the hands of her hateful half-brother, and she felt shame that she had been unable to protect the pregnant girl that Roddy – yes, and Sandy too – had entrusted to her care.

Even so her mind was made up. 'Tell him to be gone. I have no wish to speak to him.'

At that Hugh took her free, unbandaged hand in his, kissed it and held it to his chest.

'Listen to me, daughter. You don't understand, lass. Roddy is our friend, perhaps the only one we can truly rely on in this land of hypocrites and deceivers. Let me tell you what happened. 'Tis better that you should know, dreadful though the story is. Wheesht now, lass. Just close your eyes and listen.'

He then related the events of the disastrous Moore's Creek battle of February 27th, telling how General MacDonald, seized of an ague, had fallen from his horse in a dead faint and his command had been taken over by the younger, rasher Colonel MacLeod.

'We had been doing well up till then,' Hugh said. 'The general's plan depended on avoiding confrontation until we met up with the British forces, and so far we had out-manoeuvred Caswell's troops, which was none too easy because the creeks were full and we had to get wagons across the likes of Corbet's Ferry and the Black River. But our scouts gave us the wrong intelligence about the enemy's whereabouts when we got to Moore's Creek. They told us the Americans were in an exposed position on the west side when actually Caswell had retreated over the creek to meet up with Lillington. He left a detachment, though, to rip the pine planking off the bridge and grease the sleepers with tallow.

'MacLeod and the younger hotheaded officers couldn't resist the challenge and decided to attack despite their superior's advice. Oh, lass, I can hear it yet, the eerie sound of the pipes in the still misty dawn and the rallying battle-cry of 'King George and Broadswords!' as the cream of our army, seventy-five picked men, swarmed on to the bridge and were gunned down one by one. They hadn't a chance, Florrie. The sights and sounds will be with me till my dying day. The lads screaming and the horses whinnying. The blare of the cannon and the beating of drums. The ridge behind belching fire and the water of the creek running red with blood. And the feeling of sheer confusion and helplessness in the smoke and fog and agony of it all.

'And Sandy was there, Florrie! Allan sent him with twenty men armed with poles, to pull out the floundering clansmen. And – you'd better hear it all, Florrie, painful though it is – and he grabbed hold of Neil's corpse and wouldn't let go. I'm sure Neil was dead, have seen enough dead people in my time to know, but

Sandy held on and got a musket ball in his leg for his pains…'

Flora felt the pressure of the old man's hand on her knuckles and shivers of fear crept up her spine. He was breaking the bad news gradually, so as not to send her into shock. Her son was crippled for life, perhaps enduring the excruciating pain of an amputation. She saw him stumbling along with a wooden stump where his leg should be. And Hugh expected her to welcome Roddy Boyd!

'Tell that traitor downstairs to leave my farm! I'm amazed at you, father, letting yourself be seen in his company!'

'Wheesht, lass. Wheesht. Hear me out. It was then, I say, that Roddy came running from the other bank, waded into the water and rescued Sandy. Aye, Flora, but for Roddy Boyd you wouldn't have your son this day. He loosened Sandy's hand from the corpse – the lad had fainted by then – and carried him away to wherever they were treating the wounded. And Sandy's well and whole, never fear. Roddy personally removed the ball from his leg, cleaned the wound and put on an oil-and-lint dressing. And all the time of that terrible march north to Halifax, through the heat and fever and exhaustion Roddy cared for him and for us, Florrie. He it was who insisted I be sent home, and he would have had them send the others too, but former tacksmen are too valuable to them as bargaining tools when it comes to exchanging prisoners. Roddy Boyd is a true friend. Please believe me, Flora.'

And at last she did. 'Tell him to come up.'

It was spoken as by a queen who had, after much persuasion by a courtier, agreed to grant a subject an audience. She scarcely knew that physically she was in a much worse state than ever before in her life. Even on the Atlantic crossing she had been a privileged traveller and had had Allan and her maids to tend her, but now she had been virtually alone for days – or was it weeks? She had quite lost count of time. She realised suddenly that the rank smell in her nostrils came from her own body. How long had she been wearing this ragged old shift? She must have been too ill and tired to undress, let alone wash.

Overcome now by a wave of shame and self-disgust she saw herself as an objective observer would. She lay on a straw pallet that stank of her own sweat and urine, her body so feeble and emaciated that it could have been that of an eighty-year-old. Her once-lustrous hair straggled lankly, encrusted with grease and crawling with lice. Her face was the colour of old lard. A succession of restless nights had left her eyes dark-rimmed and bruised-looking, their sole expression, when they were not dulled by pain and fatigue, a wild and terrible harassment.

And when she turned those eyes on Roddy Boyd he was hard put to it to master his anger and shock.

'Flora. Thank God you're alive.' His voice shook. 'We have to get you out of here, and fast.'

Grim and tight-lipped, he turned to Hugh then.

'You can help me carry her downstairs? I have to examine this arm but we need more light. To think she has been living in this dark hell-hole of a place and that devil stepson of mine was responsible for it! He has brought naught but grief to me, that Alastair, and I have made it clear that he is no longer my adopted kin. I have banned him from my hearth, from my land, and from my consideration. He is beneath my contempt.'

As they raised her they carefully avoided putting pressure on the injured arm and although temporarily overcome with giddiness Flora was able to stumble along between them to the top of the narrow wooden stairs. She also managed to ask the one question that had been beating on the barred cage of her mind ever since Roddy's arrival.

'Jenny?'

'She does as well as one can hope. Callum MacDonald and Malcolm MacLeod had the sense to know what side their bread was buttered on – or maybe their better nature asserted itself for once. Anyway, they took her to Callum's wife, Catriona, and she's still there, bearing the scars of her battering I fear but heartened to know that Sandy is alive. I've dared anybody to lay a hand on her.'

'And the babe?'

His face darkened. 'Nobody can tell, Flora, but at least she did not miscarry. She may bear a grandchild to us yet.'

Yet another occasion for joy, tempered though it was with anxiety and doubt. To think that no matter what befell there could yet be established, here in North Carolina, a generation that bore the mingled blood of a Boyd and a MacDonald. None of their descendants would know for sure, but if Roddy were truly the son of the martyred Earl of Kilmarnock this new line was illustrious indeed. Her own fate now was of no account. She was merely a link in the chain. But how blessed to know that Roddy was part of it too.

They were tackling the stairs now.

'Careful now, man. Morag! Come and help here! I hope you have some hot water on the fire, for I'll be needing it. There, Flora: thank goodness we've got you safely down. Now let's see. This arm first. The wound has not festered, miraculously, thanks maybe to your maid's arcane knowledge of simples …'

Flora's heart missed a beat. Did this man even know that Stella had been tending her? But no matter. Stella and Hannibal must be miles away by now.

Then she saw his brows knit together in perplexity and realised that Stella's whereabouts were the last thing in his thoughts.

'This is a bad fracture, I fear. 'Tis broken in three places, and this flimsy sling is totally inadequate, apart from being foully contaminated with pus and dirt. Turn your head away and grit your teeth. I'm going to give you a shot of rum to ease the pain while I do this. I'll be as gentle as I can.'

While the hot, comforting spirit trickled through her body she fixed her gaze on Roddy's portable box of surgeon's aids, with its neat divisions for lint, bandages and instruments, and thought of how Sandy had also benefitted from its contents. She tried in vain not to scream when a strong hand wrenched her arm and seemed to rearrange every bone and tendon in it.

'Hold on now, Flora. I'm nearly done. Good girl.'

A sense of binding and tightness now, and she looked down to see her forearm enclosed in two hollow pasteboard splints covered with thin leather, the inner one longer to hold the palm and the whole held together with leather straps secured with brass studs.

'There. That's more substantial altogether. We'll leave you to rest now while I talk to your father.'

While the arm still ached abominably she felt more relieved and cared for than she had done in months, and the sleep that came to her in the lightness of that April afternoon had the perfume of jasmine on its wings. She woke suddenly aware of the whole magnificent pageantry of spring outside, of fiery azeleas flaunting themselves and magnolias in tender bud. And she was missing it all, lying here in a fusty old mill amidst sacks of flour and rats and woodlice. It would not do.

But while Hugh and Roddy had come to the same conclusion their remedy went beyond a mere walk around the farm to view the damage Alastair had wrought and see whether it could be remedied. Their plan was much more drastic than that.

'We're taking you to Glendale. To Anne. Her birthing-time is close – she may well have had the babe already – and she needs a mother's love. Besides, there are servants there, farm hands and neighbours to help ward off the marauders that infest the countryside these days.' Hugh's voice was low and urgent.

Roddy too was adamant. 'The land is swarming with desperate men, Flora, men who kill and maim without a thought for God's commandments or the judgement to come. Here you are at the mercy of thieves and cut-throats. We fear for your life. You will agree to it? Don't gainsay us in this. Please!'

The move to Glendale was such a radical suggestion that she balked at it and set it to one side. She felt like someone taking an old, lost treasure from a drawer and hesitating to examine it in case it would fall apart in her hands.

'And you, Roddy? Won't they be on the lookout for you? For I am indeed right in thinking you have defected from the rebel ranks?'

'Maybe so, Flora. I don't know how they would classify me and I don't care. All I know is that I was not made to kill. My mission as a physician is to succour and serve. The side my patients fight on is of no vital importance. You of all people must understand that, for we are of one mind on it, you and I.'

'They will not come at you, being with me?'

'That is in the hands of God.'

'Then gin it depends on His good grace I will go with you to Anne's.'

They piled blankets on the wagon and lifted Flora on to them. She breathed the sweet spring air and resolutely refusing to look at the ruins of Kingsburgh she turned her eyes towards the distant hills. I will lift up mine eyes unto the hills, from whence cometh my help. My help cometh from the Lord, which made heaven and earth.

'Feeling better, you in the back there?' Roddy's voice was bright with confidence.

'Much better.'

And to her amazement she realised that she was smiling.

AFTERWORD

What happened to Flora afterwards?

I fear that if I detailed the repeated robberies, evictions, and bandit attacks she suffered in the next two years it would make gruelling and ultimately monotonous reading, but a brief summary is perhaps in order.

She did indeed stay with Anne, whose fourth child, another girl, was safely delivered, but Glendale was sacked by patriot marauders. Alex MacLeod was still at large in the swamps – it took six weeks for him to reach Governor Martin – and so his wife's safety was of no account to Ebenezer Flosom, the sadistic patriot commander at Cross Creek. My description of Flora's treatment at the hands of Alastair Boyd stems, in fact, from a grim legend in which Anne has the rings snatched from her fingers and her clothes slashed. It is said that her children might have perished had not their nurses fled with them into the woods and pretended they were their own.

Succoured now by Kenneth Black at Nick's Creek, Flora and the family endured further tribulations, a prey to food shortages, an outbreak of smallpox and constant harrassment. Perhaps letters from Allan and hopes of eventual rescue kept the women going, however, for in the summer of 1777 Flora was still game enough to defy a court order that she take the oath of allegiance, and as a result Allan's estates were confiscated.

Eventually it was Glendale who at great expense to himself rescued his wife, his mother-in-law and his family from North Carolina. He arrived at Brunswick in February 1778. Caswell, the new governor, accepted his flag of truce and they all travelled by sea to New York.

Meanwhile Allan and Sandy had endured all manner of deprivation and humiliation as they were marched from gaol to gaol. Despite being officially pardoned shortly after the battle of Moore's Creek they were taken from Halifax North Carolina to Philadelphia. The prison there overlooked the State House and they probably saw members of Congress going about their business, and heard the bells ring when Jefferson's Declaration of Independence was first read in public in July. At last their parole was recognised and they went to Berks County to await news of an exchange. That took all of a year, but they were already in New York when Flora and Anne arrived. Remarkably, too, Charles and Ranald were not all that far away, both being stationed in Nova Scotia. Unfortunately, however, Flora's sons had inherited their fathers' prodigality, which caused Allan's cousin there, Captain Alex MacDonald, some concern.

In the summer of 1778 Allan rejoined the army and was also posted to Nova Scotia, where he was in charge of the garrison at Fort Edward, Windsor. Despite having her family and John Bethune there, life was far from idyllic for Flora. The living quarters were cold and dreary, the young men chafed with boredom, and Flora lost her only female friend when Captain Alex's wife Susie, née Livingstone, died in childbirth. Flora had another fall and damaged the wrist of her good arm. She cannot have been sorry to sail for home in October 1779. Sandy, who was also far from well, was sent home shortly afterwards but was lost at sea when his ship foundered.

Ill, sad and lonely, Flora languished in London for six months before tackling the journey back to Skye, where she was reunited with Anne and Fanny, now a strapping fourteen-year-old. As the American war continued word must have filtered through only slowly. Living at Dunvegan she would hear how Charles, Jamie and Annabella's son Donald were serving with Tarleton's British Legion in the southern campaign, and then, in 1782, she would hear that Ranald had perished off Newfoundland. He had been on board the surrendered French flagship, the *Ville de Paris*, when it came to grief.

Allan did not get home until 1785. Still optimistic, he had hopes of making a life for them in Nova Scotia, where he had been granted seven hundred acres of Crown land, but this would depend on the level of compensation the government was prepared to pay him for his losses in the war. The grant, when it came, was derisory. Allan had to stay in Skye. I suspect that Flora was not sorry.

For the next two years the MacDonalds had no settled home but in 1787, thanks to their son Johnny's generosity, they were able to take over Penduin, just north of Kingsburgh. Johnny, the most successful of Flora's family, was already distinguishing himself in the Indian Army, and was destined to become a famous map maker and writer on engineering. The same year saw both Charles and Jamie married. Jamie took the lease of Flodigarry.

Flora died on 4th March 1790. The islanders gave her a heroine's send-off, as befitted a woman of great courage and sensibility. The line of mourners stretched for over a mile to Kilmuir Cemetery, the whisky flowed and massed pipers played the coronach. Sad that she did not live to see developments that would have gladdened her even then, for Alex and Anne were to take the lease of Waternish, Annabella and Cuidreach were to take over Kingsburgh, and Fanny would indeed marry Donald, whom she had stayed loyal to since childhood.